BOSSMAN'S BABY SCANDAL

BY
CATHERINE MANN

DID ~~YOU PURCHASE THIS BOOK WITHOUT A COVER?~~ **ER?**
If you ~~did~~ ~~you should be aware that it is~~ ~~orted~~
unsold ~~and destroyed~~ ~~does not~~ the ~~blisher~~

All the ch~~aracters in~~ ~~to existence~~ ~~nation of~~
the autho~~r~~ ~~me name~~
or names ~~they are not even distantly inspired by any individual~~ ~~nown or~~
unknown ~~to the author~~ ~~all the incidents are~~ ~~ccurrence.~~

All Righ~~ts Reserved~~ ~~the right of reproduction in~~ ~~ole or in~~
part in a~~ny form. This edition is published by arrangement with~~ ~~Harlequin~~
Enterprise~~s~~ ~~MAYS ard. The text of this~~ ~~blication or any part~~ ~~reof may~~
not be reproduced or transmitted in any form or by any means, electronic or
mechanical, including photocopying, recording, storage in an information
retrieval system, or otherwise, without the written permission of the publisher.

This book is sold subject to the condition that it shall not, by way of trade or
otherwise, be lent, resold, hired out or otherwise circulated without the prior
consent of the publisher in any form of binding or cover other than that in
which it is published and without a similar condition including this condition
being imposed on the subsequent purchaser.

® and ™ are trademarks owned and used by the trademark owner and/or its
licensee. Trademarks marked with ® are registered with the United Kingdom
Patent Office and/or the Office for Harmonisation in the Internal Market and
in other countries.

Published in Great Britain 2011
Harlequin Mills & Boon Limited,
Eton House, 18-24 Paradise Road, Richmond, Surrey TW9 1SR

© Harlequin Books S.A. 2010

Special thanks and acknowledgment to Catherine Mann for her contribution
to the KINGS OF THE BOARDROOM series.

ISBN: 978 0 263 88089 2

51-0111

Harlequin Mills & Boon policy is to use papers that are natural, renewable
and recyclable products and made from wood grown in sustainable forests.
The logging and manufacturing processes conform to the legal environmental
regulations of the country of origin.

Printed and bound in Spain
by Litografia Rosés S.A., Barcelona

I'm truly blessed to work with an AMAZING group of writing industry professionals! Hugs and thanks to the fabulously talented Emilie Rose, Maya Banks, Michelle Celmer, Jennifer Lewis and Leanne Banks. Ladies, it's been a delight and an honor to collaborate with you on this project. Abundant appreciation to my brilliant editor, Diana Ventimiglia, and my savvy agent, Barbara Collins Rosenberg. And my unending gratitude to the whole publishing team for bringing my books to life!

RITA® Award winner **Catherine Mann** resides on a sunny Florida beach with her military flyboy husband and their four children. Although after nine moves in twenty years, she hasn't given away her winter gear! With over a million books in print in fifteen countries, she has also celebrated five RITA® Award finals, three Maggie Award of Excellence finals and a Booksellers' Best win. A former theater school director and university teacher, she graduated with a master's degree in theater from UNC-Greensboro and a bachelor's degree in fine arts from the College of Charleston. Catherine enjoys hearing from readers and chatting on her message board—thanks to the wonders of the wireless internet that allow her to cyber-network with her laptop by the water! To learn more about her work, visit her website, www.CatherineMann.com, or reach her by snail mail at PO Box 6065, Navarre, FL 32566, USA.

Dear Reader,

Receiving an invitation to participate in a continuity series is such a thrill and honor for me! I especially enjoy the opportunity to work with other authors to build an exciting new story world—in this case, the world for KINGS OF THE BOARDROOM. In *Bossman's Baby Scandal*, it's my pleasure to introduce you to the driven men and women at Maddox Communications, an ad agency in scenic San Francisco.

Ambitious ad exec Jason Reagert expects a fresh start on the West Coast, a chance to make his mark outside his wealthy family's influence. But all too soon his ties back east tighten when he learns his ex-lover, Lauren Presley, is carrying his baby!

I hope you enjoy the glitz, glamour and high-powered dealings in KINGS OF THE BOARDROOM. I love to hear feedback from readers, so please feel free to contact me via my website, www.catherinemann.com, or write to me at PO Box 6065, Navarre, FL 32566, USA.

Happy reading!

Catherine

Prologue

New York City, four months ago

Lauren Presley wondered how a man could be so deeply inside her and yet totally distant at the same time. But no doubt about it, the sated, half-dressed man tangled up with her on her sofa at work had emotionally left the building.

She would boot the rest of him out of her deserted office as soon as she could breathe again.

The butter-soft leather of her turquoise couch stuck to the backs of her legs through her thigh-high stockings, sweat still slicking her body from their frenetically passionate—and surprise—hookup. At least her fledgling graphic-arts business was closed for the day, the workplace empty.

Everything seemed out of sorts, disconnected like a Salvador Dali painting. She couldn't blame Jason for regretting their impulsive act, since she was pretty much freaking out, too, over how fast her panties had landed on the floor, her dress up around her waist while she'd torn at his belt buckle and zipper. Jason Reagert was a business colleague, one half of a working alliance they may very well have wrecked. She needed to get through this awkward post-sex moment ASAP with her pride intact.

A low drone filled the quiet of the empty office. Lauren tensed. "Your pants are vibrating."

Jason arched back and raised a dark eyebrow, his close-cropped hair mussed on top from her fingers. "Pardon?"

She clapped her hand on his warm hip—beside his BlackBerry. "Seriously. It's buzzing."

"Damn." He disentangled himself, cool air brushing her bared legs. Jason swung his feet to the floor, his Testoni loafers thunking against the scarred wood as he sat and unclipped the handheld. "Helluva bad timing."

Avoiding his eyes, she slid upright and adjusted her silky black wrap dress, putting it in place again. Her panties would have to wait. She kicked the scrap of ebony satin under the sofa. "Your pillow talk leaves something to be desired."

"Sorry." His zipper closing rasped, overloud in the late-night silence. "It's my reminder alarm."

"Alarm for what?" She stared nervously at the white brick walls, the easel in the corner, the artwork on lit screens.

"My flight to California."

Right.

He was leaving.

Lauren stood, smoothing her dress and looking for her favorite Manolo leopard pumps that she wouldn't be able to wear again without thinking of this stupid, impetuous night.

She and Jason had been wrapping up final details on a graphic-art design project she'd freelanced for his last ad campaign at the New York firm—he was leaving his NYC job and heading to greener career pastures in California. The job at Maddox Communications in San Francisco was a great opportunity for him. She'd known about this for a couple of weeks. And as she'd hugged him goodbye tonight, she'd been knocked off balance by how upset she was over his impending move.

One second she'd been looking up at his leanly handsome face while blinking back tears, and the next second they'd been kissing…and more. Pleasure prickled down her spine, settling low, as she remembered the bold sweep of his tongue and his hands, his strength as he'd cupped her bottom and lifted her against him. Already her body ached to reach for him again, grab hold of that tie she'd never quite managed to undo and tug him toward her. The impulse was too much, too strong.

Too overwhelming.

Gathering her shredded self-control, she looked away from his strong cheekbones and tempting mouth. She didn't know where all these frenetic feelings had come from and wasn't sure how to undo them now that he was leaving.

She spied her leopard-print shoes under the desk and welcomed the chance to put some space between herself and Jason and a sofa that smelled of good sex. She knelt, pulling one pump free, but the other stayed annoyingly out of reach.

"Lauren—" his loafer-clad feet stopped beside her, making her all the more aware of her ungainly butt-up position "—I don't make a habit of—"

"Stop." She sat back on her feet, willing away one of those awful blushes that came with her auburn-head complexion. "You don't need to say anything." Echoes of her mother's humiliating pleas for her husband to stay bounced around in Lauren's head.

"I'll call—"

"No!" Standing, she gave up on her shoes, her toes curling against the cool wood floor. "Don't make promises you aren't certain you'll keep."

He scooped his suit jacket from the back of a contoured metal chair. "*You* could call *me*."

"What would that accomplish?" She faced him full on for the first time, taking in his prep-school good looks, hardened with an edge from his years in the Navy. He came from old money and had made his fair share of new, as well. "You're moving to California, and New York City is my home. It's not like we have any kind of real connection beyond being work acquaintances who happened to get caught up in a fluky hormonal maelstrom. Nothing to disrupt our entire lives over."

Shaking her long, loose hair back, she opened the door to the larger studio outside, empty but for vacant rolling chairs pushed haphazardly up to tables.

He braced a hand on the door frame, his arrogant brown eyes revealing a hint of surprise. "You're giving me the brush-off?"

Apparently Jason Reagert wasn't told no often. Of

course she'd been mighty quick to say yes, something she intended to change starting now.

"I'm simply being realistic, Jason." She stared him down, her spine straight in spite of the fact he stood at least a head taller.

Later, away from him, she would hole up in her cute little one-bedroom apartment in the Upper East Side. Or better yet, hide out in the Metropolitan Museum of Art for the entire day, crawling into the world of each painting. Her art was everything. She couldn't forget that. This business—bought with a surprise inheritance from her dear elderly aunt Eliza—was her big chance to make her dreams come true. To prove to her mother she was worth something more than a debutante slot and lucrative marriage.

She refused to let any man derail her.

Finally Jason nodded. "Okay, that's the way you want it, that's the way things will be." He skimmed back her hair with his knuckles, his callused thumb stroking her cheekbone. "Goodbye, Lauren."

She settled her features into a portrait worthy of any Dutch master—solemn and unrelenting. Jason turned away, his jacket hooked on one finger over his shoulder, and she fought back the urge to call out to him.

Hearing he was leaving New York had brought a surprise pinch of regret. But nothing compared to the twist in her gut as she watched him walk out the door.

One

San Francisco, Present Day

Working Lauren Presley out of his system had turned out to be tougher than Jason Reagert thought when he'd left New York. But up until sixty seconds ago, he'd been giving it a damn good try.

Clinking glasses, frenetic conversation and blaring eighties music in the high-end bar swelled more tightly around him. He looked up from the photo on his Black-Berry to the woman he'd been flirting with for the past half hour, then back down at the just-in image of Lauren Presley celebrating New Year's Day.

An unmistakably *pregnant* Lauren Presley.

He wasn't often at a loss for words—he was considered a major player in the advertising business, after all.

But right now? His mind blanked. Maybe because his brain was suddenly filled with visions of that impulsive encounter in her office. Had that surprise—mind-blowing—night produced a baby? He hadn't spoken to Lauren since then, but she hadn't called, either. Certainly not with any pregnancy news. He blinked twice fast, the bar coming into focus again.

Pink mirrored walls cast a rosy glow as he studied the shocker image just sent by an NYC pal. He schooled his face to remain neutral while he figured out the best way to make contact with Lauren. She'd sure shown him the door fast enough the last time they'd seen each other.

Some guy gyrating to overloud music jostled him from behind and Jason angled to shield the BlackBerry screen from the packed clientele at the local martini bar on Stockton Street. Rosa Lounge was small and quaint and very expensive, pretty dim on the inside but still classy, with green glass tables and black-lacquered chairs.

A white marble bar took up the majority of one wall with bottles suspended overhead, while tall tables lined the other wall, dark wood floors stretching between. Since Rosa Lounge was just a block away from Maddox Communications, right on the park, MC employees tended to gather here when they closed a big deal or finished a major presentation.

His grip tightened on the BlackBerry. This gathering had been called in honor of him. What rotten timing to be the center of attention.

"Hello?" Celia Taylor snapped her manicured fingers in front of his face twice, her Key Lime Martini sparkling through the crystal glass in her other hand. "Hello? Earth to Jason."

He forced his thoughts and focus to Celia, another ad agent at Maddox Communications. Thank God he hadn't even started drinking his Sapporo. He didn't need the top-shelf brew messing with his head. "Right. I'm here. Sorry to zone out on you like that." He tucked the BlackBerry into his suit jacket. The stored photo damn near seared through his Armani jacket and shirt. "Can I get you a refill?"

He'd been about to offer her more—a date—but then the photo had buzzed through. Technology sure did have an ironic sense of timing.

"I'm good." Celia tapped her painted nail against her martini glass. "That must be one hefty work e-mail. I could get insulted by the fact I'm not warranting your full attention, except I'm just jealous my cell phone isn't buzzing."

Celia flicked her bright red hair over her shoulder and perched a hand on her slender hip.

Red hair.

Green eyes.

Like Lauren. Damn. Realization kicked him in the conscience.

He'd deluded himself into thinking he was putting Lauren behind him this evening, only to try to pick up the lone redhead in the room. Of course, Lauren had darker, auburn hair and softer curves that had driven him crazy exploring....

Jason set his bottle on the bar and eyed the door, mind made up. Delaying wasn't an option. He had to know. But he also didn't want to alienate Celia.

She was a genuinely nice woman who tried to put on a tough facade in order to be taken seriously in the workplace. She deserved better than to be seen as a sub-stitute for another woman. "Sorry to cut out, but I really need to return a call."

Celia cocked her head to the side, her nose scrunched in confusion before she shrugged. "Sure, whatever. Catch you later." She fanned a wave and pivoted on her spiky heel toward fellow ad exec Gavin.

Jason shouldered sideways through the crush of people in power suits, looking for the best way to duck out so he could place a few phone calls. And find answers.

A hand slid from the press of bodies and clapped him on the shoulder. He turned to find both Maddox brothers, the heads of Maddox Communications—CEO Brock and VP Flynn.

Flynn waved other MC employees nearby to join in and then lifted his drink in toast. "To the man of the hour, Jason Reagert! Congratulations on landing the Prentice account. You've done Madd Comm proud."

"To the wonderboy," CFO Asher Williams called.

"Reagert rules," Gavin cheered.

"Unstoppable," Brock declared, his executive assis-tant echoing the toast.

Jason pulled a smile for appearances. Bringing in the Prentice Group was undoubtedly a coup, although tim-ing had certainly come into play in winning over the country's largest clothing manufacturing company. Landing Prentice was the next best thing to nabbing Procter & Gamble. Jason had only just moved to Cali-fornia in the fall when Walter Prentice dumped his other PR firm for moral-clause violations.

The ultraconservative Prentice had a rep for ditching firms for anything from hearing that the account exec had visited a local nude beach to realizing an exec was dating two women at once. Jason's eyes flicked to Celia.

Brock dipped a wedge of pork quesadilla in mango sauce. The workaholic had most likely missed lunch. "Spoke with Prentice today and he made a point of singing your praises. Good move sharing those war stories with him."

Jason's feet itched to get to the door. And damn it, he hadn't shared the war stories as a schmooze move. He'd simply discovered a connection there since Prentice's nephew had done a tour about the same time as he had. "Only making polite conversation with the client."

Flynn lifted his glass again. "You're a hero, man. The way you and that SEAL team took out those pirates back in the day…epic."

He'd served his six years in the Navy after college graduation. He'd been a dive officer with a specialty in explosive ordinance disposal, attached to a SEAL team. Sure, he'd helped take out some pirates, saved a few lives, but so had the others around him. "I was only doing my job, same as anyone else."

Brock finished off his dinner with a final bite. "You're definitely on Prentice's radar. Keep your nose clean and you'll go far with his influence. Landing Prentice's clothing line couldn't be better timed, especially with Golden Gate Promotions breathing down our necks."

Golden Gate was their main rival, another family-owned advertising agency with quite a pedigree and still helmed by its original founder, Athos Koteas. Jason understood well the specter that rival cast. This job at Maddox—this chance in California—was everything to him. He wouldn't let anything screw it up.

His BlackBerry buzzed again from inside his jacket. More pictures? Was the guy sending him an ultrasound photo, for crying out loud? His gut pitched. He liked kids, sure, wanted some of his own.

Someday.

Flynn ducked in closer. "We consider it quite a coup, you charging in with a winning pitch after that lame ass was fired."

Brock smiled sardonically. "Lame ass? Sunburned ass maybe, after hanging out on that beach au naturel."

Low laughter rumbled up from the clustered bunch of MC employees. Jason slid his finger along the neck of his shirt. What a time to remember that Walter Prentice had reportedly disowned his own granddaughter for refusing to marry the father of her kid. Prentice lived by his motto Family Is Everything.

Performance on the job should be all that mattered, damn it. He'd already been dubbed the golden boy at Maddox Communications, a title he'd worked hard to achieve and would do anything to keep. The key word? *Worked.* He'd earned his way to the top, determined to shed the trust-fund label that had dogged him growing up. He wouldn't allow an impulsive move from four months ago to wreck his chances for the success he'd damn well paid for.

He'd walked away from the carrot of joining his old man's advertising company and took a Navy ROTC scholarship to college instead. After serving his six years, he'd launched out on his own in the ad world. While he'd tackled the New York City job, he could still feel his father's influence breathing down his neck. The offer from San Francisco–based MC had put a whole country between him and the old man's far-reaching shadow.

And just that fast, inspiration hit.

As soon as he finished up here at Rosa Lounge, Jason would be on the red-eye to New York. By morning, he would be on Lauren Presley's doorstep for a face-to-face with her. If that baby was his, she would simply have to come to California.

Any possible rumors would be taken care of when he introduced her as his fiancée.

The icy January wind kept most people indoors. Normally Lauren would have been in her apartment in warm wooly socks, tending her plants. But the cold helped calm her nausea. So she worked on the roof, checking the winterizing on the community garden she'd started a couple of years ago.

Kneeling, she tucked the plastic tighter along the edges of the rooftop planter while roaring engines and horns announced that the Big Apple was waking up. The city in winter wore the neutral palette of an Andrew Wyeth painting, a world reduced to blacks and whites, grays and browns. Icy-cold concrete stung through her jeans as she knelt, a bitter breeze whipping off the East River. She huddled deeper into her wool coat. She flexed her numbed fingers inside her gardening gloves.

Her stomach fluttered from more than the baby.

She'd gotten a panicked call from her friend Stephanie informing her that her husband had let Jason know about the pregnancy via a photo taken at last week's New Year's party.

And now Jason was on his way to NYC.

No amount of cold air or gardening would stem the tide of nausea this time. Her world was totally falling apart. Jason was on his way to confront her about the baby she hadn't gotten around to informing him was due in five months, and oh, by the way, her business was all but in ruins.

Lauren sagged back against the concrete fountain, water frozen in the base, icicles dripping from the stone lion's mane. A week ago she'd learned her bookkeeper, Dave, had used her sick leave as an opportunity to embezzle half a million dollars from her fledgling graphic-design business. She'd only found out when she hired a temp bookkeeper to take over while Dave went "on vacation." Now they all knew he wouldn't be returning from whatever island haven he'd taken up residence at using her money. Authorities didn't hold out much hope of finding him—or her funds.

She rubbed a hand over the growing curve of her belly. A child completely dependent on her and she'd royally screwed up her life. What kind of mother would she make? A total coward, up here hiding.

Things had changed so much in a few months. She missed the color palette of spring and summer, but her artistic eye still appreciated the monochromatic starkness of a winter landscape.

The rooftop door creaked a second before a long shadow stretched over her. She knew before she looked. Jason had found her anyway. There was no more delaying this confrontation.

Lauren glanced over her shoulder and... She felt a shiver of awareness.

Jason's lean, looming presence added the final touch

to the stark skyline, his swimmer's build, dark hair cut short, thicker along the top and just lifting in the harsh wind. He stood tall, immovable, uncompromising— physically and emotionally.

She turned away and tucked her gardening tools back in her bag. "Hello, Jason."

His footsteps grew louder, closer, and still he didn't speak.

"I guess the doorman told you I was up here," she babbled, her hands frantically busy.

He knelt beside her. "You should be more careful."

She inched away. "You shouldn't sneak up on people."

"What if it hadn't been me coming up here? That door creaks mighty damn loud and you were in another world."

"Okay, you're right. I was, uh, distracted." By his impending arrival, the baby on the way, and oh, yeah, she had an embezzler on her payroll. So much for her insistence she was ready to take on the world.

She could almost hear her parents' disapproval about everything in her life. Except for Jason. He was exactly the sort of man her socialite mother would pick for her, with his blue-blood lineage, fat bank account and good looks.

Hell, most any mom would be happy to have Jason Reagert as a son-in-law. But he was also stubborn and controlling and she'd fought too hard for her independence to risk it in a relationship with this man. No doubt that was why she'd succeeded in ignoring the attraction for the past months.

She clutched her bag to her chest. "What are you doing here? You could have just called."

"And *you* could have called." He looked at her

stomach and back up again. "When I spoke with a friend of mine back here last night, he told me you've been working from home because you're not feeling well. Are you all right? Is the baby all right?"

And there it was. Her pregnancy news out there with a simple statement. No huge confrontation or shouting match like her parents would have had before—and after—their divorce. All the same, her fingers shook, so she hitched her bag over her shoulder and stood.

"Only morning sickness." She stuffed her hands in her pockets. "The doctor says I'm fine. I'm just more productive if I work from home. The worst is past."

"I'm glad to hear that."

The nausea had been debilitating for a couple of months. Entrusting so much of the office routine to others had been nerve-racking, but there hadn't been any other choice. Too bad it had cost her so much. "I made it back up to half days in the office last week."

"Are you sure you're ready? You look like you've lost weight." A protective gleam lit his eyes. He grabbed an iron chair and hauled it over to her.

Lauren glanced at him warily before sitting. "How much do you know about the pregnancy?"

"Does it matter?" He shrugged out of his trench coat and draped it over her shoulders.

The familiar scent of his aftershave mingled with his body warmth clinging to the fabric. Too tempting. She passed his coat back because she couldn't handle even one more obstacle in her life. Not now. "I guess not, as long as you do know."

He stepped closer, his dark eyes intense in a way that

sent shivers up her spine and had even led her to ditch her panties four months ago.

She forced herself to look away, reminded too thoroughly of the feelings that had propelled her into his arms the first time. "Thank you for believing me."

"I would say thanks for telling me, but you didn't." The first hint of anger tinted his tones.

"I would have, eventually." Before the kid graduated from college, at this rate. "The baby isn't due for five more months."

"I want to be a part of my child's life, every moment. Starting now, we'll work together."

"You're moving back to New York?"

"No." He flipped the collar on his trench coat up over his ears, his suntanned face declaring how much he'd already acclimated to the more temperate California weather. "Let's take this conversation to your apartment where there's heat."

Then a sneaking suspicion seeped in deeper than the damp cold. "You're not moving back to New York, but you want us to work together bringing up the baby. You can't actually expect me to move to San Francisco, can you?"

His silence confirmed her suspicion.

Her anger rose. "I'm not going anywhere with you. Not to my apartment and not to California. You really expect me to uproot my life? To abandon the company I've put my heart and soul into?" If there was even a company left to look after.

"Fine—" the word burst from his mouth in a gust of cloudy cold white "—yes, I want you to come to San Francisco. I want us to be together for our baby. What's more important—your company or your child?"

She wanted to shout that she had put her child's welfare first at the cost of her business. And she knew she would do the same all over again. She only wished she'd shelled out extra dollars for someone more reliable to watch over the shop, instead of worrying about her tight budget and blindly trusting the people she'd hired to do their damn jobs.

"Jason, why are you being so pushy so fast?" Some— okay, a lot—of her anger and fear from work directed itself at Jason. "There's time for us to talk through this, months, in fact. What's really going on here?"

His face closed up, all frustration hidden until he looked as cold as the frozen lion fountain. "I don't know what you mean."

"There must be a reason for the sudden hard sell to put me in the same state as you." Wind whistled louder, almost drowning out the sounds of street traffic below. "Was your mother abandoned by some scum bucket of a man? Did a woman do you wrong in the past?"

His laughter burst out in a fresh gust of puffy clouds until he shook his head. "You have an active imagination. I can assure you that I have none of those tortured scenarios in my past."

His laughter was infectious—and distracting. "That's not a complete answer."

"I'm not here to fight with you." He stepped closer, the ocean-fresh scent of him teasing her pregnancy-heightened senses.

Warmth radiated off him in a welcome wave and contrast to the bitter cold. She ached to burrow against his chest and feel the lean coil of his muscles rippling against her. Tension gathered low and hot and fast as it always had around him, but even more so now that she knew how explosive they could be together.

She raised her hands between them, stopping just shy of actually touching his chest. Wary of even touching him to nudge him away. "You're moving too fast for me. I need time to think."

"Well, while you're thinking, keep this in mind." He slid a hand into his pocket and pulled out a black velvet ring box. He creaked open the lid to reveal…

A platinum-set solitaire diamond engagement ring.

Two

Jason held the velvet box in his hand and waited for Lauren's answer. Getting a jeweler to open up after hours had been a challenge, but he'd managed in time to catch the red-eye flight.

The shock on Lauren's face wasn't a great sign, but he was used to overcoming difficult odds. Wind stirred dry leaves around their feet, so frigidly different from the summer evening they'd spent working after hours in her office.

He extended his hand with the engagement ring, knowing he was being impatient, but time was short. "So? What's the verdict?"

"Whoa, hold on." She gathered her long straight hair back from her face and exhaled—hard. "I'm still stuck back on your idea that I would uproot myself to come to California and now you're tossing an engagement into the mix?"

"Does this look like I'm joking?" He lifted the diamond. The morning sun refracted off all three carats.

The gardening bag slid from her shoulder and thudded to the ground. "You really expect us to get married just because I'm pregnant? That's archaic."

He hadn't meant marriage. He'd been thinking more along the lines of an engagement to shut up any gossips, something she might appreciate, too. But telling her as much probably wouldn't go over well. "If agreeing to marriage moves too fast for you, I'll settle for a trial engagement."

"Trial engagement? You're out of your freaking mind and I'm freezing." She turned toward the door. "You're right about one thing. We should move this conversation to my apartment."

He picked up the canvas bag she'd left on the ground—the only sign she might be nervous—and followed her down two flights of stairs to the third floor. Her place was safe by New York standards, but somehow that didn't seem like enough now. And where would an active toddler play?

He'd had a lot of time to think on that flight, and one thing he'd settled on for certain—he didn't want to be a bicoastal dad. He wanted to be a larger part of his child's life. Sure, he worked hard, but he wasn't going to be like his father, who'd expected Jason to be a carbon copy of him, while never spending any time with his son to actually get to know him.

He needed to lure Lauren to California for more reasons than the Prentice account. He tucked the ring back in his pocket—for now. His goal set, he waited while she unlocked the double bolts and swept the door wide.

Her one-bedroom apartment reflected her personality. Vibrant. Alive. Packed with flowers, plants and colorful framed fabrics, an oasis in the middle of winter. Each area was painted a different color—the living room yellow, the kitchen green.

A hint of pink showed past her partly open bedroom door. He'd joined others from work for drinks at her apartment before, out here in the living area, but he'd never seen the bedroom up close. Something he intended to change down the road.

He set her bag on the hall table and followed her inside, wiping his feet on a rag rug. "We were friends for months, and we're obviously attracted to each other." He gestured toward her stomach. "Can you honestly say you never considered a future between us?"

"Never." She hung her coat on one of the vintage doorknobs mounted on a strip of wood, glancing back over her shoulder at him. "Now could you wrap this up, please? We can talk later about logistics for after the baby is born, but right now, I need to get ready for work."

"Wow, no worries of a guy getting an inflated ego around you." This didn't seem to be a wise time to bring up how fast she'd kicked him out of her office four months ago. Besides, she looked tired. Fine lines of exhaustion furrowed her forehead. His instincts went on alert. "Are you sure you're all right?"

She hesitated a second too long before walking away toward the green galley kitchen. "I'm fine."

He tracked her movements as she poured a glass of milk, her silky red hair swinging along her back and inviting his hands to test the texture, to discover if it was as soft as he remembered. "There's something you're not telling me."

"I promise the baby and I are both totally healthy." She lifted her glass in toast, her back still toward him.

She was dodging something, he was sure, but he could also sense she wouldn't share more now. He would be best served by a temporary retreat before advancing his cause again in a few hours.

He was an ad guy, after all. He knew how to make a pitch, and for now, he needed to back off. The right opportunity would present itself.

Jason pulled the box out of his pocket and set it on the small butcher-block counter. "Just hang on to this for now. We don't have to decide anything today."

She eyed the box as if it contained a snake. "I already know there's no way in hell we're getting engaged, much less married."

"Fair enough." He nudged the box forward until it rested beside an apple-shaped ceramic cookie jar. "Save the ring for our kid."

Turning toward him, she sagged back against the counter, her T-shirt with paint splatters hugging her pregnant belly—and her fuller breasts. "You seem sure it's a girl."

His eyes dropped back to her stomach, his own gut clenching tight as an image of a little girl with red curls filled his head. This baby was real and growing inside Lauren just an arm's reach away. He'd barely had time to process the idea of being a father, much less see the proof so visibly. His hands itched to touch Lauren, to explore the differences in her.

To feel the baby kick?

His throat went tight. "It could be a boy, who'll one day need an engagement ring to give some girl."

She tipped her head to the side, her silky hair gliding over the rounded curves of her breasts. "Do you want a boy? Seems that most men prefer to have a son first."

"Is that how things were with your dad?" His own father sure as hell had wanted a mini-version of himself, someone to mirror his every move, decision, thought.

Her face closed up. "This isn't about my father."

"Okay, then." He gave in to temptation and stroked back a lock of her hair, sliding his hand away before she could protest. "You look beautiful but tired, and I seem to recall you saying something about needing to go to work." He dropped a kiss on her forehead, resisting the urge to linger and, instead, making a beeline for the door. "Goodbye, Lauren. We'll talk later."

He stepped into the hall, her confused face stamped on his memory, fueling him in his decision to retreat for the moment, keep her off balance. She had doubts and he could play on those.

She may have said no this morning, but he wasn't down for the count. Without question, by the time he took the last flight out on Sunday night, Lauren would be coming to California with his child.

Lauren pushed through the glass door leading into the fourth-floor offices that housed her graphic-design business. Not much space, actually, just a common room with tables, a receptionist desk by the door and her own office in back. Where she and Jason had made this baby.

At the moment she couldn't blame the pregnancy for her churning stomach. Her insides swirled around like a Jackson Pollock color extravaganza.

The small velvet ring box seemed to weigh ten tons in her purse—a sack of a bag made from an old sweater she'd found at a consignment store. She'd packed up the jewelry so she could call Jason, schedule a lunch and return the ring. An engagement was a ludicrous idea.

She had enough on her plate, anyhow, finding a way to save her business from bankruptcy.

Franco, her secretary, passed her a stack of memo sheets. "Ms. Presley, your messages."

"Thanks, Franco." She forced herself to smile.

Lauren shuffled through the inch-thick pile; calls from prospective clients were mixed in with phone numbers from creditors.

Franco stood, smoothing down his NY Giants tie. "Before you go into your office—"

"Yes," she answered, opening her door at the same time. The floral scent wafted out.

Franco shrugged and leaned back. "They were delivered just before you arrived. And, uh…"

His voice dwindled off in her mind as she turned to find her office packed with at least five vases of white rosebuds with pink and blue ribbons. On the corner of her desk, she saw a carafe of juice and basket of muffins. She spun back to hear what else Franco was saying.

Movement drew her attention to the far recesses of the reception area, where Jason lounged, assessing her with sexy, hooded eyes. How had she missed him when she came in? And why hadn't Franco told…? Okay, so Franco had tried.

Lauren nodded Jason into her office. "Come on. You might as well eat with me."

He shoved away from the wall, slowly, lean and lanky, like a predator cougar as he strode toward her. Franco, the new accountant and the two interns from NYU looked from Jason to her with undisguised curiosity.

Jason slid his arm around her waist. "I wanted to make sure the mother of my child is well fed and happy."

She stiffened under his touch. Damn his presumptuous ass. Just that fast he'd announced their relationship to the world. Well, not the world, but to her employees and three waiting clients.

"The baby and I are fine, thank you." She planted a hand in the middle of his back and pushed. "Can I speak with you in my office, please?"

"Of course, dear," he said with smooth affection and a charming smile that had the two interns giggling and blushing.

She closed her office door, sealing her in the room with Jason. Alone. With the turquoise sofa. With a host of memories.

Lauren opened the white metal blinds and let the sun blast through. Not that it did much to defuse her anger. "What the hell was that all about?"

"Only letting people know I care about you and our child." He picked up a fat blueberry muffin. "Breakfast?"

"I've already eaten. Don't you think you should have checked to see if I'd told the folks at work about the baby?"

He paused. "You've told them. You've been on sick leave."

"Fine, you're right. But the clients in the waiting area didn't know, and this is my announcement to make to the world when I'm darn well ready."

"You're right, and I'm sorry." He waved the muffin closer, near enough for her to catch a whiff. "Now would you like something to eat? The bakery made them fresh this morning. I saw them come out of the oven."

She wanted to tell the pushy man what he could do with his muffins. But damned if she wasn't starving all over again as she looked at those plump blueberries straining at the sides, the sweet crumble topping making her lick her lips in anticipation. While she loved her baby, sometimes she really resented these hormones that seemed to have such Herculean control over her body.

That same hormonal storm was making her go all teary-eyed over the flowers and food because, God, this was what first-time parents did for each other. The past few months had been so damn hard without the support of a partner. She didn't even want to think about how difficult the coming months—years—might be.

For now she just wanted to enjoy her muffin.

Her feet carried her closer, until she stood toe to toe with Jason. Sniffing back her tears, she could smell him and the flowers and the muffin, and, gracious, but all of it smelled mouthwateringly good. Jason pinched off a piece and brought it to her lips. She parted for him before she could think, pretty damn much the way she'd done on that sofa four months ago.

What was it about this man that made her act so out of character? She wasn't wildly impulsive like her erratic mother. She had control over her emotions. Except for a most memorable lapse around Jason.

She took the bready bite and her senses exploded with pleasure over the sweet fruit melting on her tongue. Jason's thumb traced along her bottom lip, stroking, stirring a whirlpool of want inside her until her breasts tightened in response beneath her brown wool sweater-dress. She arched up on her toes inside her burnt-orange pumps, a whisper away from his mouth—

A knock rattled her office door.

"What?" Her voice came out breathy and impatient. She didn't move. Neither did Jason, the heat of his brown eyes sizzling through her.

The knocking continued, more insistent now. Lauren cleared her throat and tried again. "Yes?" she said, stepping back, not a hundred percent sure who that "yes" was for. "What do you need?"

Jason smiled, wicked and sexy as if to say exactly what he needed. Here. Now.

Lauren clasped the doorknob, willing her professional composure back into place. "What can I help you with?"

She found the grandmotherly accountant she'd hired to sort through the financial mess. The brisk woman waited, hand raised for another knock. Talk about a splash of ice-water reality to douse her passion! She needed to tend to this now, but didn't need Jason to hear.

Lauren said, her voice low, "I'll be with you in five minutes."

The accountant tucked the files against her chest. Her keen eyes proclaimed loud and clear that no one would steal cookies from the jar on her watch. "Good, good. We can go over the preliminary financial state-ment, with a list of the most pressing creditors."

"Of course." She glanced at Jason, nerves gnawing.

She needed him gone. "Jason, we'll have to talk later. Tonight, after work."

He frowned. "Creditors?"

"It's not your problem," she said, dodging his question.

His chest expanded in a manner she'd come to recognize as territorial. "You're the mother of my child. If something pertains to you, it's my problem too."

She angled toward the accountant. "I'll meet you in your office in five minutes."

Lauren closed the door and leaned back against it, facing Jason. The genuine concern in his eyes caught her off guard. She was so on the defensive these days, she'd all but forgotten what a champion he could be. In their year as friends, more than once she'd seen him go to the mat for someone else—a guy fired unjustly, a woman with a stalker boyfriend, even taking on the account of a company pro bono when he'd learned the owner's kid had inordinately high medical bills.

Jason Reagert was pushy, but a goodhearted kind of pushy. It wasn't surprising he'd found his way to military service for so many years.

She could cut him some slack while still keeping her boundaries in place. "It will be public knowledge soon enough when charges are filed, so you might as well know. My accountant, the one before this new lady, embezzled half a million dollars from my company."

His eyebrows shot up toward his dark hairline. "When did this happen?"

"While I was working from home." She pushed away from the door and sagged to sit on the sofa, suddenly weary all over again. If she couldn't tell the guy who'd knocked her up, who could she tell? "I had some suspicions about Dave just before I got sick and planned on firing him. Then I spent a week in the hospital for dehydration. I was relieved when he turned in his resignation. I gave him two weeks' paid vacation and had him escorted out of the office. Three days later I hired a new accountant, the one I should have hired in the first place, but I was trying to save money." She shrugged. "I guess it's true that you get what you pay for."

He sat beside her, not touching, not crowding her for once since he'd shown up on her roof. "I'm so damn sorry."

"Me, too."

"No wonder you were upset this morning." He clasped his hands loosely between his knees, his Rolex glinting in the light shining through the open blinds. "You don't need this kind of worry, especially when you're pregnant. Let me help."

So much for not crowding her. "Whoa, back up. I may be in trouble, but I'll handle it."

"There's nothing wrong with accepting help." He stretched his arm along the sofa back, wrapping her in his scent if not his arms. "In fact, that's why I'm here. I need *your* help."

"With what?" she asked warily, wondering if she was talking with the altruistic Jason, who went to the mat for people.

Or the shark of an ad man who won accounts through his unerring ability to make people believe anything he said.

"I'm new at Maddox Communications and times are tight. No job is secure." His chocolate-brown eyes seemed sincere, intense.

"I can understand that."

"I'm not sure how much you know about MC...."

"It's a family-owned business." She hadn't worked with Maddox before, but the grapevine said they'd hooked some hefty clients. "Run by two brothers, right?"

"Right, Brock Maddox is the CEO and Flynn is the vice president. The one thing standing in the way of the company's domination out West is Golden Gate Promotions."

"That's a family-owned advertising business, too, isn't it?" She relaxed into the sofa, more comfortable in their familiar ground of talking shop. "Athos Koteas still runs the show. I haven't worked with him, but I've heard he's quite a force to be reckoned with. Absolutely ruthless."

"But successful." His arm on the back of the sofa radiated a warmth that made the roots of her hair tingle. "He's a Greek immigrant who made quite a splash, which brought in many European connections to give his company a leg up in these tough last few years. Now he's trying to encroach on Maddox's clients." His face went tight with irritation. "He's put some rumors out there to make Maddox Communications seem untrustworthy and now they're losing business. It's causing Brock even more headaches."

"Are you regretting the move to California?"

"Not at all. Things are going better at work. I've brought in some new clients, one big fish in particular. But that client is extremely conservative. You may have heard of him—Walter Prentice."

Holy crap. "Congratulations, Jason. That's amazing. Landing Prentice isn't just reeling in a big fish. The Prentice account is a freaking whale."

"A whale with the motto Family Is Everything.

Prentice fired his last ad guy for going to a nude beach."
Shaking his head, Jason pulled his arm back. "He
disowned his only granddaughter for not marrying the
father of her baby."

Wait, he couldn't really be suggesting… "You can't
expect me to believe they'll fire you because you have
a pregnant ex-girlfriend." Okay, so she'd never been his
girlfriend. But still. She flopped back on the sofa. "Give
me a break."

He held up both hands. "I'm serious as a heart attack.
The guy's offering up a seven-figure ad campaign in
tough economic times. He gets to call the shots and
choose whoever he wants."

She eyed her bag with the ring inside—a ring that
hadn't been romantic at all. It hadn't even been offered
out of old-fashioned chivalry. He wanted to keep his job.

A cold core grew heavy in the middle of her chest.
"You're that ambitious."

"Aren't you?" He leaned closer, eyes intent. "You and
I are like-minded. We both want to prove to our families
we can make it without their help. So let's work together
for the good of our kid."

"Leave my parents out of this!" she snapped before she
could think, but her heart hurt when it totally shouldn't
have. She knew better than to expect anything from Jason.
There had never been talk of feelings between them.

In fact, she preferred her life be less emotional. Less
like her mother.

"Fine," he conceded, "it's not about our parents.
We'll make this about securing our baby's future by
securing our own. I need you to agree to a temporary
engagement, just until I've finished with the Prentice

account. I'll give you the money you need to tide over your business until you regain your footing."

He was starting to make sense and that scared her. She shoved to her feet, pacing, restless. "I don't need your money. I just need time."

"You can call it a loan if it makes you feel better. A half million, right?"

She toyed with the strap on her purse, all too aware of the ring inside. His offer of money made it all sound so awful. "Do you know what would really make me feel better?"

"Name it." He walked up behind her, quietly, looming without touching. "It's yours."

She spun to face him. "If you took your almighty money and—"

"Okay, okay, I get the picture. You're not interested in saving your company."

She jammed her arm elbow-deep in her purse and fished out the ring. "I'm not interested in handouts."

He clasped his hands behind his back. "I'm offering you a trade."

She thrust the ring toward him. "How can you be so certain this big-account client will even know the baby is yours? We can just stay silent."

His chest expanded. "There's no way in hell I'm denying my own kid for even a day. I may be ambitious, but there are lines. That one's not negotiable."

She pressed the back of her wrist to her forehead, ring box still in her grip. "This is all too much to absorb at once. I just don't know…"

He clasped her shoulders lightly. "Fine, we'll let that ride for now." He massaged gently, his touch both soothing and stirring. "We have more pressing concerns, anyway, making plans for the baby. I'll pick you up after work."

She struggled not to loll into his caress, his comfort. His help. She'd been so tense and scared her whole body ached from knotted muscles. "Do you think for once you could ask rather than command?"

He smoothed his hands down her arms, plucked the ring box from her and set it on her desk. Then he linked their fingers, the first real connection they'd shared since they'd made love in this office four months ago. "Would you like to go out to dinner after work?"

"To discuss plans for the baby."

He nodded, still holding but not moving closer, not crowding, only tempting.

She should know better. But they did have to talk. She couldn't avoid him forever. "Pick me up at my place at seven."

As she watched him leave her office, she couldn't help but wonder if she'd made a mistake bigger than the rock resting in that ring box.

Three

Phone tucked under her chin, Lauren hopped on one foot, tugging on her purple boot. "Hi, Mom." She dropped onto the edge of her bed. "What can I do for you?"

"Lauren, dear, I've been calling and calling and you never pick up at work, or home, or on your cell," her mother said, rambling a thousand miles an hour at the other end of the line. Her flat New England accent was more pronounced, a sure sign she was worked up. "I'm beginning to think you're dodging me."

"Would I do that?" She'd spoken with her mom just a couple of days ago. Jacqueline Presley had logged in about thirty-seven messages since then. Lauren had enough trouble dealing with her mother in a manic cycle during a regular day.

These days were far from regular.

"I don't know what you'll do, Lauren, I don't know anything about you lately." Her mother paused. For air? To gather her thoughts? "Have you spoken with your father?"

Ah, hell. She needed to steer clear of that ticking bomb. "No, Mother, I haven't given Dad a single minute more of my time than you've gotten."

"There's no need to be snippy. I don't know why you get so uptight. Sometimes you're just like your father's sister, and she ended up alone. And fat."

Great. Just what she needed to hear, her mother's obsession with her daughter's curves. Lauren had probably been the only ten-year-old on the planet who'd known what the term *Rubenesque* meant.

"Didn't mean to offend you, Mom." Perched on the edge of the mattress, Lauren zipped one boot, then the other, glancing at the clock. Jason would be ringing the doorbell any minute now. She'd barely had time to yank on the black stretch pants and long sweater after her workday had run late. She'd tossed her purse onto her bed and the ring box had tumbled out. "Things are just hectic at work."

"You don't have to grind yourself into the ground trying to prove yourself to me." A chain jingled on the other end of the line as Jacqueline Presley undoubtedly fidgeted with her jewel-studded glasses chain. "I can tell your father to release a portion of your inheritance now. Or you could have simply invested that money from Aunt Eliza and had a nice little nest egg while you pursued real art."

Lauren's chest went tight. A typical stress reaction around her mom, especially when Jacqueline went down this path...

"You could be as good an artist as I was, Lauren, if you just applied yourself."

Lauren twisted her fists into her satiny damask bedspread. The debacle with the accountant would only fuel her mother's arguments. She felt ill. "Mom—"

"I'm going to be in the city next week." Jacqueline plowed ahead. "We can lunch."

Good God, once her mother was on a roll with her list of all the ways Lauren wasn't living her life right, it usually ended with a list of eligible young men she'd met. Men Lauren would just *love*. Men like Jason.

Her mother was going to have a cow when she learned about this pregnancy.

"Mom, it's been great talking to you—" she stood, tugging her sweater over her hips "—but I really have to go."

"You have plans?"

And if she didn't? Her mother would keep talking. Might as well be honest. "I do have a dinner date with a work associate. Not a *date* kind of date." Babbling only made things worse, and worst of all made her fear becoming like her mother.

"Please, dear, do go and pretty yourself up. And remember, pink is not your color. Ta-ta." Her mother hung up.

"Argh!" Lauren thumbed the off button so hard her nail polish chipped. She tossed the phone on the bed, pacing and shaking her hands as if she could somehow flick away the irritation.

The hurt.

After all these years, she should have gotten used to her mother, and actually, this conversation hadn't even really been that bad in the big scheme of things. But she could hear the mania building, knew how close her mother was to the edge. One small nudge would send her flying into a full bipolar swing. Since her mother refused medication and therapy lately, the highs and lows grew more extreme.

Finding out about the baby would be more than a small nudge for Jacqueline Presley. Add the embezzlement, and who knew how her mom would react? One thing was certain, her mother wouldn't handle any of the news calmly.

Passing a potted fern under the window, Lauren snapped off a dry frond. What would it be like to have a mother she could turn to right now? Her hand slid to her stomach. She would do whatever it took to be that kind of support for her child.

Lauren turned the fern stand so the other side of the plant received equal time in the sun. If only she could have a few weeks to regain her footing outside the high drama. If she just had some space to gather her thoughts, plan, put her life on track again…

The ring box in the middle of the mattress drew her eyes like a magnet. Her feet followed, leading her toward the bed.

Jason's offer of a temporary engagement spiraled through her mind. Tempting. Dangerous. Could she risk that much time in California in close quarters with him?

Then again, with her life in New York ready to implode and her own health a bit touchy, could she afford not to?

Jason guided the rental car along the two-lane road leading into a quaint small town about forty minutes out of the city. Lauren sat beside him, her head resting back, that crazy sweater purse of hers cradled in her lap against the gentle curve of her stomach.

Of their baby.

He finally had Lauren alone for a few hours and he needed to make the most of them. He'd dug deep for everything he knew about her, had approached the evening as an account he needed to win.

Yeah, thinking of this analytically was a helluva lot easier for him than contemplating how important it had become to win this point. The more he thought about the crook who'd stolen from her business, the more pissed off he got. She was so damn talented. He'd recognized her extraordinary artistic gifts from their very first meeting.

His fist tightened on the luxury sedan's gearshift. The urge to do more than protect—to take action—fired through him, stronger than anything he could remember since he'd been on assignment in the Navy.

Of course, persuading Lauren would be easier if she was awake. She'd been out like a light before they hit the city limits. If she didn't wake up by the time he reached their destination, he would simply circle the block until she woke up or he needed to refuel the car. As much stress as she'd been under, she undoubtedly needed the sleep. And he could press his point better with a well-rested Lauren.

Vintage streetlamps dotted the roadside, casting dim orbs for a shadowy view of the small stores and shops. Snowflakes skittered in front of the sweeping beams of the headlights, the occasional car swishing past in the other lane.

Ring, ring. Her cell phone cut through the silent car with soft wind-chime tones, buried deep in her funky sweater purse. Too deep for him to fish out. Would she simply sleep through it?

She stirred, then jolted awake, her long eyelashes sweeping wide and blinking fast. Lauren grabbed her purse and stuffed her hand inside. She pulled out the cell just as the ringing stopped. She frowned.

He turned down the radio, jazz music fading. "Do you need to take that call?"

She shook her head and stuffed her phone back in her bag. "No, it's fine. I can call back later."

"I understand if you have work commitments."

"It's not work." She fidgeted with the handle on her purse, the strap looking as if it was made from the arms of a sweater. "My mother. She calls. A lot."

From her tone it didn't sound as if she looked forward to those calls, but still, they talked. He hadn't spoken with his parents since his dad disowned him, vowing he'd broken his mother's heart by turning his back on everything they'd done for him. Hell, he didn't want to go there in his mind. Better to focus on Lauren. "What did your family have to say about the baby?"

She pitched her purse on the floor. "I haven't told them yet."

Strange. "She calls but she doesn't visit?"

"We haven't seen each other in a month. I only started showing a couple of weeks ago."

"They're going to hear soon. Hell, I heard clear across country. I'll go with you when you tell them."

A laugh burst free. "Who said you're invited, ego man? Besides, they're divorced."

He eased up on the accelerator as they approached a curve, careful to keep the car well below the speed limit. He had precious cargo on board. "I thought we were going to try and get along for the baby's sake."

"Sorry." She folded her arms under her chest and stared out the window, trees stretching ahead in the historic suburb, full of whitewashed fences and brick colonials. "I'm upset about work and taking it out on you."

He wanted to remind her he could fix that work problem in a flash, but decided not to push his luck. Better to go at this from a different angle. "You can't genuinely expect to keep it a secret that I'm the baby's father, can you? Your parents will find out eventually. If they're going to get upset, maybe it would be best to run a preemptive strike. We tell them as a unified front, catch them off guard, then head out before they have a chance to ask questions."

"That sounds good in theory, but the odds of getting both my parents in the same room together are slim to none. And the second one of them finds out, that person will be on the phone blaming the other." She shook her head, her booted feet crossing and uncrossing restlessly, her purple footwear drawing his eyes, not to mention his interest. "I just don't want to put myself through that if I can possibly avoid it."

He couldn't recall her mentioning much about her parents before. They'd mostly talked about work and nightlife in New York. He'd always been attracted to Lauren, but the timing never seemed right to pursue it. First she was seeing someone else, then he was. Although he couldn't even remember who that other woman was now. "Sounds like your parents have really hurt you since they split up."

"Maybe in the past." Her chin tipped, her green eyes glinting from the dashboard glow. "But I don't let them have that kind of power over me anymore."

"Are you sure?" He glanced at her purse with the cell phone. "Just because they had a contentious relationship doesn't mean we'll play out the same problems."

The glimmer in her eyes turned cooler than the snow-flakes picking up pace outside. "And just because you've been inside my body doesn't give you the right to crawl inside my head."

"Fair enough." He liked her spunk most of all. When he thought about it, he liked a lot of things about her. Her smarts, her ambition, even her obsession with packing every square inch of her apartment with plants. Then there was the way her cool exterior lit on fire when he'd least expected it.

"That's it? You're backing off?" She looked over at him, her full lips parting in a pretty O of surprise that invited him to lean across…

He held strong. Better not push his luck. Especially when he had thoughts filling his mind of her wearing nothing but her hair.

"You asked me to back off. I'm listening to you." Very closely. Details were important with so much at stake.

He slowed on the tree-lined road, nearing his destination.

She watched him through narrowed eyes. "I've seen you at work. You never give up, you merely change tack. Remember when you went crazy for the sailboat ink drawing I did and vowed to work it into the cologne campaign even though the client was dead set on a cowboy graphic?"

Okay, so that sailboat was now stamped on male cologne bottles around the world—the original drawing framed in his computer room at home. But all that was beside the point. He focused on the goal.

"This is more important than work. I want you calm and happy." Honest enough, and while he was going for truthfulness… "Hell, and it just so happens that I also want you. You were beautiful before, but now you're absolutely stunning."

"Back down, Romeo," she said, but still smiling, as he guided the car up to a small cabin restaurant. "You've already worked your way into my bed."

"It's been a while." Four months that felt like longer and still he hadn't been able to forget her. Irritation nipped. Damn it, he'd had to force himself to offer to buy another woman a drink. A drink, for Pete's sake. He hadn't even asked her for a date.

Lauren pulled out her cell phone and thumbed the keypad.

Jason reigned in his irritation and focused on Lauren. "Your mother again?"

"No, I'm checking the call history." She pursed her lips. "Hmm…four months and not a single call from you. Doesn't seem like you've been pining for me."

Had she been mad that he hadn't called? He'd considered it, but she'd been fast to show him the door after they had sex. Maybe he'd misread her. As much as he prided himself on gauging people, this time, he wouldn't mind being wrong one damn bit.

Maybe she did want a repeat. God knows, he'd

wanted more of her then, wanted more now. Her flowery scent drifted across the car, her soft curves warm, inviting him to pull off somewhere more secluded and tangle up with her. The pregnancy complicated matters, sure. But maybe sex could simplify them again.

Pure want pounded through his veins. "You made it clear our plans for the future didn't jibe."

"That hasn't changed."

"Everything has changed." He shifted in his seat, the leather creaking as he leaned closer to her.

Her pupils dilated. She swayed nearer. Still he waited, taking his time to breathe in the fresh scent of her, the flowers and greenery she worked with.

He slid an arm along the back of her seat, just cupping her shoulder, absorbing the feel of her, remembering. Her curves fit into the curve of his arm, softer, fuller with the swell of pregnancy between them.

He forced himself to move away. "This baby puts a whole new spin on priorities, and the sooner you accept that, the sooner we can move on to the good stuff."

She flopped back with a frustrated sigh. "You have a one-track mind."

He wasn't going to make the same mistake twice. If there was a chance she wanted to resume the sexual relationship, he wouldn't mess it up again by pushing too fast or walking away too soon. Time to start romancing the mother of his child.

Jason flipped his coat collar up and unlocked the car doors. "Let's put this conversation on hold until after supper. I have a surprise for you."

He was certain the specially chosen restaurant would charm her. He just had to hope his best powers of persuasion would be enough to sway this coolly inscrutable woman.

The stakes were too high to consider a loss.

Where had she lost her self-control?

Lauren gripped the banister of the front steps leading up to her apartment building, a restored brownstone. The dinner with Jason had been amazing. His choice of a family-owned Italian restaurant full of plants charmed her. The rustic old homestead was like a warm vineyard inside. Having him notice her love of greenery touched her. He was trying.

She climbed the steps, aware of him at her back. Of course he was trying. He wanted to get his way. Jason Reagert was a driven, ambitious man. Everyone in the ad business knew nothing could stop him when he set his mind to do something. She'd found it admirable when they were work friends.

But as the target of his campaign? She wasn't so sure anymore. What would have been an enjoyable, intimate evening bothered her somehow, made her want the real thing.

No. She wasn't ready to go that far. The ring would stay in her purse a while longer.

She glanced over her shoulder as a car slushed past. "Thank you for the thoughtful dinner. You actually managed to take my mind off the mess at work for a couple of hours."

He turned up his coat collar, his dark hair shiny in the glow of the outdoor lights. "You need to eat. Glad I could be of service."

Lauren twisted her key in the lock. "You're not going

to use my comment as an excuse to press your plan for a fake engagement?"

"You know where I stand. What more is there to say?" He followed her into the building's hallway, apparently in no hurry to call it a night. "And before you ditch me on the stoop, I am going to see you safely to your apartment door."

"For safety's sake?" She gestured around the entry-way, soaring ceiling echoing the low voices of a couple down the corridor and the older lady in 2A calling to her poodle for a walk. Nobody would get mugged here. Too many witnesses.

"Somebody's gotta protect you from that vicious pup." He smiled, his five-o'clock shadow adding a bad-boy air to go along with the glint in his eye.

She rolled her eyes and started up the stairs, trying not to think about how long those three flights would feel once she was in her third trimester. "Come on, then."

He followed, a wooden stair creaking under his foot. "I'm not asking for coffee or anything. Although if you invite me, I'll pick you up and carry you inside for a night you won't forget."

"I had forgotten how persuasive you can be."

"I didn't forget how good you smell." He eye-stroked her. "Have I told you how much I like the scent of flowers on you?" He dipped his head. "Taking you to that restaurant was as much for me as it was for you."

"Dinner was nice and I appreciate that you picked a spot to win me over, but I don't like being manipulated. Your honesty calls out to me more than anything."

A grin creased the corners of his eyes as they reached

the third floor. "I forget sometimes that you and I are in the same business."

"Just be straight with me."

"I can do that."

Could she believe him? Leaning back against her door, she searched his eyes for some sign of his deeper thoughts and feelings. She looked and found…passion.

Not a surprise, but unsettling all the same, with her own emotions in such a whirl that she felt the least upset could send her spinning. Before she could think, she reached to dust melting snowflakes off the lapel of his jacket. Hard, male muscles twitched under her touch. Her pulse raced, stirring that pottery wheel inside her faster.

"Whoa!" She jolted back, pressing a hand to her belly.

Frowning, Jason braced a palm against her back. "Are you all right? Give me the key. You need to lie down."

"I'm fine, totally fine." She stepped away before she succumbed to the temptation to lean against him. The baby's swift kick brought her back to reality. "Our kiddo is just exercising off that fabulous chicken marsala."

His gaze dropped to her stomach. His fingers flexed. The way he didn't ask for what he so obviously wanted nudged her to offer. "Do you want to feel?"

He nodded curtly.

She took his hand and flattened it to the spot where… "I'm not sure if you'll be able to feel—it's still kinda early." And no way was she inviting him to touch her bare stomach. Would he be at her doctor appointments down the road? Too much to think about. She needed to stay in the moment, one thing at a time. "Wait, just a little to the left." She guided him. "Right there."

His eyes widened. He looked up at her quickly, then back to her stomach. "I think I… Yeah. Wow."

"Sometimes I just lie in bed and feel the baby move until all of the sudden I see an hour has passed. Wild, isn't it?"

"I had no idea what that felt like. I've never…" He looked up at her again, holding her gaze, no shutters in place for the first time. "Thank you."

All noise around her faded, the other couple, the barking poodle, became a dull din drowned out by the drum of her pulse in her ears. She linked her fingers with his, wondering what it would be like to follow this attraction.

The heels on her boots brought her closer to his face. He only needed to duck a little, or she could arch up. Only a kiss. Nothing more. A simple…brush of his mouth against hers. She could feel his breath already touching her in a phantom caress and, God, how she wanted this, just this much. Why even bother worrying about whether they would take it further?

She nipped his bottom lip. He growled low, then took her mouth with his, fully, no way to tell who'd opened for whom first because the hunger just took over. They'd kissed in her office before landing on the sofa. It hadn't been a totally impersonal hookup, but they certainly had made out. Not like this, standing in the hall outside her door, necking with the man who'd taken her to dinner. There was something wonderfully romantic about it. Something that made her want to sink in for a while and just enjoy the moment.

Her fingers tested the texture of his short hair still damp from snowflakes. He smelled of the cool crisp winter air and a hint of oregano from the restaurant, and her ravenous senses lapped up every bit.

"Lauren," he whispered, scattering kisses up her cheekbone, over her ear, "this is getting more than a little out of control for a public hallway. Do you want to move inside?"

Did she? She inched back to stare up into his face.

Her apartment door swept open, startling her back a step and into the present. Jason stepped in front of her protectively, his back tense under her fingers. When had she touched him again? Her fingers curled deeper into the fabric of his jacket, taut muscles flexing under her grip.

She peered over his shoulder and winced. "Mom?"

Four

Lauren stared at her mother, framed in the open doorway, and tried not to panic. How long would it take those keen maternal eyes to notice the baby bulge under the baggy sweater? She really should have taken care of informing her parents before now.

Second-guessing herself served no good. She needed to focus on how to best handle the moment, which began with gauging her mother's current mood by how she dressed.

Jacqueline Presley had always been a strange mix of junior league meets avant garde. She wore her standard Chanel suit—plum purple today—but with chunky jewelry in an animal theme. A family of ruby lizards climbed up one side of her jacket. Her emerald cape with silver fringe was draped haphazardly over her arm. She must have just arrived.

How she'd talked her way past the super to get inside, Lauren didn't even want to know.

She had more pressing concerns, anyway. Her mother's clothes said she was in an up mood, but her tousled hair, chipped nails and shaking hands testified to a frenetic edge. Sure, they were minor signs, but Lauren had learned long ago to catalog every detail, read the nuances, prepare herself for anything.

As she struggled for what to say, Jason stepped forward and thrust out his hand. "Hello, Mrs. Presley. I'm Jason Reagert."

"Reagert?" She shook his hand, then tapped the air with a rhinestone-studded fingernail, chewed down on one corner. "Are you related to J. D. Reagert of Reagert Comm?"

His smile tightened but didn't disappear. "My father, ma'am."

"Oh, no need to call me *ma'am*. I'm Jacqueline." She took his arm and hauled him into the apartment, not even looking back at Lauren.

What the hell?

She'd been so freaked out worrying that her mother would learn about the baby—only to be ignored completely. But then, Jason represented everything her mother wanted in a son-in-law. Lauren followed them inside, closing the door behind her.

Jacqueline's laugh bounced around in the vaulted ceiling. Her mom had many wonderful qualities, and she could certainly be charming when she wanted. And the times she'd taken meds, life had been level, happy. Lauren couldn't quite say "normal," because her mother was always quirky and artsy, but when she took care of her health, those eccentricities were actually fun.

God, she hoped this was one of those times.

Lauren inched her purse around over her stomach and followed Jason and her mother deeper into the apartment, the pair still with their backs to her. Jason pulled out a chair for her mother at the dining table. Odd choice, but Lauren wasn't going to argue, since sitting at the wooden ice-cream-parlor-style table would conveniently hide her pregnancy.

Had Jason known that? A sharp and watchful edge in his eyes indicated he was very aware of everything going on around him. Realization washed over her. Jason was shielding her from her mother. He'd maneuvered everyone so Lauren's stomach was never visible, while keeping her mother distracted—offering to take her wrap, pulling out her chair, asking about her trip down.

Could they actually pull this off without her mom finding out about the baby in such an explosive way tonight? It looked increasingly possible as Jacqueline seemed enraptured with quizzing Jason about his new job in California. Neither of them spared so much as a glance across the table at Lauren. Jacqueline was too busy soaking up the attention to even fidget with her glasses chain dangling from her neck.

How strange, not to mention different, to have someone run interference with her mom. She'd never had that before—her father had been more concerned with hiding out than containing the situation. Okay by her. She was an adult now.

Still, it felt good to breathe. Of course, Jason offered

only a temporary reprieve. The news would come out soon enough, but in a more controlled setting.

Fifteen or so minutes of small talk later, Jason clasped Jacqueline's hand. "Jacqueline, it's been a delight meeting you. I hope you don't find me pushy here, but I've just gotten in from California to visit Lauren and have to leave soon…"

Her mother scooped up her cape and passed it to Jason to hold open for her. "Oh, don't let me keep you two lovebirds. I'll just head back to my suite at the Waldorf." Stepping into her cape and shaking out the fringe, she turned to Lauren. "Lunch, dear, you and I, as soon your guy here returns to California."

"Sure, Mom. We really do need to talk."

"I know a great place with all organic foods. It'll help you with that water retention. Your face is a little puffy." Jacqueline leaned close to press her cheek to Lauren's. "He's a keeper. Don't mess it up this time, dear."

Lauren secured her purse over her stomach. "Of course, Mom."

She so didn't want to have a conversation with her mom about finding an "acceptable catch," especially in front of Jason. She could even let the "puffy face" comment pass if it meant getting through this visit without a confrontation. Come to think of it, her mother would probably see this baby as an opportunity to reel in that "catch."

Lauren shivered in disgust at the thought of her child being used that way.

Jacqueline breezed toward the door with a wave over her shoulder but not even a backward glance at Lauren as Jason escorted her out to the hall.

Lauren sagged in the chair, her purse sliding to the hardwood floor with a hefty thump. She smoothed her hand over the slight bulge of her stomach, the baby rolling under her hand. No child of hers was going to be seen as merely an opportunity to climb up some social ladder.

A tear dripped off her chin.

Damn. She scrubbed the back of her wrist along her face. She hadn't even known she was crying. She heard the creak as Jason closed the door, and she swiped her fingers under her eyes again, praying she'd cleared away any mascara tracks.

As he stepped into the apartment again, she scavenged up a smile. "I can't even begin to thank you."

"For what?" He pulled a chair closer to her and sat.

"For running interference with Mom, for not saying anything about the baby or my slimy accountant."

"I'm all about making things easier for you and our baby."

Our baby.

His words sent a shiver through her. Of excitement or fear?

She thought of their kiss in the corridor and how quickly she could land right back in his arms again, in his bed. Jason had a way of making her lose control, and that scared her most of all.

Lauren clenched her hands together to keep from clasping his hand on the table. "You've been great. Really. Coming here the minute you found out, dinner, handling Mom." In so many other ways, but still she couldn't forget the past months of no communication, not even so much as an e-mail. They needed to talk about that night sometime. Discussing it seemed less daunting now in light of the land mine she'd just dodged with her mother. "You haven't asked how I ended up pregnant."

He scratched his jaw, leaning back. "I figured the condom must have failed."

Memories of their frantic coupling churned through her mind, her body still humming from their make-out session in the hallway. Four months ago they'd torn at each other's clothes. And yes, they'd kissed then, too, deeply, frantically, desperate to connect. Then the mad fumbling through his wallet to sheath him before… "We were pretty preoccupied at the time." Lauren shifted in her chair, suddenly unable to get comfortable. "I appreciate you not questioning me about it."

Her eyes lingered on his strong neck as she remembered the strength of it under her lips, savoring the bristly texture of his late-day shadow.

"We've known each other for a year and worked together most of the time the last month before I left. And I realize you weren't seeing anyone else around the time we, uh, landed on your office couch."

"I wasn't seeing you, either." Yet they'd ended up having impulsive sex, something she'd never done before. She'd only ever been with two men before, both long-term relationships, both men she'd considered marrying.

He angled closer, skimming his knuckles up and down her arm. "We may not have been dating, but I sure as hell always noticed you."

His stroking hand moved slower, shifting from soothing to sensual, the heat of his skin searing through her sweater. She wanted him so damn much.

Too much.

She inched out of reach before she did something impulsive like draw him down to the floor with her. God, why hadn't someone warned her about how out of control her hormones would be during pregnancy? Crying one minute and ready to jump Jason's bones the next.

He rested his hand back on the table, giving her the space she needed. Okay, she would need a couple of states between them to disperse the tangy scent of his aftershave.

Lauren cleared her throat, settling on a subject sure to douse any passion. "How did you manage that whole scene with my mother so perfectly?"

His eyes smoked over her, assessing for three very loud beats of her heart before he relaxed in his chair again.

"A while back," he said, apparently willing to concede her abrupt change of subject, "I landed an ad account for a new makeup line. The spokesmodel got pregnant. They still wanted her face on their product but not her stomach. We did some very inventive posing on that photo shoot."

"Well, I appreciate your help all the same." She toyed with a peppermill in the middle of the table. Maybe if she ground some flakes she could explain away the tears stinging behind her eyes. "I know I'm just delaying the inevitable."

He tugged a linen napkin out of the basket and passed it to her. "Telling your mother about her first grandchild should be a happy event—at a time and place of your choosing."

"Thank you for understanding." Taking the napkin from him, she dabbed at her eyes, cursing the hormonal flood yet again. The weight of everything going on overwhelmed her—from saving her company to being pregnant on her own. It all felt like too much and Jason had offered her help. What did she have to lose by going to California with him, just for a couple of weeks to get her world in order and work out logistics for their life as parents? "Okay, Jason."

"Okay what?"

She drew in a deep breath and crossed her fingers as the words bubbled out. "I'll go to California with you for two weeks and pretend to be your fiancée."

His eyes flashed with surprise briefly, then his face smoothed into his best calm-executive expression, which she'd seen him plaster in place often in the past. "Two weeks?"

So he'd caught that part. "I can't leave my business indefinitely." And she couldn't let herself get caught up in playing house with Jason. "Look what happened when I was out of the office for a few weeks because of the morning sickness. My slimy accountant ran off with half a million dollars."

"Valid point." His features hardened, more angular with his negotiating face. "And you're willing to accept my offer to infuse some cash into your business?"

"A loan. With interest and a payment plan." Her pride would only let her go so far with this crazy idea. "I wouldn't feel right otherwise, especially since I'm not agreeing to move to California permanently."

"We could consider the money an investment for our child."

"Jason, don't push your luck. Even if half a million dollars isn't much to you, it's the principle here."

"Fine," he conceded. "I hear you."

"I'll accept a low interest rate." She wouldn't allow her pride to push her to the point of bankruptcy again.

"Good business decision. I'm obviously not going to argue, since I would have given you the money."

"I'm going to be more careful this time in choosing who will watch over the business while I'm away. I considered hiring an office manager when the morning sickness first set in, but opted to cut corners to save money. That's a mistake I won't be repeating."

She'd gotten a second chance, one she couldn't afford to lose. Her baby deserved a strong, capable mother.

Lauren jabbed Jason in the chest with a finger. "But I really mean it when I say two weeks. I'm nervous enough being away from the office for that long."

"You come back to New York in two weeks, but we leave the engagement on the books to quiet your mom and my client." He clasped her finger and folded it against his chest, enfolding her in the warmth of his touch and chocolate-brown eyes.

"After a while, we can say time apart took its toll."

"Hey, we just became engaged." His thumb rasped along the inside of her wrist, her pulse leaping in response. "Do we have to plan the breakup already?"

"Quit trying to make me laugh." *And quit trying to turn me on.*

He linked their fingers, holding her as firmly with his molten brown gaze. "But you have the most beautiful smile. Call me a selfish bastard, but I like to see it."

The heat of his hand and his eyes stoked the barely banked fire inside her. She needed to hold strong.

Lauren eased her hand away. "I have one final condition."

"Name it. I'll make it happen."

Lauren clasped the arms of her chair to keep her hands off him and her resolve in place. "Under no circumstances will we be sleeping together again."

She'd agreed to go to California to give herself breathing room to regroup, to save her company and, yes, to help him secure his job. But she refused to let him blindside her a second time. She couldn't risk the way sex with Jason stole her ability to think straight.

As she stared at his broad shoulders and steamy brown eyes, she wondered if she'd cut off her nose to spite her face.

Jason had known he would win in the end. Still, he was damn glad to be pulling up to his home in San Francisco's Mission District with Lauren firmly planted in the seat next to him. Sure, she'd tossed that "no sex" clause into the agreement, a frustrating turn. Not unexpected, though. And not insurmountable. He'd seen the arousal in her eyes, the tightening of her nipples under her sweater.

He had hope.

Their day traveling together had gone well in a chartered flight with a catered supper on Sunday night. He'd bided his time and kept things low-key. He had two weeks to win her over, and he wasn't going to blow it on the first day by pushing too fast. Right now, he needed to focus on getting her settled into his restored Victorian house for the night as smoothly as possible.

The streetlamps brightened the inside of the sedan. Lauren pressed her hand to the window of his Saab, her eyes widening. "You have a house."

"I don't live in my car."

She laughed lightly, then looked back at the house as he drove around to the garage. "I just expected you to live in some cool condo in a singles' complex." She looked closer and gasped. "And look at that window box next door. They already have some flowers in January. This is all so…domestic."

He hadn't thought of it that way and wasn't sure he was comfortable with the label. He turned off the ignition and closed the garage door. "When I was in the Navy, I spent so much time on a cramped ship and on the road. I'm ready for a space of my own."

"Babies are noisy and take up lots of room."

"Unless you're pregnant with a dozen sailors, I don't think we're going to have a problem with space." Winking, he stepped out of the car and opened the door for her, leading her out to the covered walkway connecting the new garage to the historic, million-dollar home.

He'd bought the property for its location. As he walked up the steps to the side entrance, he saw the details anew through Lauren's artistic eyes—an old remolded Victorian home, gray with white trim. Hardwood floors stretched throughout, the newly refinished sheen gleaming as he flicked on the lights. Crown molding and multipaned stained-glass windows had made it too good an investment to pass up.

"This is absolutely gorgeous." She spun on her heel, her loose dress swirling around her calves. Her pinup-girl curves and beauty sucker punched him.

Jason loosened his tie. "I like being at the center of things."

"Does that mean you're not a workaholic anymore?"

She skimmed her fingers along the marble fireplace mantel, her gaze skipping around the room with obvious appreciation.

He'd known the vintage home would appeal to her. He hadn't been shopping for the two of them when he'd bought the house, but appreciated the dumb luck of owning a home she liked. Or would that qualify as having something in common?

"My time for recreation is very limited. Having restaurants and nightlife more accessible makes sense."

She traced the chair rail down the hall. "What a find."

He set her luggage at the foot of the stairs. "The couple who lived here before remodeled the whole place, wiring and all. They even gutted and updated the kitchen and baths."

"So how did you luck into it?" Her auburn hair swished along her back as she looked over her shoulder at him.

"Apparently the renovations put a strain on their marriage and they ended up in divorce court. It looked like they broke up in the middle of a project. The upstairs guest bath still had the materials for wallpaper stripping set up in the tub." He'd been working so hard landing the Prentice account, he'd only gotten around to clearing out that guest bathroom the week before. "Neither of them could afford to keep the house on their own, so they sold it."

"How sad." She wrapped her arms around her waist, accentuating her lush curves. "Don't you worry about stepping into all that bad karma?"

"I would worry more about paying the extra cash to get the same house down the road."

"I guess so," she said, her soft voice bouncing around the nearly empty space. "What about furniture?"

He glanced at the bare walls and mostly vacant rooms. A few moving boxes were stacked in a corner in each room. He just pulled out what he needed as he needed it. "I haven't had time to pick anything out and my old place came furnished. So once I got here, I bought the bare basics and went to work. I figured I might as well wait to do it right rather than buy a bunch of crap I regret later on." He gestured for her to follow him. "Come on back to the kitchen. I have seats and food."

"You could hire a decorator." Her footsteps echoed down the hall on her way into the kitchen. Her gasp of pleasure at the spacious layout made him smile.

"I can wait. I have everything I need." He steered her toward one of the two bar stools at the mammoth island between the kitchen and eating area. "A recliner, a big TV. There's a bed upstairs with a top-of-the-line mattress."

Her lips went tight as she sat, resting her elbows on the Brazilian-granite countertop. "Where will I be sleeping?"

"In my bed of course." His temperature spiked at just the words. He opened the refrigerator. "Bottled water? Fruit?"

"Yes, please." She stood and took the drink and grapes from him. "Then I hope for your sake that your guest room has a comfy bed or sofa."

God, he loved the way she didn't take his bull, just quietly lobbing the serve back to him. "No furniture there, either. I'll sleep in the recliner for now and have another mattress delivered."

"That really sucks for you tonight, because I am not

going to feel sorry for you and invite you to share the bed." She tipped back her water.

"You're heartless." He slid a hand behind her waist and brought a grape to her lips.

"I'm fairly certain I made myself clear about the sleeping arrangements before we left New York." She plucked the grape from his hands and popped it into her mouth.

"Can't blame a guy for trying." His thumb stroked along her spine as he watched her eyes for any signs of arousal—like the widening of her pupils, the pulse along her neck quickening.

"Jason, we can't just sleep together for a couple of weeks and then have a civil relationship. It's not logical. We have a child to think about. We can't afford to take risks."

Since she hadn't shoved him away, he urged her a little closer until she stood between his knees. "Don't you think our kid would like to see us together?"

"Are you suddenly magically ready for a long-term relationship? Because you damn well weren't prepared for that four months ago."

His eye twitched. "Sure, why not?"

"How charming." Her lip curled. She shoved his arms away and charged toward the stairs.

"Hey, I'm trying here." He spread his arms wide, following. "This is uncharted territory for me, too."

She gripped her roll bag. "I'm going to bed. Alone. Enjoy your recliner."

Not a problem, since he doubted he would sleep, anyway.

"I will. Thanks. I'm a deep sleeper." He slid the

suitcase from her hand. "And I'm also a guy who can't watch a woman—especially a pregnant woman—lug a suitcase up the stairs."

Without another word, he loped ahead of her. He had her in his house and he had two weeks to work his way into her bed. And once he got there? He intended to make sure she wasn't so quick to boot him out again.

Five

Loneliness echoed around her in the empty bedroom.

Lauren slumped against the closed door, Jason's footsteps growing softer as he made his way to his recliner. Sure, she jammed too much furniture and plant life into her apartment back in Manhattan, but this space? It was beyond sparse.

A mattress on a frame.

One brass side table for a lamp and alarm clock.

And a closet full of clothes hanging from the racks and neatly folded on the shelves.

She pitched her purse on the bed, the bag bouncing to rest on the brown-and-blue comforter. Again the ring rolled out like a bad penny that kept turning up. Lauren placed it on the brass table. The generic piece of furniture.

Damn it, she didn't want to feel sorry for him. Jason

was known as a shark in the business world, and stakes were too high for her to be caught unawares. But something about this place made her sad, made her want to bring flowers and color and noise to his world.

His whole house looked forlorn, for that matter, all the sadder given the home absolutely shouted out for love and attention, parties and family. Although he did have two bar stools in the kitchen. Had they come with the place or had be bought them with the notion of entertaining someone?

Kneeling, she unzipped her suitcase and pulled out the silky nightshirt that still fit. But for how much longer? She smoothed a hand over the growing curve of her stomach. Certainly not femme fatale material.

Her eyes scanned the empty walls, the barren bay window that cried out for a pair of comfy chairs, perfect for a couple watching a sunrise together. But other than those bar stools, it didn't appear he'd brought anyone here.

Anyone except her.

He knew she hadn't been dating anybody for the last six months he'd lived in New York—but *he* had been. Well, up until a couple of months before he'd left, that was. She wouldn't have slept with a guy who was seeing someone else, no matter how swept up into the attraction she may have felt.

Lauren peeled off her travel-weary clothes and slid the nightshirt over her head. The silky fabric teased her breasts to pebbly peaks, leaving her achy. Wanting. God, it would be so easy to walk down those stairs and satisfy the ache between her legs.

She eyed the door and actually considered taking

what she wanted. She even stepped forward. Her toe hooked on the strap to her computer bag.

Her computer. Her work. She needed to remember her reason for coming here in the first place—to give herself time to plan, to save her business, to save her pride.

Too bad a laptop and pride made for very chilly bedfellows.

Jason stepped over the serpentine computer cord, Lauren's laptop closed and resting on the bedside table by his alarm clock. The ring box sat by the clock, closed. Her ring finger was still bare. She'd agreed to be his fiancée, even flown to California, but she hadn't committed one hundred percent to the plan.

He set the breakfast tray on the corner of the mattress and took his time studying the sleeping woman in his bed. Her auburn hair was spread over the brown cotton pillowcase, the sheets tangled around her legs. Her lemon-yellow nightshirt rucked up to the top of her thighs. He remembered well how soft those legs were to the touch, how strong when wrapped around his waist, insistently urging him along. Keeping his hands to himself with her in his space all the time was going to be tougher than he'd expected, but the game went to those who were patient.

Jason sat on the edge and indulged himself by stroking her hair away from her face. He hated to disturb her, but also didn't want to leave her alone in a strange place without checking on her. "Wake up, sleepyhead."

She rolled to her back and stretched, the nightshirt pulling taut over the growing curve of her stomach.

Feeling the baby move the other day had been…amazing. And unsettling.

Persuading Lauren to stay became all the more important.

Her eyes flickered open, vague and unfocused. She smiled, reaching up to him, and just that damn fast he forgot about careful plans and brushed a kiss over each beautiful eye. Her soft skin enticed him to hang around a while longer, kiss the tip of her nose, her chin. He would have liked to work his way lower, but she wasn't fully awake yet, and he wanted her aware and consenting the next time they had sex.

She wriggled slowly, sensuously, beneath him, waking him up hard and fast, harder still as she sighed sweetly. He rested his forehead against hers.

And then she froze, her eyes snapping open wide. "Jason—" she shoved at his chest and slid to the side "—I thought I told you to stay out of my bed."

He eased back, frustration pulsing through his veins. *Patience.* "You're in *my* bed, remember?"

"A technicality." She tugged her nightshirt down to her knees with one hand and pulled the sheet up higher with her other.

"I remember you being more of a morning person." He lifted the black lacquer tray from the corner of the bed.

"That was back when my stomach didn't live in my throat." She eyed the breakfast tray packed with juice, milk, toast and eggs. "Thanks, though. This is nice of you."

"I'm sorry you're not feeling well."

"I'm better now. At least I can keep food down." She plucked up a piece of toast and nibbled at the corner.

Content she was going to eat, he stood, for the first time in…well, ever wanting to delay leaving for the office. "I'll be back at lunchtime."

"You don't need to. I can entertain myself." She sipped her milk. "I have work on the computer and calls to make."

"All right, then. We'll meet up for supper. Tomorrow I need to introduce you to my boss, and there's a big shindig in the evening later this week."

"Ah, so I'll get to meet the people who don't like the fact that you have a pregnant girlfriend." She scrunched her slim nose. "Great. I can't wait."

"Actually it's the client who has the problem, not my coworkers." He tugged a tie out of the closet, slid it under his collar and began knotting it.

"Oh, that's right. The old-fashioned guy."

He flipped his collar back in place and reached for his suit jacket, the intimacy of the morning stealing over him and she'd only been in his house one night. "It's his money to spend how he chooses. If we want his account—and we do—then we have to play by his rules, especially with Golden Gate Promotions nipping at our heels. Surely the businesswoman inside you understands that."

"I hear what you're saying."

"It would really help convince people to buy into our engagement if you would wear this." He scooped the ring box off the table and placed it on her breakfast tray. Winning a point was all about the presentation. If he offered her the diamond nestled in his palm, it seemed too much like a real proposal. Hopefully, by casually dropping it on the tray, she would feel less crowded.

Lauren nudged the box with the tip of her index

finger. "You can't really expect to marry someone just to please a business associate."

Her question churning in his brain, he decided honesty would work best. She was smart and insightful, two things he enjoyed most about her.

"Honestly, Lauren, I'm not sure how far I would go with this. I'm still taking things a day at a time, working to make the best decision possible to secure the baby's future, which means smoothing out your world and mine. Making the engagement as official as possible— including flashing this ring around—will go a long way toward taking care of those concerns. It could keep your mother off your back for a while, too."

Lauren lightly punched his arm. "Now you're playing dirty pool."

"I'm a man on a mission." He tapped the little velvet box.

She hugged her knees and stared at the ring as if it was a bomb, not a three-carat, flawless rock.

Nice. He restrained the urge to laugh. Especially since it really wasn't all that funny.

Lauren tore her eyes from the ring. "What will I say if someone asks when we're getting married?"

He cricked his neck from side to side, working out the stress already knotting its way up and it wasn't even seven o'clock yet. "Tell them your mother is planning the wedding. Tell them we're looking for a date that fits in with our work schedules. Tell them we're thinking about bolting to Vegas and will keep them posted."

She scooped up the box and held the ring so it reflected the morning light streaming through the stained-glass window. "You're really, really good at lying."

Lying? He prided himself on being a man who stuck to the truth, even if he did his best to make that truth something others would buy into. "I'm just an ad man spinning the product."

She stayed silent, but her eyes said loud and clear she thought he was lying to himself.

Steam from the shower still coating the air, Lauren tucked the towel more snugly around her body and raced to the telephone. God, she felt like a teenager rushing to catch a call from a guy.

Gasping, she snatched up her cell phone from the bedside table, her wet hair a dripping rope over her shoulder. "Hello?"

Her mother's voice popped through the airwaves, loud, high-pitched and frantic. "Lauren, I got a call from the lawyer for Aunt Eliza's estate today."

Lauren dropped to the edge of the bed, her stomach knotting as she mentally kicked herself for not checking caller ID. "Why is he speaking with you, instead of phoning me directly?"

Could something actually be wrong? The money from Aunt Eliza's estate had already been transferred to her—and stolen by the crooked accountant.

"He said he's looking for you and can't find you. Where are you?"

"I'm on a business trip, but I have my cell phone and am checking e-mail. I'll give him a call. Thank you for the heads-up," she said quickly, hoping to end the conversation.

"Dear, he says you're having financial troubles."

Lauren measured her words carefully. Her parents

had plenty of money and didn't hesitate to share it with her, which was generous. Except that money came with big strings attached. And quite frankly, she didn't want to be a trust-fund kid, living her entire life off Mom and Dad's hard work, never accomplishing anything on her own. "Things are tight at work, but I'm settling that out."

"Tight? Most businesses fail in their first year, you know, dear." Her mom's jeweled glasses chain clicked in the background as she fidgeted.

"Yes, Mother. I know the statistics." And she prayed her business wouldn't add to the failed numbers on that list. "Thank you for passing along the message."

Jacqueline pressed ahead. "You know, I'm going to call my accountant to talk to you. Make sure to keep your cell phone with you."

"Thank you, Mom, but I can handle it." And she would. She hugged her towel closer, shivering.

"You've never been good with money, dear."

Staying silent, she bit her lip. Hard. The barb dug deeper than her teeth.

Her mother continued. "Remember when you blew your entire savings on that watch?"

"Mom—" the words bubbled up in spite of the fact she knew better than to argue with her mom on a rant "—I was in the third grade. My savings fit in a piggy bank."

Her mother's voice cracked on the start of a sob. "Of course. What do I know? I only care about you." Jacqueline gasped again and again between words, her voice bobbling. "There's no need to attack me. You're just like your father, always picking, picking, picking at everything I do."

"Mom, I'm sorry—"

"Yes, well, at least I have somewhere to go to relieve the stress. Did I tell you about my new vacation home?"

Lauren closed her eyes. Already weary and it wasn't even lunchtime. Her mother's mood swings were nothing new, but exhausting all the same. She just listened and hmmmed when her mother shared the details of the latest perfect place to get away to.

Which actually meant a new place to start over, since she'd alienated the people in her old vacation community. Lauren had seen it play out time and time again. While she half listened to her mother, she stared at the little velvet box.

Jason had been so calmly helpful in dealing with her mother. He'd helped her with her business troubles and her mother. He was certainly trying to understand what *she* needed, as well, even down to small details like the flowers in her office and the toast for the morning.

His reasons for becoming engaged might feel calculated, but what did she really have to lose by simply wearing his ring? Just by sliding that diamond on her finger, she could help him secure his job, which made for a more secure future for their baby. He was already doing everything he could to help stabilize her business, too.

She slipped the velvet box from the side table. The ring winked suggestively from the bed of velvet.

It was just a formality, really. She was here, in his house, pregnant with his child. What did it matter if she wore the ring?

Phone tucked under her chin, Lauren slid the ring in place and closed her fist. She knew this was the right thing to do, but the thought of sitting around here all day staring at that ring and second-guessing herself made her nerves churn so fast she feared losing her toast.

Jason wanted his office to know about their engagement. He'd given her time to gain her footing even though the delay could cost him. So why bother waiting? She could meet the people he worked with and even surprise Jason with a casual meal out where they could start on their path of a smoother relationship for the baby's sake.

Decision made, she stood. "Mom, it's been great talking to you, but I have a lunch date I just can't miss."

Staring out the taxi window, Lauren took in the towering white buildings of Union Square's posh shopping district. Somewhere in that concrete jungle with palm trees waited Maddox Communications. She'd done more research on the Internet about MC before leaving Jason's house. She was a businesswoman in her own right and knew to arm herself as well as possible before entering any new camp.

The Maddox patriarch, James, had founded Maddox Communications more than fifty years ago. He'd married Carol Flynn and they'd had two sons: Brock and Flynn, who each went into the family business. When James died eight years ago, Brock took over the helm, with his brother acting as vice president.

Lauren leaned forward, reading signs, watching for Powell Street, and, more important, the building referred to as The Maddox. Finally the cab cruised to a stop in front of the seven-story, Beaux Arts–style building constructed in 1910. The article she'd found said the building had been set for demolition when James

Maddox saved it from the wrecking ball and had it lovingly restored in the late seventies.

Now the building was reputed to be worth ten times his purchase price.

She tipped the cabbie and stepped out of the taxi. Automatic doors whooshed wide. The first floor was home to the trendy New American cuisine restaurant Iron Grille and several retail stores. At the elevator, she consulted the building legend and found the second and third floors were rented out to other businesses.

Floors five and six were the corporate offices. Directions indicated that clients and visitors to Maddox Communications should enter the offices on the sixth floor.

Elevator Muzak piped jazz horns, floors chiming smoothly and quickly. The elevator opened directly to a reception desk and total opulence and edginess, from the black-stained oak floors to the stark white walls with original art. Two seventy-inch plasma screens sat on either side of the large reception desk, showing videos/commercials with a small scroll of words along the bottom proclaiming they'd been produced by Maddox Communications.

Jason had landed well in his new job. A sense of pride in his accomplishment beyond his parents' wealth stirred. She sure understood how tough it could be to step out of the shadow of influential parents to make your own mark in the world.

Lauren's low heels clicked along the high-sheened floors.

The receptionist smiled. "Welcome to Maddox Communications." Her short brown hair swished with every perky twitch of her head. "How can I help you?"

Lauren glanced down at the woman's name plate—Shelby—and smiled. "Hello, Shelby, I'm here to see Jason Reagert. My name's Lauren Presley."

"Yes, ma'am, if you'll wait over there?" She gestured to the large white leather sofas.

Lauren flickered her thumb over the engagement ring nervously as butterflies stirred. Shelby eyed her with undisguised curiosity. Lauren's stomach flipped again.

Suddenly Lauren wasn't so sure this had been a good idea, after all. What kind of game had she been expecting to play? She'd wanted to show Jason she was in charge and had only succeeded in looking erratic.

She cringed inside. Maybe she should just leave. She inched her purse around to cover her stomach, starting to stand.

A shadow stretched from the hall and she hesitated. Was it Jason already?

A lean man, around forty with black hair, came into sight, stern and very obviously not Jason. The man stopped at the desk, passing a note, his voice low. Lauren decided to make her big escape—

Shelby whispered back and pointed to Lauren. He straightened and walked toward her. Damn.

He extended his hand. "Hello, I'm Brock Maddox." The CEO. The big boss and obviously one confident son of a gun. "I understand you're here to see our wonderboy."

Busted. She shook his hand. "Lauren Presley. I'm a friend of Jason's. I'm also a graphic designer. We worked together on a couple of projects back in New York."

He eyed her stomach briefly. Sheesh. Was it that obvious? Apparently so. "Are you in San Francisco on work or vacation?"

"Both," she answered noncommittally. "Shelby was just about to let Jason know I'm here."

"Follow me. You can surprise him." Brock gestured over his shoulder and began plowing deeper into the Maddox offices, making low small talk she barely registered.

She was committed now to seeing this through. She quelled her nerves as he stopped in front of a door with a brass plate: Jason Reagert.

Inhaling a bracing breath, she pushed open the door and stopped short. Jason stood with his back to her—with a woman. *A smiling, stunningly beautiful red-haired woman who had her hand placed intimately on his arm.*

Fluttering nerves morphed into stone-still anger and a possessiveness that unnerved her to the tips of her toes.

He couldn't actually be seeing someone else? For a guy who cared about causing a scandal at work, he sure was playing with fire on a lot of levels.

Lauren stiffened her spine, feeling as frozen as the chill seeping into her heart. As she took in the couple standing together in his sleek office full of nautical prints, she couldn't believe she'd actually allowed herself to be hopeful simply because he'd brought her some toast and milk.

God, she was too easy. She'd had it with passively letting people walk all over her—her mother, her accountant, now Jason. She twirled the ring on her finger. At least she'd gotten a wake-up call when it came to the father of her baby.

He'd brought her here, damn it. And she wasn't going to scamper off like some scared rabbit. He wanted a fiancée? He was about to get one. Big-time.

"Hey there, lover." Lauren rested her hands on her stomach. "I'm absolutely starving. Are you ready for lunch?"

Six

Damn it all.

Jason stepped back from Celia so her hand fell from his arm—something he'd been a second away from doing, anyway, right before Lauren walked into his office. What was she even doing here? And to make matters worse, Brock stood just behind her, scowling.

What rotten timing all the way around. Celia had stopped by his office to ask if he was going out for drinks after work, and he'd been preparing the words to clear the air between them when the door had opened.

He needed to do some damage control ASAP.

Lauren stepped farther into the office, her green eyes flashing like kryptonite, ready to take down Clark Kent. Her loose-fitting teal-colored dress swirled around her legs, brushing against her curves. The woman was total sensual confidence. She thrust out her hand—her left one—engagement ring glinting. "I'm Lauren Presley, Jason's fiancée just in from New York. We're getting married tonight."

"Married?" Celia squeaked.

"Tonight?" Jason needed air because keeping up with the surprises Lauren dished his way was an Olympic sport.

Brock cocked an eyebrow and leaned deeper into the doorway for a front-row seat.

Lauren breezed up to Jason's desk and hooked her arm in his. "I know an elopement is supposed to be a secret. Sorry for spilling the beans, honey, but I'm just so darn excited. We're catching a hop to Vegas. Hokey, I know, but, well—" she caressed her stomach "—it's obvious we don't have a whole lot of time to plan unless I want to get married wearing a tent."

Brock stuffed his hands into his pockets, his face inscrutable. "We all had no idea. Congratulations."

Jason adjusted his tie. "Thank you."

Lauren smiled apologetically. "Blame me for that secrecy part, Mr. Maddox. I tend to be very private about my social life. I'm working on being more open." She smiled up at Jason, her fingernails digging trenches into his arm, the only indication her joy was anything other than authentic. "Did you tell them you'll be late for work tomorrow?"

He patted her hand, easing her nails away. "Uh, not yet."

Brock straightened. "Sounds like you two have some plans to make. We all look forward to celebrating with you when you get back. Congratulations again." He held the door open for wide-eyed Celia to follow.

Man, Jason owed her an apology. But he also owed Lauren his loyalty. Had she been serious about eloping? If so, why the sudden change of heart?

Once the door clicked shut, Jason turned to Lauren, eyeing her warily. Her hand rested mighty darn close to the pewter antique compass he used as a paperweight. Was she the kind of person who threw things? She was usually so calm he wouldn't expect behavior like that from her. Although he also wouldn't have expected her to announce to the world they were jetting off to Vegas in a few hours.

He closed the gap between them, watching her stoic face for the least sign of her mood. "Were you serious about eloping tonight?"

"Serious as a heart attack." She set the pewter paperweight down with an extra-hefty thud.

"That's great, really great." He wasn't sure what had caused her change of heart. Hell, he wasn't sure what had propelled her to come to the office in the first place, but he didn't intend to argue. He brushed her hair back over her shoulder, lightly, intimately. "You have nothing to be jealous about with Celia."

"Who said I'm jealous?" she snapped.

"You're obviously upset." He cupped the back of her neck, massaging, hopefully soothing.

She shrugged free of his hand. "I don't like being made a fool of."

"There's nothing going on between Celia and me." And there wasn't.

"Does she know that?" Lauren jabbed a finger toward the door.

"I was making sure when you walked in."

Her eyes narrowed. "So there *is* something between the two of you."

"Whoa, hold on. Let's back this up." His feet damn near paced the shine off the black floors. "You're confusing the hell out of me. I try my ass off to charm you, and you all but toss my ring in the Bay. But when you think I'm flirting with another woman—which I was not—you're ready to elope?"

"As soon as you can pack your bags and book the flight." She closed the gap between them, blocking his pacing. Her jaw jutted aggressively. Which also happened to thrust out her full, kissable bottom lip.

She was hot when she was mad. Her eyes glimmered and her hair all but crackled from the heat radiating off her.

He was trying to do the straight-up best thing for their baby, and she was jerking him around nonstop. "If you're so pissed at me, why did you announce to the world we're headed to a Vegas wedding chapel?"

"Before—" she inched closer, tipping her head back until there was only a whisper of static-charged air between them "—I was worried about our feelings getting tangled up. But believe me, you've laid to rest all my fears about broken hearts and muddying the waters with an emotional train-wreck marriage like my parents went through. Now I know without question, there's not a chance in hell that I could fall in love with you. So let's go to Vegas."

Lauren held it together all the way through the introductions to Maddox Communications employees as Jason escorted her to his car. At least Jason had seemed to get the message she didn't want to give anything other than simple yes and no answers as he chartered a flight to Vegas.

She even managed to stay dry-eyed during the flight and through the sham of a wedding ceremony, difficult as hell to do since Jason had somehow managed to find a garden chapel service.

"I now pronounce you husband and wife. You may kiss the bride." The wedding chapel official closed his book of vows, running his hand over the floral cover. His Hawaiian shirt was a little over-the-top, but there were flowers and plants everywhere, just as she would have wanted, which made her all the more emotional.

Jason brushed her lips with a kiss, nothing overly dramatic and yet still perfect. Although the feel of his mouth against hers, even closed and only lightly touching, sent heat sparkling through her veins.

And made tears prick her eyes.

He palmed her waist gently, his thumb stroking so lightly but enough to send her spine arching toward him. Her stupid, stupid traitorous body.

She broke away, looking down quickly, needing space. "Excuse me."

Lauren raced to the washroom, desperate to leave before she embarrassed herself by falling completely apart in front of Jason. The whole day had been like a ride on a high-speed roller coaster, with more than a few loops tipping her life upside down. And somehow she'd zipped right along with it, never once calling for a halt, or even a slow down.

What in the world had she just done?

Lauren rushed into the restroom, potted palms and hanging ferns packing the space. She sank onto the rattan sofa and yanked tissues from the box on the end table. Finally she let the tears flow, tears she'd bottled up since the minute she'd found out she would be having a baby alone. Tears collected from worry about how all of this would affect her mother. Tears over the possibility of losing her business.

And tears over Jason?

This was her wedding night and as much as she wished she could allow herself to enjoy the fringe benefits without worry, she simply couldn't throw caution to the wind that easily.

She would do what it took to save her business. And yes, she would help Jason advance in his career, as well, because that was in the best interest of her child. Once this farcical marriage was done, she was through with Jason Reagert.

But first, she had to get through her wedding night.

Jason had a backlog of work waiting on his laptop propped by his seat on the plane. Normally flights made for the perfect time to play catch-up, and the pilot had just given them the all clear to use electronics.

Tonight he had no interest in what waited on that hard drive.

He shifted in the large leather chair, the aircraft droning softly through the dark, and studied his new bride reclined in a seat, talking on the plane's phone. She'd just finished telling her father about their elopement, making him swear not to tell Jacqueline that he'd been called first.

And although this wasn't a traditional wedding night by any measure, that didn't stop him from aching to share a good old-fashioned honeymoon suite with Lauren.

The single-engine plane offered enough room to move around and a small galley kitchen, but no sleeping quarters other than the chairs that reclined all the way back.

His wife—he paused at the surprise jolt to his pulse at just the word—dialed again and pressed the phone to her ear. She tucked her legs up to the side, adjusting the folds of her teal-colored dress.

"Hey, Mom," Lauren said, fine lines of stress and exhaustion fanning from the corners of her eyes. "Sorry to bother you so late, but I've got some really important news." Her gaze flicked over to him briefly, brushing him like the tips of a flame crackling over his body. "Remember Jason Reagert… Right…you met him at my place last week. Well, he's actually more than a friend. We just got married in Vegas.…"

Jason thumbed the simple gold band on his finger. The wedding chapel had supplied it at the last minute, and he figured the ring would only help cement their case. He hadn't expected to notice its weight quite so much.

Lauren continued, nodding. "Yeah, Mom, I know you would have liked a heads-up so you could attend. But, uh, prepare yourself for more amazing news. Time was kinda tight for us. We're expecting a baby—"

A shriek sounded from the phone, followed by a long string of indistinguishable babbling. Lauren looked over at him briefly with a light wince before continuing. "I'm due in a little less than five months from now— No, I don't know the baby's gender yet— Uh, honey-moon? We have work…" She stopped, interrupted for what must have been the tenth time.

"Mom, that's really—" Sighing, she squinted her

eyes closed while the voice on the other end rambled louder and louder.

Jason took the phone from her hand. Lauren gasped, but he wasn't backing down. "Jacqueline? This is your new son-in-law, Jason, and I'm about to assert my marital rights. We'll be turning off this phone until at least noon tomorrow."

"But wait—" Jacqueline interrupted.

Jason interrupted right back. "Good night, Jacqueline." He turned off the phone.

"Wow," Lauren said. "Just flat-out wow. I don't know how to thank you for making that easier for me."

He wanted to… Hell, he didn't know what he could do to shield her from this sort of fall-out. "Are you all right?"

She smiled shakily. "At least that's done now."

"But are you all right?" he pressed.

"Of course." She straightened, the effort of gathering her control so obvious and laborious he wanted to pull her to him.

Protect her.

But she radiated stand-back vibes.

Calling her parents really had her freaked out, beyond just tense family relations like he had. "What's really going on here?"

"I'm not sure what you mean." She toyed with her purse, avoiding his eyes.

"You're obviously stressed over that phone call." He stroked her chin, tipping her face toward his. "I realize your mother is, uh, wired rather tight, but I think I'm missing something."

"I might as well tell you. You'll find out, anyway, over the years since she's the grandmother of your baby." She gripped the armrests in white-knuckled fists. "My mom was diagnosed as bipolar at twenty-two."

Damn. Not at all what he'd been expecting. "I'm really sorry. All this time we've known each other and you've never mentioned it."

But then, he'd been equally dodgy about his own past, which probably accounted for why he'd never probed too deeply about hers.

She rolled her head along the rest to face him full on, her expression wry. "It's not the sort of thing to come up in the workplace or during after-hour drinks—'Hey, my mom's manic-depressive.'"

What if he'd taken the time to talk to her more over the past year, to really listen, beyond discussing work and exchanging lighthearted banter? Could they have reached a point earlier where she would have shared this with him? He had no way of knowing, since apparently it took a forced marriage to coerce her into opening up.

He hadn't dug more deeply before, but he'd be damned if he'd make the same mistake again. "You said she was diagnosed at twenty-two?"

"She's been in and out of a doctor's treatment for a long while." Only going when her husband pushed or her daughter pleaded. "There were some good times when I was kid. But the past couple of years, she's decided she doesn't want to take any more of it— therapy or meds." Lauren straightened the drape of her dress again and again, restoring order. "Don't get me wrong, I'm not whining. Growing up with those sorts of mood swings was difficult, sure, but I like to think I'm a stronger person for it."

He respected the way she tried to put a positive spin

on things, but he suspected Lauren had done that so often no one noticed when she needed help. "Still, it must have been beyond tough for you as a kid, never knowing what to expect."

She plucked at a stray thread on the hem of her dress, nibbling her bottom lip. "I used to worry I would be like her. Since she never seems to accept she has a problem, what if I'm just oblivious? I've even visited doctors—shrinks—to have myself evaluated."

"And what did they say?"

She hesitated, folding her hands in her lap and studying him intently, then smiling. "You don't look like you're ready to run for the door."

"Given we're in an airplane, that would be damn reckless."

Thank God, she laughed. The sound stroked over him, arousing him as much as her soft hands. Hell, everything about her seemed to turn him inside out lately. But he wouldn't let that distract him. Her vulnerable eyes said she needed something from him now, and he was determined not to come up short.

"Lauren—" he measured his words as carefully as he had in any million-dollar presentation "—I've worked with you for over a year and I haven't seen anything to lead me to believe you have similar issues. I may not have any kind of psych degree, but I do know enough about you to be sure if there was ever a problem, you would do everything possible to take care of it."

Her throat moved in a long swallow as she blinked back tears. "I appreciate that. I like to believe that about myself. But when people learn about her illness, I feel

like they look at me differently, as if my feelings are dis-
counted because I'm just—"

"Hey—" he reached for her hand, unable to resist
touching "—I take you seriously." And he did, person-
ally and professionally. He trusted his judgment and for
a year he'd seen the depth of her stability. If anything,
he wondered how to break through her calm stoicism.

"Thank you." Linking their fingers, she squeezed his
hand, her engagement ring and wedding band glinting
in the low lighting overhead. "So far the doctors have
all said they see no signs of bipolar disease in me. It
usually crops up in your teens and twenties. I know
there are no guarantees, but you won't hear me complain
about turning thirty."

"That must have been a relief to hear."

"More than you can imagine." She curved her hand
over her stomach. "Although now I'm worrying all over
again. What if I've passed along the gene to our child?"

How did he feel about it? He'd barely processed he
had a kid on the way. His thoughts had been focused on
securing the baby's future, luring Lauren to California,
steering clear of a career crash for both of them.

There were so many aspects of his child's life to
worry about. And there were some things he absolutely
couldn't control. His energies were best spent focused
on dealing with what he *could* control.

"You're aware. I'm aware. We'll watch and provide
whatever help our kid needs if the occasion arises." He
squeezed her hand, enjoying the way her pulse leaped
under his thumb. Or was that his heartbeat kicking up
a notch at the feel of her silky-soft skin? "Hell, I've got
a family history full of diabetics and a sister with

dyslexia. There are few families with perfect medical histories."

A tear trickled down her cheek. "God, you can be so wonderfully logical and sweet both at the same time."

"Sweet? That's a new one for me."

"Hey, I'm serious here." She slid her fingers free and cupped his face in her hands. "Somehow you knew just the right thing to say and I could tell you meant every word."

"Just this morning you told me I'm the consummate ad man, good at making the sale even if I have to lie." He wasn't sure why he would try to wave a damn red flag in front of her when she was finally seeing something worthwhile in him. Since when was he into self-sabotage?

And then it hit him. Lauren was too important to him to be anything but completely honest. Could it be that he wanted more than just this wedding night from her?

He forced his focus back on her words, tough to do when it felt like the deck was rolling under his feet even though he knew the plane was flying steady on.

Her hands caressed his face lightly. "Maybe I'm starting to trust my instincts more and my instincts are telling me you're a good man."

She pressed her lips to his.

Her fingers slid back into his hair and he angled his head sideways for a better, fuller fit. The soft give of her mouth against him stirred a barely banked fire. He'd wanted her—hell, dreamed about being with her—since that night in her office. As much as he'd tried to tell himself he was merely immersed in the mayhem of starting a new, high-powered job, no one caught his eye or attention the way she had.

The way she still did.

Lauren leaned into him, her amazing curves pressing close. He burned to get his hands on her again. Skin to skin, touching and traversing every dip and valley, watching her skin flush from wanting him.

Damn it, his hands were shaking.

She smiled against his mouth a second before she eased away. The kiss wasn't an invitation into her bed, but it was a step in the right direction.

"Good night, Jason," she whispered, her hands gliding off him as she settled into her seat again. Her lashes fluttered closed and that fast she was asleep.

He, on the other hand, was wide-awake on their wedding night. Jason adjusted his pants, not that it helped ease the pinch of erection straining at his fly. Not much he could do about that now. He'd been so focused on working that wedding band onto her finger and getting her into bed, he hadn't realized the tougher part was still ahead of him.

Keeping the ring in place.

Seven

How would she just pick up her old life in a couple of weeks?

Lauren sagged onto the edge of the bed, alone on her wedding night. What was left of it, anyway. By the time the chartered flight had landed and Jason drove them back to the house, the sun was already fighting to break over the horizon, oranges and yellows painting a hazy glow in the distance. She would have liked to watch the dawn with him, but he was already showering before he left for the office—some unmissable meeting, he said, but he vowed to come home early. She'd assured him she had business calls and work on her computer.

Strange wedding day. Strange honeymoon. Yet neither of them could afford to take time off. They were both struggling to launch careers. It was silly to want something more.

Too restless to go back to sleep just yet, she kicked off her shoes and wandered back into the upstairs hall. She didn't dare go near where Jason showered. She wasn't sure she could resist the temptation to slide under the spray with him in his luxuriously remodeled bathroom. Everything she'd seen in the house thus far was top-of-the-line, from the kitchen to the three bathrooms, to the master suite with a sitting area. She hadn't checked out the other bedrooms, but suspected they were just as sleek.

She creaked open the room to the door next to the master suite. *Empty.* Just hardwood floors, intricate crown molding and a few packing boxes. The view would make it a lovely guest room.

The next room—equally as empty—had a domed ceiling that called to her fingers to create a little Sistine Chapel with angels for a nursery. Swallowing hard, she closed the door behind her.

One bedroom left. She opened the door and found he actually had furniture here. Not much. Just a cherry table with an elaborate computer, printer and fax machine set up. A tangle of wires led to a power bar on the floor.

A nautical scene scrolled across the screen. Jason had talked about being near recreation, but the only personal items she saw in his house were business suits and work materials. As much as she understood the satisfaction work could bring, a part of her itched to fill his house—his world—with more. Furniture. Plants.

Lazy mornings watching a sunrise.

Sunbeams eased thicker and stronger through the sheers in the window. She needed sleep, for the baby if not herself. She pivoted on her heel—

And stopped short when a frame on the wall snagged her attention. It couldn't be. She stepped back into the room, closer until she saw clearly. Her stomach tightened. Framed on the wall across from the desk…

…the pen-and-ink drawing of a sailboat for a cologne campaign, a drawing created by her.

Her hand shaking, she traced the edges of the image and thought back to how he'd left her office without any argument, hadn't called in four months. Yes, she'd told him to leave, she'd pushed him away.

But could he have been thinking about her just as often as she'd dreamed of him?

Later that day in the MC boardroom, Jason wasn't any closer to figuring out how to keep Lauren in San Francisco. He seesawed his pen on the large oval acrylic table, turning the red leather chair ever so slightly from side to side.

Fellow ad exec Gavin Spencer eyed his rocking pen and raised an eyebrow.

Jason stilled. Damn. He felt like a kid hyped up on a pack of Pixy Stix, all because he wanted to be home with his new wife.

Instead, he was stuck at a mandatory meeting at work. Located in the center of the sixth floor, the boardroom was a huge space, with all four walls made of clear glass that turned opaque with the touch of a button. One wall was currently lit up as a huge screen for the computer-generated presentation of the day.

Brock clicked away the final image on his PowerPoint presentation before turning to the table again. "That's all for now." He turned to his assistant, Elle Linton. "You'll forward the specs from my presentation to everyone?"

She nodded efficiently, her brown hair clasped back smoothly and unpretentiously. "Will do, Mr. Maddox."

Brock tapped the button, transforming the opaque walls back into clear windows. "Jason?"

He forced his attention front and hoped like hell the CEO wasn't about to ask what the last slide was about. "Yes?"

"Let me be the first to officially congratulate you on your wedding. On behalf of everyone here at Maddox Communications, we wish you and Lauren a long and happy life together." Brock started a round of applause.

As the cheers and clapping subsided, Flynn stood. "Everyone here at Madd Comm is looking forward to getting to know your new bride better at the company dinner party."

"Absolutely, we'll be there." The dinner gathering would be more formal than their get-togethers at Rosa Lounge. Wives were expected to attend. Rumor had it that Flynn's estranged wife had chaffed under all the pressure that came from the hours demanded by MC to stay ahead of Golden Gate Promotions.

Jason cricked his neck from side to side, not sure how anyone managed to balance it all, especially in today's competitive market where there were plenty of hungry dogs ready to take his portion. Success had an added edge for him now that he had a wife and baby depending on him.

Gavin clapped him on the shoulder. "What the hell are you doing here leaving that pretty new bride of yours alone?"

"Don't be eyeing my accounts while I'm away," Jason answered, only half joking.

"Wouldn't dream of it," Gavin said, his own competitiveness shining through. But that edge would keep MC on top, which was good for both of them.

Jason rolled his large leather chair back, his feet itching to hit the road. He couldn't afford to take his eye off the ball at work, but an afternoon away the day after his wedding seemed more than reasonable. In fact, it would look strange otherwise. And he did need to make inroads with Lauren to keep her and the baby in San Francisco. "I'm knocking off early today. Lauren and I are planning our honeymoon for later. She understands I have the Prentice account to contend with right now. In fact, she's looking forward to meeting Walter Prentice at the big bash."

Brock studied him through narrowed eyes, assessing. "Perhaps we'll have a chance to get to know your bride in a more informal setting, maybe for an after-work drink at Rosa Lounge sometime this week."

"I'll speak with Lauren and let you know."

Brock nodded shortly. "Sounds like you have a real keeper there, sharp business lady, to boot."

"Thank you. Lauren's a special lady. I'm happy she's willing to follow me out here to California, especially given she has a company of her own back East." There. He'd laid the groundwork for her returning to New York as he'd promised her he would do, but damned if he would give her up that easily.

Her?

It was about their baby, right? About being a full-time father to his kid in a way his father had never been for him and his sister. Hell, time to stop lying to himself. He wanted Lauren here. He wanted her in his bed and in his life. She fit. They'd already proved they got along well as friends and at work.

They definitely were in synch sexually.

California was the right place for her to stay. He could ease the stress for her at work and in her family. They could have it all here in San Francisco. He just had to convince Lauren.

Now that he thought about it, she knew as well as he did that they had chemistry. He'd put all his effort into seducing her when he should work on convincing her on a practical level, showing her the ways their lives could fit together. He needed to think less about returning to his wife's bed and more about persuading her they could make a real family here together in San Francisco.

So for now, he would keep his hands to himself while he romanced his wife.

Lauren tugged her bathrobe tie tighter as her foot hit the last step leading into the hall. Supper with Jason had left her edgy, the carry-in Latin cuisine amazing, their legs brushing against each other at the kitchen island frustrating. She'd hoped a shower would help ease the tension, but no luck. She'd spent the whole time under the spray imagining inviting him to sit on the seat opposite her.

Then joining him to straddle his lap, instead.

A trickle of water slipped from her hair down the V of the robe, between her breasts, heavy and achy with desire. She stared through the carved archway into the living room. A fire crackled in the fireplace. Jason knelt in front, jabbing at the logs with a poker. Jeans pulled taut across his lean hips, the muscles in his thighs rippling against the faded denim and calling to her fingers to explore his strength up close and personal. The blaze in the hearth and between her legs both beckoned. She walked closer, the wood floor chilly beneath her bare feet.

His back still to her, Jason stood. He reached into a cardboard packing box and pulled out a thick striped comforter. With a snap of his wrists, he whipped the spread out and let it rest on the floor in front of the crackling fire.

"Did you finally give up on the chair and opt for the floor?"

He smiled back over his shoulder. "You seemed pretty awake at supper, so I thought you might want to hang out and talk."

"Talk. You want to talk?"

"Sure. Why not?"

Thinking of her sailboat drawing he'd kept framed in his home office gave her the courage to step into the romantic setup he'd prepared. On the corner rested the same black lacquer tray he'd used to bring her breakfast. A couple of cooking utensils—grill tools?—rested on the edge. This time, the wineglasses contained…

"Grape juice. I thought it was only fair you enjoy grapes in some form, since you have to bypass California's amazing wines for a few more months."

Tucking her robe around her knees, she sank onto the comforter. "How was work? Was everyone grilling you for details about the Vegas nuptials?"

"Some natural curiosity. Lots of congratulations." He glanced over his shoulder quickly, then went back to work on the fire. "Everyone wants to get to know you better, of course. There's a dinner party this weekend for the big Prentice account."

"Of course I'll be there. That's why we did this whole marriage thing, right?"

He jabbed the fire, his pause overlong. "The office also goes to a local hangout for drinks every now and again. We don't have to go this week if it's too much for you. You're working all day, as well."

"Drinks are fine—well, water with lime—but I don't have a problem spending time with the people from MC." Except for Celia. That could be damn awkward now that she thought about it. Suddenly she didn't want to talk about work anymore. "You have a way of making the no-furniture thing work…well, other than your furnished office upstairs." She glanced out the corner of her eye, watching for any telling reaction from him.

"I brought a few things from New York with me." He nodded toward the packing boxes. "Linens. Kitchen supplies. My clothes and some books."

"And your computer desk?" And the sailboat she'd drawn.

"Sure." He pressed a hand to the plush comforter. "This was my bedspread back in New York."

"For freezing winters, but not milder San Francisco temperatures, so it's stayed in the box so far." How strange to lead an unpack-as-you-go kind of existence.

"Exactly. Not so cold here."

"But chilly enough for a fire tonight." She angled forward to inhale the rich woodsy scent of an authentic fire. No gas logs here.

"And warm enough for gardens." He rolled up his shirtsleeves as the temperature in the room rose. "I was wondering if you would take a look at the flower beds and offer some suggestions."

A full-out plan already grew through her mind like vines clinging to a trellis, much like the one she could envision in his backyard leading to a hot tub. But this wasn't her house. She wouldn't be staying, and right now she wasn't sure she could take having more things to regret leaving behind when she returned to New York. "Wouldn't you rather hire a landscaper?"

"I would rather have my highly talented graphic-artist wife draw up a plan and put the landscaper to work. But only if you have the time, of course." He dipped his head into her line of sight. "I mean it. I'm not BSing you here."

She would probably regret this later, but… "Okay then, I'll take a look and sketch some ideas." She stared at her wedding rings. "It'll be fun thinking of things the baby will enjoy when we come to visit."

"Great," he said, smiling—another thing she would miss seeing when she left. "And speaking of the baby, I brought late-night snacks to go with the grape juice, if you're hungry." He reached behind the packing box and lifted a small grocery sack.

"I'm always hungry at the end of the day now." The baby fluttered inside her as if already anticipating whatever he had inside that bag.

"I'm glad you're feeling better." He pulled out graham crackers, marshmallows…

…and Godiva chocolates.

Her mouth watered. She eyed all the ingredients in his hands. "We're making Godiva s'mores?"

"Unless you don't want them. I understand about

finicky cravings." He tucked the gold box against his chest. "I can eat them myself."

"Do it and die." She snatched the box of chocolates, tore off the ribbon and popped one of the truffles in her mouth. "Mmm."

His smile went downright wicked. "I take that to mean you do want a s'more."

"Or three," she said, relaxing into the makeshift camp. Although they hadn't stocked Godivas in the tent when she'd been a Girl Scout.

She sat cross-legged on the thick comforter, leaning back on a packing box, the fire warming her as much as the romanticism. Jason put together the s'more and rested it on a grilling spatula with efficient hands. The way he read just what she needed touched a part of her she hadn't known sought tending. She prided herself on her independence, her competence. And while she could have fed herself, she never would have come up with Godiva s'mores.

While she may have known Jason for a year already, he was still surprising her more and more by the second. Like how well he'd handled the discussion on the plane about her mother's mental-health issues. "Thank you again for everything."

He glanced back over his shoulder. "Wait until you taste it first."

"I meant thank you for how understanding you were about my mother."

"I'm sorry she upset you on the phone." Firelight illuminated the genuine concern in his brown eyes. "I wish there was something I could do."

"It's okay. I don't really need her approval anymore."

"But she still has the power to hurt you," he observed too damn astutely.

"I guess maybe there's a part of us that never gets past wanting to see our artwork on Mom's refrigerator. The problem is, my mother only wants me to paint *her* kind of pictures. Her dreams." A dry laugh slipped free. "Although she certainly can dream big."

"Big is good." He placed the heated s'more on a small plate, chocolate and marshmallow oozing from the sides, and passed it to her.

"No. I mean big. Mount Everest big." She smiled her thanks and took the plate. "My mother had those grandiose kinds of fantasies. Two days into my tap lessons she was making plans for Broadway. A dive into the pool and she was talking Olympics."

"That's a lot of pressure for a kid."

"She had the same sort of plans for herself and her artwork. She always talked about how marrying Dad—" she dipped her finger into the warm, soft goo seeping from the treat "—and having me cost her Paris."

"Your mother is an artist?"

"An amazing talent, but the high-brow kind, which means she thinks I'm a sellout."

She popped her finger in her mouth and sucked off the chocolate-marshmallow mix just a smidge purposefully, enjoying the way he reached to loosen the neck of his shirt—only to find the top two buttons already undone. She couldn't deny the rush of pleasure, even the slightly hopeful edge after the torment of showering alone.

"You're a sharp businesswoman." His eyes tracked her every move, eyes turning as dark as the charred wood.

She couldn't help but revel in the appreciation in his

gaze. What pregnant woman wouldn't be happy to feel desirable and sexy? "So sharp my bookkeeper is enjoying all my profits on some island retreat."

She took a bite of her s'more, her tongue chasing every drizzle. Was that moan from her or from Jason?

"Crap like that happens. You're recovering." He shifted on the blanket, adjusting his jeans covertly. Well, almost covertly, except she couldn't miss the growing bulge pressing at his fly. An answering heat flamed inside her.

At least until her thoughts went back to her mom.

"I just question myself at times like this, examine every move I made for mistakes, carelessness. Lack of focus." She set her s'more back on the plate. The fun of the evening faded. "What about your parents? Have you called them yet?"

"I don't speak to my folks." He turned back to the grocery sack, preparing a second graham-cracker treat for the fire.

"That's sad."

"Why would you think that's sad? Wouldn't you be glad to dodge those judgmental confrontations with your mom?"

As much as her mother frustrated her, even hurt her sometimes, she couldn't imagine cutting her mom completely out of her life. What had driven such a wedge between Jason and his family?

"She's still my mother." Although she had to admit the extra distance between them California provided eased some of the pressure.

"You're mighty forgiving—except when it comes to me, of course."

Thinking back to her scene in his office, she winced.

"I thought you said you hadn't done anything wrong with Celia."

"I was talking about the way I handled the whole after-sex issue four months ago." He shoved aside the cooking gear and moved closer to her. "I should have missed the damn flight and stayed to talk to you."

"I told you to leave."

He stroked back her hair, his knuckles leaving a tingling path on her cheek. "And I should have asked if you meant it."

"At the time, yes." She'd been terrified of how out of control she'd felt in his arms, so much so she'd shown him the door as fast as she could. She'd thought at the time he felt the same way.

How they'd both only been able to let down barriers with each other when they had the assurance he would be leaving.

"What about now, Lauren?"

No chance of booting him out of her life again. "We're connected forever through the baby."

The air between them grew thick, the scent of him and the fire, the intimacy of the conversation all too much. She craved air. Now.

Arching back, she reached into the pocket of her robe and pulled out a copy of the ultrasound image. "I brought something to show you."

His eyes went wide, awe wide, as he glanced back up at her, then down at the picture again. "That's our baby?"

She nodded, determined not to let tears clog her throat. She could win this one battle over her damn hormones. The miracle of seeing the ultrasound for the first time washed over her again.

His thumb worked along the edge. "Do you know if it's a boy or girl?"

"They couldn't tell. The baby played shy, but the doctor said if they do an ultrasound later, they can look again. Do you want to know?"

"I'm fine either way." He looked her in the eye, his full attention a heady aphrodisiac. "I just need to know that you're both healthy."

His hand slid along her waist, rubbing the small of her back, soothing the ever-present ache, his touch and thoughtfulness stirring another ache altogether. Fire kindling inside her, spreading, she rocked forward. Everything he said and did tonight made her question her decision to stay in New York, made her want to throw away all she'd worked for just for a chance with him....

She snapped upright again and scavenged for the tattered remnants of her control. "The baby and I are both fine. There's nothing for you to worry about." Snatching up her s'more, she shot to her feet. "Thanks again for the dessert and the picnic, but I need to go to sleep."

He let her go with a low laugh that followed her all the way up the stairs. Damn him for being absolutely perfect tonight, enticing her with visions of what they could have together if she stayed in San Francisco. She stomped up the last two steps, not that it helped release the tension coiled inside her.

There was only one way to work that out of her system. She just didn't know if she was brave enough to risk taking it—*taking Jason.*

Eight

Rosa Lounge wasn't at all what she anticipated.

She'd known ahead of time it was a martini bar, but she'd expected something along the line of New York high brow. Instead, she'd walked into San Francisco retro funk.

Loud music reverberated.

Pink lighting cast a hazy glow.

Black and white accents added a crisp edge.

The artist in her lapped up the visual contrasts.

And the food was to die for. She dipped an oozing grilled-cheese triangle into a cup of tomato soup. Her nausea a thing of the past, it seemed her appetite was making up for lost time. She nibbled a bite. Ah-mazing. Still, nothing beat Godiva s'mores with Jason.

Nothing about this time in San Francisco was turning out the way she expected. Did she dare risk more surprises by launching into an affair with Jason? The thought felt big and scary, so damn silly, really, when she already carried his baby. But there it was and she didn't know how to get past the hurdle to take what she wanted.

A light hand on her shoulder pulled her out of her reverie. Lauren turned quickly. "Yes?"

"Hello, we didn't get to speak earlier." A slim woman with dark brown hair clamped back unpretentiously thrust out her hand. "I'm Elle Linton, Brock's assistant."

"Lauren Presley…uh, Reagert. I'm still getting used to the new name."

"Of course." Elle smiled with understanding. "Elopements give you a little less time to get used to the changes coming up."

An elopement that came about in a very public and embarrassing fashion, thanks to her anger. Lauren looked across the bar and sure enough, Celia still stayed well clear of her on the other side at one of the tall tables.

Lauren turned back to Brock's assistant. "Jason and I have known each other for over a year."

"I'm sorry if my comments came out wrong. I didn't mean to sound nosy or imply anything." Her blue eyes lit with sincerity—and curiosity. This woman had a knack for getting people to spill their guts. "We're all just wondering about the lady who managed to land Jason Reagert."

Anger pulsed anew in time with the thrum of the music. "You mean since Celia Taylor was hitting on him just a few days ago?"

"Wow, Lauren—" Elle's eyes blinked wide "—you really know how to lay it all out there."

"Unless I'm mistaken, you all had a front-row seat to the scene in the office. I was a bit histrionic, I know." She winced at even describing herself that way, but God, she wanted out of this with her pride intact. And while creating a plausible cover story for Jason, damn his handsome ass. "I guess I just go a little catty when it comes to my man."

Ick. Had she really said that? And even worse, it was true. Her eyes gravitated to Celia again. The too-gorgeous redhead smiled tightly at the guy hitting on her, then eyed the door. She clearly didn't want to be here but couldn't seem to figure out how to leave. She had an outward confidence, but her agitation didn't quite match the way Elle had portrayed her.

"Lauren—" Elle rested her hand on her arm, angling sideways to let a waiter pass with a tray balanced on one hand "—nobody blames you for getting pissed. Celia's gorgeous and more than one person around here has wondered if she tried to sleep her way to the top."

Lauren hated the twinge of sympathy she felt for Celia. She knew how tough it was to get ahead in the business world without those sorts of rumors flying around. "That's pretty harsh."

Elle sipped her martini, eyeing her over the rim. "Unless it's true. I'm only saying, this is a very competitive crowd. Be careful."

Lauren watched Elle and found the woman's gaze skipped over to her boss, lingering. Could the assistant have some jealousy issues of her own? Regardless, Elle had a point. Lauren needed to step warily, especially around Brock's right-hand person.

And especially when she had a big fat secret of her own to hide in the form of a *fake* marriage. "Thank you for the heads-up, Elle. I appreciate your looking out for me and I'm sure Jason will, too."

"No problem. Just call me the troubleshooter."

Jason slid up behind her. "Hello, ladies. Can I get you refills?"

Lauren could smell his warm aftershave mixed with something distinctively him before he even announced himself. "I'm good, thank you."

"Me, too." Elle lifted her green martini in toast.

His arms slid around her as he stood against her back. "Everyone having fun?"

Lauren glanced up at him. "Just getting the lowdown on everyone at MC from the lady in the know."

Jason smiled. "That would be Elle."

Brock's assistant laughed dismissively, then eyed Lauren's sandwich. "I'm going to order one of those for myself. Nice talking with you."

Once the woman left, Lauren turned in Jason's arms, careful to balance her plate of food. "I think this is going well."

"Beyond well. You've more than done your bit for the evening. How about we relax?" He plucked her plate from her hands and set it on a nearby table. "Want to sit and eat, or dance?"

She almost blurted out a vote for her food, but then the heat of Jason's hands on her waist stirred a deeper hunger. More than anything, she wanted to be in his arms. What better way to test the waters on whether or not to pursue her sensual longings than to take to the public safety of the dance floor?

After all, what could happen there?

Three gyrating songs later, Jason pulled Lauren into his arms as a slow song came over the loudspeaker. She stiffened almost imperceptibly before sighing against him, a light sheen of perspiration adding an extra glow to her skin. The musky scent reminded him too quickly of sex. Of course, that tended to be a common thought for him whenever he saw Lauren, much less pulled her close.

She was temptation personified.

The dance made for the perfect chance to move forward with his plan to persuade her while holding back a while longer. He wanted her in his bed with no regrets this time.

He rested his forehead against hers. "Thank you for being so great this evening."

"Just holding up my end of the bargain." Her legs brushed lightly against his, her breasts pressed to his chest.

Okay, so maybe this hadn't been the brightest of ideas, after all. But hey, in for a penny—

"You really are amazing, and not just in a work setting. Do you know that?" He angled to skim his mouth against hers. Holding. Not so long as to make a sideshow event of things, but long enough for her to soften against him as he grew hard against her. Her lips tasted like a sweet ripe cheese and the lime from her water. And he didn't want to stop.

A couple jostled them and he eased his head away with more than a little regret.

Lauren looked up at him through thick eyelashes. "Are you trying to seduce me?"

Her voice came out husky and sexy, her chest rising and falling faster against him.

He slid his hands low along her waist, his finger aching for a more thorough exploration. "I only kissed you."

"You call that only a kiss?"

Her words revved the adrenaline zinging through him. "I do believe you complimented me."

She swatted his chest lightly, her cheeks a pretty pink. "You know full well what you were doing, what that was doing to me."

"You liked the kiss." He nestled her closer.

"Again, obvious." She swayed against him. "My body turns traitor when it comes to you. So *are* you trying to seduce me?"

Too obvious would lose the day here. He needed a more subtle, more romantic approach. "Who said a kiss has to lead to bed?"

She blinked back at him, surprise stunning her quiet.

"What?" He tucked her away from the crowded floor toward the outer edges, away from the speakers. "You disagree?"

Lauren shook her head quickly. "I don't disagree at all. I just didn't expect to hear something like that from you. From a man."

"I can assure you I am most definitely a man."

"I know." She rocked her hips lightly against his erection pressed undeniably against her soft stomach.

"Kissing you—" he brushed his mouth against hers lightly with promise "—brings me much pleasure."

And torment. But he didn't want to lose precious ground here by mentioning that.

MC's CFO—Ash—strode past on his way to dance

with his longtime girlfriend, a local law student. Did Ash remember that not more than three weeks ago right here at Rosa Lounge, they'd both declared themselves confirmed bachelors? Of course, Ash already had a failed marriage behind him.

Jason thumbed his wedding ring, reminding himself of the importance of patience. Keeping Lauren here in San Francisco required finesse. They'd already gone the route of jumping each other's bones at warp speed and that had not ended well for him.

He did not repeat mistakes.

The band cranked up the pace and Jason linked fingers with Lauren, leading her away from the increasingly packed space. He ducked closer to her ear. "Want to drive up to Twin Peaks for a romantic view of the city, perfect place to make out? I promise not to take advantage of you on our first date."

She snorted a laugh. "It may have escaped your notice, but we've already had sex."

"Believe me, I noticed." And remembered. And wanted more. Which meant sticking to his plan. "I take it that's a no to making out. Damn shame."

Her eyebrows pinched together in confusion. "Jason, I don't understand you tonight. I'm not sure what you expect or want—"

"Shh." He pressed a finger to her lips. "And by the way, nobody asked you for sex tonight. I'm an ad man, remember? You need to pay close attention to my words."

He stepped back and kissed her hand before letting go. "Thank you for a most enjoyable dance, Mrs. Reagert. I'll think about you all night long…while I'm sleeping in my chair."

* * *

Two restless nights later, Lauren mingled at the MC dinner party. As unsettled as she was in her personal life, this business party did remind her of all the things she enjoyed about her job, the wheeling and dealing, the exchange of ideas with the best in the industry. She thrived on it.

Of course, that provided a whole new layer to her frustration.

Because this party also reminded her of all the reasons she wanted and needed to go back to her business in New York City, especially when her body screamed even more loudly for satisfaction with Jason. He was tormenting the hell out of her with his "accidental touches" and surprise kisses at every turn. Her skin felt on fire.

The live band segued from the swing music they'd played during dinner to classic rock. She wasn't sure she could hold out through another dance with Jason. Except it wasn't just on the dance floor where they were so in synch. In the upheaval of the past few months, she'd almost forgotten what an awesome team she and Jason made professionally. Tonight's gathering brought that all back to her.

Swaying to the beat, she nodded her thanks to the congratulations zinging from all sides as she made her way to the bar for a refill on her water. For the first time this evening, she and Jason worked opposite sides of the room, dinner finished, the mingling and dancing just beginning to crank into full swing. She felt his eyes following her, though. Her copper satin dress swished around her legs, each brush teasing her already overloaded senses, the beaded top suddenly itchy and uncomfortable against her breasts. God, she so needed to get her mind in the moment and off the way Jason made her feel with just a look.

The dinner party—catered by Wolfgang Puck's local Postrio—was being held in an exclusive yacht club that sported a fabulous view of San Francisco Bay. Through the wall of windows, she could see the Golden Gate Bridge through the mist.

It was one hell of an impressive party, from the five-star dinner to the A-list guests, everything running smoothly, thanks to Brock's ever-efficient assistant zipping to and fro.

Growing up in Connecticut, Lauren had wined and dined with influential families and major players in political circles. Even so, she was impressed. Maddox had pulled out all the stops.

With her nausea totally abated, her appetite had kicked into full gear. She could well enjoy everything from the crusted Alaskan halibut to the sweetheart plum dessert. Too bad she couldn't pack a doggy bag.

For another picnic in front of the fire? She shook off the memory.

The best of California wines flowed. Not that she'd been able to drink any, but the fragrant bouquets wafted through the room, mingling like the high-end guests. She sipped her sparkling water with lime.

"Mrs. Reagert," a voice called from behind her, "may I refill your drink?"

Lauren glanced over her shoulder to find the offer came not from a waiter but from Jason's big-catch client, Walter Prentice. Apparently even the ultrauptight client enjoyed a vintage wine on occasion.

"Thank you, Mr. Prentice. I was just making my way over."

"Then let me help you with that." He snapped his fingers impatiently and a waiter magically appeared to take her order, as well as a refill for Prentice's wife. The poor woman looked as if she could use a shot of something stronger to lift her spirits. Her husband was obviously devoted to her, but the worry lines across the woman's brow, the sad frown that didn't appear new hinted that Angela Prentice wasn't as happy as her husband.

Taking her fresh sparkling water from the waiter, Lauren smiled her thanks.

Prentice rocked back on his heels. "Sharp group of up-and-comers working with Maddox. It was a close competition between them and Golden Gate Promotions, but I'm pleased to be with such a dedicated and savvy group of young people."

Lauren glanced around the room at the major movers in the business. "I'm still getting to know everyone, but they've been wonderfully welcoming."

CFO Asher Williams placed his empty wineglass on a tray and led his law-student girlfriend onto the dance floor. Gavin Spencer shifted restlessly from foot to foot, the musclebound guy tugging at the neck of his tux absently as he listened intently to a cell-phone-company heiress.

Angela Prentice touched Lauren's arm lightly. "Tell me your name again, my dear."

"Lauren Presley, uh, Reagert now, of course." She smiled. "But the Presley part is no relation to the King."

Walter laughed full and loud. "I imagine you get asked that often."

"Often enough." She thought through what she knew

about Prentice and zeroed in on his company mantra. *Family Is Everything.* "Although my family is from Connecticut, nowhere near Graceland."

"Lovely country in Connecticut. I have a place on the coast." The billionaire probably had places on every coast. "You knew Jason in New York?"

"I own a graphic-arts business. We collaborated on a few accounts, and our relationship formed from there." True enough, even if the details might have sent Prentice into an apoplectic fit.

Angela pressed two fingers to her furrowed brow. "How will you manage your business from clear across country now that you and Jason are married?"

Prentice frowned. "I hope you don't intend to try one of those bicoastal relationships. They never work, you know. That's why I have my wife and children travel everywhere with me."

No wonder the woman had bags under her eyes.

"A lot can be accomplished with a good office manager, a computer and telecoms." She'd actually been thinking through some possibilities already, since making sure Jason was a part of their baby's life would require a great deal of travel on both their parts, especially for the next few years.

Which would also necessitate spending time together. A lot of time. Her eyes gravitated to Jason, speaking with Flynn, MC's vice president. The VP's broad shoulders and swagger drew more than a few female eyes in the room, but Lauren preferred Jason's lean swimmer's build. She could almost smell the salt air and sun on his skin.

Lauren yanked her focus back to Walter Prentice, who was speaking.

"You're a modern-day businesswoman."

She stiffened. Was that good or bad in his eyes?

Angela rested a gentle hand on her arm. "Congratulations again, dear, to you and Jason on the marriage and the baby. Walter and I are happy for you and your growing family."

"Hear, hear." Walter lifted his glass in a toast. "Now if you'll excuse us, Mrs. Reagert?"

"Of course. Nice speaking with you both." Lauren relaxed as the older couple walked away. Jason had read the situation right. All was well. She thumbed her wedding band, watching the Prentices. Forty years married. What would that be like? Staying with one person for more than half your life? While the Prentices seemed to have everything, Angela's sad eyes made Lauren think about all she had in New York.

Shaking her head, she pivoted and came face-to-face with…the very woman she'd been avoiding most of the evening.

Celia Taylor winced visibly.

Lauren considered making a quick excuse and speedy exit, then changed her mind. Running or evading would only fuel possible rumors. And weren't there already enough rumors about this woman floating around? While she should hate Celia, instead, she felt kind of sorry for her. The business world could be catty and vicious to beautiful women.

So Lauren plastered a big—hopefully genuine-looking—smile on her face. "Hello, Celia. I was just looking for you. I'm still new in town and was wondering if you could recommend a good hairstylist."

Sheesh, that sounded lame. So much for ignoring

the issue of looks. Why hadn't she thought to ask about work? Or consult on some other business matter? Or even ask for a freaking art gallery? Hell, she was committed to the conversation, so might as well forge ahead. She really wanted to smooth over any awkwardness with Jason's coworker.

Celia blinked fast, scrunching her too-darn-perfect nose. "Sure, sure, I'll e-mail you the name of my salon and spa."

"I appreciate it." She also needed to find a new ob/gyn out here, as well, if she was going to visit Jason again. Or maybe stay longer.

"I'm sorry about the other day," Celia said softly, leaning closer, her cologne expensive and probably delightful, but pregnancy heightened Lauren's sense of smell in a fickle way. It had to be the pregnancy, right? Not the fact that right now she resented the woman for merely existing.

Now wasn't that utterly ridiculous? Celia Taylor hadn't done anything wrong. The jealousy was totally Lauren's issue, not this woman's. "Really, there's no need for things to be awkward."

"Of course not. I just wanted to make sure you know there's nothing between Jason and me. I mean, I was asking about after-work plans…if he was going to Rosa Lounge with others from the office."

Celia wouldn't have asked in the first place if there'd been an inkling Jason was already in a relationship. Except he hadn't been. Not really. If their mutual friend hadn't sent Jason that photo showing Lauren pregnant, would he have accepted Celia's drink offer?

Jealousy nipped all the harder, after all. Reminding

herself it wasn't Celia's fault didn't seem to be helping. "Seriously, it's okay. I was the one who insisted on keeping our relationship quiet. If there's anyone to blame for it not being obvious Jason was already taken, the fault is mine."

Celia exhaled long and hard. "I'm so relieved to hear that. I hate office gossip. God, you're a really nice person."

Then why was she obsessing over how Celia didn't have to wear a tent of a dress to hide her stomach? No water retention on that woman, for sure.

And why was she thinking about impressing the Prentices? And finding an ob/gyn in San Francisco?

Because like it or not, she was drawn to Jason. For four months she'd been trying to work him out of her system—unsuccessfully. Ignoring him hadn't worked.

Lauren looked across the room again, finding him, wanting him. Jason's chin tipped as if he sensed her watching him, sensed *her*. He turned his head almost imperceptibly and his intense eyes locked with hers. A delicious tingle of awareness prickled over her, tightening her nerves with a deep need to wriggle against him skin to skin.

She couldn't run from the truth any longer. Her passion for Jason hadn't even begun to be tapped out. Denying it—denying herself—only made the ache grow stronger as pressure built.

She understood all about hormonal rushes from pregnancy, and maybe that added an edge, but still she knew it was something beyond just the raging hormones. She certainly hadn't tried to jump any of the other men who crossed her path, and heaven knew there were plenty of hot, high-powered men in this room.

But she only wanted Jason.

Starting tonight, she would try a new approach. Indulging every fantasy she'd ever entertained about her brand-new husband.

Nine

The MC dinner had been a success. Jason had every-thing he'd wanted.

So why was he so damn irritable?

Stuffing his hands in his tuxedo pockets after locking up the house for the night, he stared at his sexy wife on the other side of their living room, fairly certain she was the cause of his frustration. The ride home had been off somehow. He'd pointed out scenic spots of interest along the way, trying to show her the upside of living here, but she stayed silent for the most part, staring at him with an intensity he found unsettling, since he didn't have a clue what she was thinking.

Lauren stood in the bay window, moonlight stream-ing through and glinting off the metallic beads on the bodice of her evening gown. She was both stunning and elegant at once. She was perfect in every regard. So much so, she made *him* see just how well their lives could fit together.

This hands-off idea of his was growing old fast. He wanted it all—wanted her—now. Her dress showcased her generous breasts until his hands shook from restrained desire. Gathered high on her waist, the loose folds hid any evidence of the baby, satin fabric pooling around her feet in low heels. Her hair was smoothed into a sleek twist with one long strand grazing her cheek like the stroke of the backs of his fingers along her jaw.

Male eyes had followed her all night long, damn near making him crazy with the need to remind them she was with him. She carried *his* baby. But he wouldn't behave like some kind of possessive ass.

Besides, he was too proud of her. He'd almost forgotten what a savvy businesswoman she was. She'd won over not only Prentice, but had worked the room, charming people and making contacts that would help her, as well as him. What a surprise to find her serene confidence turned him on just as much as her lush curves.

He stopped behind her, cupping her bare shoulders, determined to help her see how well their worlds were in synch. "You were amazing tonight. You absolutely had Prentice eating out of the palm of your hand."

She looked back, the lone strand of hair caressing her face the way he longed to do. "He seems a nice enough man, nicer than I expected, actually, after how rigid he seems in his criteria for how other people should live their lives."

"He certainly took to you." Jason slid his arms around her, encouraged that she didn't protest or stiffen. He linked his fingers over her stomach. The baby rolled lightly, then settled. "His wife did, too, for that matter."

"She seems like such a sad lady." Lauren leaned back against him, the sweet scent of her shampoo seeping deeper inside him. "I can't help wondering if the high-powered lifestyle suits her as much as it does him."

"How about you? Do you enjoy that kind of gig?" An important part of his life that could cause a real problem. The MC work-grind-and-party circuit had certainly tanked Flynn Maddox's marriage.

"Are you kidding? You've known me for a year. I thrive on that sort of wheeling and dealing." She shifted to fit more firmly against him, her bottom nestling intimately until there was no damn way she could miss his throbbing response.

"You certainly keep your cool under pressure." His blood pressure, however, was skyrocketing over just the feel of her brushing back against him. Right now he just wanted to sink into the moment. With her.

She glanced at him. "What are you thinking?"

Might as well be honest. "Just can't look away from you. You're absolutely gorgeous."

"Stop. You don't have to flatter me." Her hands slid over his on her stomach. "I know my waist disappeared a couple of weeks ago."

"I wasn't the only one who noticed you." Primitive possessiveness pumped through him all over again. "You're sexy as hell. That pregnancy-glow stuff is for real." His wayward thumbs brushed the undersides of her breasts. "All week long I've been aching to touch you."

She laughed lightly, turning in his arms to face him,

giving him a clear view of creamy cleavage. "Ah, so it's all about the extra cup size."

"An extra cup?" Hell, call him Cro-Magnon, but he absolutely couldn't tear his eyes off her chest, couldn't stop the thoughts of how much he wanted to peel her clothes from her and see every inch he'd missed during their hurried, half-clothed, one-time coupling. "Do you know what I'd give to see you out of that dress? God, Lauren, I heard what you said about no sex, but I'm about to die from wanting you. I don't know how much longer I can keep my hands off you."

She toyed with his tie, her fingers soft and enticing against his neck. "Maybe I've revised my thinking on the no-sex notion."

Her words slammed through him. He'd been hoping to make progress with Lauren, but could the dinner have shown her the same practical synchronicity of their lives that he'd observed?

Regardless, he certainly wasn't going to question the awesome opportunity of having her warm and willing in his arms.

Jason brushed a kiss along her ear, nuzzling aside the loose strand of hair. "*Maybe* revising your no-sex policy?"

She turned to meet his mouth, her body fluid against him, her arms sliding up around his neck. Her pupils widened with desire, urging him on. "*Definitely* revising."

Growling his relief, he kissed her, finally and fully, finding her open and ready and boldly seeking. It had been too long, too many nights waking up hard and unfulfilled from dreaming about her.

Lauren clutched at his shoulders, her hands strong

and insistent, like a woman who knew exactly what she wanted. Her fingers crawled up his collar and furrowed into his hair, urging him closer. Not close enough, since they still wore too damn many clothes.

He cupped her bottom, bringing her flush against him—which reminded him of his need for restraint. "What's the best way to make this happen that's safe for you and the baby?"

With nimble fingers, she swept aside his tuxedo jacket. "At four and half months, it's really not an issue yet. The books and my doctor all say to get inventive with positions down the road. Perhaps we should start practicing ahead of time?"

"You're putting some mighty powerful images in my mind." Of her now…of her later. Would they still be together then? He had a chance to sway her and he intended to make the most of it, because he was quickly learning that just a taste of Lauren was nowhere near enough. "How is it that you can turn me inside out with just that sexy voice of yours?"

"Words can be an aphrodisiac, too. I have some fantasies I'd like to share."

With one hand, he reached past her and whipped the curtains closed. "Listening to you talk about anything beats the hell out of oysters any day of the week."

Sighing her agreement, she nipped his bottom lip. He tugged the zipper down her spine, the expensive gown parting, sliding free to reveal…

His mouth went dry.

Lauren stood in a strapless lace bra and tiny matching bikini panties that sketched just below the gentle curve of her stomach. Metallic gold threads glinted in the off-white lace, drawing his eyes to alluring curves and creamy skin. He touched, stroked, couldn't think of anything more gorgeous than Lauren swelling with his child. The woman was a walking fertility goddess. He went so hard he thought she could very well bring him to his knees.

Her eyes heavy lidded with undisguised excitement, she plucked pins from her hair and shook the sleek updo free in a tumble over her shoulders. "One of us is vastly overdressed. Ditch the clothes, wonderboy. I have definitely been fantasizing about having you pose for me naked."

"Pose?" His hand hesitated on his buttons.

"I took art classes in drawing the male body while in college, you know."

He frowned. "I'm not so sure I like the idea of nude guys hanging out with you."

She trailed a nail down his chest. "Then get naked."

"Happy to accommodate." His eyes locked on hers, he shrugged out of his shirt, toed off his shoes and socks. Urgency pulsed through him, but taking his time meant he got to stare at her all the longer. They'd gone at each other so fast in her office, there hadn't been a chance for him to memorize the look of her.

Although the feel of being buried deep inside her silken walls was seared in his mind.

He kicked aside his pants and boxers, and extended a hand for her. She clasped his hand in one of hers and with her other, scratched a manicured nail down his chest. His heartbeat surged in response.

He tugged her toward him and she leaned against his chest, giving him easy access to unhook her bra and sweep it away. Satin and lace glided over his hands before sailing to the floor.

She arched against him, flattening her generous breasts to his chest with a moan of pleasure. "I don't think I can wait any longer. Can we go slow the second time?"

"My pleasure." Because a second encounter meant she wasn't going to boot his ass out right away afterward.

He backed her against the wall, grateful for the blank space, not that he would have given a damn if they'd knocked a Monet to the floor. She kissed him, bit him, scored her finger down his back as she shared ideas for the two of them together—white-hot fantasies—that let him know loud and clear she burned for this as much as he did. He swept away her panties, allowing himself a leisurely second to feel her warmth still lingering on the scrap of fabric. Amazing, but no substitute for the real thing, which happened to be right here in his arms.

Lauren hooked a leg on his hip and he didn't need any further invitation to explore. He found her slick and ready. He dipped his head to her breasts, drawing a taut nipple between his teeth carefully. The sound of her sigh, the way she tightened in his mouth, sent a charge through him until he throbbed against her stomach.

She cupped him, stroked him, her intent clear.

"Now? Here? You're sure?" Even clearly seeing the passion in her eyes, the same wild want he'd found four months ago, he needed to hear her say it, to confirm she wanted frantic sex against a wall as much as he did.

Her grip tightened ever so slightly. "If you don't take the edge off, I'm going to explode without you in about ninety seconds."

He throbbed in her hand. "Ninety seconds?"

"Eighty-nine." She circled her thumb over him.

He hitched her other leg up until she locked her ankles around his waist. He cupped her behind and lifted, positioning… She braced her hands on his shoulders and lowered, taking him inside her again…the way he remembered, except better, because nothing could have felt this amazing.

Her head fell to rest on his shoulder.

"Everything all right?" he said against her hair, holding himself in check, barely. The room around them faded as his world narrowed to the silky warm clamp of her body.

"Seventy-one seconds," she gasped, "and counting." Her chest rising and falling rapidly, she rocked her hips. He didn't need any more encouragement than that.

He thrust while she wriggled to get closer. She whispered urgent pleas, her voice growing breathier, her skin flushing, and yes, he was watching every nuance of her face. They might be rushing, but he wasn't going to miss the opportunity to see her, a gift he'd lost out on their first time.

Now, he savored the graceful arch of her neck as she threw her head back. The perspiration dotting her brow, her eyes shutting tighter with each increasingly loud moan. The way she bit down on her lip until the cry of completion burst free in an awesome expression of just how high he'd taken her. Lauren's heels pressed deeper into his back, vise-gripping them together. Her voice ricocheted into the high ceilings, their coming together noisy and uninhibited in a way they hadn't been able to indulge in at her office.

Who'd have thought his reserved wife would be a screamer? And the knowledge that he'd been the one to bring those sweet cries from her mouth sent him slamming over the edge in explosive release.

His forehead resting against the wall, he slumped against her, her legs still wrapped around him. Sweat sealed them skin to skin, linking them together. But for how long?

Because in just ninety seconds, he'd realized he couldn't ever let her go.

God, she needed to run.

Lauren straddled Jason's lap as they sat on the wooden seat in the spa shower. Spray pelting her back, she kissed water from his shoulder while he throbbed inside her.

Aftershocks from her own completion still shuddered through her, her mind full of images of how he'd loved her through the night with his hands, his mouth, his body. Even his words as he told her over and over how much he wanted her, how hot she made him feel, how he couldn't wait to have her again. She'd been totally out of control.

And that scared her to her dripping-wet toes.

Her skin cooling in the aftermath, she still couldn't bring herself to move off his lap.

She'd remembered sex between them being good, but this tangled, combustible passion they'd explored again and again was beyond good. It was reckless and messy and mind-numbing, so much so that she could lose reason altogether and forget the independent life she'd painstakingly built for herself. She'd worked so hard to break free of the smothering, constricting family life she'd grown up in. Would she have the strength to assert herself with Jason when he could so quickly reduce her to a puddle of pleasure?

When they'd stepped into the spa shower together, she'd been sure she couldn't make love again so soon, but he'd vowed they could make their way through one more of her fantasies before morning. All too quickly the stroke of his hands over her lathered body had sent her spiraling again until their oh-so-vocal coming together had echoed around the tiled walls.

Slowly, intensely. This was different from their frantic coupling on her work sofa, where he'd left her too quickly. She'd ached for more.

Now? He wrung every last orgasm from her, taking her to new heights after an already sensual night of lovemaking. She was so damn scared. She shivered against him.

Jason kissed her ear. "You're cold. Let me take care of that for you."

He lifted her off his lap gently, settling her on the other seat across from him before turning off the shower, brass fixtures steamed over. He stepped out onto the plush bath mat, opened the warmer drawer and passed her an oversize towel.

"Thank you." She didn't bother explaining that her shiver had come from another source altogether.

Lauren wrapped the heated folds around her and moved closer to the small fireplace in the bathroom. While this one had gas logs, instead of real wood, still it crackled with warm decadence. She'd been blessed to grow up in an affluent home, but even so, this remodeled bathroom impressed her.

That poor couple who'd broken up while decorating

this home sure had put a lot of time and care into their renovations. Had they gotten a chance to enjoy the place at all before their marriage fell apart?

Toweling his back dry, Jason leaned to kiss her, firmly, but briefly. "Would love to linger, but I'm late for work."

"Just blame me and my darn fantasies." She forced herself to smile and go along with his lighthearted mood.

The faster she could get him out the door, the sooner she could restore order to her jumbled emotions. She could barely think now, much less trust herself to be reasonable.

All but impossible to do while watching his lean, muscled body saunter away into the walk-in closet. She recalled him explaining there had been a fifth bedroom on this floor, but a wall had been knocked out to create the spacious master bath and walk-in. How much daring it must have taken to boldly whack out walls, making such an irrevocable change in the hope that all would turn out the way you'd envisioned—a reckless daring she was pretty damn sure she didn't possess.

Towel wrapped around her body, she combed through her hair as he rushed to dress.

He slipped into his loafers and snagged his briefcase on his way across the room toward her. "Sorry I have to work on Saturday, but I'll be home by six. I have plans for the evening, so don't bother with supper. I'll be thinking about you."

He kissed her again, longer this time, lingeringly— lovingly?—his tongue bold and possessive. The fresh taste of his mouthwash, the tangy scent of his aftershave, all sent her senses into overload. The man did know how to kiss and kiss well. And somehow the kiss meant all the more right now, because it obviously wasn't going to lead to sex. They were both wrung out and he had to leave for work. The tender attention he gave to her lips, the time to just connect, spoke of something somehow as intimate as when he'd been buried deep inside her.

Her eyelashes were just fluttering open as the door closed behind him on his way out.

She sank onto the edge of the whirlpool tub. Even if she found the resolve to return to New York, she would come back here for visits with the baby. He would have to travel East, too.

How could she be in the same room with him in the future and not want him? Want this. Want more and more. For how long? Surely a fire this hot had to burn out.

And if it didn't?

She'd had a front-row seat to the way her parents' high-intensity emotions had consumed each other. She would be damned if she would relive it in her own marriage.

Ten

He was making headway. He could feel it as surely as the sting of salt spray off the Bay.

Jason slid his arm around Lauren's shoulders as they walked along the pier outside the yacht club where they'd consumed one helluva big dinner. He winced with guilt over making a pregnant woman wait an extra hour for supper.

Damn, he hated running late, but this afternoon he hadn't been able to avoid it. Prentice suddenly changed his mind about signing a teen pop star to endorse a line of beachwear. Not to mention Jason was juggling four other new accounts that needed settling in. At least they'd gotten to go out together on a Saturday night for an official date. And he intended to make the most of every minute to show her the many ways San Francisco living rocked.

How better to show her a number of sights at once than from…

"You have a boat?" Lauren exclaimed, her feet slowing along the dock. Waterfowl flapped overhead, local marshes rich and teeming with migrating birdlife during the winter months.

"Did I forget to mention that?"

"Uh, yeah, you did overlook it, because I'm sure I wouldn't have zoned out this." She swept her hand toward his Beneteau fifty-foot, performance/racing sailboat.

"I got a good deal on it from a guy whose business went belly-up. The custom-made boat had only just been delivered and in the water for a couple of months before he realized he would have to consolidate to avoid bankruptcy court."

"It's new, then?"

"Less than six months off the truck." Zipping up his windbreaker, Jason could already feel the lulling give-and-take of the deck beneath his feet. He hoped she wasn't the type to get seasick. It wasn't a deal breaker, but it sure would suck, given this was his only real form of recreation. "Would you like to go out for a spin?"

"Uh, sure. Why not?" She blinked at his surprise shift in the evening plans.

Did she have a problem with being impulsive? He wouldn't have thought that from the way they made love when and wherever the mood struck. On the way to supper, he'd had to pull off onto a deserted road or risk a wreck. She been frenetic and demanding and he'd enjoyed the hell out of every minute of it.

Come to think of it, that could have also played into why they were late for dinner.

He helped her aboard, nodding his thanks to the club employee who'd prepped the sails so he could head straight out with Lauren. So far, she seemed at ease on the boat. Her feet steady, she settled into a seat and tipped her face into the wind. The slap and ping of sails and lines soothed him after a tense day at work.

Lauren seemed content with silence—something he appreciated since most people he knew felt the need to fill up quiet spaces. He guided the boat out into the Bay. The moon overhead and lights along the shore show-cased a top-notch view of the shopping at Fisherman's Wharf and historic Alcatraz.

After an hour of cruising, he set the anchor and joined her on the bow of the boat. The boat's running lights sparked off the crest of waves, the shoreline lit with nightlife.

Jason draped a blanket over her shoulders and sat behind her. "Are you cold?"

She shook her head against him. "I'm fine. Lots of layers, just like you instructed before we headed out." She burrowed more deeply into the quilted folds. "But leave the quilt. It's getting colder."

He pulled her closer, enjoying the feel of her body tucked against his even through the blanket. "Did you have a productive afternoon working?"

"Not particularly creative, but busy. I'm taking care of creditors since your infusion of cash came through." She rested her hand on his bent knee. "Thank you again. My company means a lot to me."

"No thanks necessary." And he meant it. "You're paying me back, remember?"

She chuckled. "At an absurdly low interest rate."

He hoped they could just write off that whole damn debt soon. He'd meant to help her, and now he hated the way she seemed hung up on not taking anything from him. With luck, the private detective he'd hired to hunt down her accountant would turn up something soon. If she got her money back, then she would have stability in her company, which afforded flexibility.

He knew there wasn't a chance in hell she would accept more money from him, but perhaps he could persuade her to keep the original loan for their kid, expand her business with a San Francisco base. Best for the baby, right?

And damn great for him.

She glanced back at him, wind whipping her long auburn ponytail over her face. "I'm glad you suggested this. I imagine it's no surprise I've been a little stressed out lately."

"The water has a calming effect." Waves lapped the side of the boat, fish plopping a few feet away. Lights from a couple of other crafts glittered in the distance, but no one close enough for him to see details in the night.

"You could live here. The boat has more furniture than your house."

He decided the time had come to press her for more. According to her preset deadline, he only had a week left before she returned to New York. "Maybe Sunday we can wander around Fisherman's Wharf, do some furniture shopping."

"Jason, you're pushing." She traced the outline of his kneecap, her eyes still set on the horizon. "What made you decide to get out of the Navy? Prentice mentioned something over dinner about you being a hero during a pirate incident. You went really quiet."

He tensed at her surprise charge into his past. Then decided to let her subject change go unnoted, since she hadn't left his arms. "I was just doing my job. I only mentioned it to Prentice because he has a nephew in the service."

"What happened?"

His Navy time seemed such a world away now, but it was a part of him, giving him a discipline, drive and focus his old man had always insisted he needed, but was never around to teach or model. Jason felt his baby roll lightly under his hands and vowed to do better, to be present. "It was a hostage situation off the coast of Malaysia. We were called in to help."

"We?"

"I was a dive officer attached to a SEAL team, working EOD."

"EOD?" she prodded.

"Explosive ordinance disposal."

She shuddered against him. "Sounds scary."

Scary? In the early days, but in later years, the shakes usually didn't set in until after a mission. "There were some tense times, sure, but you train hard, then go on autopilot for the mission."

"Your job must seem tame now."

"Just different. Sometimes I miss it, but for the most part I'm content with what I offered my country. I'm ready to move on. This is what I studied to do in college. It's what I've always wanted to do. I was just so determined to be different from my old man that I chased other dreams for a while before coming back to what's in my blood."

"You've certainly stepped well out of your dad's

shadow, here and back in New York, too. You're your own man."

He appreciated that she saw that. He'd sure as hell tried. "I took a Navy ROTC scholarship to college since my inheritance from my grandparents wouldn't come through until I was twenty-five. After I graduated, I owed years of service in return. I like to think I would have joined even if I hadn't needed the money."

"Your parents wouldn't pay for you to go to college?"

"Oh, they would have paid, but there were too many strings attached."

"Like what?"

"Go to my father's alma mater, join the family firm. I appreciate the advantages my family provided while I was growing up, but I couldn't be a spoiled trust-fund kid."

"You definitely proved yourself."

"It's an ongoing process." Lifelong, in fact. He thought about her mother who'd so devalued Lauren's art because it wasn't the same as hers. Maybe Lauren understood his problems with his parents better than he would have realized before. "Overall, I'm happy here, with the locale and the job."

"Given your obvious love of the water, San Francisco is a good fit for you, then, much more so than the cold northern winters back in New York."

"I've been diving since I was in elementary school. It's convenient having my boat here rather than losing time jetting to a vacation spot." He rested his chin on top of her head. "The sunken ships are fun to explore, and the coral reefs are amazing here. I'd like to take you after the baby's born."

"Jason—" she pinched the inside of his thigh lightly "—you're pushing again."

And she was so warm and beautiful in his arms, he decided to nudge her a little further. "We can't take this one day at a time forever. Eventually we have to make plans."

She turned in his arms, her face luminous in the moonlight. "You know what? I have a plan, a really great plan for how we should spend this night together."

Damn it all, he was serious here. He wanted her to see all the ways their lives fit together as perfectly as their bodies. The determined glint in her eye gave him only a second's warning before she tackled him back against the deck.

Lauren tugged the blanket over them. "I think we should climb underneath this quilt and see who can make the other scream with pleasure first."

Lauren planted her hands on the deck on either side of Jason's face and kissed him, letting her body and her passion have free rein. The stunned expression on his face gave her the advantage she needed. But he didn't lag behind for long. Growling low, he rolled her underneath him, the blanket tenting over them.

All his talk of the future had increased the panicked need to flee until she decided to act. To shut him up the best way possible.

She didn't want to talk. He should already know full well she had dreams, a business, a need to make her own way in the world. And yes, even a need to look out for her mother, who had no one else to care for her, nobody to make sure she didn't slide completely over the edge.

And, oh, God, it hurt to think about that. But those needs were all calling to her to return to New York.

Her time here with him was running out. She only had a week left to store up memories, and then she would have to set boundaries in place if they were to have any hope of peacefully bringing up their child.

Right now, she just wanted to feel, to savor the lean, long stretch of his body over hers, memorize the sound of his voice hoarse with desire for her.

The boat undulated gently beneath them, nature's waves mimicking the motion of their bodies rocking against each other. She tore at his clothes with frantic hands until he brushed them aside and worked his jeans open and her pants down to her ankles. She wrapped her fingers around the throbbing length of him, his open zipper rasping against the back of her hand as she guided him.

And then, yes, thank heavens, yes, he was inside her, moving, loving, angling his weight off her. The spicy scent of him mingled with the salt air and her own floral perfume until her senses went on overload.

She gripped his butt through denim and urged him harder, faster, needing to be closer than her swelling stomach would allow. His hand slipped between them and he touched her. Tormented her. Eased her and drew her tighter both at once as he worked her with his fingers and his thrusting body.

Already they were developing an instinctive rhythm of their own, an understanding of each other's needs that excited and scared her. How could something be so amazing and so discombobulating at the same time?

He made her yearn to do scandalous things, like make love out in the open on the deck of a boat.

He nipped at her ear, his face in her hair as he continued to coax her, rubbing tight circles, his callused skin heightening the sensation. "So, Lauren, who's gonna scream first?"

She pressed her knees against his hips, massaging him with gentle squeezes until he groaned in her ear. "I don't know," she gasped, "you tell me."

He loomed over her, his face taut with restraint. "I think we're gonna make this a simultaneous thing."

His confident promise of synchronized satisfaction sent her closer to the edge.

He captured her shout with his mouth and she could have sworn she took in his hoarse growl of fulfillment, as well. Pleasure flowed through her veins like a molten rainbow palate, melting every muscle and bone and nerve until she sagged back on the deck.

Dragging in air, he slumped beside her, hauling her against his chest wordlessly. He tucked the blanket more securely around them both before hooking his arms around and under her breasts.

Lights winked on the San Francisco shore, a world away from New York. Yet with each slap of the waves against the hull, she couldn't escape the fact that with every second that ticked away, she was growing weaker where Jason was concerned. He'd presented his campaign well in showing her how perfectly their lives could fit together.

As much as she embraced cool logic and calm in her world, with her heart pounding out of her chest right now, she just kept thinking about how he'd never once mentioned the possibility of love. And she couldn't escape the churning sense that she was falling irrevocably in love with Jason.

Eleven

Jason loped belowdecks after double-checking that the boat was secure for the night. Having Lauren all to himself in a bed until morning was a pleasure he intended to make the most of.

If he could keep up with her. The woman was damned near insatiable.

He smiled.

Pushing open the door to the main sleeping quarters, he stopped short. The sheets were rumpled, but the bed was empty. Where the hell had she gone? It wasn't as if there were many options.

He pivoted back toward the galley kitchen and flicked on the light this time. Sure enough, Lauren sat curled in a corner of the sofa, her eyes red from unshed tears. Wearing one of his T-shirts and not much else, she hugged her knees to her chest.

"Lauren?" he asked warily. "Everything okay?"

She straightened quickly, her smile overbright. "Of course. Why wouldn't it be?" She smoothed the U.S. Navy shirt over her legs, the cotton faded and soft from years of washing. "I've just had amazing sex under the stars and I suspect I'm going to get more great sex before the night's played out."

That was a bet she would damn well win. Soon. But not yet. Especially not until he figured out what had upset her.

Jason sat beside her, not too close, though. Something about her tense shoulders shouted she would crumble if touched her. "You seem distracted. And call me a selfish bastard, but when I have a woman in my bed—when I have *you* in my bed—I want your complete and undivided attention."

"It's nothing." She tugged at the hem of the shirt with nervous fingers, so unlike his normally confident wife. "Really."

"You're obviously upset." He rested his hand on hers, stilling her nervous fidgeting. "Why can't you just tell me?"

She reached under her leg and pulled out her cell phone. "My mother called again."

Rolling her eyes with a dismissive bravado that didn't quite play out, she pitched the phone to the end of the sofa. A light dip of the boat sent the cell tumbling to the floor.

Her mother? Good God, it was after midnight here, which meant it was later than three in the morning in New York. What was her mother doing calling Lauren so late? Inconsiderate to her pregnant daughter, who could have already been asleep.

Then it hit him. Jacqueline must have been in one of

her manic moods. He didn't know much about bipolar disease—something he intended to rectify ASAP—but he figured tonight's call couldn't have been pleasant.

He couldn't change the past, but maybe he could lighten her present. "Well, hell, Lauren, you should have thumped from below and I would have come to your rescue."

A wobbly smile eased over her face. "Thanks, truly, but you can't yank the phone away from me forever."

"What did she say?"

"Nothing all that horrible, really. Her timing just sucks, is all." She leaned a little closer. A promising move. "She's wigging out over the baby news. The wedding was okay in her eyes—not the baby. Or rather not the whole having-to-get married thing."

He tugged a lock of her hair gently. "I thought you said you found that kind of view archaic."

Her mouth went tight. "She told me to make sure I get a good divorce settlement, and after she hung up, she texted me the number of her attorney."

He stayed silent for three caws of night birds outside to keep from saying exactly what he thought of Jacqueline's interference. It was all he could do not to pick up the cell phone and toss it into the Bay. "Not exactly a supportive call from Mama, huh?"

Her hands clenched into fists. "I know it sounds silly. It's not like we're planning to stay married or anything. I just resented the way she expected me to take you to the cleaners. She made me think of that half-million dollars and it felt so damn wrong." She thumped the cushions with a fist. "I should have stood strong, let the company go under if that's the way things had to be. I screwed up."

"Whoa, whoa, slow down a second." He cupped her shoulders and turned her to face him fully. He might have some issues of his own he would like to press with her, but no way in hell was he going to let Lauren doubt herself this way. Damn Jacqueline for cutting such a wide swath through this amazing woman's confidence. "Let's unpack these thoughts one at a time. First, the creep stole from you. That happens to the most competent, smart people in the business world all the time. Hell, even entire cities get ripped off. Second, we are attached through this baby, which means we have to work together and help each other. If my ass lands in the fire, I damn well expect you to come help me. Got it?" He tapped her chin. "Do you hear me?"

She nodded, her smile a little steadier this time. "I do hear you, and I have to admit I like what you're saying."

"And lastly—" this one was for his own satisfaction, as much as hers "—quit giving a crap what your mother thinks. I don't want her upsetting the mother of my kid."

Her hands cupped either side of his neck as she cocked her head. "That point's not quite as reasonable as the first two, you know."

Yeah, and he felt a bit like a hypocrite since he'd let his father's opinion matter for most of his life. "Maybe when it comes to you I'm not as reasonable as I would like to be." Wasn't that the understatement of the year? "Now come to bed."

Her smile was slow, sensuous and full out this time. "Are you seducing me?"

"God, woman—" he slid an arm around her shoulders, his knuckles skimming the side of her breast "—you have a one-track mind."

She nibbled along his jaw. "Are you inviting me to make out again?"

Was he? Truth be told, he wanted something more from her right now. "I'm asking you to sleep with me."

"Sure, sounds great." She yawned her agreement, her voice offhand, totally missing the significance of what he was trying to say.

She wasn't even looking at him. She was already walking toward the cabin, her head tucked under his chin.

He tried to tell himself it was his impatience kicking into overdrive. This was no big deal. Yet even as they slid under the covers and she tucked close against his chest, Jason could sense she was holding a part of herself back. Playing out fantasies was fine for her.

But after the way she'd been burned in the past, he was beginning to see that Lauren ran like hell from the messiness of real life.

Long after Jason drifted off to sleep, Lauren stared at the moon and stars playing around in the sky just beyond the portal. The gentle rocking of the boat would have lulled her to sleep on any other night, but now? Too much turmoil churned inside her.

Tugging the comforter more securely over them, she tucked her leg between his, tangled up in the sheets, and savored the warm, bristly weight against her. If only they could stay on this boat, maybe move a little farther out to sea where her cell phone wouldn't pick up a signal.

She didn't cry. She wouldn't let herself. These middle-of-the-night calls from her mother weren't anything new, and she should have expected it. After all, there had to be fall-out for not telling Jacqueline about the baby. She'd just hoped this time…

Squeezing her eyes shut, she mentally kicked herself for expecting too much from her mother. She should know better after all these years of ups and downs. How damn stupid to get emotionally wrecked because she wanted to pick out nursery decorations with her mom. To talk about baby names, even. Instead, she'd been given the name of a divorce lawyer.

She was fairly damn certain she wasn't going to name her kid Horace—after her mom's current favorite attorney.

Lauren tucked herself closer to Jason and his arm slid around her waist in his sleep. Sighing, she snuggled even nearer, taking some of the comfort she hadn't been able to let her guard down enough to accept earlier.

Keeping things light was much better in the long run—it meant her heart wouldn't be as broken when they had to say goodbye.

"Damn it, Jason, a subject is supposed to be still. You're making this so much more difficult than it has to be."

A valid point. But he didn't think he was cut out to be a nude model. Of course, given he was the subject *and* the canvas, staying motionless was a little tougher than normal.

His muscles twitched from the effort, almost impossible with Lauren watching and touching him. "Aren't you out of syrup yet?"

Lauren stood naked just outside the small shower belowdecks while he "posed" inside the aqua-tiled stall. Halfway through their Belgian waffle breakfast, she'd eyed the remains of their food with glee. The next thing he knew, she'd scavenged a basting brush from the galley kitchen and returned with a bowl of warmed syrup. When she pointed to the shower, he hadn't argued.

She waved the brush, a droplet of maple syrup landing on top of his foot. "Don't move or I'll stop."

"You're wicked."

"Just indulging in another fantasy."

"Have your way with me, then." He winked, imagining a lifetime spent exploring more fantasies together. "I'm all yours."

The bowl rested in the sink and she dipped the marinating brush in the rich brown liquid. She swirled the heated glaze over his heart, slowly along his pecs, circling tighter and tighter until she flicked his nipple. His heart kicked up, harder, faster. He pulsed hot and ready to flip her onto her back and plunge inside her. Her eyes, however, warned him again she would stop if he so much as flinched.

With a sweeping stroke, she trailed lower, the sugary scent coating the air. She traced his ribs, dipping lower again until his abs contracted. He bit his lip.

"Are you ticklish?"

Not that he would ever admit. "No. What are you painting, anyway?

"A big, powerful tree." Her teasing touch brushed closer to his sides with branchlike sweeps. That sure was one leafy tree. "I think you *are* ticklish. I think the big strong guy has a weakness, after all."

He held still through sheer force of will. "It's only a weakness if I let it affect me."

"Is that a dare?"

He simply arched an eyebrow. Then he saw the impish intent in her eyes and prepped himself to hold still. She moved. Stroked.

Lower.

Not tickling at all, but boldly painting a bristly path over the hardened head of him straining up his stomach. He slumped back against the tile wall and this time she didn't rag him about moving. Lauren smiled with womanly power, continuing down, coating him all the way to his base.

Her grin broadened before she knelt and took him in her mouth. At the slick glide of her tongue, he forgot how to think or form rational thoughts. Sensation swept over him as she suckled and laved away every last bit she'd so torturously applied. Her moan of appreciation echoed a deeper one rumbling up his chest. Need pounded through him until his blood turned as thick as the syrup in the bowl beside them.

The brush fell from her hand and clanked against the tile floor a second before her cool fingers cupped him, massaging. His jaw clamped closed, and he planted his palms flat against the stall wall to keep from falling to his knees. And he couldn't even blame the rocking of the boat under his feet. Much more of the dual torment and he would lose control—before he made sure she was every bit as turned on as he was.

Jason gripped her waist and drew her away from him with more than a little regret. Regret quickly dispersed as he saw her dilated pupils, the flush of arousal tinting her skin, all signs that being with him affected her on a deep and visceral level, a level he intended to take even deeper. He cranked on the shower and plunged them under the spray. Icy pellets needled along his oversensitized skin, then quickly warmed.

Fitting his mouth over hers, he tasted syrup and desire and heat, and he couldn't get enough of her. They were messy and sticky, but nothing with Lauren had ever been simple. And he did so enjoy showering with her afterward.

Maybe after they finished in here, he could wring a promise from her to stay longer…then longer…until they settled into a life together.

Water rolled down them in a syrupy whirlpool spiraling into the drain. He hooked her leg over his hip until he nudged the moist core of her. Lauren dug her heel into his butt, leaning against him for balance. She writhed against him harder, her need for release evident in her insistent wriggles and breathy moans echoing with the call of early-morning birds outside the portal.

"Stay, stay here in San Francisco." The command fell out ahead of his brain. Damn. He'd meant to wait until after.

Jason sealed his mouth to hers, determined to distract her. It was just one lame-ass little sentence, after all.

Lauren went still against him, water streaming from her sopping-wet hair.

"What did you say?" she whispered, water spiking her eyelashes.

"We can talk later." He splayed his hands over her shoulders, down to cup her slick breasts, hoping to distract her and cursing himself. He knew timing was everything in an ad presentation, and winning her over was the most important campaign of his life.

She angled back, water sealing them together for a

moment before giving way. "I heard what you said." Her face was wary and closed and offered little clue to her thoughts, but she'd sure as hell put a stop to getting busy. "I just don't understand why you're changing the rules."

"You're the one who rescinded the no-sex ban." He palmed her back, keeping his touch low-key while reconnecting. "And I don't know about you, but for me, what we've done together changes everything. I want more."

She nibbled her lower lip, uncertainty clouding her eyes as she stared back in the narrow space. Hope steamed through him and he guided her between his legs.

She slid her hand up to cradle his face, her expression sad. "Why? Why do you want more?"

Not the answer he'd been angling for, but she hadn't slammed the door in his face. He scavenged for arguments to change her mind and came up blank. He'd used his best ammo from the minute he'd stepped into her apartment a week ago. Still, there had to be something—

His BlackBerry chimed softly, rattling against the galley-kitchen counter. He let it play out. Seconds later it chimed again.

Lauren stepped away, snagging a towel from the hook and wrapping it around her. "Just answer it."

"No—" he clasped her elbow "—we're in the middle of something important. I want you and the baby with me. I'll pay the relocation costs to move your business here, anything I can do to make the transition easier for you, because bottom line, New York is just too far away for the life I want us to build in San Francisco." Frustration clawed up his throat as he searched for the right way to persuade her. "Damn it, Lauren, this is the logical thing to do."

As soon as he finished his tirade, he realized he

hadn't come close to hitting the right button with her, and he still didn't have a clue what the answer might be.

Was she just that stubborn? That proud? A dark sense of foreboding crept over him like ants coming out to feast on the sticky sweetness drying on his skin.

"We're not in the middle of anything anymore." She snatched up his BlackBerry and thrust it toward him.

Left with no choice, he took it from her with the intent of just turning the damn thing off. The e-mail address scrolling across stopped him cold.

The private investigator he'd hired to find Lauren's crooked accountant.

Jason clicked on the message.

Have located the subject, his Cayman account and other holdings of interest. Details are ready to turn over to police. Please advise how you wish to proceed.

Keeping the information from her wasn't an option, even if tossing it aside increased her chances of staying. His opportunity to win Lauren had passed.

Now that her business was secure and she didn't need his money, there was nothing holding her in San Francisco.

Lauren had no reason to stay. Jason didn't love her, and she had no reason to believe her too-logical lover ever would.

From Jason's car, she looked at the houses leading up the steep street to his home. Her home, too, even if only for another week. She'd initially promised to stick around for two weeks to help solidify the Prentice account, and she would keep her end of the bargain, even if she didn't need his money anymore.

After the message had come in on his BlackBerry, Jason had told her about hiring a private investigator, about finding her slimy old accountant and the missing money, now tucked away in a Cayman account. Authorities were on their way to pick up the bookkeeper, and his assets in a number of other countries had been frozen. It didn't matter if they could get to the Cayman account or not, or how sticky extradition might be; the crook had enough cash stashed in other places she would have her money returned in the end.

In a week she would return to her little apartment in New York, her icy winters and her business. Thanks to Jason and his private investigator, she had her old life back. Eventually she could repay Jason what she'd borrowed. She had everything she wanted.

So why did she feel so empty?

It was going to be a long and miserable final week in Jason's house. How had she ever thought she could simply play out her fantasies with him, then leave without a mark on her heart?

Jason sat silently beside her, driving the car, the scent of his freshly showered body riding the light gust of his car heater. The morning was chilly, but nowhere near as cold as the knot freezing up in her chest. She just wanted to get to her room, away from Jason and the temptation to ignore reason and throw her carefully planned life away to move in with a man who'd never even told her he loved her.

Love?

Yes, she loved him, a certainty that was settling more

deeply inside her. But the simple word still scared her down to her toenails. She'd seen what love did to her parents and she wanted no part of that. Apparently Jason was as cautious with his emotions as she was, since he'd never alluded to feeling something so complicated and inconvenient—and wonderful—for her. What if she took a chance and told him? Maybe once they got home, over supper in front of the fireplace she could take that risk on the outside chance…

Jason crested the hill leading to his place. Lauren squinted for a better view in the early-morning sun, and sure enough a sleek luxury car was parked directly in front of Jason's house. He cursed low and long beside her. Lauren sat up straighter and peered through the window. A man leaned against the car, a tall guy with jet-black hair. His face became clearer as they neared.

None other than Jason's boss, Brock Maddox, waited for them. The man wore a suit. Was he on his way to church or work? Either way, finding him waiting here couldn't be a good sign.

Jason pulled up behind Brock's car, parking on the road. "I'll meet you inside in a few minutes," he said to Lauren before sliding out of the vehicle. "Good morning, Brock. What can I do for you?"

Lauren closed the sedan door, curiosity holding her on the sidewalk as Jason approached Maddox. She would go inside shortly.

Straightening from the car, Brock jammed his hands into his pockets. "Prentice is not happy."

Jason frowned. "What are you talking about?"

"This fake marriage you two tried to pull off."

Lauren stiffened. She might be torn by her decision

to go back to New York, but in no way did she want to cost Jason his job. She stepped alongside him, sliding a shaking hand in the crook of his arm. "Who says it's not real?"

Brock looked back and forth between the two of them as if weighing the wisdom of including her in the conversation. He didn't seem interested in going inside, though, opting instead to hold this meeting outdoors. Maddox was one cool customer, distant and perhaps even a bit uncaring. Was that what Jason had to look forward to becoming?

She rubbed the goose bumps prickling her arms. At least the neighborhood was quiet and deserted for the most part, other than a Jaguar driving past, engine growling low. Four doors down a small family piled into a car, all dressed to the nines for church. A lump swelled in her throat.

Jason's face went taut with tension. "Anything you can say to me, you can say to Lauren."

They always had managed well when it came to the business arena. The bittersweet thought tugged at her aching heart.

"Okay, then." Brock nodded. "The financial world is a small community. Did you think your half-million-dollar transaction wouldn't be noticed? Let me see if I can put this together just right, given the rumors floating around from Wall Street all the way to key players at Golden Gate Promotions. Lauren's accountant ran off with her operating capital, also a half-million dollars."

Hearing how clearly Brock saw through their ruse sent a bolt of panic through Lauren. She glanced at Jason, but he still kept his face impassive, apparently much better at tamping down freaked-out feelings than she was. Lauren forced herself to listen carefully to Brock.

"I'm guessing you bailed Lauren out in exchange for a pretend marriage to keep Prentice from going off the deep end over the pregnancy."

Lauren searched for the right words to save Jason's career. How damned ironic that just as hers came back together, his fell apart. "Ours may not have had a more traditional romantic beginning, but things have changed between us."

Not that it was any business of his. How could Jason manage a work environment that was so claustrophobic? Hell, so downright nosy? She considered blurting out how much she loved Jason.

Brock glanced back at Jason. "So Lauren's staying?"

Jason hesitated a second too long. "She doesn't have plane reservations."

Brock cocked an eyebrow. "You'll have to come up with better than that. Hell, I already know the police are involved and they locked in—what?—an hour ago?"

"My wife and I share finances. Her business is my business. What's wrong with my investing in her company?"

"That's not the way Prentice is seeing things. He's not too hyped on trusting a guy who paid a woman to participate in a pretend marriage just to save an account."

She bristled, prepared to tell Brock off, but held back for Jason's sake. Besides, for once the gossips were right on the mark.

Jason's shoulders braced with military bearing. "How do you intend to proceed?"

"It's your account. You brought it in, so it's yours to

manage. I won't lie—we've never needed an account like Prentice more than now. Competitors—Athos Koteas in particular—are breathing down our neck."

"I understand that and want to do what's best for MC."

Brock glanced at Lauren, then back. "It's obvious how far you'll go, and while a part of me admires that, I also expect you to cover your ass better." He scrubbed a hand over his jaw. "I'm kicking myself for not figuring this out sooner."

Jason pinched the bridge of his nose. Lauren felt like a fool, a heartbroken fool who'd stupidly fallen in love with her relentlessly ambitious husband. Thank God she'd resisted the urge to blurt out her feelings for him.

Brock pulled out the keys to his car, jingling them in his hand. "That's all for now. I just wanted to give you a heads-up in person, offer you time to come up with some way to pull your ass out of the fire. Prentice has called a meeting for tomorrow afternoon. But I'll see you in my office first thing in the morning." He nodded quickly to Lauren before sliding back in his car, all business.

Jason didn't even look at her, his gaze fixed on Brock's receding car. "I guess that's it for us, then," he said. "You won't even need to wait until next week for that flight out."

It was what she wanted. What she'd planned from the start. Her eyes shot back to the family down the street, her gaze lingering on the dad buckling the baby into a car seat.

If she had everything she wanted, why did it hurt this much to watch that little family down the street drive off together?

Twelve

The next morning Jason left Brock's office after a damage-control meeting to prep strategy for the Prentice powwow later today. His brain was too numb to do more than operate on autopilot to salvage what he could at work. He'd lost Lauren and would be relegated to parceled-out visits with his kid.

Last night he and Lauren had been back to sleeping separately, with him in the recliner and her in the bed. She'd made it clear it would best if he was gone before she woke up. She would keep in touch about the baby, but she didn't want any big emotional goodbyes.

He turned away from Brock's door. Brock had pretty much given him a speech to memorize, a pack of convoluted lies about how things had shaken down, but well-constructed lies Prentice might well buy into. His job was all that was left. A bigger office with a better window view was all he had to look forward to.

Brock's secretary sat outside in a waiting area at a modern acrylic desk like the rest of the floor—and Flynn leaned against a sleek filing cabinet built into the wall.

The Maddox VP shoved away and clapped an arm around Jason's shoulders. "Walk with me. Let's grab some food, then head back up to my office."

Like he had a choice. Jason suspected that Flynn was about to play his role of good cop after his brother's bad cop. Except he got the feeling it wasn't a game so much as their natural personalities.

Jason walked with Flynn as he jabbed the elevator button for the fifth floor. That floor contained all the other departments: public relations, art, financial. The offices were smaller than on the sixth, but still modern with stark-white walls and acrylic desks. Flynn smiled and waved as he walked past the rows of cubicles, calling each person by name, stopping to speak briefly with a couple of employees.

Finally they reached the large lunchroom with its modern kitchen. Brock Maddox kept the fridge well stocked, realizing that creative types enjoyed snacks while brainstorming in one of the soundproofed breakout rooms.

Flynn opened the fridge and pulled out a sack of Chinese food. "There's enough to share. Do you want water or soda?"

"Water, thanks."

Flynn's approach was definitely more laid-back than that of his brother, who didn't so much as offer a chair, much less a causal walk around followed by food. They took a service elevator back up to the sixth floor, making tracks to Flynn's office. The space used to be Brock's from back when their father was alive, but Flynn had made it his own, much homier than Brock's current digs. Airy with live plants, a glass desk and several cream-colored sofas for impromptu meetings.

Just the sort of place Lauren would like.

God, did all roads lead back to her now? Would it always be that way for him? He needed to get over it fast, because she would be gone when he returned home tonight.

Maybe he would stay at the office and sleep on his sofa rather than torment himself with the scent of her lingering on his sheets. He would throw himself into work and salvage his career.

Flynn sat behind his desk and gestured for Jason to sit across from him. He passed a carton of sweet-and-sour chicken and a pair of chopsticks. "How are you holding up after the ass chewing from my brother?"

"He has a right to be pissed. It's going to take some masterful manipulation and a dash of luck to pull off the meeting with Walter Prentice this afternoon."

Flynn stirred the wooden sticks through his food. "Brock can come off pretty harsh sometimes, but it's because he lives for this place. He worshippped our father. He's determined to keep his legacy alive through the business. MC is his life. I don't agree with his way, but I understand." Flynn swung his feet up on the desk, unwrapping an egg roll. "I have what he calls a lacka-daisical attitude toward the company."

Jason twisted open a bottled water. His old man would have gotten along great with Brock. Brock would also be one hell of a tough guy to have as an older sibling, always walking around in his shadow. But even though things were strained between the brothers, Jason didn't intend to risk siding with one or the other either way. Better to just let Flynn play out whatever it was he wanted to say.

Flynn finished off the egg roll in two bites. "Things are tight all the way around, but the business is basically secure. There's no cause for concern. Once we knock Koteas off his pedestal, we'll have a lock on this sector of the country."

"Okay, then." That wasn't the picture Brock had painted, but then, the Maddox brothers rarely got along smoothly.

"The tension between me and Brock is that obvious, huh?"

Jason shrugged noncommittally, swigging back his water.

"Brock and I need to work on not letting that show. Bad for business to put up anything other than a unified front." Flynn swung his feet back to the floor, leaning forward on his elbows. "I imagine you're wondering why I brought you in here."

"I'm the man of the hour." And not in a good way today.

Flynn's face went serious, tension making him resemble his brother all the more. "Let's put the Madd Comm crap aside for a second." He plowed a hand through his hair as he seemed to struggle for words. "Hell, I'll just come right out and say it. Don't let your work come before your wife."

Jason set his food aside carefully. That wasn't at all what he'd expected to hear when he walked in here, and he didn't know what to make of it.

"Lauren's heading back to New York this afternoon." He could already hear the empty echo of his house. He scratched under his tie, his chest going tight. "There are no other demands on my time." Not until the baby came.

"It's not too late for you, man. There're no divorce papers signed. Listen to me, I'm speaking from experience here. I let my family and my work come between me and Renee, and I've regretted it more times than I can count." More of that regret coated his voice even now. "Do you really want to end up like Brock? Breathing and eating the job so much he even lives here?"

Brock's primary residence was none other than an apartment in the Powell Street office building. A luxury setup, sure, but Jason preferred his house.

His empty house that wasn't even close to becoming a home until Lauren stepped inside with her ideas for filling it with furniture and plants. "It's all a moot point. She and I went into this with our eyes wide open. We were working some damage control of our own, trying to find the best possible solution."

"You're not even talking like the Jason Reagert we see around here. I can't see you giving up this easily."

What the hell did Flynn know? Jason had worked his ass off this past week to show Lauren all the ways their lives blended, the great life they could provide for their baby.

A whole week?

Damn.

Realization slammed through him. He didn't want to be *that* guy, the man who regretted not doing everything in his power to fight for the woman he loves. And hell, yes, he loved her. He wasn't emotionally closed off like his old man. His father would never have cared whether Lauren was happy, and his dad certainly would never have gotten choked up over an ultrasound photo.

A week might not be much time when it came to winning something as big as a lifetime together, but it was enough for him to be sure his feelings for Lauren were real. Lauren was perfect for him in every way, as a friend, lover, wife, mother of his child. He wanted it all with her.

Flynn was right. Nothing, no one and certainly no job should come between him and his wife. He'd be damned before he would let his life be dictated by business the way his father's was. He would follow Lauren all the way to New York, even if it meant starting up his own ad business there to be with her.

Once he finished his meeting with Prentice this afternoon, he would book the first flight out to reclaim his wife.

Lauren watched Jason's house in the rearview mirror as the taxi pulled away from the curb. Her suitcase was packed, her flight back to New York booked, her brief marriage over. She'd even gotten her wish for a no-scenes exit since Jason had honored her request to leave for work before she awoke.

Her life was such a mess she felt like a Picasso painting with her nose on crooked.

The city unfolded ahead of her, already crammed full of memories she'd made with Jason in only a week. Amazing memories. All those moments together merged in her mind in a bittersweet portfolio. She loved him, but didn't know how to build a life with him if he didn't love her back.

Her cell phone rang in her purse, jolting her. Could it be Jason? She fumbled fast to fish it out, read the screen.

Mom.

Lauren considered just pitching the cell back into her bag. They'd talked just yesterday about nursery murals, after all, and she really didn't have the emotional energy to deal with her mother now. Except she was only delaying the inevitable.

She brought the phone to her ear. "Hi, Mom. What do you need?"

"I'm just checking up on you. How are you feeling?"

Lauren stilled in the taxi seat. There was a calm in her mother's voice she hadn't heard in a long while. Instinctively she flinched away from hope. Most likely her mother was headed for a downward spiral instead.

"I'm feeling a lot better these days." Physically, anyway. Her nerves and heart, however, were in tatters. "In fact, I'm ready to work at full speed again. I'm, uh, heading to New York right now to tend to some business." She would deal with explaining about the divorce later.

She waited for the sure-to-come advice and demands to spend every minute of every waking hour together. Her hand tightened around the phone.

"That's fantastic, Lauren. I'm glad you're doing well." Jacqueline paused, inhaled a shaky breath on the other end of the line. "Listen, dear, I have a specific reason for calling."

Lauren's stomach clenched. Here it came. Although you never knew what that something might be with her mom, except that it usually included high drama, a lot of tears and then lashing out. "I'm listening."

"This is very difficult for me to say, so please don't interrupt."

Lauren restrained a slightly hysterical laugh at the notion of her interrupting when most of the time she could barely get a word in edgewise. "Whenever you're ready, Mom."

"I went to see my doctor today. Not my GP, but my *other* doctor, the one I stopped going to a while back." Jacqueline's words picked up speed. "We've scheduled some follow-up appointments, as well."

A rushing sound started in Lauren's brain. She couldn't have heard what she thought. But she had. Hope was a scary thing. "That's good to hear, Mom, really good."

"Don't interrupt, dear."

"Of course." She shook her head, stunned at this turn of events. "Sorry."

"He also wrote me a prescription, some new drug on the market, and I'm going to take it. This isn't easy for me to do or even tell you, but I want to be the best, healthiest grandmother I can. I want to enjoy that baby you're having." Her glasses chain rattled on the other end of the phone. From nervous fidgeting? Probably. This was a huge step for Jacqueline, seeking help on her own rather than because her family pushed. "All right, dear, you can speak now."

Her mother had been in and out of a doctor's care before. Lauren prayed this new initiative on her mom's part would lead to a long-term healthy outlook. "I know how tough that was for you, and I'm really proud of you. Thank you for calling to let me know."

Never before had her mother discussed going to the

doctor, and of course privacy was her right. But she'd also expected everyone had to pretend the problem didn't exist.

That Jacqueline could talk openly about seeking help? Trusting in this new start would take a while to fully set in, but they'd taken a major first step today.

Lauren cleared her throat. "I love you, Mom."

"I love you, too, dear," her mother whispered, her glasses chain clinking faster.

The line disconnected.

She cradled the phone to her chest, trying to hold on to that tenuous new connection with her mother a little longer. She'd told Jacqueline she was proud of her, but the enormity of it rolled over her even harder now that she had time to process the surprise news.

Then she started to wonder. If her mother could be so brave in setting her life right, in taking control of her own happiness, why couldn't she? Lauren sat up straighter, the cell phone falling to her lap. She didn't want to leave San Francisco. She didn't want to leave Jason. She was his wife, pregnant with his child, and she loved him. Totally and completely.

Why was she running away from the promise of a life together? True, he hadn't told her he loved her, but had she even bothered to ask? Or told him *her* feelings?

She stared out the window at the town she was only just beginning to explore. An SUV packed with a family and pulling a boat passed in the other lane, reminding her of Jason's yacht and all the weekend trips they could take, trips she'd never let herself think about even though Jason had tried to get her to look beyond this week.

The cab passed a restaurant, and she thought of licking

maple syrup off Jason's body. A plant nursery brought visions of him helping with a garden. She saw possibilities everywhere. It was as if the cap had come off a genie bottle once she gave herself permission to think "what if," and now she couldn't get the genie back in. She was wishing for a future with Jason all over the place.

She'd only given their relationship one simple week. No time at all in the big scheme of things. Running away was a cowardly thing to do. How ironic to spend all her life trying not to be her mother, yet now, she knew, she had a thing or two to learn about bravery from Jacqueline.

Starting today.

Lauren tapped on the plastic partition between her and the cabbie. "Excuse me? Could you turn around, please? I don't want to go to the airport, after all. I need you to drive me to Powell Street. The Maddox Building."

Standing in the MC boardroom at the head of the table, Jason thought of that "damage control" speech Brock had spelled out.

And he couldn't give it.

If he wanted to win his wife back, it had to start now, even when she wasn't around to hear what he was saying. "Mr. Prentice, while I value having you as a client, there's nothing more important than Lauren and our baby. I would rather pass your account to someone else in the firm than let anything come between me and my wife."

Walter Prentice rocked back in the red leather chair, his eyes narrowed, inscrutable. "Do you realize, Reagert, that I might very well take you up on that offer of another ad exec? I don't much like people misrepresenting themselves."

A gasp sounded from across the room. Jason pivoted fast and found…

…Lauren standing in the open doorway.

Chairs squeaked around the table as the MC executive staff jockeyed for a better view. Surprise rocked Jason all the way to his Testoni loafers, followed by caution. Then he saw Lauren's eyes filled with determination.

"Mr. Prentice." She strode into the room confidently, sliding her hand in the crook of Jason's elbow. "I can assure you that Jason and I are in one hundred percent agreement."

Prentice's chest puffed full of bluster. "Are you planning to lure this bright young star away from MC and back to New York?"

"I have no intention of taking Jason away." She tucked herself closer to his side. "Mr. Prentice, my marriage is rock solid. Nothing will budge me from San Francisco or from Jason's side."

She sounded as though she meant it. If this was some kind of act to pay him back for insisting on the fake engagement in the first place… Then he looked into Lauren's eyes.

And he saw love staring right back at him. Relief rocked him so hard he damn near forgot about the other people in the room until Gavin coughed helpfully, tuning him in again to Walter Prentice.

"What about all these rumors I'm hearing about a marriage of convenience?" Prentice's face creased in disapproval. "Mrs. Reagert, did you really take a half-million dollars to pose as his wife?"

Jason wanted to tell the old guy it was none of his business, but Lauren squeezed his arm lightly in restraint. "Mr. Prentice, apparently it's no secret my business had a rough patch, and Jason was willing to do anything, absolutely anything, to help me. Just as I'm willing to do anything to help him. We're that devoted to each other's happiness."

All eyes moved back to Prentice. Everyone seemed to be holding their collective breath, too, because the room went completely silent while the clothing magnate mulled over Lauren's declaration.

Finally, Prentice threw back his head and laughed, the sound booming around the room along with all those hefty exhales.

Jason's included. Lauren was pulling this off. He'd been prepared to go to the mat for her, only to have her step in to fight for him. God, she was magnificent!

Prentice slapped Jason on the back, holding on to his shoulder with a paternal air. "I like people who live out my motto Family Is Everything. You're a couple made to be an advertisement for that."

The stunned look on Brock's face was priceless. No doubt he hadn't expected Prentice to be swayed that easily. Especially given Brock's personal motto had always been Company First.

"Maddox," Prentice barked, "give the newlyweds the rest of the week off. My orders. Surely there's some busywork for my account that the rest of your people can handle while these two start their marriage off right."

Everyone around the office table applauded and whooped agreement. Brock even clapped, albeit slowly. Lauren blushed but, man, was she ever smiling.

He rushed her out of the boardroom and into his office, slamming the door closed and locked behind them. Lauren's laughter filled the room, mixing up with his as he hauled her into his arms. He kissed her and she kissed him, no hesitation, no distance, just all-out passion and connection and relief. Knee-buckling relief that she wasn't leaving him.

Jason backed his seriously hot wife against his desk, an ordered day off sprawling ahead of him invitingly. But first, he needed to know. "Did you mean everything you said back there with Prentice?"

"Every—" she kissed him "—single—" she kissed him again "—word."

A sigh shuddered through him. "Thank God, because I realized today I can't let you go."

"Good thing I'm not leaving, then." Lauren tugged his tie, bringing him closer. "It's not exactly professional to make love in the workplace."

"We're married." The need to seal their newfound commitment surged through him. "It's not only okay, but completely in the best interest of my future success. Anytime I'm sitting at this desk, I'll be reminded of you, which will make me plow through work all the faster so I can get home to my family, to my wife, the woman I love."

Then tears filled her eyes. Her chin trembled; her smile damn near blinded him. "Well, then," she breathed against his mouth, "ditch my panties and get me on that desk."

"Keep talking like that and this time will go so fast, no one will suspect we've been up to anything."

"Since you never leave me wanting, I have no problem with that. We'll just get home all the sooner."

"Home." He tunneled his hands into her silky hair, growing longer and fuller, blooming like the rest of her.

"Are you sure you're okay with staying in San Francisco? I don't know if you heard what I said before you interrupted Prentice, but I told him I'm willing to move back to New York if that's what it takes to make you happy. I have the financial resources to locate wherever you want. I'm not going to lose you over a job."

He and his father had let work and prideful stands come between them. He wouldn't make that mistake again.

"Oh, Jason." Her voice shook, heavy tears welling up in her eyes. "I feel the same way. I realized I've been hanging on to an idea of success and happiness, limiting myself out of fear of losing control. Here, with you, is exactly where I want to be."

"You're more than I deserve." He hauled her against his chest, inhaling her sweet floral scent.

"Hey, you can keep right on romancing me to make it worth my while," she said teasingly. "Actually, I've been thinking. Why not take that money you dropped into my company and start a branch out here?"

"I like the way you think." He looked into her eyes. "We could work with each other again like we used to."

"We were mighty damn good together."

"Still are." And they would be in the future, as well. "You've always been incredible, special, but this week has made me realize just how much I love you. How much I need you in my life. I'm glad you decided to stay, but I would have come after you. I couldn't let you boot me out of your life a second time."

One of those tears trickled down her cheek into her smile. "I love you, too, you know. So much. The way you make love to me, the way you help me while making it clear you know I can take care of myself. I should have realized sooner, but I've been so scared. You make me lose control, you know."

Her hesitant admission slid a piece of the Lauren puzzle into place for him, making him see how her tightly controlled surface hid so much passion beneath. But knowing that—understanding her—would help him navigate their relationship down the road. "The last thing I want to do is frighten you."

"I've been running from the intense way you make me feel, so afraid that I'll turn out like my mother, that we'll end up like my parents. But I know better now. We bring out the best in each other."

And she was right. Only with Lauren had he been able to find the joy of a future and family he'd never expected. "Sounds like you did a lot of productive brainstorming in the past few hours."

"And I haven't even begun to tell you the plans I have for the gardens." Her fingers crawled up his jacket lapel. "Now that I've finished with business for the day…"

He lifted her onto the edge of his desk, in perfect synch with her as always. "It's definitely time for some recreation."

Epilogue

San Francisco, two weeks later

Lauren Presley wondered how a man could be so deeply inside her body and mind at the same time. But no doubt about it, her sated, half-dressed husband, tangled up with her on the sofa, was one hundred percent emotionally in the moment.

She would make the most of a second go-round in their newly furnished living room as soon as she figured out how to breathe again.

The butter-soft leather of their burgundy-colored couch stuck to the backs of her legs through her thigh-high stockings, sweat still slicking her body from their frenetically passionate hookup.

Jason nuzzled aside her hair to her ear. "I have an idea. Let's break in every piece of new furniture this way."

She arched her neck to give him better access. "That could get a little tricky when that antique, upright piano you picked out arrives."

"We can just practice more of those inventive positions." He trailed a fresh bloom from the front yard over the swell of her stomach where their child grew, healthy and strong. "The flowers look great. I can't believe how fast this place is turning into a home."

"I'm only just getting started." She'd placed two topiaries by the front door and planted some cooler-weather snapdragons and diascia in the flower boxes, a nice beginning. But she looked forward to landscaping the garden in more detail over time. She had that now with Jason.

Time. Forever. Together.

She'd hired a full-time manager for her New York offices and had started the ball rolling for opening a San Francisco branch. Since she would soon have her money back, she and Jason had decided to use the half-million-dollar loan he'd given her as seed money for her expansion to California. It truly was a smart investment for their future and for their child. Lauren was already looking into plans for building an architecturally matching office behind the home.

Life was coming together perfectly.

She had her friend, her lover, her partner, her husband—and he also happened to be the love of her life.

They'd even invited her mother to come out and look at vacation condos for winter visits with her grandchild. Having Jason at her side made dealing with Jacqueline easier. While he still had a ways to go making peace with his own parents, she knew she would never be comfortable cutting her mother completely out of her life, especially now that her mother seemed ready to embrace help.

Lauren didn't delude herself. Dealing with Jacqueline would still be tough—to say the least—but she had a new level of confidence in her ability to avoid explosions by drawing better boundaries.

"Love you," she whispered against his mouth.

"Love you, too," he answered, and she never grew tired of hearing it.

Prentice's Family Is Everything motto was working well for them. Sure, their start had been for practical reasons, but they'd both been so stubborn and locked into their workaholic, cold lives, they'd needed a good shaking up.

Lauren shuffled, twisting around until she straddled Jason's lap. "I've got a hankering for pecan pancakes with lots of maple syrup. How about you try your hand with the basting brush this time?"

He stood, holding her in place as she wrapped her legs around his waist. "I say you are absolutely the best partner to work with, Mrs. Reagert. Absolutely the best."

* * * * *

Advertising Media Volume 184
FEATURESPOTLIGHT

This Week in Advertising…

The VP:
Flynn Maddox
His New Campaign:
Cribs & Cradles—for the man who has it all…
except the baby!

Scandal is threatening Maddox Communications yet again and this time Vice President Flynn Maddox is the target. According to sources, Mr Maddox is now living with his ex-wife—who apparently was never his "ex" at all. Rumor has it that Mrs Renee Maddox relocated from Los Angeles to the house she and Mr Maddox shared seven years ago. But what's even more interesting is that she recently tried to gain access to her husband's sample at a sperm bank. So…what exactly is going on between husband and "ex-wife"?

EXECUTIVE'S PREGNANCY ULTIMATUM

BY
EMILIE ROSE

Published in Great Britain 2011
Harlequin Mills & Boon Limited,
Eton House, 18-24 Paradise Road, Richmond, Surrey TW9 1SR

© Harlequin Books S.A. 2010

Special thanks and acknowledgment to Emilie Rose for her contribution to
the KINGS OF THE BOARDROOM series.

ISBN: 978 0 263 88089 2

51-0111

Harlequin Mills & Boon policy is to use papers that are natural, renewable
and recyclable products and made from wood grown in sustainable forests.
The logging and manufacturing processes conform to the legal environmental
regulations of the country of origin.

Printed and bound in Spain
by Litografia Rosés S.A., Barcelona

To Cathy, Maya, Michelle, Jen and Leanne.
Ladies, it was great being part of your team.

Bestselling Desire™ author and RITA® Award finalist
Emilie Rose lives in her native North Carolina with her
four sons and two adopted mutts. Writing is her third
(and hopefully her last) career. She's managed a medical
office and run a home day care, neither of which offers
half as much satisfaction as plotting happy endings.
Her hobbies include gardening and cooking (especially
cheesecake). She's a rabid country music fan because
she can find an entire book in almost any song. She is
currently working her way through her own "bucket list,"
which includes learning to ride a Harley. Visit her website
at www.emilierose.com or e-mail EmilieRoseC@aol.
com. Letters can be mailed to PO Box 20145, Raleigh,
NC 27619, USA.

Dear Reader,

Who hasn't spent time rehashing a conversation or event after the fact and come up with a much wittier response or better ending? Wouldn't it be great if life had a "do over" button?

I recently heard country song lyrics that talked about how a rock and a hard place can make a diamond. I am a firm believer that everything in life—even the bad stuff—happens for a reason, and we have lessons to learn from the events. Once we've learned those lessons we are often stronger and better equipped to deal with the next stumbling block in our path.

Executive's Pregnancy Ultimatum gave me the opportunity to grant Flynn and Renee Maddox a second chance at love when Renee's longing for a baby brings her "ex" husband back into the picture. This story also afforded me the opportunity to revisit San Francisco, one of the most romantic cities in the US.

I hope you enjoy the trip as much as I did.

Happy reading,

Emilie Rose

Prologue

January 11

"What do you mean I'm still married?" Renee Maddox struggled to keep the hysteria out of her voice as she stared aghast at her attorney.

Unflappable as usual, the older gentleman sat back in his chair. "Apparently your husband never filed the papers."

"But we've been separated seven years. How could this happen?"

"Failure to file is not as uncommon as you might think, Renee. But if you want to know the real reason, then you'll have to call Flynn and ask him. Or let me do it."

The pain of failure, of love gone so horribly wrong, still hurt. She'd loved Flynn with every fiber of her being. But in the end her love hadn't been enough. "No. I don't want to call him."

"Let's look at the big picture. You're entitled to half Flynn's assets when we file again, and those assets are considerably more now than they were then."

"I'm not any more interested in Flynn's money now than I was then. I want nothing from him."

The quick flattening of her lawyer's lips told her the news didn't make him happy, and no doubt she'd hear more about the subject. "I understand that you want a quick, clean break, but remember, California is a community-property state. You could get more since you didn't have a prenuptial agreement."

Another wave of worry rippled over her. "Does that mean he could also get half of my business? I've worked too hard to make California Girl's Catering a success to give it away."

"I won't let you lose CGC. But let's revisit what brought you here today. You can change your last name regardless of your marital status."

"My name is the least of my worries right now." Her plan to take control of her life had seemed so simple, beginning with taking back her maiden name, then starting the family she'd always wanted. But Flynn had refused to...

Her thoughts skidded to a halt as an elusive memory teased her. Grasping the arms of the cool leather chair, she struggled to recall the details of the story he'd confessed over too much champagne on their honeymoon, and slowly the pieces fell into place.

Hope flickered to life inside her. She'd been aching for a baby, and when she'd turned thirty-two last month she'd decided to take matters into her own hands and quit waiting for the mythical Mr. Right to appear. Like the heroines of some of her favorite romance novels, she'd decided to get artificially inseminated via a reputable sperm bank.

She'd been reading donor profiles for weeks, but had never expected to find a donor she'd known—and once loved. She knew how many unanswered questions—some important, some not—she and her child would face down the road if she went through with her plan. She'd grown up not knowing her father's identity because her mother couldn't—or wouldn't—name the man who'd impregnated her.

"Renee, are you all right?"

"I—I'm fine." Swallowing to ease her dry mouth, Renee studied the wizened face of the man on the opposite side of the desk. "You said I'm entitled to half of everything Flynn's?"

"Yes."

Her heart raced with excitement. She struggled to regulate her quickened breaths. The idea of having Flynn's baby without his consent was ludicrous and even sneaky. It certainly wasn't the nicest thing she could do, but she desperately wanted a child, and she would never ask him for support. He'd probably forgotten about that college dare, anyway.

She wiped her damp palms on her pant legs. "While Flynn was in college he made a deposit at a sperm bank on a dare. He said he asked them to hold it 'for future use.' If the sperm bank still has his…stuff, can I have it? Or at least half of it?"

Kudos to her lawyer for not showing surprise by so much as a twitch of an eyelash. "I don't see any reason we can't pursue that option."

"Then that's what I want. I want to have Flynn's baby. And then as soon as I've conceived, I'll want a divorce."

One

February 1

The pencil snapped in Flynn's fingers Monday morning. Ledgers forgotten, he rose with the phone still pressed to his ear and walked around his desk to close his office door. He leaned against it. No one on the sixth floor of Maddox Communications needed to hear what he thought the woman on the other end of the line had just said or his reply to her statement.

"I'm sorry. Could you repeat that?"

"I'm Luisa from New Horizons Fertility Clinic. Your wife has asked to be inseminated with your sperm," a cheerful female voice enunciated precisely as if he was an idiot. At the moment he felt like one.

His *wife?* He didn't have a wife. Not anymore. A familiar hollowness settled in his chest.

"Do you mean Renee?"

"Yes, Mr. Maddox. She's asking for your sample."

Head reeling, he tried to break down this crazy conversation and make sense of it. First, why would Renee try to pass herself off as his wife when they'd been apart seven years? She'd been the one to file for divorce the minute the one-year waiting period had passed. And second, there was the donation he'd made on a stupid dare back in college. Not a wise decision. Linking the two separate incidents boggled his mind.

"My 'sample' is fourteen years old. I thought you would have disposed of it by now."

"No, sir. It's still viable. Semen, if properly stored, can last beyond fifty years. But you stipulated that your specimen not be used without your written consent. I'll need you to sign a form to release it to your wife."

She's not my wife. But he kept the rebuttal to himself. The advertising agency dealt with some extremely conservative clients. One whiff of this story getting out and they could lose business—not something Madd Comm could afford in these tight economic times.

He scanned his office—the last happy project he and his ex-wife had completed together. When he'd resigned from his previous job and joined the family advertising agency, he and Renee together had chosen the glass desk, the pair of cream leather sofas and the profusion of plants. Plants he'd managed not to kill—unlike his marriage. He and Renee had been a good team.

Had been. Past tense.

He intended to get to the bottom of this fiasco, but one thing was certain. Nobody was getting his frozen, fourteen-year-old sperm.

"Destroy the sample."

"I'll need your written consent for that, too," the faceless voice quipped back.

"Fax over the form. I'll sign it and fax it back."

"Give me your numbers and I'll get it right to you."

Flynn's mind raced as he gave the numbers by rote. He tried to recall the awful months surrounding Renee's moving out, but much of it was a blur. He'd lost his father, his architectural career and then his wife all within six miserable months. A year after Renee had moved out he'd received the divorce papers, reopening an unhealed wound. The old anger returned—anger toward Renee for giving up on them so easily and toward himself for allowing it to happen. He detested failure. None more than his own.

The fax machine in the corner beeped, signaling an incoming missive. He checked the letterhead. "It's here. I'll return it before the ink dries."

After ending the call, he whipped the sheets off the machine, read, signed and then faxed them back.

His last memory of the divorce papers was of his brother promising to mail them after they'd sat on Flynn's desk for a month because Flynn hadn't had the heart to mail them and break that final link with Renee. What had happened to the documents after Brock took them?

The back of Flynn's neck prickled. Wait a minute. He didn't remember receiving a copy of the divorce decree. Hadn't his divorced friends said something about getting an official notification in the mail?

He was divorced, wasn't he? But if so, why would Renee lie to the clinic?

Lead settled in his gut. Renee had never been a liar.

He reached for the phone to call his lawyer, but stopped. Andrew would have to track down the information and call back, and Flynn had never been good at sitting and waiting.

Brock was closer.

Flynn yanked open his door so quickly he startled his PA. "Cammie, I'll be in Brock's office."

"Do you want me to call and see if he's free?"

"No. He'll make time for this." He'd damned well better make time.

Flynn's feet pounded on the black oak floors as he strode down the hall to the opposite side of the sixth floor and Brock's west corner office. He nodded to Elle, his brother's executive assistant, but didn't slow down as he passed her desk. Ignoring her squeak of protest, he barged into Brock's office without knocking.

His brother, with the phone to his ear, looked up in surprise, then held up his finger. Flynn shook his head and made an *X* with his forearms in the universal "shut down" signal, then closed the door. Brock wrapped up his conversation.

"Problem?" he asked after he'd cradled the receiver.

"What did you do with my divorce papers?"

Brock jerked back in his chair. Surprise filled eyes the same blue as Flynn saw in the mirror every morning, and then the surprise turned to wariness.

Flynn's gut clenched. "You did mail them, didn't you, Brock?"

Brock rose, exhaling a slow breath. He unlocked and opened a file-cabinet drawer, then withdrew a sheaf of papers and swore under his breath. "No."

Shock rattled Flynn to the soles of his feet. "What?"

"I forgot."

His heart hammered in his chest and in his ears. "You *forgot?* How is that possible?"

Clutching the back of his neck, Brock grimaced. "I stalled initially because you were so broken up over losing Renee that I hoped once you two calmed down you'd resolve whatever issue drove you apart. I felt partially responsible for the demise of your marriage because I pressured you into leaving a career you loved to come aboard as Maddox's VP. And then I forgot. Stupid of me, but if you recall it was a tough time for all of us after Dad died."

Flynn's legs went weak. Flabbergasted, he sank into a leather chair and dropped his head in his hands.

Married. He was still married. To Renee.

A confusing swirl of responses swept through him. Tamping them down, he focused on the facts.

If Renee was passing herself off as his wife, then she must have known they weren't divorced. The question was, how long had she known, and why hadn't she called and chewed him out for not mailing the forms, or at the very least, sicced her attorney on him?

"Flynn, are you okay?"

Hell no.

"Of course," he answered automatically. He'd never been one to share his problems. He wasn't going to start now.

As his shock slowly subsided, a completely different emotion took its place. Hope. No, it was more than that. Elation filled him like helium, making him feel weightless.

He and Renee weren't divorced.

After years of silence, he had a reason to contact her. A reason besides finding out why she'd tried to pull a fast one with his sperm. But for now it was enough to know they weren't divorced and she wanted to have his baby.

The surreal feeling left him reeling. "I'll call my lawyer and find out where I stand. I'm going to take a few days off."

"You? You never take time off. But as much as I hate to say it, now is not a good time."

"I don't care. The situation has to be dealt with. Now."

"I guess you're right. Here. Again, I apologize. If you'd ever demonstrated any real interest in another woman, maybe it would have tripped my memory. Maybe not. It's a lousy excuse, but there it is. What brought on this sudden interest in your divorce? Is Renee planning to remarry?"

Flynn flinched. Logically, he knew Renee had probably dated since their separation, as had he, but the idea of her with other men filled him with a possessiveness that should have died long ago. He rose to his feet and took the document that should have ended his marriage and made an instant decision not to share the sperm news. His family was better off not knowing.

"I don't know Renee's plans. I haven't seen her in years." She'd wanted it that way. But now he would see her. His pulse accelerated at the prospect.

"Flynn, I'm sure I don't need to warn you that we need to keep this quiet, but I'm going to, anyway. News of this getting out won't help our cause against Golden Gate Promotions, and I'll be damned if I want to hear that bastard Athos Koteas crowing in glee if we lose more clients."

The mention of their rival almost dampened Flynn's excitement. "Understood."

He returned to his office and crossed straight to the shredder. Through the window above the machine, the sun glowed just above the roof lines in the distance. The symbolism of a new day and a new beginning didn't escape him. Losing Renee had been the biggest regret of his life. His older brother's negligence had given Flynn the perfect opportunity to see if the attraction was still there and if so to win her back.

He fed the papers through the slot one page at a time, enjoying the whine and grind of the machine turning his biggest failure into crosscut paper fragments. When he finished he felt like celebrating. Instead, he sat down at his computer.

He needed to locate his wife.

MADCOM2.

The light blue BMW's license plate snagged Renee's attention as she turned into her driveway. She almost clipped her mailbox post with her minivan's front bumper and quickly jerked the wheel to the left.

MADCOM equaled Maddox Communications.

Her stomach churned like a dough mixer as she parked beside her visitor. She knew the identity of the car's owner from the "2" part of the tag before her ex— her *husband*—climbed from the driver's seat.

Ever since she'd heard the clinic's message on her answering machine informing her that her request for Flynn's sperm had been denied, she'd known it was only a matter of time before he came looking for her. The clinic must have contacted him. Her attorney had warned her of the possibility.

But nothing could prepare her for Flynn looming over her car even before she could pull the key from the ignition. The moment she disengaged the locks, he opened her door. Heart racing and her mouth going dry, she fought to appear calm, grabbed her purse from the passenger seat and stepped from the vehicle, ignoring the hand he offered in assistance. She couldn't touch him yet, and wasn't sure she'd ever be ready for that again even in the most casual way.

Dreading the conversation ahead, she tipped back her head to look up at the man she'd once loved with all her heart. The man who'd broken her.

Flynn had changed. And yet he hadn't. His eyes were still impossibly blue and his hair inky dark, but a few strands of silver now glimmered at his temples. His shoulders were as broad as she remembered and even with him wearing his suit, she could tell he hadn't added any fat to his lean torso. If anything, his jaw looked more chiseled.

But the past seven years had been hard on him. There were grooves beside the mouth she'd once lived to kiss, and a new horizontal crease divided his brow. She didn't think those were laugh lines fanning out from his eyes, although he used to smile often during the early days of their relationship, before he'd begun to work for Maddox Communications.

"Hello, Flynn."

"Renee. Or should I say, wife?" His deep, gravelly tone filled her tummy with the sensation of scattering butterflies. "How long have you known?"

She could have played dumb, but didn't see the point. "That we weren't divorced? Only a few weeks."

"And you didn't call me."

"Like you didn't call me when you decided not to file the papers?"

He frowned at her snippy tone. "There's more to it than that."

"Enlighten me." And then she remembered the

Wednesday-morning fish-market cargo in her cooler. "But you'll have to finish this riveting story inside. I have to get the seafood into the fridge."

She opened the van's back door. His hip and shoulder bumped hers when he nudged her aside to grab the cooler. Her senses went wild over the contact. The way they used to. Darn it. Her reaction didn't mean anything. She was over him. Well and truly over him. He'd ripped out her heart piece by piece before she'd left him. No feelings remained other than regret and disappointment.

"Get the door," he ordered.

His words shocked her into motion. She locked the car and hustled up the flower-lined brick sidewalk of her bungalow, scanning the exterior and trying to see it through Flynn's eyes. He hadn't been here since the early days of their short marriage when this had been her grandmother's home. Renee had made a lot of changes since then as she'd turned a private retreat into an inviting place of business.

She'd added flower beds beneath the lemon and orange trees, as well as a bubbling fountain, and she'd hung multiple trailing-flower baskets and a swing on the porch. The stone foundation and shingled exterior had been pressure-washed last year and the trim freshly painted a rich emerald-green, but she'd done the majority of her work inside.

She unlocked and pushed open the front door, then followed him through the foyer and living room to the kitchen, her masterpiece.

He stopped abruptly. "You've expanded."

"I needed a larger kitchen for my catering business, so I enclosed Grandma's back porch and redid every-thing. I'm using her old bedroom for an office."

Stop babbling.

She closed her mouth and focused on her stainless, commercial-grade appliances, acres of granite counter-tops and bright white cabinet—a cook's dream. Her dream. Something she had not been allowed to pursue as Flynn's wife.

"Nice. What made you decide to open your own business?"

"It was something I'd always wanted. Granny talked me into taking the leap before she passed away four years ago."

From the shock in his eyes, she guessed he hadn't known about her grandmother's passing. She probably should have notified him, but she'd had enough heart-ache to deal with over losing Granny without having to face Flynn at the funeral.

"I'm sorry for your loss. Emma was a wonderful lady."

"Yes, she was. I don't know what I would have done without her, and I still miss her. But she would have loved this—another generation of Landers women working with food and feeding the masses."

"I'm sure she would."

In the silence that followed, Renee looked across the kitchen to the ladder-back chair that had been her granny's favorite. There were days when it felt as if Emma were watching over her, but then, Emma had been more of a mother to Renee than her own had been. Her grandmother had certainly been a rock of support when Renee had arrived brokenhearted on her doorstep after leaving Flynn. Emma had opened her arms, her heart and her home, offering Renee a sanctuary for as long as she needed one.

"Where do you want the cooler?" Flynn asked.

"On the floor in front of the fridge." As soon as he

set it down, she transferred twenty pounds of shrimp and six large salmon filets into her Sub-Zero refrigerator, then washed her hands and faced him. "So…what's so complicated about slapping a stamp on the envelope containing the divorce paperwork?"

"Brock thought he was doing us a favor by giving us cool-down time. He put the papers in a file cabinet."

"For six years?"

"They'd probably still be in the drawer if you hadn't tried to get my sperm." Eyes narrowing, he leaned against the counter and crossed his arms and ankles. "So you still want to have my baby."

His speculative tone put her on guard. "I want to have *a* baby. You just happened to be a donor I knew."

"And you planned to have my child without informing me?"

She grimaced. "Probably not one of my best decisions. But after going through page after page of other potential donors, I had too many unanswered questions. But now that you've refused I'll go back to my anonymous candidates."

His unblinking gaze held hers. "Not necessarily."

"What do you mean?"

"Renee, I always wanted you to have my baby."

"Not true. I asked seven and a half years ago. Correction, I begged. You said no."

"The timing was wrong. I was trying to adjust to my new job."

"A job you hated. One that made you miserable."

"Brock and Maddox Communications needed me."

"So did I, Flynn." She hated the telling crack in her voice, but the sadness of watching their love unravel hit her all over again, making her throat tighten. "I needed the man I fell in love with, the one I married. I was more than willing to help you deal with your grief over losing your father. But I couldn't stand by and watch that job destroy you. You gave up your dream of becoming an architect and in the process became a silent, uncommunicative stranger. We didn't talk. We didn't make love. You were barely ever home."

"I was working, not cheating on you."

"Watching our love die was more than I could bear."

"When did it die?"

"You tell me." When she'd caught herself turning to alcohol to dull the pain of her unhappiness, she'd known that no matter how much she loved him she'd end up just like her bitter, unhappy alcoholic mother if she didn't get out. If she'd stayed, Flynn would have ended up hating her the way each of her mother's lovers had eventually despised her mother over the years.

The childhood memories of loud arguments, slamming doors, cars roaring off and "uncles" who never returned had been too vivid. She couldn't live that way and she would never raise a child in that atmosphere.

"I loved you right up until the day you left me. We could have made it work, Renee, if you'd given us a chance."

"I don't think so. Not as long as you had a job that sucked the life out of you. Out of us." She tried to shake off the bad memories. "I'll have my attorney draw up another set of divorce papers. Like last time, I want nothing from you."

"Except my child."

Another dream dead. They'd once planned to have a large family—at least three children, maybe four, because she'd hated being an only child. "Like I said, I'll go back to my donors."

"You don't have to."

Her heartbeat blipped out of rhythm. "What are you saying?"

"You can have my baby."

She forced a breath into her tight chest. "The clinic said your sample had been destroyed. Are you planning to make another donation?"

"I'm not talking about frozen sperm or artificial insemination."

Her tongue felt as dry as parchment paper. "Then what are you suggesting, Flynn?"

"I'll give you my baby—the usual way."

Stunned by the idea of making love with Flynn again, she staggered backward into the counter. But an undeniable wisp of desire snaked through her. They'd been so good together. She'd experienced nothing remotely close to that level of fulfillment before or since Flynn. But she couldn't risk it.

"No. That isn't an option. I didn't do casual sex before and I'm not going to start now."

"It's not casual sex when we're still married. I know how much not knowing anything about your father bothered you. This way you'll know who fathered your child, and you'll have my complete medical history."

Tempting. And dangerous. "Why would you agree to that?"

"I'm thirty-five. It's time to think about kids."

Alarm ripped through her. "I'm not looking for someone to be a part of my child's life."

"Your catering business takes up what? Fifty, sixty hours a week? When are you going to have time to be a parent?"

Had he been checking up on her? "I'll make time."

"Like Lorraine did?"

She winced as the barb hit deep. "That's low—even for you, Flynn."

Her mother had worked long hours as a chef in a series of swanky L.A. restaurants and would then come home to drink until she passed out. Typical of a functional alcoholic, only her family had suffered. Her mother had hidden her addiction well from her employers and the rest of the world.

"It will be easier to raise a child with two parents and better for the child. It's also a good backup plan in case something happens to either of us."

Horrified by his implication, she backed away. "We might still be married, but we're not staying that way."

"I want to share every aspect of the pregnancy and delivery and be a part of the baby's first year. After that we can go our separate ways—other than sharing custody. We'll keep the option open for our child to have the siblings you never had."

"More children? Are you crazy?" But what he said appealed on so many levels. Too many levels.

"I want to be a father, Renee. I want a family."

"Don't you have a girlfriend or someone your mother would approve of who could—"

"I could ask you the same question. No men in the picture?"

"I'm not seeing anyone." She'd be insane to risk her heart and her health again. Shaking her head, she paced to the opposite side of the kitchen. "Thanks for your generous offer, but I'll stick with my donor catalog."

"You'd rather depend on a questionnaire that's probably no more truthful than a personal ad?"

Another direct hit. She had wondered how factual the

donor data might be. Sure, the lab results would be accurate, but she'd done enough online dating in the past few years to know that answers applicants provided rarely resembled the truth. "I'll choose carefully."

"Think about it, Renee. The plans we made. The house we bought and restored together specifically with raising a family in mind. The fenced yard. The dog. The whole deal. Your baby could have all that."

Her heart squeezed. "You still have the house?"

"Yes."

They'd spent the first six months of their marriage working side by side renovating the beautiful Victorian in Pacific Heights. She'd spent the second six months wandering around the empty rooms alone trying to figure out how to save her dying marriage. In the end, all she could do was save herself.

"Flynn, it's a crazy idea."

"So was us running away to Vegas to get married. But it worked."

"For a while. And judging by your license plate, you still work for Maddox Communications. Nothing has changed."

"The job is under control now. It doesn't consume me like it used to. Move in with me. Let's make a baby, Renee."

She gaped at him. "Move in with you? What about my business? I've spent years building California Girl's Catering. I can't walk away for a year and expect my clientele to be waiting when I come back. And I can't commute. It's a five- or six-hour drive each way without traffic."

"I checked out your Web page. You have 'an amazingly talented assistant' who helps you, or so you claim on your blog. Leave the L.A. business in her hands temporarily and expand into the San Francisco area. I have connections. I'll help you."

He certainly knew which buttons to push to get her acquiescence. She didn't doubt for one second that Tamara could handle the L.A. side of the business, and having the Maddox clout behind CGC would certainly get her foot in the door of the highly competitive San Francisco marketplace faster.

But were the risks worth the potential rewards?

"Have my child. Allow me to spend the baby's first year under the same roof, and then I'll give you an uncontested divorce and pay full child support."

A tiny, sentimental part of her wanted to agree. Renee had always believed Flynn would make a wonderful father—the kind she wished she'd had. She'd experienced firsthand how patient and encouraging he could be when he'd taught her the skills of restoration. But letting him back into her life was scary and risky.

You're older, wiser and stronger now. You can handle it.

She had to be crazy, because she was actually considering his suggestion. But maybe…just maybe this insane idea could work. Focus on the result. A baby. Someone to love and come home to each night. But if she was going to keep her head and her sanity, she needed to lay ground rules.

"Flynn, hooking up just to have a baby is crazy."

"It could work—for both of us."

"If I agree to this, then I'll need help finding kitchen space in San Francisco."

"I'll get right on it."

She rubbed her cold hands together. Her heart

pounded wildly out of rhythm. She gulped, trying to ease the knot in her throat. "Okay, I'll consider it, but I have a few conditions."

Victory flared in his eyes, giving her a moment's panic. "Name them."

"We need time to get to know each other again and make sure this crazy scheme can work before jumping back into bed together."

"How much time?"

"I don't know. A month, I guess. That should be long enough to determine whether or not we're still compatible."

"Agreed."

"If it's not working, then either of us can back out and you will sign the divorce papers."

He dipped his chin. "I'll sign."

The sense of panic squeezed tighter, as if she was drowning and desperate for air. Was she crazy to plan on bringing a baby into a broken marriage? But she and Flynn had never had the kind of volatile arguments her mother and her mother's lovers had had. Their child would not feel like a bone of contention. Her baby would know from day one that it was wanted, planned, not a mistake that derailed her life.

"I—I want my own bedroom. We'll get together… when it's time…*if* we decide to go through with the plan."

The crease in his forehead deepened. "If you insist."

"I do." She smothered a wince at the words she'd spoken so many years ago. Back then her heart and head had been filled with happiness, dreams and possibilities, instead of a stomach-twisting fear that she was making a huge mistake.

"Anything else?"

She searched her brain for more protective barriers to build, but her thoughts churned so chaotically she could barely think. "Not at the moment. But I reserve the right to revisit this later, if need be."

"I accept your terms and have a few of my own."

She stiffened. "Let's hear them."

"I want to keep the real reason for our living together between us. It is critical that our family, friends and business associates believe we are trying to reconcile rather than temporarily hook up to make a baby."

Could she fake that kind of happiness? For a baby she could do almost anything. "I guess that would be better in the long run—especially if there is a child."

"Then we have a deal?"

Doubts swirled through her like fruit pureeing in a blender.

Think of the baby. A beautiful blue-eyed, black-haired, chubby-cheeked baby.

She nodded and extended her hand. Flynn's long fingers encircled hers. He simultaneously tugged and stepped forward, then covered her mouth with his.

Shock crashed over her like a waterfall as his warm, firm lips moved against hers. Familiar sensations deluged her, sweeping her back into a current of desire and far out of her depth. Even though he was six feet and she was barely five foot three, they'd always fit together like perfectly cut puzzle pieces. His thigh spliced between hers, his strong arms enfolded her, tucking her into his chest. It felt as if she'd never left his arms, and she was right back where she was supposed to be.

Horrified, she broke the kiss and shoved against his chest. Gasping for air, she backed away, but she couldn't deny the turbulent flood of hunger sluicing through her. "What was that about?"

"Sealing the deal."

"Don't do it again."

"I'm not allowed to touch you?"

"No. Not until…it's time."

"Renee, to make our reconciliation look real, we're going to have to touch and kiss and act like we're in love."

"I'm a caterer, not an actress."

He dragged a knuckle down her cheek and over the pulse hammering in her neck, then along the neckline of her top. She shivered and her nipples tightened.

"Let your body do the talking. You still want me and it shows."

She gasped at his audacity. Unfortunately, he told the truth. Her reaction to a simple kiss told her she still wanted her husband. And wanting Flynn was the worst possible thing that could happen.

If she wasn't careful, Flynn Maddox would break her heart all over again or worse, drive her to self-destruction. And then she'd be no good for anyone—especially her child.

TWO

There's no place like home.

But this wasn't her home, no matter how it felt, Renee reminded herself Friday evening. A knot of apprehension formed in her stomach as she stared up at the tall, Queen Anne Victorian house painted brick-red with cream-colored balusters and gingerbread trim.

The wooden front door with its oval, beveled-glass insert opened and Flynn stepped onto the porch. He must have been watching for her. In faded jeans and a blue T-shirt, he looked so much like the man she'd fallen in love with eight and half years ago that it felt as if someone had dropped a fifty-pound bag of sugar on her chest.

But that love had died. Painfully. And it wasn't coming back. She wouldn't let it.

A volatile cocktail of emotions churned inside her as he jogged down the steep stairs toward her, then stopped on the concrete driveway a foot away. "I'll take these bags. You grab the rest of your stuff."

Her gaze dropped briefly and involuntarily to his lips before she ripped it away. "This is all I brought."

She'd only brought the minimal requirements. She was only a visitor here, and she didn't want Flynn—or herself—to get the wrong idea that this was anything more than a temporary residence. "I'll pick up anything else I need when I make my weekly visits to check on Tamara and CGC."

He didn't look pleased, but he didn't argue. "Would you like to park your car in the garage?"

"No, thanks. Did you ever do anything with the rest of the basement?" They'd been debating what to do with the large space behind the garage after he finished using it for a workroom during renovations. Since the area was on the downhill side of the house and had plenty of windows overlooking the back garden, the empty space would be wasted as a storage room.

"Not yet, but I have some ideas."

She scanned the exterior of the house, loving every line of the gingerbread trim and dental moldings, the steep roof and the round turret. "It doesn't look like you've made any changes to the exterior."

"It's hard to improve on perfection. We did well with Bella."

Bella. The pet name they'd given the beautiful house.

Flynn's fingers covered hers on the handles of her suitcases, sending sparks shooting up her arm. He stood too close and he smelled too good and too familiar. Memories of happier times pushed their way forward. She battled them back, released her luggage and moved a safer distance away.

He carried her luggage up the steps as if the heavy bags weighed nothing. She followed him but paused on the porch to turn and look at the view. Other restored nineteenth-century Victorians lined the east-west ridge like a brightly painted rainbow of color. On days like today when the sky was clear, she could see the Golden Gate Bridge, Alcatraz and the Marin Headlands to the north. The shopping and dining districts were down the steep hill and around the block.

"Come in, Renee."

Dread slowed her reaction time. Turning her back on the gorgeous view that made real estate in the area so expensive, she stepped into the foyer. Nostalgia washed over her. She could have walked out just yesterday, instead of an aeon ago. The warm, rich, jewel-tone colors they'd chosen welcomed her exactly as she remembered. Even the scent of the vanilla and cinnamon potpourri she'd loved lingered.

Gleaming hardwood floors stretched in every direction. The staircase with its delicately carved ivory-painted spindles rose up the side wall from the center of the foyer. The formal parlor took up the front left corner of the first floor and the dining area the right.

She pulled her thoughts back to the present. "Have you finished the third floor yet?"

"There didn't seem to be much point."

Their children's rooms would have been on the third floor. Three bedrooms and a playroom.

"You can't quit, Flynn. Bella deserves to be finished."

"Now that you're back, maybe we'll get around to it."

We'll. She rejected the word.

The house had been a wreck when Flynn bought it ten years ago. He'd been restoring the first floor when they met in a local paint store where she'd driven just to find a specific brand of unscented paint that the L.A. stores hadn't carried. He'd asked her opinion on an exterior color, and the rest, as the cliché said, was history.

They'd spent many of their dates and the first six months of their marriage finishing the first floor and then the second. They'd been about to tackle the third when he'd lost his father and changed jobs, and renovations had ceased to matter to him. Just like their marriage and her. She'd continued working on the house, but it hadn't been the same. Without Flynn by her side, her heart hadn't been in the project, and when he'd refused to have a baby, there had been no point in finishing the nursery.

He climbed the stairs. "You have your choice of bedrooms—the guest room or the master."

And sleep with the memories of making love with him in that big bed and in the master bath's claw-foot tub? No, thanks. They had eventually "christened" every room in the house, so there were literally memories to suppress every way she turned, but she still wanted to be as far away from Flynn as possible.

"I'll take the front room with the balcony." The one where they'd made love on a paint-spattered drop cloth. She'd found paint in her hair and other interesting places for weeks afterward. But that day and the drop cloth were long gone.

He frowned. "Are you sure? The guest room's on the street side."

"One of us has to sleep there, and it's not like you have a lot of traffic noise here. I always thought the balcony would be a great place for guests to sit and sip coffee in the morning. You have to admit the view is incredible."

He carried her luggage into the guest quarters and set it on the iron bed. "You know where everything is. Help yourself."

"Thank you," she said as stiffly as if she was a stranger, instead of the one who'd chosen the decor of this room—right down to the wedding-ring quilt on the bed and the rug beneath her feet.

"When you're finished unpacking we'll have dinner at Gianelli's."

Memories of the quaint Italian restaurant lambasted her. "Don't even think of trying to act like everything is the same, Flynn. It isn't."

"Those who know us will expect us to celebrate our reconciliation at our favorite restaurant."

Unfortunately, Flynn was right. To make this look real she was going to have to face the demons from her past.

"Our *pretend* reconciliation," she corrected.

He inclined his head.

Resignation settled over her like a cold, wet tablecloth. The charade was going to force her into places she didn't want to go.

"Give me thirty minutes." Maybe by then she'd find the courage to do what she had to do.

Flynn loved a good plan and thus far his was coming together nicely. Renee was home. She wasn't in his bed yet. But she would be. Soon.

He laced his fingers through hers as they strolled to Gianelli's the way they'd done so many times before. She startled and tried to pull away, stumbling over an expansion joint in the sidewalk in the process. He tightened his grip, halting her fall and pulling her closer to his side.

Her wide, blue-violet eyes found his. "What are you doing?"

"Holding your hand. You can tolerate that for appearances' sake, can't you?" Having her close felt good.

"I guess so."

He inhaled, letting her familiar Gucci Envy Me perfume wash over him. He wanted to tangle his hands in her long, blond curls and kiss her until she melted against him like she used to, but that would have to wait until she was more receptive. The initial kiss had answered his primary question. The chemistry between them hadn't faded, and as long as they had chemistry to work with, he had a good chance of fixing what he'd broken.

He could feel Renee's tension through her fingers and sought a way to distract her. "I've done some research on available properties in the area for you to lease."

Her beautiful, blue-violet gaze flickered his way. "And?"

"There are a few prospects, but everything depends on your budget. I'll show you the data when we get back, along with my ideas for the basement."

Genuine interest brightened her face. "What did you decide to do with it?"

"That will have to wait until we get home."

"Tease," she said with a smile that faded almost instantly.

She no doubt remembered the occasions when she'd used the same word in the past—times when he'd aroused the hell out of her but delayed her pleasure repeatedly until she'd begged for mercy.

His skin flushed with heat and his groin grew heavy. He focused on what he planned to show her after dinner.

Drawing the blueprints for her business had filled him with an energy and excitement he hadn't experienced in a long time. He'd wanted to share them with her earlier when she'd asked about the space. But first he needed to ply her with good food, good wine and good memories to make her more receptive.

He opened the restaurant's heavy wooden door, and Mama Gianelli, thanks to a heads-up text from him, waited by the hostess stand. The women had bonded years ago when Renee had asked the restaurant owner's advice on a recipe.

Mama Gianelli squealed and bustled forward to hug Renee and kiss her cheeks. "When Flynn asked me to reserve your table, my heart overflowed. It makes me so happy to have you back where you belong, Renee. I've missed you and that beautiful smile," she gushed in her heavily accented English.

Renee's smile made its first appearance since she'd come back into his life. Too bad it wasn't aimed at him, because like Senora Gianelli, he'd missed it and the way it made Renee's eyes sparkle. "I've missed you, too, Mama G."

"And this one." Mama G pointed at Flynn and he stiffened. "He has not been eating like he should. Look at him. Skin and bones."

Flynn shifted uncomfortably, then Renee's gaze coasted over him, slowly, thoroughly. The appreciation he saw in her eyes made him stiffen for an entirely different reason.

Mama G linked her arm through Renee's. "Come, I have your special table ready."

He followed the women to the back corner, taking the time to admire his wife's petite shape from behind.

Renee had gained a little weight since their split, but it had landed in all the right places, and her white wraparound sweater and gray trousers that accentuated her figure awakened his libido in a way no other woman had been able to do since Renee had left him.

"I will bring a bottle of your favorite Chianti to the table," their hostess said.

Renee shook her head. "None for me, thanks."

Surprised, he studied her face, but he could roll with her decision. "I'll pass, as well."

Mama Gianelli departed and Renee opened her menu. He didn't know why she was wasting her time unless hiding behind the menu was her way of avoiding him. She'd ordered the same dish each time they'd eaten here in the past, claiming no one made spinach manicotti as well.

"Aren't you ordering your usual?"

"I want to try the chicken romano. It's stuffed with shrimp and fresh mozzarella and covered in a lemon cream sauce," she replied without looking at him.

"That's a change."

She peered at him over the menu, her gaze serious. "I've changed, Flynn. I'm not the quiet little mouse who's eager to please and afraid to make waves anymore."

Was there a warning in her tone? "Everybody changes, Renee, but the fundamentals that make us who we are remain the same."

The Gianellis' granddaughter arrived to take their order. After she left, Flynn lifted his water glass. "To us and our future family."

Renee hesitated, then raised hers. "To the baby we might make."

He noted the way she stressed "might," but let it

pass, and reached across the table to capture her free hand. She stiffened. "Is this really necessary?"

"We always held hands while we waited for our food in the past."

Her fingers remained stiff in his. "Why is it so important that everyone believe we're a happy couple?"

Not the relaxing conversation he'd planned, but she needed to know the facts. He stroked his thumb across her palm. "The tight economy is pinching advertising budgets for even the largest firms. Our closest rival, Golden Gate Promotions, is encroaching on our turf and not above using underhanded methods to steal our accounts."

"For example?"

"Athos Koteas, the owner, will do anything to make us look unstable, immoral or untrustworthy."

"How can he do that?"

"Gossip. Innuendo. We don't know where he's getting his information, but it's almost as if he has an inside source. Some of our biggest clients are ultraconservative. They'll go elsewhere at the first hint of scandal because they can't afford to have their names attached to anyone who might cause them to lose customers and revenue. That's why the truth behind our personal project needs to be kept confidential."

"That's like living in a glass house, Flynn. You can't keep it up indefinitely."

"Koteas is seventy. He won't live forever. But enough about my work."

"I like hearing about your work. You never used to discuss it…well, not after you joined Maddox."

"I had enough of the advertising jungle during the day. I didn't want to rehash it at night." But she had a point. When he'd been at Adams Architecture he'd been so excited about his work that he'd often recounted the highlights of his day over dinner. "How is Lorraine?"

Her stern expression told him she'd recognized his change of topic, but then she shrugged. "Mom's the same. She's working at a five-star restaurant in Boca Raton now."

"Does she still change jobs every few years?"

Renee nodded. "She moves on as soon as someone gets on her bad side."

"That's the negative side of her alcoholism. You're very lucky to have had your grandmother to provide a more stable environment." He scraped his thumbnail across her palm. Her breath hitched. She yanked her hand free and reached for her water—but he didn't miss the goose bumps on her arms.

"You look good, Renee. Owning your own business must suit you."

"Thanks. There are advantages to being the boss, and I admit, I prefer having the freedom to be creative, instead of always being stuck with the tried-and-true recipes."

When they'd met she'd been employed by a well-known L.A. caterer. After they'd married she'd quit her job and moved to San Francisco.

He'd had a lot of time to think about the demise of their marriage, and he'd concluded his first mistake had been in asking Renee to focus full-time on their marriage and home. Much to his mother's disgust, Renee had come from a working-class family. Her grandmother had owned and run a trendy diner, and then Renee's mother had become a top chef. Both jobs required long hours, exhausting work and a willingness to get their hands dirty.

Renee was no stranger to hard work. She'd practically been raised in a bustling restaurant kitchen. At fourteen when he'd been building models and acting like a typical teenager, she'd been busing tables at her first job. She'd been accustomed to earning her own money and had never been comfortable coming to him for cash to buy groceries or anything else.

Lunch and shopping expeditions, unless related to home improvement, had never excited her, and she wasn't the type to laze in the spa. Being a lady of leisure hadn't come easily to her, and she'd had nothing to distract her when his hours increased.

Nothing except premature ideas about a baby.

He'd asked himself a hundred times if they would still be married if he'd let her take another job or if he'd said yes to the baby. But he'd refused to start a family because he hadn't wanted to be the absentee father his had been.

Children. How many would they have had by now if he hadn't said no? He brushed the thought aside. The past couldn't be undone. The only thing he could do was learn from his mistakes and move on. And this time, he didn't intend to let her go.

It would be far too easy to forget this reconciliation wasn't real, Renee decided as Flynn let her into the front door of their—his house.

During dinner he had been attentive, witty and conversational—just as he'd been during the beginning of their relationship. But he'd changed once and he could again, she reminded herself. Besides, he wasn't the real problem. She was.

"I have a set of keys for you," he said so close to her ear that his breath stirred her hair.

Awareness shivered over her. Uh-oh. She put a yard

of space between them in the foyer. "You said you'd show me your ideas for the basement."

"They're in my study, along with the keys. Go on in. I'll join you in a moment." He headed toward the kitchen.

Renee wandered down the hall to the room tucked beneath the stairs. Flynn's office smelled like him. She caught herself inhaling deeply and stopped. His drafting table still took up most of the space beneath the bay window. She was surprised he hadn't gotten rid of it since it represented the life and the dream he'd abandoned.

It seemed such a waste that he'd thrown away four years of college and four and a half more of his internship. He'd been so close to getting his credentials and ready to fulfill his dream of designing homes. Saddened, she let her eyes skim over the architectural texts and titles still occupying his floor-to-ceiling shelves, then they skidded to a halt on the framed photograph taken on their wedding day.

Melancholy thickened her throat, trapping her breath in her chest. She and Flynn looked so happy standing in front of the little white Vegas wedding chapel with their blinding smiles and love-filled eyes. But that had been before the threads of their marriage had begun unraveling, before his mother's confidence-eroding attacks had started hitting their mark and before his father had died.

In that blissfully ignorant moment frozen in the photo, Renee hadn't had a clue how silent and lonely being married to the man she loved could be. Or how weak she could become. Discovering she had feet of clay had not been one of her better moments.

A pop startled her into spinning around. Flynn entered the room carrying a bottle of wine. He had two glasses pressed against his body in the crook of his arm.

She held up a hand. "None for me."

His brow pleated. He set the bottle and glasses on a side table. His strong hands worked the cork free from the corkscrew. "Dr. Loosen used to be your favorite Riesling."

"I don't drink anymore unless I have to sample something for work. Even then, I sip and spit."

"You used to love wine."

She shrugged. "That was then."

"Did you quit because of your mother?"

He didn't know about the morning Renee had woken up on the sofa after drinking herself into oblivion while waiting for him to come home. And he never would. "Partly. The basement?"

"In a minute." He recorked the wine and, still frowning, settled behind his desk. He opened a drawer, withdrew a key ring and offered it to her. She remained frozen in place. Taking that set of keys would be another giant step forward, a blind leap over the edge of a cliff. Gathering her will, she took them from him. The cold metal bit into her hand as she closed her fist.

Next he opened a file folder and then slid it across the desk in her direction. "These are the nearby available properties that could be made to suit a catering company."

She leaned forward and scanned the first page, gasping at the numbers, then she turned to the second. He'd taken the time to list the pros and cons of each property along the margin in his familiar script. Heart sinking, she continued turning and skimming pages. Each one had high monthly rents she didn't even want to contemplate for a new business and renovation requirements that staggered her. She glanced up at Flynn and found his narrowed eyes focused on her face.

"None of the leases includes the improvements you'd

have to make to get the building up to code for California Girl's Catering. Since you've recently done that type of work, you know better than I what kind of expenses you'd incur."

Mind racing, she ticked through possibilities. Even if she used her emergency money, she didn't have the kind of cash a project of this size required. She'd have to get a loan.

Did she really want to go into debt for something that might not pan out? The San Francisco market was notoriously tough. Borrowing a large sum would also leave her trapped in San Francisco if this bargain of theirs went sour and she wanted out in a hurry. She wanted to kick herself for not checking into the costs before agreeing to Flynn's bargain.

"I don't have that kind of budget," she admitted.

"There is another less expensive option." He rose and crossed to his drafting table.

Her pulse quickened as he flipped over a large sheet of blueprint paper revealing a page covered in sketches. "You've drawn up plans."

His gaze met hers, and for the first time in ages the fire of excitement that had initially drawn her to him in that paint store gleamed in the blue depths of his eyes. "Take a look."

A little leery of her body's breathless reaction to a glimpse of the old Flynn, she edged closer. He'd sketched out a kitchen very similar to hers back in L.A., only this space was larger and had more work surfaces and bigger windows in one corner. The layout also included an office area where she could work or meet with clients and an outside patio complete with tables and a fountain.

"This is beautiful, Flynn. Where is it?"

"Our basement."

Alarm sirens screeched in her head. "But—"

He held up one broad palm. "Hear me out. The basement is a rent-free space with a separate entrance. You could work downstairs and have a nanny keep the baby upstairs. You'd be able to slip away to visit our child whenever you wanted."

Our basement. *Our* child. *Her* panic.

Her stomach fell faster than a soufflé. The words implied a long-term commitment—one she wasn't prepared to make. "Investing that much money into a temporary workplace is not a good idea, Flynn."

"Who says it has to be temporary?"

Panic prickled through her anew. "I do. Even if the San Francisco branch succeeds and I decide to keep it, I'll have this baby and then I'll hire a manager and move back to L.A. We agreed to divorce after the baby's first year."

"Think about it, Renee. You won't find a better location or price than this one. It's a trendy address with the right demographics, and it's close enough to the dining and shopping district to make it convenient and easy for clients to find."

Not only was he right, he'd literally and figuratively drawn a tempting, almost irresistible picture.

She wanted to refuse, but she'd go crazy living in San Francisco with nothing to do but wait for the sound of his car turning into the driveway. Having failed at that life already, she didn't dare risk it again—not even for a baby. Living vicariously through him and his job wasn't enough. She needed her own interests and her own financial security.

She had to work, and working for another caterer

wouldn't allow her the freedom to help Tamara in L.A. when the need arose. Not to mention, it would be a conflict of interest. It was unlikely anyone would want to risk her stealing their ideas for her own company.

Unfortunately, what Flynn proposed was both the best and worst option out there, and opening CGC in his Victorian might be the only way she could make expanding into the competitive San Francisco market a financially feasible option.

But did she really want to eat, sleep and work in Flynn's shadow? Setting up shop in his basement while living in his house would mean exactly that. Was she strong enough to handle that kind of pressure? Last time she'd crumbled under the stress.

For sanity's sake, housing CGC here would have to be a temporary solution, and if this branch succeeded she would find an alternative property as soon as she had an idea of her income and budget. That way she'd be nearby whenever her child visited his father, and her baby would never feel as if Mom couldn't wait to get him out of her hair.

You can do this. You're strong. You won't drink, whine or bemoan how the world is against you. Your son or daughter will know from day one that it is wanted, planned, not a mistake that derailed your life.

You are not your mother.

She looked down at the data Flynn had spread before her and then back at him. "It's not that I don't trust your research, but I've learned to do things for myself. I'll check around and get back to you."

Three

Flynn hadn't lied.

With a mug of coffee in hand and a sense of doom weighing heavily on her shoulders, Renee stood in the cool basement Sunday morning studying the empty, unfinished space. Flynn's plans lay on the nearby worktable for reference.

She'd spent all day Saturday looking at properties with a real estate agent only to reinforce Flynn's findings. But then, she'd always been able to trust Flynn. *She* was the one she had to worry about.

Property in the area was out of her price range unless she took on more debt than she wanted or leased space in an area where she wouldn't feel safe coming and going alone early in the morning or late at night.

She credited her grandmother for her frugal nature. Even after Granny had earned a large sum by selling her secret oatmeal cookie recipe to a national company, she'd kept the diner and lived within her means. Granny's only luxury had been the bungalow she'd bought with a fraction of the windfall. The remaining "saved for a rainy day" cookie money had been Renee's start-up fund.

The stairs creaked behind her. She turned. Flynn's long, bare legs came into view as he descended. His running shorts displayed his muscular calves and thighs to mouthwatering perfection, and his sleeveless T-shirt revealed powerful shoulders and arms. Desire flickered to life inside her. She tried to snuff it out with little success.

His gaze raked her, making her self-conscious of her old jeans, long-sleeved knit shirt and bare feet. "Good morning, Renee."

"Good morning. Do you still run every day?"

"Rain or shine. Care to join me?"

Déjà vu. She smiled. "You know the answer to that one."

He'd always asked. She'd always refused. She likened running to getting a paper cut—something she avoided whenever possible. But the invitation was a game they'd once played, and it worried her how easily they had fallen back into the banter.

He tapped his hip. "I have my cell phone if you need me. I left the number upstairs on the table." He nodded toward the blueprint. "Did you make a decision?"

She took a deep breath and then a sip of coffee, delaying the inevitable and maybe hoping for divine intervention in the form of a better idea. "You're right. Using the basement is the best option."

Satisfaction gleamed in his eyes. He nodded. "I'll make the call to the contractor first thing in the morning.

I know one I trust implicitly. Monday afternoon we'll go out and look at tile, cabinets and countertops."

"Don't you have to work Monday?"

"I'll take the afternoon off. Come by the office after lunch and we'll leave from there."

That surprised her. He'd never taken time off from Madd Comm before, and he certainly hadn't liked her popping in and interrupting his day—a circumstance that had only reinforced his mother's snippy comments about him having other "more suitable" women.

"Look over the preliminary plans while I'm out and see if you want to make any changes."

"Your drawings are as wonderful as always." He'd had so much talent back then and shown so much promise that big firms had been trying to recruit him even before he had his certifications.

A frown flickered across his face. "I'll have to ask a licensed architect from my old firm to sign off on the plans."

"You do that." Maybe in talking to them he'd remember how much he used to love the work.

He crossed to the exterior door and opened it, letting in a cool rush of air. "I'll be back."

The door closed behind him, leaving her in silence—a reminder of the long, lonely days and nights she'd once spent in this house while Flynn worked. She couldn't help but believe their marriage would have survived if he'd stayed with his beloved architecture, instead of becoming the VP at the family firm. But because he'd minored in business administration and been groomed to work there until he'd rebelled and refused, he'd been familiar with how Madd Comm worked, and he'd been the only one considered for the job after their father's death.

She shook her head. The loneliness she'd experienced back then wouldn't happen again. She wouldn't allow it. She had her own business and interests, and her life and happiness would never again be completely wrapped up in Flynn.

She took the last sip of her coffee, then rolled up the blueprints and climbed the stairs. In the past she would have cooked breakfast while Flynn had his run, and she'd have had it waiting on the table when he returned. Cooking for him and doing things for him had filled her with satisfaction. She debated raiding his refrigerator to see what ingredients she could find, but she resisted. This was not the old days.

Instead, she refilled her mug and sat down with a pad of paper. Starting up a new branch would be a lot of work, but she had experience under her belt now. She needed to make a shopping list, a to-do list and a general list. Once she combined her lists and got an estimate from a contractor, she'd be able to tailor her budget.

The doorbell rang, breaking into her concentration. Had Flynn forgotten his key? Did he still keep a spare behind the ornate wrought-iron house numbers? She glanced at the clock. He'd only been gone forty minutes. He used to run for closer to an hour. But that had been years ago.

She rose and shuffled barefoot to the front door. The glass distorted the person on the other side, but not so much that she couldn't see her visitor was too petite to be Flynn. Who would visit so early?

Renee opened the door. Her mother-in-law stood on the doormat. Dislike crawled over Renee. Carol Maddox. There wasn't a polite way to describe her. "Hello, Carol."

Blonde and thin to the point of emaciation, Carol managed to show disapproval despite her stiff, overly botoxed face. "So it's true. You're back."

"Yes." One single word shouldn't provide so much satisfaction, but given the number of times Flynn's mother had deliberately made her miserable, Renee took great pleasure in knowing she'd ruined Carol's day—probably her entire week.

Carol's condemning gaze ran over Renee, from her tangled morning hair and unmade-up face, to her jeans and department-store polo shirt to her bare feet with un-painted toenails, then returned to her mug. "I'd like a cup of coffee. That is, if you've learned to brew a decent pot."

Renee's temper rose, but she bit her tongue rather than stoop to Carol's level. "Come in, but if you're ex-pecting Kopi Luwak you'll be disappointed," she said, naming the most expensive coffee in the world.

She led the way to the kitchen rather than the parlor, where she had entertained her mother-in-law in the past. Without ceremony, she filled a sturdy mug, instead of the good china, and brought it, the sugar and the milk carton to the table.

In business, presentation was everything. But with Carol there was no point trying to impress her. No matter what Renee did it was never good enough. A lesson Renee had learned the hard way.

Carol made a production out of preparing her coffee, then sipped and grimaced. She set the mug down. "What game are you playing by coming back into Flynn's life when he finally has someone he cares deeply for and who suits him?"

Dismay and denial rippled through Renee in quick succession, surprising her. But the acid burn in her belly was not jealousy. She had no right to be jealous if Flynn had found someone during their separation. To be jealous she'd have to still care. She didn't. "Does he?"

"Yes. You're wasting his time and yours. She's our kind. You are not."

"By 'your kind' you mean rich, rude and backstabbing?" The words popped out of Renee's mouth before she could curb them. While a part of her was horrified by her disrespect, another part took pride in the fact she'd finally stood up for herself with this bully. Civility had never worked with Carol. The harder Renee had tried to make her mother-in-law like her, the more obnoxious Carol had become.

Carol's eyes widened in surprise, then narrowed in calculation. "So you've finally grown a backbone. How commendable. But you're too late and it's not enough. You'll lose Flynn the same way you did before. He loves Denise and plans to marry her."

The cauldron of toxic feelings bubbled in Renee's stomach. Anger. That's all it was. Anger toward this hateful, malicious woman. "That might prove a little difficult since he's still married to me because *he* never filed the papers."

Carol stiffened. "An oversight, I'm sure. You may have him temporarily distracted, but whatever the reason you came looking for him, sooner or later he'll see through your innocent act to the opportunistic tramp you are."

Renee's nails bit into her palms as she fought to control her temper. She yearned to tell the supercilious witch that stud service and a desire to dilute the Maddox pedigree was the only thing on her agenda, but Renee bit her tongue. She'd promised to try to make the reconciliation look real.

During their marriage she'd been so afraid of losing

Flynn or turning him against her that she'd never told him about his mother's barrage of insults. Today she didn't have those concerns. In fact, if they were going to split up, it would be better if they did so before she invested her time and money in expanding CGC and before she became pregnant.

"FYI, Carol, Flynn came looking for me. In fact, my moving back in was completely his idea. He drew up these plans for me to convert the basement into my business." She gestured to the blueprints. "And he asked me to have his baby. We're discussing trying right away since we've already wasted seven years."

"You're lying."

"I'm not. We're going to make you a grandmother. Granny Carol. How do you like that?"

The horror in the older woman's eyes didn't alter her chemically paralyzed face, but Carol looked as if she had caught a whiff of something malodorous. "If you care anything for Flynn, you'll go back where you came from and let him find happiness with Denise. He loves her," Carol repeated, "and the marriage plans are already under way."

The arrow hit its target with another burning barb. *Don't let her get to you.*

She stared her mother-in-law down. "And if you care anything for your son, you'll keep your nasty comments to yourself. Because I'm warning you, Carol, if you dare to play any of your spiteful, undermining mind games with me this time around, I won't hesitate to tell your son how hateful you've always treated me."

"Tell me now," Flynn said from the basement doorway, startling Renee. Slapping a hand to her chest, she spun around.

"Flynn, I didn't hear you come in."

"I used the basement entrance. I thought you might still be down there studying the plans." He walked deeper into the room, his blue gaze unblinking on hers. He didn't even acknowledge his mother's presence. "Tell me what you meant about my mother playing spiteful undermining games."

Renee winced. "How long have you been standing there listening?"

"Long enough to know you kept something from me during our marriage. Something important. Spit it out, Renee. All of it."

She wasn't a tattletale. Her words had been mostly bravado, and one glance at Carol's superior, daring look told Renee her mother-in-law didn't believe she had the guts to reveal the truth. Resignation and determination settled over Renee. If she didn't follow through with her threat, then Carol would walk all over her. Again.

Speak now or forever hold your peace.

Flynn had never gotten along well with his mother, but still… She *was* his mother.

Renee tried for diplomacy. "Your mother has never made it a secret that she didn't approve of me or our marriage. If you recall, she tried to talk you out of marrying me. That's one of the reasons we went to Vegas."

"Was she rude to you when we were married before?"

Renee hesitated. But again, she couldn't back down without losing ground. "Yes. And more than once she implied that you weren't working late. That you were with another woman. This morning she informed me you were in love with someone named Denise and that I needed to step aside and let you marry her as planned."

"What?" The genuine astonishment on his face said more than any denial could have. Carol was lying.

"I take it you haven't proposed to Denise?" Renee asked, just to be sure.

"No. How could I propose to another woman when I'm still married to you?" He closed the distance between them and lifted a hand to firmly cup her face, then he looped an arm around her waist, pulled her close and kissed her so tenderly her knees nearly buckled. He pulled back until his forehead rested on hers. She smelled fresh sweat and Flynn's unique scent—a devastating combo. Her heart pounded.

What was he doing?

"You are the love of my life, Renee. I don't want any other woman." His soft voice and gentle touch melted her, but pure command filled his eyes. He leaned forward and nipped her earlobe.

"Play along," he whispered in a rush of warm breath across her skin.

She shivered as arousal raced through her like water through a broken dam. Did he mean what he'd said? He couldn't. Otherwise, why would he have stayed away until now?

When he kissed her again, she kissed him back. Not because he said to, but because she couldn't have resisted even if she'd wanted to.

Trouble. SOS.

Slowly, he released her, then turned to his mother. He loomed over Carol, his body language threatening. "Get the hell out of our house and don't come back. You are no longer welcome here, Mother. If I find out you've so much as looked hard at Renee, you'll regret it."

"You can't possibly believe her?"

"I have no reason not to. Renee has never lied to me. You, on the other hand, have a habit of doing and saying whatever it takes to get your way."

"Flynn, I do not lie," Carol protested.

He grasped his mother's bony arm and frog-marched her out of the room. "You just did when you said I was going to marry Denise." Flynn's voice carried from the foyer. "She and I dated twice, nothing more, and you know it. There won't be a wedding. I already have a wife."

The front door opened, then slammed a moment later. Flynn returned to the kitchen, his steps heavy with anger.

"Thank you, Flynn."

"Why didn't you tell me?"

She plucked at the seam of her jeans. "I didn't want you to have to choose between me and her."

He assessed her through narrowed eyes. "You thought I'd take Mother's side."

Yes. "She is your mother."

Heaven knows she'd been forced to cover for hers often enough.

"Because she's my mother I know how she operates. She's a bitter, unhappy person who infects those around her with the same ill temperament. I'm sorry she worked her sorcery on you, but if you'd told me, I would have put a stop to it."

Touched by his support, Renee pressed a hand over her heart. Would he have been as supportive if she'd told him about his mother's nastiness years ago? Moot point. She'd never given him the chance. "You had enough on your plate then, trying to learn a new business and grieving for your father."

"I insist on total honesty from you this time, Renee. I'll settle for nothing less."

"And for better or worse, you'll get it."

Flynn looked into the pleading blue-green eyes of Celia Taylor.

"Flynn, please let me put together a pitch for Reese Enterprises. Other Maddox ad execs may have failed, but I know I can get to Evan Reese."

"What makes you so sure?" The male ad execs of Madd Comm believed the attractive redhead used her looks to lure new clients. Flynn wasn't so sure. While Celia was beautiful, she seemed too sharp to rely on something so superficial. And while her looks might be a great asset, appearance alone couldn't deliver the goods the way Celia did time and time again.

"I've met Evan several times over the past few months. We've…connected."

He frowned, not liking the sound of that. "Is this going to be a conflict of interest?"

She shook her head and her hair swung over her shoulder. "We're not dating or sleeping together, if that's what you're asking."

"I wasn't, but thanks for clarifying. We can't risk pissing off a potential client due to a romance with one of our staff going sour."

"Not an issue. I'll put together an irresistible package—if you'll give me a shot."

Her enthusiasm and confidence were admirable and made him inclined to believe her. "Why come to me, instead of Brock?"

"Because Brock is so obsessed with landing Reese Enterprises that he only wants to send in someone like

Jason, our current Golden Boy. Brock's not willing to let an underdog like me take on the task."

Celia was right on one count. Brock was obsessed, and if his brother's grouchy attitude and the bags under his eyes were an indicator, Brock hadn't been getting enough sleep. Flynn had been meaning to talk to him and remind him how destructive tunnel vision could be. Brock's broken engagement and Flynn's failed marriage were perfect examples.

Speaking of his marriage, his wife was due any minute. He checked his watch and rose. "Give it your best shot, Celia. I'll speak to Brock on your behalf and let him know you have my support."

Celia sprang out of her chair, raced around the desk and threw her arms around Flynn's neck. "Thank you. You won't regret it."

"Make sure of it or Brock will have both of our heads."

The exterior of the seven-story building housing Maddox Communications on ritzy Powell Street hadn't changed, but Renee's feelings about entering the building had undergone a drastic transition. The joy and anticipation she'd once experienced when meeting Flynn at work had turned to trepidation. Entering those doors meant entering a web of deception.

Flynn hadn't been born when his father had purchased the soon-to-be demolished Beaux Arts–style building back in the seventies, but Flynn had told her the photo documentation of the renovations had fascinated him from an early age and launched his interest in architecture. He'd never intended to join the family advertising agency. He'd wanted to design buildings. And then his father had died and his priorities had changed.

She neared the doors and her muscles tensed. Trendy restaurants and retail stores still occupied the first floor. In the past Madd Comm had occupied the second through sixth floors, and the top floor had contained a penthouse suite with a huge roof garden. Who lived there now?

Renee entered the building and made her way to the elevators. A dark-haired muscular man about her age held the doors open for her. Renee stepped into the cubicle. "Six, please."

He nodded and pushed the button. "Are you a Maddox client?"

"No." She hesitated, unsure who this guy was or what Flynn had told his coworkers and clients about her. But Flynn had said to make the marriage look real. *Let the games begin.* "I'm Renee Maddox, Flynn's wife."

If her response surprised him, his gray eyes didn't show it. "Gavin Spencer. I'm an ad exec for Maddox. Flynn's a nice guy."

"Yes. He is." She shook the hand he extended. "It's nice to meet you, Gavin."

The elevator shot up, then the doors opened. Gavin motioned for her to precede him. "Nice meeting you, Renee."

She stepped out. A slim woman with short brown hair sat behind the reception desk directly ahead of Renee. Swallowing the nervous lump in her throat, Renee scanned the area while she waited for the receptionist to end her phone call.

In the waiting room white sofas faced two monstrously large flat-panel TVs streaming advertisements—Madd Comm's work, no doubt. The stark white walls and acrylic tables combined with the black oak floors gave the place a contemporary edge. The other walls held extremely colorful modern paintings, some new to Renee like the TVs, some not.

"May I help you?" the receptionist asked in a cheer-leader-chipper voice.

"I'm Renee Maddox. I'm here to see Flynn."

The woman's eyes widened. "I'm Shelby, Mrs. Maddox. Flynn told me to expect you. It's great to finally meet you."

"Thank you. You, too, Shelby. Should I head back or is Flynn with someone?"

"He doesn't have an appointment, but I'll call and let him know you've arrived."

Before she could dial, an attractive auburn-haired pregnant woman approached from the offices section. The receptionist perked up. "Lauren, this is Flynn's wife, Renee," she blurted as if she couldn't contain the news.

Smiling, the newcomer stopped. "Hello, Renee. I'm Lauren, Jason's wife."

Renee scanned her memory and came up empty. "Jason? I'm sorry, you'll have to forgive me. I haven't been here in…a long time. I've been living in L.A., so I'm a little out of the loop."

"I'm new here, too. I just moved from Manhattan last month. Jason is an advertising executive. We'll have to get together sometime and do lunch."

Lauren seemed warm and friendly and Renee could use a few friends in the area. She had no intention of re-peating her past mistake of isolating herself. Also, an insider could give her an idea of what Flynn's life was like now. "I'd like that."

"Good. Can I reach you at Flynn's home number?"

"Yes. Or you can call my cell number. I'll be in and out a lot." She dug into her purse for a business card and passed it over. "I'm trying to open a branch of my catering business here in San Francisco, and I have a lot of running around to do while I set up."

"Something else we have in common. I'm opening a branch of my graphic-design business here, too. We will have a lot to talk about. But I have to run to an appointment now. I'll call, okay?"

"I'm looking forward to it."

Lauren ducked into the open elevator and the doors closed. The receptionist seemed to be hanging on their every word and then startled as if she'd suddenly remembered she was supposed to be calling Flynn. "I'll let Flynn know you've arrived."

"Don't bother. I'll just go back." Renee's heels tapped on the wood floors as she made her way to the east corner office as she'd done so many times before. This time her pulse raced with nervousness instead of excitement. If Flynn had changed offices, this would be embarrassing.

The chair behind his PA's desk was empty, but Cammie's nameplate on the desk told her at least Flynn's assistant hadn't changed. Cammie had been with him since his first day at Madd Comm and Renee had always liked her.

Flynn's door stood open. But Flynn wasn't alone. A woman with long red hair had her arms around his neck.

Shock stopped Renee in the outer office. She struggled to inhale, but her tight chest resisted.

You're not jealous.

Oh, yes, you are.

And that did not bode well for her mental health or the temporary nature of this assignment.

Four

Was Flynn involved with another **woman**?

The poison Flynn's mother had spread **in the past** and again yesterday percolated through Renee, **filling her** with doubts. About him. About herself. About **their plan** to make a baby.

Renee's throat tightened. Could she stand knowing that while he held her, made love to her and impregnated her, he was thinking of someone else?

The woman backed away from Flynn and bent to scoop a file folder from the visitor chair. "Thank you again, Flynn. I'll keep you abreast of the project."

"Do that. You'll need to run the proposal by Brock before pitching it." Flynn glanced up and caught sight of Renee. Her expression must have given away her chaotic thoughts. His gaze sharpened on her face.

Smiling tightly, Flynn came around his desk, took

Renee in his arms and kissed her without warning. She stiffened automatically as his hot body pressed hers and his warm, firm lips moved over her mouth. Conscious of their audience, she had to fight to relax and look as if this was a regular occurrence.

Getting used to being touched by him again was going to take some work. Not that she didn't enjoy his kisses and caresses. She did. Too much. Even now, despite the other woman in the office, desire curled in Renee's belly and her pulse fluttered wildly. But she had to hold herself in check. She couldn't let herself crave him or surrender to him the way she once had.

Flynn eased back and turned her toward the woman. "Celia, I'd like you to meet my wife, Renee. Renee, this is Celia Taylor, one of our ad execs."

The beautiful redhead grimaced. "Sorry about the hug, but he just let me break the good ol' boy barrier. I got a little excited."

Celia's words and contrite expression seemed genuine. And what Renee had seen after the hug had looked innocent enough. There had been no lingering body or eye contact. Tension leeched from her knotted muscles. "It's nice to meet you, Celia."

"Nice meeting you, too, Renee. Now, thanks to your husband, I have a lot of work to do, and trust me, that is not a complaint. Excuse me." She left, the quick tap of her heels receding down the hall.

Renee looked everywhere but at Flynn while she grappled with the strength of the emotions that had hit her when she'd spotted him in another woman's arms. No matter how much she might want to deny it, she had been jealous. That was not good.

The office looked exactly as it had seven years ago—

right down to the photograph of the two of them on the shelf and the remains of a half-eaten lunch on his desk. Back then she'd brought him meals time and time again because he often forgot to eat, and in a matter of a few months he'd dropped a lot of weight despite her TLC.

Flynn looked her up and down, making her heart skip. "You're right on time, and you look great."

"Thanks." She brushed a hand over her light, garnet-red, cowl-neck sweater and simple black twill trousers. "You have several new staff members. I met Gavin in the elevator, Shelby in the lobby and Lauren on the way in. I forgot who she said she was married to, but it was someone I don't know. She suggested we have lunch together soon."

"She's married to Jason Reagert, another ad exec. You'll meet him later. But Lauren is a good contact. She can probably recommend an obstetrician since she's pregnant."

Panic skipped down Renee's spine. She wanted a baby. She even wanted Flynn's baby. But tying herself to a man who made her weak still scared her more than a little—especially given her emotional reaction moments ago. Was she strong enough to endure a temporary marriage and a permanent link through a child without breaking and turning to alcohol again? "I'll keep that in mind."

"You'll have to join us next time the office staff goes out after work to meet everyone at once."

"What did you tell them about me…about us?"

"That we'd worked out our differences and our trial separation was over."

Her gaze flicked to the photo. "Have you had that sitting there the whole time?"

He frowned. "No. I dug it out of storage when you agreed to move back in."

For some reason that seemed like the perfect answer to soothe her rattled nerves. He hadn't been pining for her, but he hadn't thrown away the picture. She still had the box of mementos from her marriage that she hadn't been able to part with, either. As much as she'd wanted to put Flynn out of her mind, she hadn't been successful.

If you haven't succeeded in forgetting him in seven years, will you ever?

The nagging voice in the back of her head didn't ease her worry that this entire plot could blow up in her face.

Renee's head spun with combinations of paint samples and fabric swatches, cabinet configurations and countertop surfaces as she shoved her key into the front door Monday evening. Just like old times. And it felt good. Eerily good.

She'd forgotten what an effective team she and Flynn made, but today, watching his sharp mind work and his eyes gleam with intelligence and excitement as they discussed the basement conversion had brought all those bittersweet memories stampeding back.

"Do you want to eat in the kitchen or in the den in front of a movie?" he asked from behind her.

Another flashback. In fact, the past had hung over her like a rain cloud the entire day. Déjà vu moments had unexpectedly spattered down on her. Some like big, fat warm droplets and others like icy cold drizzle. There had been no escaping the deluge of memories.

In the early days of their marriage they had ended many a day of labor by having dinner on the sofa in front of the TV with an old movie. Sometimes they'd even watched the entire film before climbing all over each other. But most of the time they'd missed the last half because they were too absorbed in making love to hear it playing in the background.

Her skin flushed and her hands trembled as she dropped her keys into her purse. "Kitchen."

His gaze held hers and his pupils expanded, telling her he remembered, too. Her chest tightened. She couldn't get enough air into her lungs and had to open her mouth to breathe. "Flynn, don't."

He moved closer, then lifted his hand and cupped her face. "Don't what? Tell you that I want you? That I can't stop thinking about losing myself in the softness of your skin and the scent of your body, in the heat of you?"

A shiver of desire rippled over her.

"Don't tell you that I've barely slept for the past three nights because I've lain awake listening for sounds of you moving around our house?"

She'd done the same, listened for him.

"Your house," she corrected automatically.

"Our house. Your touch is in every room, Renee."

She told herself to back away, but her legs refused to move. "I'm not ready, Flynn, and I'm still not convinced this is a good idea."

"It's a good plan. A baby. *Our* baby. Us doing what we do best. Making a home. Making love."

The husky pitch of the last phrase only increased her desire. But her defenses were too weak to give in now. Before they did this, she had to find a way to make this about sex and procreation, instead of making love. Gathering every ounce of strength she possessed, she ducked out of reach and hurried into the kitchen. He followed.

They'd stopped by their favorite Chinese restaurant for

takeout on their way home. She took the bag from him, set it on the table and opened it. The aromas of hot and sour soup, Yu-Hsiang pork and Hunan chicken and shrimp filled the air. But her appetite had taken a vacation.

"For this to work you have to want it, too, Renee."

"I do. I mean, I will. But not yet." She had to change the subject because she was very, very close to giving in, and that could be the death of her—literally. "I'd like to keep your design, but I think the island should be movable, instead of fixed."

"*Re*movable, you mean."

Uncomfortable with the edge in his voice, she bit her lip. "You always talked about having a games room or a home theater downstairs. You still might one of these days. Making things portable, instead of built-in would make that transition easier."

"You're keeping one foot out the door."

"What do you mean?" she asked, but she knew. He'd seen her ambivalence, her fear.

"Nothing nailed down. No permanent fixtures other than the required plumbing. You refused to sign the builder's contract today. He might have believed your excuse of double-checking finances, but I don't. Either you're in or you're out. Which is it?"

Stalling, she retrieved plates from the cabinet and returned to set them on the table. "I'm in. I think."

"Once we conceive this child, you can't change your mind. I will be a part of my baby's life—a part of *your* life for at least eighteen years and very likely longer."

That's what scared her. That and the fact that she'd almost signed contracts today committing to investing a substantial sum of money in Flynn's basement. Doubts had hit her as soon as she'd lifted the pen. The contractor had been understanding and agreed to give her a few days to think over his estimate.

"I know how long we'd be tied together, Flynn. Let's eat before dinner gets cold." *Coward,* her conscience gibed.

"Let it." He came up behind her and wrapped his arms around her middle and she jumped.

"It wouldn't be the first time." His palms spread low over her abdomen, pulling her flush against him, then his lips grazed her neck in that spot that had always driven her crazy. "Let's make a baby tonight, Renee."

Hunger for her husband raced through her and temptation chiseled away her will to resist. Her breaths hiccupped in, then shuddered out. She desperately sought any reason to resist. "I don't know if it's the right time of the month."

His hands caressed upward, stopping short of her breasts, then back down again to her hips. "Forget about timing. Focus on how good we are together."

He skimmed up her torso again, and her nipples tightened in anticipation, but he stopped short of them to trace the elastic band on the bottom of her bra before descending again.

Up. Down. Up. Down. With each rise her breath caught. With each descent she exhaled…in disappointment, it shamed her to admit. Despite everything that had happened in the past, she wanted his touch. *Craved* his touch.

But she wasn't ready. She wasn't strong enough. Why was that, exactly? She couldn't concentrate on the reasons this shouldn't happen yet, with his hands on her body. Flynn had always known exactly how to arouse her. Physically, they'd always been in perfect tune.

Up. This time he cradled her breasts, instead of leaving her hanging. His thumbs brushed across the puckered tips and her womb tightened. Why was she even bothering to fight? She was going to give in eventually, anyway. Wasn't she?

Down. She caught his hands, halting their descent, and lifted them back to where she needed them. Flynn rewarded her by simultaneously rolling her nipples with his fingers and scraping his teeth lightly along the shell of her ear. A shudder racked her.

She pushed her hips back against him and encountered his erection, rigid and hot against her spine. Her resistance crumbled. She turned in his arms, her hip bumping deliberately over his arousal and making him inhale sharply.

His nostrils flared, and then he stabbed his fingers into her hair, framing her head and holding her steady. His mouth covered hers. Their tongues clashed in a kiss as wild and passionate and breathtaking as any they'd ever shared. Each successive kiss and caress grew more urgent, more desperate. His hands skimmed down to cover her bottom and yank her closer.

She dug her fingers into his waist and held on until her head spun from lack of oxygen and disorientation. The past and the present blurred in a wash of want and hormones. But if she couldn't distinguish between reality and old fantasies, then how would she survive this relationship? Flynn had been her greatest joy, but also her greatest weakness. She ripped her mouth from his and touched her fingers to her still-tingling lips.

Desire darkened Flynn's eyes and his cheekbones. His palms branded her upper arms. "Make love with me, Renee. Now. Tonight."

Her heart battered against her rib cage and her mouth went dry. If she had sex with him now, there would be no turning back, no time to gather her strength. She'd be surrendering without making one single attempt at self-preservation. "I can't. I'm sorry."

And then she did exactly what she'd done seven years ago when she'd woken up on the sofa with two empty wine bottles lying on the floor and no memory of opening the second. She ran.

Flynn couldn't wipe the smile off his face. He'd awoken hard, horny and miserable as a result of last night's nutknotting kisses, but he wasn't complaining. He considered the prelude to his nearly sleepless night progress.

Renee was almost his. It was only a matter of time before the chemistry between them became explosive.

Balancing the tray on one hand, he knocked on her door with the other. She didn't answer, but that didn't surprise him. Renee had always been a sound sleeper. He turned the knob and pushed.

She lay on her side, with the covers bunched at her feet. She'd always preferred to sleep without getting tangled in bedding. One long, bare leg was hooked over a pillow she clutched to her chest. Her position stretched the fabric of her nightshirt tight across her bottom, making it easy to determine she wasn't wearing panties. During their early days, he'd been her pillow, and her leg would have been hitched over his hip and thigh. And she would have been naked. His groin pulsed at the memory.

The temptation to wake her the way he once had— by caressing her skin, running his palm up her leg and smoothing over her round butt—was almost irresistible.

"Renee. Wake up."

She startled awake and rolled over, shoving her curls out of her face. "What? What's wrong?"

"Nothing's wrong. I brought breakfast."

Squinting, she scrubbed the sleep from her eyes. Knowing her as well as he did had its rewards. He took advantage of her usual morning fog to hustle forward and plant himself on the bed beside her before she awoke enough to realize she was giving him one hell of a good view. If he anchored the sheets in the process, making it impossible for her to cover up, he considered it a fringe benefit. She had to get comfortable around him again and the only way to achieve that goal was through exposure.

"Sit up."

Blinking owlishly at the tray, she scooted up against the pillows. "You cooked for me? You've never brought me breakfast in bed before."

He didn't miss the suspicion in her morning-husky tone. "Our relationship before was a little one-sided. You always cooked for me. But times have changed. If we're both going to be working, we're going to have to share the chores. Especially after the baby comes."

She bit her lip, worrying the soft, pink flesh and making him ache to lean in and kiss her again. But moving too fast could cost him the battle, so instead, he settled the tray across her lap and enjoyed the sight of her nipples tenting her thin sleep shirt. The little nubs drew his gaze like a power outage does looters and hit his gut with a brick of desire that splinted through him like a broken store window. He blinked and tried to focus on his goal—getting her to let down her guard. He nudged the coffee mug in her direction.

"I've adjusted the blueprints based on the comments you made yesterday."

She picked up a piece of toast slathered in raspberry jelly. "What do you mean?"

"You wanted temporary. I found a compromise."

She chewed her toast, then sipped her coffee. "Explain."

He slid the sketch out from under the plate containing her scrambled eggs, Canadian bacon and fruit. "Instead of built-in standard cabinets, the island will have legs. It will look like furniture and can be moved against the wall like a sideboard or out to the patio when necessary. But that means you'll lose the prep sink in the island. I've moved it to the corner."

Renee took the page from him. Her hair fell across her face as she bent to study the sketch. He caught a strand and twined a curl around his finger. Her chin jerked up. He tucked the lock behind her ear, taking the time to run his finger down the side of her jaw and over her pulse point. The beat quickened beneath his fingertip.

"You always did look good in the morning."

She leaned out of reach and put a self-conscious hand to her tousled curls. "My hair's probably a mess."

He shrugged. "A little messy. But that's always more interesting than a woman with every hair in place."

Her cheeks flushed, then her eyes narrowed on his. "Did you sleep at all last night, Flynn?"

Busted. "You know I can't sleep when I have ideas I need to get onto paper."

Sympathy turned down the corners of her mouth, then her attention returned to his rendition of the kitchen. "It's beautiful, Flynn, but the contractor has already given us his estimate."

"This early on it's easy to amend the numbers."

"It's a good idea. Thank you for making the changes. I'll, um, think about them."

He nodded. "Finish your breakfast. I have a meeting with Brock this morning. I'll be leaving in twenty minutes."

"Is everything all right?" He shouldn't be surprised she'd picked up on his tension. Renee had always been perceptive. And he'd been a fool to neglect her.

"He's obsessing about a client. I need to talk him off the ledge."

"You're good at that."

If he'd been better at talking sense into people, he would have been able to talk her out of leaving. But then, she'd given him no clue of her plans. One day she'd been there and the next she'd been gone.

"I'm good at a lot of things." His gaze fell to her breasts.

Her breath hitched and her nipples puckered. "If you'll excuse me, I'll take my shower and then deal with the contractor. You take care of your brother."

He patted her thigh, savoring the warm silkiness of her skin and fighting the urge to slide his fingers north into the warmth between her legs. Her quadriceps tensed beneath his fingers, reminding him of his goal—getting her pregnant.

But this was the one time he'd welcome failure on the first few tries. Hell, he wouldn't mind if it took a year…or two. As long as he had Renee in his bed he'd be happy.

"So Renee is back," Brock said as soon as Flynn closed the door marked CEO. "Why?"

"What do you mean why? I told you."

"C'mon, Flynn. Level with me."

"You don't believe she missed me and what we had and wanted to try again?"

"No. You burst in here eight days ago asking questions about your divorce out of the blue. Four days later Renee moved back into your house. The question is, what started that domino fall of events?"

He didn't intend to tell Brock—or anyone—the whole truth. Telling the truth meant admitting failure. "We still care about each other and we're going to try again."

His brother's expression turned from disbelief to disgust. "You're sticking with that lame story?"

"Yes."

"For the record, the rest of the staff may buy it, but I don't." Brock rocked back in his chair. "This isn't about your inability to accept you're fallible like the rest of us, is it?"

Tension invaded Flynn's spine. "I don't know what you mean."

"You have no tolerance for weakness or failure. That goes double when it's your own. I credit Dad for that. He rode you pretty hard."

Flynn had been a failure in his father's eyes. He knew it and accepted it. Brock, on the other hand, could do no wrong. The old resentments percolated beneath his skin, but he ignored them and focused on what had brought him to Brock's office. "Sounds like we're talking about you, not me. You can't let this Reese Enterprises thing go. You're obsessed."

"You're mistaken. You always blamed yourself for the failure of your marriage," Brock added. "You couldn't accept that Renee might have gotten tired of playing house."

Flynn's surprise that Brock had read him so well vied with his anger at the unjust accusation, but he wasn't going to be so easily distracted. Worry for his brother had brought him to the lion's den. "If you must rehash the past, remember one thing. You've already lost a fiancée because of your obsession with work."

Brock folded his arms. "Good riddance, but we were talking about you."

"You might have been, but I wasn't, and I'm the one who scheduled this meeting." He parked his butt in the chair facing Brock. "Judging by the matching set of baggage beneath your eyes, you're not sleeping."

"What, are you a psychiatrist now?"

"You need to get your mind off work and get laid. Find someone to take the edge off. Isn't there a woman you can speed-dial for an unemotional quickie?"

He could use a little of his own medicine. The trouble was, now that Renee was back, he didn't want anyone else, and even if he did, he couldn't risk a scandal that might cost them business.

Living with Renee was like walking a tightrope stretched between heaven and hell. One wrong step and he could fall and land on the wrong side of the rope. She'd insisted on sticking with her get-reacquainted stipulation, which resulted in him having one hell of a time concentrating on work.

The only upside: the lack of sheet time forced him to focus on less carnal aspects of his beautiful wife—like her new strength and confidence. Not to mention her recently acquired curves. A very sexy combo.

Brock pitched his pen onto the desktop. "Sex isn't the answer."

"Maybe not, but it relaxes you enough to get the blood flowing back to your brain."

A knock preceded the door opening a crack. Elle Linton, Brock's executive assistant, poked her head through the gap. Her gaze flicked between Flynn and

Brock and then settled on her boss. "Your next appointment is on his way up."

Flynn turned back to Brock and caught a quick glimpse of something on his brother's face he hadn't seen before. But then Brock blinked and straightened, his mouth reforming into a tense line, before Flynn could decipher the expression. "Thank you, Elle. Give me five minutes."

"Yes, sir." The door closed.

His own lack of sleep had him imagining things. Was there something between his brother and Elle? No way. Brock would never condone an office affair. Maybe thoughts of another woman had brought that hungry expression to Brock's face just before his assistant had knocked. Did he have a speed date in mind already?

Flynn rose. "Think about what I said. Get a little R & R before you crack up. I don't want your job."

"I'm fine. You watch your step. I don't want to have to clean up again after hurricane Renee blows out of town."

"Not going to happen." Flynn intended to make damned sure of it. He might be fallible and he did make mistakes.

But he never made the same one twice.

Five

Renee's cell phone vibrated in her pocket, making her jump. She grimaced at Lauren. "Oops. Sorry. My phone buzzed me."

Lauren waved her hand. "No problem. Go ahead and see who it is. Like me, you're waiting to hear from contractors and can't afford to miss something important."

Renee checked the caller ID. *Flynn*. Her pulse took a *ba-ba-boom* misstep.

"It's my husband." She had to force herself to say the H-word. In her head Flynn had been her ex for so long it would take some time to get used to his new/old status.

"Take the call. Believe me, if Jason called I'd answer."

"Thanks." Renee punched the button. "Yes?"

"Join me for lunch," Flynn's deep voice said, and her heart clenched in regret.

"Too late. I'm just finishing brunch with Lauren. As soon as we pay our checks we're going shopping."

"We'll do it another time." Did he sound disappointed? "Don't forget to get the doctor recommendation. See you tonight, baby."

That "baby" shimmied down her spine like a feather-light caress. Renee disconnected and pocketed her phone. As much as she liked Lauren and believed they could be friends, Renee had no intention of asking for an obstetrician's name, because a very insistent part of her subconscious kept yelling, *Run before it's too late!*

She dabbed her mouth with her napkin. "How long have you and Jason been married?"

"Three weeks," Lauren replied with a smile that lit up her face.

Surprise hiked Renee's eyebrows. "You're newly-weds."

"That, of course, leads to the next question." Lauren pointed to her baby bump. "Jason and I worked together in New York and had a brief affair before he moved out here for the Maddox job. It wasn't supposed to be more than that. The pregnancy caught me by surprise, and I debated not telling him. I was prepared to have my baby on my own. But when Jason found out, he wanted more. Our explosive chemistry returned and we got married." She winked. "He is pretty irresistible when he puts his mind to it."

Love and pregnancy combined to give Lauren's face a beautiful glow that Renee had read about but never seen. An itty-bitty twinge of jealousy nipped at her heels. She would never have that glow with Flynn. She couldn't afford to let herself love as deeply as she once had ever again.

"What about you and Flynn? You do realize you're the hot topic in the Maddox break room at the moment, don't you?"

Renee grimaced. "I suspected that might be the case. Flynn and I met, fell in love and ran off to Vegas eight years ago."

"I sense a story there."

Renee shrugged and decided it wouldn't hurt to share a little background. "Carol Maddox will never be a big fan of mine. She claimed I wasn't worthy of her son and said she'd boycott our wedding. Flynn and I took that option away from her by eloping."

"How did your family feel about missing the wedding?"

Renee winced. "I hated not having my grandmother there, but she understood, and all she wanted was my happiness. Since I loved Flynn she supported my decision."

"It was just you and your grandmother, then?"

"And my mother. But Mom…well, she's sort of in her own world." Lauren's brows lifted in a silent question. "She's a chef. Brilliantly creative, temperamental, self-centered—all the clichés you've ever heard about top chefs fit. So it was mostly Granny and me. But Granny was wonderful, so please don't think I'm a pity case. Far from it."

"Good to know. Do you mind my asking what happened to you and Flynn?"

A fresh wave of pain hit hard and fast. Renee glanced away. If she was over him, then why did it still hurt to think about those miserable months?

"After Flynn's father died, Flynn and I hit a rough patch and took a break. We're trying to work out our differences now." She believed she could trust Lauren and was tempted to ask her advice, but instead, she tucked the cash for her lunch into the vinyl folder with the bill and tactfully changed the subject. "Are you ready to overheat your credit card in the local stores?"

"Absolutely. I appreciate your willingness to tag along and offer your opinion. Most women's eyes glaze over when I start babbling about nurseries—unless they're pregnant." Lauren's mouth opened in surprise, and excitement widened her green eyes. "You're not, are you?"

"Pregnant? No. But Flynn and I are discussing it. We'd once planned to have a large family, so I don't mind looking."

"You said you were waiting on calls from a contractor, too?" Renee ventured as they strolled side by side toward the shop someone had recommended to Lauren.

Lauren nodded. "We're building an office behind Jason's home in the Mission District. It's a historic property, and we have to have an architecturally equivalent design to meet all the codes and regulations. Our simple addition has become quite a complicated endeavor."

Renee nodded sympathetically. "I know what you mean. Flynn and I plan to convert the basement of his Pacific Heights Victorian into a kitchen for my catering business. I don't want to do anything to violate zoning laws or devalue the property."

"It's a challenge to make new fit into old, but working so close to home will be worth it, especially after the baby comes."

Exactly what Flynn had said.

They arrived at a baby boutique catering to upper-class mommies-to-be. Renee followed Lauren in.

Inside the boutique each vignette portrayed a perfectly decorated nursery. Before she'd left Flynn, Renee used to wander through the baby departments of local stores, yearning for a family and someone to love. But she'd done her looking and yearning alone.

Then the oddest thing happened at the fourth display. A sensation of coming home settled over her like a warm blanket. She ran her fingertips over the rails of an oak crib with chubby, tumbling teddy bears painted on the head and footboards and tried in vain not to fall in love with the piece.

If the baby plan came to fruition, she had to have this furniture.

"Gorgeous, isn't it?" a saleswoman said.

"Yes." Renee looked around for Lauren, but her new friend had moved several displays deeper into the store.

"Each spindle is hand-lathed, and of course, the bears are hand-painted. It's a one-of-a-kind piece from one of our most talented and sought-after craftsmen. When are you due?" the woman asked.

"Oh, I'm not pregnant. Yet."

A polite smile stretched the woman's lips. "Ah. Then may I suggest that if you're going to wait until you conceive to make your purchase, you might not want to set your heart on this crib. This gentleman's work always sells within a week of being put on the floor."

Indecision twisted inside Renee. If she walked away now, she'd probably never have this set. But if she bought it, she'd be making a commitment to an idea that still terrified her. "I…I'd better catch up with my shopping partner."

The saleswoman's interest cooled. "Of course."

With turmoil tossing inside her like a stormy sea, for the next five minutes Renee shadowed Lauren through the store. Questions tumbled through her brain, distracting her from the task at hand.

"Renee, are you okay?"

"Can I ask you something?" She waited for Lauren's nod. "Starting a family, moving and expanding your business simultaneously is a lot to take on, and yet you seem so serene. Doesn't this much change at once make you nervous?"

Lauren chuckled. "Of course it does. And if I appear calm, it's an illusion. I adore my husband, and I can't imagine not having this baby or sharing the pregnancy with Jason now. My only concern is that Jason loves his work so much that he might miss a few things if I don't make sure he puts us ahead of business."

The words struck a chord deep inside Renee. "I understand that concern all too well. After Flynn joined Maddox he became a workaholic. I almost never saw him."

"I'll bet that contributed to your need for a break." Renee hesitated, then nodded. "For what it's worth, I make Jason take time out most weekends for a sail on his boat. That allows us some quality one-on-one time and gives me an opportunity to polish my painting skills."

The wicked glint in Lauren's eyes caught Renee's attention. "Do I want to pursue that topic?"

Lauren flashed a mischief-filled grin. "Probably not." She tapped a hand-carved toy chest. "What do you think of this piece? It's not too feminine, is it?"

"No. It's lovely." Renee realized she and Lauren were approaching pregnancy with polar-opposite attitudes. Lauren's pregnancy had been unplanned and yet she'd happily embraced the coming baby and the upheaval in her life. Renee, on the other hand, was trying to plan and control every detail and was petrified of failing and falling in love with Flynn again. She wished she possessed a fraction of Lauren's courage.

Lauren smoothed her hand over a quilt. "I don't want you to think I'm making light of your fears. I'm not. It's all terrifying—moving across the country, getting married, having a baby—but I choose to focus on the positives, and I refuse to live in fear of what *might* go wrong. There are no guarantees in life. Sometimes you just have to take a chance and believe that you can make things right."

The words wrapped Renee in a familiar embrace. "My grandmother always said the same thing."

"There you go, then. Great minds think alike." Lauren punctuated the words with a wink.

Renee had never known anyone wiser or stronger than her grandmother. When Emma's husband had gone off to war, she'd taken over running the diner and continued doing so after her husband's death in battle. She'd not only succeeded, she'd excelled.

Emma had raised a daughter alone and then stepped in to help raise her granddaughter when her alcoholic daughter couldn't cope. Renee had never heard Granny complain about the unfairness of life or how hard it was to keep a roof over their heads and food on the table. Renee wanted to be as strong as Emma.

Renee's spine stiffened as realization dawned. Carol Maddox was right. Renee hadn't had a backbone before. She hadn't stood up for herself or fought for what she wanted. But she had the strength to do so now. She could do this.

She wanted a baby, a family. And she wanted to expand her business. Flynn was offering her the opportunity to achieve her dreams. All she had to do was guard her heart for the next twelve to eighteen months or so and then divorce Flynn.

Just like her granny, she could have her baby, her career and keep her sanity. She wouldn't have to keep the San Francisco catering biz in Flynn's basement once it started making enough profit to cover a lease elsewhere. All she'd have to do is move it to a new location.

With so much to gain, how could she afford to say no?

A combination of trepidation and excitement filled Renee with three parts can-do attitude and one part yellow-bellied coward as she pulled into Flynn's driveway.

"Please don't let this be a mistake," she whispered as she shoved open the van door and slung her purse over her shoulder.

Commit to a goal and go for it, Granny's voice echoed in her head.

But she didn't have a clue how to approach her husband for a procreation-only get-together. In the past when they'd made love she hadn't minded initiating the encounters, but this time there would be no love involved—just sex and if she was lucky, a baby. She'd checked her calendar and the timing seemed right.

She slipped her key into the lock and let herself in the front door. The aroma of grilling beef reached her, making her mouth water and her tummy grumble. She stopped in surprise. Flynn was home? And cooking? "Flynn?"

"In the kitchen."

She dropped her bag, took a deep breath for courage and made her way to the back of the house. Her legs trembled like a virgin's. Crazy.

Flynn stood by the range, turning steaks.

"You're home early and you're cooking again."

He turned. "I had this great wife who spoiled me with delicious food. When she left I couldn't stomach the old bachelor fare of sandwiches or frozen stuff, and a man can't live by takeout alone. I had to learn to cook."

He twisted the cap on a bottle of sparkling water and filled two champagne flutes waiting on the counter. He brought one to her.

"Are we celebrating something?" How could he know she'd conquered her reservations and made a decision?

"The builder called. He said you'd signed the contract."

Oh. That. "Yes."

He chinked his glass to hers. "Congratulations. You'll have your new branch open in no time. May it be as successful as the first."

Her heart pounded against her chest wall. She took a sip, swallowed and then blurted, "I bought nursery furniture today."

Flynn's chest expanded on a deep inhalation. "'Bout damn time," he muttered and set his glass aside, then he took hers, too, even though she'd only had one sip.

He grasped her waist, his hands burning her through her knit dress, and pulled her body flush against his. "Wanting to hold you, touch you and taste you has been driving me crazy."

Her nervousness dissolved like sugar in boiling water—right along with her knees. She and Flynn had been good together. She should have known he wouldn't let this be awkward. The sex would be easy and natural, the way it had always been. All she had to worry about was protecting her heart.

He bent and kissed her, a soft sweep of his mouth

over hers, a gentle nip of her bottom lip, and then he settled in. His lips pressed hers apart and his tongue tangled with hers—slick, hot, wet and full of hungry passion. He tasted good, like the Flynn she remembered. Her heart raced as she ran her hands over his thick biceps, broad shoulders and strong back.

His hands skimmed over her, hitting every erogenous zone. She'd missed this. Missed him.

A timer beeped, intruding into her euphoric haze. "What's that?"

"Dinner," he muttered against her neck, then grazed the tender skin with his teeth.

Renee leaned back and met his passion-darkened gaze. "Looks like dinner is going to get cold."

A sexy, hungry smile eased over his lips. "Good plan. Give me two seconds."

He spun from her, turned off the burners and the grill. When he turned back, the need tightening his face made her gulp. He crossed the room in long, deliberate strides, and her heart rate doubled.

Flynn fisted the hem of her shirt and pulled it over her head. She gasped at the suddenness of the move. He stared down at her breasts and cupped them with his hands, sending a current of need straight to her core.

"I never thought it possible for you to be more beautiful than you were before. I was wrong."

She cupped his face and stroked his beard-stubbled jaw. "Thank you."

He bent and nuzzled her cleavage. The softness of his lips contrasting with the coarse rasp of his five-o'clock shadow caused desire to fist in her abdomen. He dusted a string of butterfly-light caresses across each curve until she ached for more. She arched to give him better access and to press her pelvis against his. His thick erection burned into her.

Reaching behind her, he released her bra and peeled the lace away, then captured a tight nipple with his mouth. Wet heat surrounded her sensitive flesh. He tugged with his lips, his teeth, his fingertips, forcing a moan of pleasure from her.

Heat radiated from her core. She raked her fingers through his soft hair and held him close. He knew exactly how she liked to be touched. Not too rough. Not too gentle. No one had ever been able to play her body the way Flynn could.

His fingers stabbed into the waistband of her slacks, making her gasp, and then the fabric loosened. The zipper rasped open seconds before he pushed her pants and panties to the floor. His palm coasted over her hip, her belly and then into her curls. Pleasure sliced through her. "Flynn."

Eager to have his skin against hers, she kicked her shoes and clothing aside. And again he pulled back a few inches to study her. His expanding pupils and quick breaths gave approval as he reached for the buttons on his shirt. "Beautiful."

A moment's self-consciousness swept her. "I've gained weight."

He hushed her with a brief, hard kiss. "Baby, your new curves make me hot."

A smile bubbled to her lips. "I'm glad. Hurry," she pleaded and tried to help him disrobe, but her hands tangled with his, slowing him down. Impatient, she abandoned his shirt to tackle his belt and trousers.

Her fingers fumbled with leather and metal, then he was as naked as she and it was her turn to feast on his wide shoulders, deep pectorals and washboard abdomen. She traced the thin line of hair bisecting his lower belly and disappearing into the denser crop surrounding his erection. She wrapped her fingers around his hard, satiny flesh and stroked, loving his grunt of approval and the blaze of his skin against her palm.

He scooped her up, swung her around and sat her on the table. His fingers found the slick seam of her body and massaged her swollen flesh, making her womb clench with want. She wound her legs around his hips and tightened her grip on his steely flesh. "That feels wonderful."

"Slow down, baby."

"I don't want to go slow." She wanted fast and furious, a sensation overload to crowd out thoughts, doubts and fears that this could be a mistake. Sex with Flynn felt so good, so perfect and so right it scared her. They were so instantly in tune it could have been yesterday, instead of a lifetime ago, that they'd made love in this exact spot. In this kitchen. On this table. While some meal grew cold.

She hooked a hand behind his nape, yanked him close and kissed him, pulling him with her as she lay back on the cool wooden surface.

Flynn's body blanketed her with heat. His thighs pressed hers apart and his fingers found her exposed center, then he took a nipple into his mouth, laved, sucked and nipped it while he manipulated her until a knot of tension twisted so tightly in her tummy that she thought she'd snap. He must know how close she was to the edge. He'd always been able to read her body language.

He worked his way down her torso, over her ribs, across her waist to her hipbone, then he circled her navel, alternately teasing and arousing her with soft lips and hot tongue and bristly chin. Renee's muscles wound tighter with each inch he covered. Then he found her center, sucked her into his mouth and flicked his tongue over her. She gasped at the intensity of sensation arcing through her. Release hovered just out of reach.

"Flynn, I want you inside me," she whispered and tried to guide him.

He lifted his head from her curls. "Not yet."

His chin rasped her tender flesh, making her toes tingle. And then he pushed her over the edge. Orgasm crashed over her.

His gaze locked with hers as she tried to catch her breath, then he captured her hands and carried them over her head, rising above her and pinning her to the tabletop. He stroked his penis against her, his silky hard flesh gliding over her slick crevice as he sawed back and forth. Each smooth advance and slow retreat moved her closer and closer to a second release until she teetered on the brink. Her muscles tensed and her back arched in anticipation. He paused with his thick tip at her entrance.

"Don't you dare stop now," she ordered hoarsely. Squeezing her legs around him, she lifted her hips.

"And if I do?" She felt him smile against her temple.

"I'll make you pay."

His chest shuddered against hers on a rumble of laughter, then he plunged forward, thrusting deep into her body and pushing the air from her lungs. He drove in again and again, and she lost command of her body. Orgasm fractured her, emptied her lungs and seized control of her muscles, making them jerk and spasm involuntarily.

Flynn buried his face in her neck. "I…can't… hold…on."

"Don't even try." She pulled her hands free, raked her nails down his back and nipped his earlobe in the way she knew would break his restraint. His groan filled her ear as he bucked against her and emptied into her.

An urge to hold him close and cuddle descended on her. But there was no place for lovey-dovey this time around. As her skin cooled and her respiratory rate returned to something approaching normal, the gravity of the situation descended upon her. They could very well have made a baby tonight, and if they had there was no turning back.

Fear made her heart pound. She'd been sure she could do this earlier. But that was before they'd made love and she'd lost sight of her goal. Get pregnant. Get out. Instead, she wanted nothing more than to make love with Flynn again. And again. She couldn't afford to let him become an addiction she couldn't live without. An addiction that could ultimately destroy her.

She pushed against his shoulders. "Let me up."

Chest heaving, Flynn slowly levered himself off her. His eyelids were heavy, his face relaxed and his hair… well, she'd wrecked it. The strands stood in dark, irregular spikes.

"Going somewhere?" A smile lifted one corner of his mouth, and the tenderness in his eyes made her tummy swoop alarmingly.

She couldn't care about him. She had to remember this was a simple case of supply and demand. A business transaction. She wanted a baby. He'd promised to provide one. But the warmth and wetness of their joined bodies felt better than any business transaction she'd ever conducted and far more personal than insemination at a clinic would have been.

She squirmed to get out from under him and snatched her clothing from the floor. This wasn't more than sex, was it? Of course not. She'd have to be a total idiot to risk loving him again. She needed space and time to get her head together. "I'm going to shower before dinner."

"Sounds good." He pulled up and refastened his pants as if he planned to join her—the way he once would have.

"Alone," she insisted and fled.

Six

He'd miscalculated, Flynn realized as he watched his naked wife exit the kitchen, her round behind jiggling and her bare feet slapping the hardwood floors as she hustled down the center hall and up the stairs.

Hit-and-run encounters were nothing new to him. He'd had several over the past four or five years while he'd believed himself to be single, but having one with Renee left a void in his chest.

He scooped up his shirt and stuffed his arms in the sleeves. His theory that reminding Renee of how good they used to be would lead to a happy reunion had missed its mark. Now what?

He grasped the back of his neck and scanned the kitchen. Dinner. After she had her shower she'd come back down and they'd discuss the situation over bacon-wrapped, medium-rare filet mignon, buttered asparagus and the *ciabatta* bread he'd picked up at the local bakery on the way home.

When he gathered new facts, he'd recalculate his strategy, because apparently it was going to take more than great sex and good food to make her forgive and forget six months of neglect.

He turned to the stove, flicked on the grill to finish the steaks and the burner to steam the asparagus. The old adage "two steps forward and one back" seemed to apply. Today she'd signed contracts and bought baby furniture, committing to spend time with him. And they'd had unprotected sex. That realization hit him with a fresh rush of adrenaline. Could their cells be on a collision course already?

So where had the reconciliation train derailed? At what point had he lost her? He could have sworn she'd been with him right up until he'd made like a geyser and blown. He knew the sex had been good. Fast, but good. He'd felt her contracting around him as she climaxed.

He tried to correlate the data and couldn't make sense of the way she blew hot and cold. Fear of pregnancy wasn't the issue, since the baby had been her idea. And she planned to divorce him. That meant she couldn't be concerned about him abandoning her again. Not that he intended to let that happen.

He didn't like her holding back even though he was doing the same. But he had to be careful. He wasn't sure he could handle loving her as deeply as he had before and then losing her again. If he hadn't been able to lose himself in Madd Comm, he might not have survived. But that was the catch-22. Renee claimed his obsession with Madd Comm had killed their marriage.

By the time he finished grilling the meat, he had a

rough idea of how to move forward. Identify the problem. Own the problem. Solve the problem.

He plated the food, but there was still no sign of
Renee. Did she plan to hide in her room for the rest of
the night? He wouldn't let that happen. He loaded the
plates on a tray and carried the meal upstairs. The
strategy had gained him ground this morning. Why not
try it again? Renee had once told him that her family
equated food with love, and this time around he'd decided to show his commitment to her by feeding her—
the way she'd once done for him. It was a language he
knew she'd understand.

He knocked on her door. No answer. She could still
be in the shower. He turned the knob and pushed. His
gaze ran over her neatly made empty bed and on to the
bathroom's open door. Empty. The shift of a window
sheer caught his eye. One French door to the balcony
stood ajar. Renee leaned against the outside railing
facing the sunset. She had a quilted throw wrapped
around her shoulders against the cool evening air.

He crossed the room and toed open the door. She
startled and turned. He ignored the lack of welcome on
her face and set the tray on the small bistro table.
"Dinner's ready."

She didn't move away from the rail. "Flynn, I'm
ovulating. I thought I might be…so I checked."

He sucked in a deep breath. "How do you check?"

"I did a test strip after my shower."

"They make tests for that?"

"Yes, and since it might already be too late to change
our minds I need to know you'll respect the boundaries
I've laid out."

He'd respect them—right up until he mowed them

down. He wanted his wife back, and he didn't intend to settle for less than a normal marriage. "Renee, I would never force you to do something you didn't want to do, nor would I ever use a child as a weapon against you."

"I'm glad to hear that."

"If you're ovulating now, how long is our window of opportunity open?"

Her gaze bounced around the room then back to his. "About three days."

That meant he had three days to let the magic between them soften her up. But each month she failed to conceive meant one more he'd get to keep her around and additional time to convince her to throw away her idea of a temporary relationship.

He pointed to the chair and waited until she sat. "I owe you an apology."

Her expression turned wary. "For what?"

"During the last six months of our marriage I used our home like a hotel room, only dropping in when I needed to shower or crash before my head exploded. And I treated you no better than a hotel maid. I took what you did for me and our home for granted, and I even left cash like a tip on the table for you."

Her brow pleated. "Flynn—"

He held up a hand. "Let me finish. My only defense is that I was afraid of failing my mother, brother and the entire staff of Madd Comm. In the end I failed you, someone much more important to me than any of them. I take full responsibility for the failure of our marriage."

Her lips parted on a gasp and then she quickly ducked her head and focused on the fingers she'd knotted in her lap.

What had caused her shoulders to hunch? Why had she flinched?

She exhaled slowly. A moment later she lifted her gaze to his again, looking at him through worried eyes under long, dense lashes. "Apology accepted. But that doesn't change our current situation. We'll have this baby and then we'll go our separate ways. I'm not looking for forever, Flynn."

Not what he wanted to hear, but he would change her mind.

"We'll take it one day at a time." He studied her face, her eyes and the tense way she perched on the chair. Renee was hiding something. But what?

He wouldn't rest until he found out what.

Making love with Flynn had been neither clinical nor emotionless—the way Renee had hoped and expected it would be. The thoughtful, romantic meal of her favorites that he'd prepared only exacerbated the situation.

Dining with him resurrected too many memories: good ones of sharing similar evenings and bad ones of sitting on the sofa in sexy lingerie and waiting for him to come home or sitting outside on this balcony drinking alone. That was one of the reasons she'd chosen this room—to remind her of how weak she'd been.

Did that make her a masochist? Maybe. But Granny had always claimed the only way to overcome a weakness was to admit it and confront it—something Renee's mother had never done with her alcoholism.

Renee lay down her fork, her tummy full but agitated, and focused on Flynn, his thick dark hair, his deep blue eyes, his determined jaw and delicious mouth. He abhorred weakness of any kind. Would he hate her if he discovered her secret? Would he try to turn their child against her?

The urge to run quickened her pulse and dried her mouth. She wouldn't find the space she needed to distance herself from Flynn in this house, not with the past suffocating her.

"I'm going home to L.A. tonight. I need to check on Tamara and lease a new van for the San Francisco branch."

He frowned. "You said you were ovulating."

Therein lay the complication. Her break would, of necessity, be a brief one. And then tomorrow night she'd come back and make lo—*have sex* with Flynn again whether or not she had her head together. But right now she needed the strength that only mental and physical distance could deliver.

Beneath the table she picked at the seam of her pants with a fingernail. "Twenty-four hours shouldn't matter. I'll come back tomorrow as soon as I've done what needs doing in L.A."

His gaze fixed on hers like crosshairs on a target. "If you leave now it will be past midnight when you arrive."

"Traffic will be lighter at this time of night."

His lips thinned, then he inclined his head. "Let me help you acquire the van. I know a salesman at a local dealership that I trust who'll give you a good price."

He'd always tried to take care of her, to protect her from difficulties. She had to make him understand she needed to stand on her own feet. "Flynn, I can negotiate a car contract without a man to help me. I've done it before."

"If you could wait a few days, I could clear my calendar and go with you."

She couldn't let herself become dependent on him. He was only a temporary fixture in her life. "The builder will be here soon, and I won't be able to get away. He's working us in between projects. I have to go now. Tonight."

Resignation flattened his lips. "Call when you arrive and before you leave to come home to let me know you're on the road."

His concern yanked at something inside her, reminding her of a time they couldn't bear being apart for more than a few hours and they'd bent over backward to please each other. But those days were long gone and they weren't coming back. She wouldn't let them.

"How was week one in purgatory?" Tamara asked from the opposite side of the kitchen work counter early Wednesday morning.

Renee dropped the sugared violet she'd been carefully placing on a petit four. "It's only been five days and it's not purgatory."

"Living with my ex would be."

"Your ex is an idiot. Flynn's a nice guy. Are you sure you can handle this weekend's wedding alone? I could come back Friday night."

Tamara's dark eyes widened and her jaw went slack in disbelief. "Are you insane? And don't change the subject. You know you don't have to do this baby-making thing. If you want a kid that badly, I'll give you one of mine. They're already housebroken and they adore you."

"Ha-ha. Aren't you the comedienne? You love your girls, so don't give me that nonsense. I'm the one who had to dry your tears when your youngest started school, remember?"

Tamara sniffed. "What can I say? I was used to her coming to work with me. I lost the little slave who lived to fetch and carry for Mommy."

Renee chuckled and used the tweezers to gently anchor more violets in the icing. She'd taken a risk on hiring Tamara as a kitchen assistant four years ago. At the first interview Tamara had warned her that her daughter Angela suffered from epilepsy, and after a few terrifying seizures at day care Tamara didn't trust anyone else to watch out for her special child. Tamara had assured Renee that Angela would be as quiet as an angel, and the name had stuck.

Angel had been a fixture in the kitchen from Tamara's first day on the job. Renee had set up a gated corner, complete with toys and a small crib, which allowed Tamara to work and watch her daughter. During lunch more often than not all of them had eaten outside so Angel could run around Granny's backyard.

The interaction with Angel had only increased Renee's ache for a baby of her own, and Tamara hadn't been the only one missing the little girl since she'd started kindergarten last fall. The toys and gate were gone now, leaving the kitchen and Renee feeling empty and lonely.

"I want a family, Tamara."

"You do realize that having a baby doesn't guarantee you'll have someone who'll love you back, right?"

Renee smothered a wince as the arrow hit home. "I'm not a high schoolkid. Yes, I know."

"And being a single parent is hard."

"I know that, too, but because of your stellar example, I know I can do it. Besides, you let me practice on your children, so I'm ready." She scanned the work surface. "What's left to prepare after these?"

"You're changing the subject again. But it's the finger sandwiches, if you must know. I won't do those until tomorrow morning. What about the witch-in-law? Is she still a factor?"

Renee rolled her eyes. There were times she regretted sharing so much with her assistant. "Persistent, aren't you?"

Tamara batted her lashes in mock innocence. "It's one of my charms. Spill it."

"Carol has already been over to spread her poison, but Flynn overheard and he threw her out."

"Wow. Impressive. Too bad he didn't have the balls to do that seven years ago."

Renee winced. "I never told him that his mother treated me like trailer trash."

Tamara gaped. "You should have. Are you sure you can handle this sex-only relationship? You certainly are quick to jump to his defense."

"Again, with your fine example, I know how to handle it."

"Pffft. My sex-only lifestyle is because there's not a guy out there I'd trust to raise my girls or one who doesn't bail when he finds out about them. But there is some freedom in knowing that you can enjoy a man without the hassles that usually come attached to one."

"I intend to do exactly that."

"Still…you should think very hard before deciding to raise a child on your own. It's a 24/7/365 job."

"I know." Renee didn't dare tell her assistant that the decision might already have been made, because she didn't want to answer the multitude of questions that would follow. "You're managing to raise two on your own."

"I have your help."

Renee shrugged. "And I'll have yours."

"What about the San Francisco branch? What will

happen to it once you have what you want? You're not going to stay in his basement indefinitely, are you?"

"Once the business is going strong I'll find a new location and then hire a manager. If all goes according to plan and I get pregnant quickly, then I estimate my baby and I will be back in L.A. permanently in less than two years."

Tamara paused with the pastry bag in her hand. "You can count on me. And don't forget to tell that husband of yours that if he hurts you again, he'll feel my rolling pin upside the head."

"Your rolling pin is safe. Flynn won't get the chance to break my heart again."

Flynn caught himself watching the clock Wednesday morning and counting the minutes until he could get out of this meeting. Work had once monopolized his thoughts, but since Renee had come back into his life, she'd taken over the top slot.

Only half listening to the discussion around the conference room table, he caught himself sketching her face in the margin of the report in front of him and shifted in his seat.

What time would she get home?

Would she even come back?

She'd appeared to have second thoughts about their bargain after the sex. Hell, she'd left town last night to avoid a repeat encounter. He would have loved to get her into his bed and make love to her again more slowly, taking the time to linger over each inch of satiny skin. He would have reacquainted himself with all his favorite places: the sensitive spot behind her knee where she often dabbed perfume; the dimples at the base of her spine that she hated; the ticklish arch of her foot.

But she hadn't been interested in round two. If she really wanted to get pregnant, wouldn't she have hung around to jump him again last night and this morning? It bothered him that she'd sent him a text message to let him know she'd arrived safely rather than call as he'd asked. Like some romantic, newlywed sap, he'd wanted to hear her voice.

He checked his watch again. He'd have a surprise for Renee when—if—she came back. She liked to do her exercising indoors. He'd ordered a treadmill and video setup for her so she could walk her miles and watch cooking shows simultaneously. The equipment would be delivered late this afternoon.

Brock continued explaining how the economic crisis had put the squeeze on potential clients' advertising dollars. Nothing Flynn as VP didn't already know. Then his brother switched to Athos Koteas's latest account-stealing stunts. Again, it wasn't a news bulletin that the Greek immigrant was a ruthless bastard. Madd Comm struggled to compete with Koteas's European connections and devious tactics. Good thing none of the old guy's three sons was as competitive.

"That's bull and you know it," Asher Williams, Madd Comm's CFO, barked in reply to something Brock said, making Flynn snap to attention.

What had he missed? Flynn scanned the tense faces around the table and tried to figure out what had set off the normally unflappable Ash.

"Ash, we have to make it work," Brock said.

"You're asking the impossible." Ash shot to his feet and slammed out of the conference room. Silence descended, broken only by Brock's muffled curse and the shuffling of papers and clearing throats of the ad executives around the table.

Damn. Flynn rose. "I'll talk to him."

He followed Ash out and down the hall to the CFO's office and knocked on the open door. "You okay?"

Ash's brows flatlined over his hazel eyes. "Brock's trying to squeeze blood out of a rock. It can't be done."

"I hear you. But we have to stay competitive."

Ash stared silently out the window, his back tense.

Flynn closed the office door. "Is this even about work?" The silence stretched. "Do you have something you need to run by me, Ash?"

"Melody's gone."

Another man with woman troubles. What was that old cliché? *Women, can't live with them, can't live without them.* They were a blessing and curse. "Temporarily or permanently?"

"I don't know."

"Any idea where she went?"

"Negative."

"Been there, done that, man. You have my sympathy. Will you look for her?"

Ash pivoted abruptly. "Hell no. We were never going to be anything but short-term, anyway. I've been paying her way through law school, but she's probably found another sucker."

"That sucks, man. Losing a woman you love—"

"I never said I loved her. I don't. I'm just pissed off."

"Right." Denial was a wonderful thing. Flynn had fed on denial and anger for years after Renee left. "If you need anything—even if it's a designated driver while you drink yourself into oblivion—I'm your man."

Ash's drawn and pale face stared back at him. The guy might claim he wasn't hurting, but his eyes told a different story.

Flynn imagined he'd probably looked the same when Renee left the first time. But that was then. He intended to right the wrong he'd committed and repair his marriage. And while he'd love to have a long-term relationship with Renee and have several more children with her, he couldn't afford to love as wholeheartedly as he once had.

He'd save his love for his child or children if he could talk her into more. At least they wouldn't leave him until college time.

Seven

Turning into Flynn's driveway in her new van shouldn't have been an aphrodisiac, but for Renee, it was. She knew they'd have sex tonight. And only sex. There would be no bonding. Just sweaty, satisfying, exhilarating fulfillment.

Familiar signs of arousal took control of her body: accelerated pulse rate, flushed skin, shortness of breath, excessive moisture in her mouth. Her hands shook as she pocketed her car keys and climbed the brick steps to the front door.

She let herself in and silence greeted her. She should have checked the garage for Flynn's car. And then she noticed the spicy, garlicky, tomatoey scent in the air. Something Italian. Mama G's lasagna? She sniffed again and smelled the yeasty scent of dough. No. Papa G's pizza. Renee's mouth watered for an entirely different reason, and her stomach rumbled in anticipation.

No one made pizza as well as Papa G, and she and Flynn had ordered many of them for takeout when their renovations had left them too grungy for dining out or too tired to cook.

"Flynn?" She followed her nose to the kitchen and found it empty. A note on the table caught her eye. Trying not to think about what they'd done on that table twenty-four hours ago, she snatched up the page and turned her back on the scene of the crime—the crime being in the heat of the moment she'd temporarily lost sight of her goal. A baby and a clean break.

"Come to the basement," Flynn had written.

Had he started work on her kitchen already? Dumping her purse on the counter, she hurried downstairs. He wasn't in the area designated for CGC. "Flynn?"

"In here," he called from the storage room across the hall.

She heard an old home-restoration program playing on the TV as she approached. At her touch, the door dragged over carpeting that hadn't been here seven years ago. She scanned the gym equipment filling the space. Some kind of weight equipment with four stations occupied the center of the room flanked by an exercise bike on a rubber mat on the left and an electric tread-mill on the right.

Flynn stood in front of a wide, flat-panel television mounted on the wall. He wore faded jeans and a snug white T-shirt and work boots. A leather tool belt hung on his hips, accentuating his muscular butt. Her heart stalled at the sexy, familiar sight.

He turned and extended his arms. "What do you think?"

That he looked delicious.

He tossed a small black object at her. She snapped

out of her daze, caught it and identified a remote control. "I didn't know you'd turned this room into a home gym."

"I hadn't until today. You can watch your cooking shows while you work out."

Surprised and touched by his thoughtfulness, she gasped. "You did this for me?"

He nodded. "I ordered the equipment the day after you moved in. They delivered it today."

A little of the wall she'd built around her heart crumbled. This was the old Flynn, the one who'd routinely surprised her with thoughtful, considerate gestures or gifts. The one she'd fallen in love with so long ago. She swallowed to ease the lump in her throat and reminded herself to guard her heart.

"This is incredibly nice, Flynn, but I could have rejoined the gym."

"Your favorite gym closed. The closest facility isn't as nice, and you always hated fighting for a parking space."

She grimaced at the memory of how she used to seize on any opportunity to avoid exercise. But that had been back when she was young enough to eat anything and not gain an ounce. When she'd passed thirty her body had changed. As much as she liked the wisdom that came with getting older, there were some parts of maturing she could do without.

"Well, yes, but…you didn't have to go to this expense. Thank you."

He pointed to an empty corner. "There's room over there for a playpen or crib. For after the baby."

Her head spun with images of Flynn's hands splayed over her swollen belly, working out beside her while she tried to get back in shape, of him cradling their tiny infant in his big, gentle hands.

A knot of emotion rose in her throat. "I—I hope you'll use some of the equipment, too."

"I will. Especially this." He straddled the weight bench. His thick biceps flexed as he pulled down on the bar hanging over his head.

She wanted him. Like this. Relaxed. Sexy. The old Flynn.

Her feet felt weighted as she crossed the room to his side and bent to kiss him. He let her take the lead, let her move her lips over his, waited for her tongue to slip into his mouth and caress his before he responded without releasing the weight bar. His tongue dueled with hers.

Her pulse raced as she sucked his bottom lip into her mouth and gently nipped the tender flesh. He grunted his approval. She lifted her head. Passion widened his pupils, the black almost obliterating his blue irises.

He shook his head. "As much as I would love to take you right here, right now, we're not rushing tonight. This time I want you in my bed. Naked, wet and breathless."

Desire made her dizzy. "You have two out of three already."

His nostrils flared, then a dangerous, naughty smile curved his lips. "Dinner first."

He exploded off the bench and brushed past her, leaving her staring at his gorgeous backside. And hungry. But not for Papa G's delicious pizza.

She wanted Flynn as badly as she ever had.

Flynn's muscles were so tense he could barely swallow. Dinner had been one long foreplay session.

With an imp of mischief lurking in her face, Renee had lingered over her food, licking dots of sauce from the corner of her mouth and fingertips and nibbling on errant, gooey strings of cheese or fallen slices of pepperoni.

He wanted that mouth on him, that talented pink tongue licking *his* lips, instead of hers. The moment she pushed her plate away, he shot to his feet, grabbed the dishes and dumped them in the sink. The scrape of her chair brought him around.

She stood by the kitchen door. Sexual hunger darkened her eyes to almost purple. Without a word she peeled her sweater over her head, dropped it on the floor and then pivoted and sauntered down the center hall to the stairs—the same way she'd retreated last night, only this time her invitation was clear in every sexy sway of her hips.

He smiled at the familiar game, and the needle of his body compass pointed north. In the early days, coming home to a bra on the foyer floor had been one hell of a welcome and the promise of a hot night ahead. When they'd wanted to make love he and Renee used to leave trails of clothing like bread crumbs leading to their location of choice. But somewhere along the way, they'd quit playing with each other and merely coexisted in the same space.

The blame for that rested solely on his shoulders. He'd been the one too exhausted to accept her sexy invitations. The disappointment he'd seen on her face when he refused had led him to sleep at the office a bit too often. He'd been so afraid of failing at work he couldn't tolerate the possibility of failing at home, too. In the end, his fear had become a self-fulfilling prophecy.

But not anymore. He had control of all aspects of his life—all aspects except his relationship with Renee. And if he felt a mild sense of discontent, then as soon as he had his marriage under control, that dissatisfaction would disappear.

He sat down long enough to untie and remove his work boots and socks, and then he followed her. Her bra draped the newel post, a pink lacy scrap of almost nothing. He scooped it up and sniffed her scent. The fabric still carried the warmth of her body. He could see his fingers through the cups. Halfway up the staircase she'd left one shoe. A few treads higher he spotted the other. He shucked his shirt and draped it over the banister. It slid down. He didn't care. Her pants puddled on the landing. He dropped his on top of them, then paused.

Which bedroom? His or hers?

The pink panties hanging on his doorknob provided the answer. Grinning, he strode toward the trail marker and hooked the lacy garment with his finger. They smelled of her. He pushed open the door. Renee reclined on a pile of pillows in the middle of his big bed with one knee bent to hide her blond curls, but that didn't make the sight of his wife, curvy and naked on his sheets, any less inviting or arousing.

He dangled her lingerie from his fingers. "Next time I want to see you in these. Then *I'll* take them off you."

She licked her lips, and he could practically feel her tongue on his erection. Heat pumped through him. Her gaze raked him, pausing at his tented boxers. "One of us is overdressed."

He dropped her undergarments, shoved his boxers down his legs and kicked them aside, then slowly stalked toward the bed. Looking his fill, he stretched out on the mattress beside her, but he didn't touch her. Not yet. Once he did he wouldn't be able to stop. A flush of arousal pinkened her cheeks, chest and breasts. Her nipples contracted under his scrutiny, and her stomach quivered slightly with each shallow breath she took.

He ached to be inside her, to pound his way to release, but he'd promised himself he'd take it slow and remind Renee how amazingly perfect they were together before letting go.

He twisted a blond ringlet around his finger, then released it to stroke her cheek, her nose, the softness of her parted lips. "I've missed this. Us."

Her breath hitched. She captured his hand, guiding it to her breast. The soft globe filled his palm, the pebbled tip pressing into him. He rolled the point between his fingers, drawing a whimper from her. Her lids fluttered closed. Propped on one elbow, he bent and replaced his fingers with his mouth, leaving his hand free to explore her other breast, her smooth stomach, her long legs and damp curls. She was already moist and hot. Need fisted in his abdomen.

She arched into his fingers, but he didn't want to rush this, so he moved on, caressing the crease behind her knee, the curve of her waist, the sensitive spot beneath her arm and the dip of her navel. She shuddered, encouraging him to follow the same path with his lips.

Her fingers tangled in his hair, alternately gripping and releasing. Her toes curled against the sheets. He relished her scent, her taste, the softness of her skin against his lips and tongue.

She slid the arch of her foot up his calf and down again. Her free hand kneaded his back, then his butt before sliding toward his swollen flesh. Determined to keep her from rushing him, he kept his groin out of reach. She detached from his hair to trace the shape of his ear and to tease the hammering pulse point below with the light scrape of her short nails. Desire rippled over him. Renee had never been a passive lover. She gave as much as she received.

He grazed his teeth along her instep and her legs tensed. He circled her ankle with his tongue, then worked his way up the back of her leg to nibble on the bottom curves of her buttocks. Her muscles tightened. She twisted beneath him, winding her legs around him and rubbing her hot center against his thigh.

Palming her knees, he pressed her legs apart, leaving her open and exposed to his gaze, to his mouth. He licked her slick seam, making her jerk and gasp, and then he nuzzled her neatly groomed curls.

Her scent filled him with the anticipation of driving her over the edge, of hearing her cries and feeling her contract around him. Slowly. He found her center again with his tongue, flicking the hot pink nub, teasing her to the brink and then backing off. Paying close attention to the tension of her muscles, he repeated the process, smiling against her thigh at her frustrated groan when he left her hanging a second time. He urged her toward orgasm again, but before he could withdraw a third time, her fingers fisted in his hair.

"Please, Flynn."

Her breathless plea sent his blood south. His penis pulsed against his thigh, reminding him who was boss and urging him to get on with it. He slid his fingers inside her and she groaned. She was so wet, so hot and tight and ready for him that it took all his restraint to delay his own gratification.

He sucked her into his mouth, making her moan and arch, and then he stroked her with his tongue and his hand until her muscles squeezed his fingers and her cries filled his ears. Her climax shuddered through her. He barely gave her a moment to catch her breath between spasms before making her come again and again.

She sank into the bed limp as he tongued her navel, giving her a break before his next planned assault. Her hand gently caressed his cheek. She lifted his chin until their eyes met. "I want you inside me for the next one. Please, Flynn. It feels so good when you're inside."

Hunger charged through him. He couldn't resist any longer. He climbed over her, hooked her legs over his forearms and drove deep. Slick heat welcomed him, and then she clutched him with her internal muscles, and it was his turn to groan as his head nearly exploded with pleasure.

He drew back and sank in again and again. Her breasts, jiggling with each slam of his hips against hers, riveted him, and then he had to feel that movement with his hands. He cupped and kneaded her, tweaking her nipples while he rocked his hips.

Renee locked her ankles behind his back and clamped her hands on his shoulders, pulling him down for a kiss that nearly boiled his brain. She devoured his mouth in a clash of tongues and teeth. To stave off his own release, he tried to focus on her, on the stiffening of her muscles, on her dampening skin and on her panting breaths, but a fuse lit in his gut, and he ignited like a roman candle. He tore his mouth away from hers as a groan roared from him. Blast after blast of ecstasy rocketed through his extremities until he was nothing but spent ash.

His elbows buckled. He collapsed on top of her, cushioned by her soft breasts, then eased to her side and braced himself on an elbow so he wouldn't crush her. A fog of satisfaction invaded his skull and weighted his eyelids.

Hitching her leg over his hip so he wouldn't have to disengage from the slick sleeve of her body, he wrapped her in his arms. Nothing had ever felt more right.

This is what they should have been doing for the past seven years. Solo sex and impersonal relationships didn't come close to delivering this level of satisfaction. He and Renee belonged together.

And as his body cooled and clarity slowly returned, he made an interesting realization. His deal with Renee wasn't just about correcting a mistake. It was about winning—winning his wife back.

There was no way in hell he was going to let her walk out of his life again. The passion was too intense. He would use whatever means necessary to keep her here. It was time to turn up the heat.

Excitement bubbled through Renee's veins Thursday evening as she stood on the patio outside the basement watching the workers pack up their tools for the day.

Everything was coming together much faster than the months of chaos she'd endured during the renovation of her grandmother's house. When Flynn flexed his influential muscles, work got done at an amazing rate. Yesterday he'd set up her gym, and today the permits had been issued and the work on her new kitchen had begun.

"How did the first day of construction go?" Flynn asked from behind her, startling her. Her heart *baboomed* wildly as his arms encircled her waist and his lips brushed her jaw. She hadn't expected him until later…if at all. Shadows of the past crept over her.

She turned quickly, simultaneously stepping out of his embrace. He looked powerful, charismatic and successful in his immaculate charcoal-gray suit, but she preferred him in the khakis and dress shirts with the rolled-up sleeves that he wore when he worked for the architectural firm, or the faded jeans and T-shirts he donned for renovation.

Memories of last night's passionate encounter rushed forward, but she muscled them back. Sexual satisfaction did not guarantee happiness, which was why she'd sneaked out of Flynn's bed as soon as he'd fallen asleep, and then she'd awoken early this morning, raced to her new gym, climbed on the treadmill and donned a pair of earphones so she could be working out when he came downstairs before work.

Yes, she admitted, she was taking the coward's way out, rather than discussing a situation that scared her.

Focus on the project, a much safer topic. "The basement tile has been laid. Tomorrow they'll grout, and then Monday the cabinets will be delivered and installed."

He strolled to the door to look around. "Looks good."

She caught herself checking out his broad shoulders, straight spine and tight butt, and forced her attention elsewhere. But diverting her gaze didn't derail her quickening pulse or the warmth pooling behind her navel. "I'm going to paint this weekend."

He faced her again, but she avoided his eyes, fearing he'd see her hunger she couldn't control. "You didn't contract the crew to do that for you?"

"No. Doing it myself saves money and gives me time to think." Time to plan and try to figure out exactly how their peculiar agreement would work out. She should have plotted the whole deal on paper—preferably in her lawyer's office with legal backup, but Flynn's need for secrecy had prevented that. "Besides, I like painting."

A smile tilted one corner of his mouth. "I know. I'll help you paint."

Butterflies took flight in her belly. Coming on the heels of the phenomenal sex, working side by side with Flynn would be a trip down memory lane she didn't need. "I can do it."

"I know you can, Renee. I doubt there's anything you can't handle when you set your mind to it, but I have a stake in how this project turns out."

The reminder that this was his house sobered her— exactly what she needed—and reminded her to ask her attorney to make sure everything she and Flynn had agreed upon was spelled out in their divorce agreement when the time came. "Yes, of course you do."

"I meant I want CGC to be up and running before your pregnancy makes it difficult for you to deal with the setup."

His thoughtfulness melted a tiny chip of her heart. "I may not be pregnant yet."

"But you will be. Soon."

The sensual promise in his words made her heart and womb contract. "I don't know what kind of strings you pulled, but the contractor thinks I'll be ready to fire up the stove by the end of next week."

"Then I'm glad I brought home a client list for you."

She blinked in surprise. "What?"

"I mentioned CGC to a few people and they're interested in talking to you about catering jobs. One wants an appointment ASAP for an emergency fill-in job."

He worked fast. "I wish I'd had you around when I started CGC. It wasn't nearly as easy to pick up clients. I pounded on a lot of doors and had a lot of rejections.

"Once the construction is completed I'll still have inspections to get through, but I need to work up an advertising plan and hire a few part-time employees."

"I can recommend a reputable employment agency to screen your applicants, and you have connections at Madd Comm for your promotional plan."

His generosity made it more difficult to keep her emotional distance. "Thank you. But Maddox isn't in my budget."

"We'll see about that." He lifted a hand and tangled his fingers in her hair. Renee's muscles locked, trapping the air in her lungs and making retreat impossible. "You have something in your hair."

He plucked at the strands, but he didn't release her after he'd tossed whatever it was aside. Instead, he cupped her head and held her as he bent to capture her mouth. Alarms shrilled inside her as his lips sipped from hers, stirring a response she wanted to deny but couldn't.

Flynn plied her mouth with gentle tugs, then when she gasped, his tongue swept inside to tangle with hers. His palms skated down her arms to rest in the small of her back, then he pulled her forward until her body rested against his. His heat suffused her.

She couldn't let herself love him again, but she couldn't stop the wanting. Kissing him felt so good, so familiar, so right. But it wasn't. Giving in to the passion he evoked was a dangerous act, like walking a tight wire without a net.

Push him away, a voice warned, but her neurons ignored the command. Her hands splayed on his chest. She felt the steady thump of his heart beneath her palm. Why hadn't she ever found anyone who could arouse her the way Flynn did? With nothing more than a kiss he made her pulse race and her knees weak.

A truck door slammed nearby—probably one of the workers. Flynn eased back, reluctance clear on his face, and checked his watch. "I'm supposed to take you to the Rosa Lounge for cocktails with the Madd Comm staff."

To continue the farce. The more people he introduced her to, the more he'd have to explain her absence to when they went their separate ways. "What is the Rosa Lounge?"

"A bar on Stockton. The team meets there for celebrations."

"Flynn, I'm not sure including me in your celebrations with your coworkers is a good idea. When I leave—"

"That's a long way off. I'll deal with it if it happens. If we want this reconciliation to look real, then you'll join me."

"*When* it happens. I hate lying to everyone."

"Would you prefer I call Brock and have him tell the staff we've decided to turn in early?"

Her cheeks heated at the implication and so did that coal in the center of her pelvis that Flynn seemed to be able to ignite at will. Would they have sex again tonight? Did she want to? *Yes.* The strength of her desire for him scared her.

He stroked her cheek, tucking a strand of hair behind her ear. "Lauren will be there."

Renee winced as he unintentionally twisted the knife of guilt inside her. Yet another person being deceived. She liked Lauren. They had a lot in common, both being transplants and opening new branches of existing businesses, and she hoped they'd be sounding boards for each other.

But what choice did she have except to play along?

She gestured to her jeans and casual sweater. "I'll need to shower and change."

And then she'd face Flynn's fellow Maddox employees and pull off the best acting job of her life. For her future child's sake, everyone had to believe the fairy tale Flynn had chosen to tell.

Eight

Renee cataloged the dimly lit bar as she entered with Flynn on her heels. Small, trendy, high-end clientele, and judging by the specials written on the blackboard in fluorescent green marker, expensive.

Flynn's hand snaked around her waist, and his lips and warm breath touched her ear. "Head for the tables in the back."

To onlookers his embrace would look intimate, but in reality he'd issued a command in a low, don't-argue-with-me tone, and his firm grip ensured she wouldn't chicken out and run.

She made her way down the center aisle between the large bar taking up most of one wall and the Rosa Lounge's green, glass-topped tables with tall, black-lacquer bar chairs lining the opposite. The voices reached her even before she spotted the long table where a half-dozen well-dressed twenty- and thirty-something patrons sat.

Lauren's auburn head lifted. She spotted Renee and Flynn and waved. Conscious of other heads turning, Renee fought off her nervousness and returned the gesture. One familiar face stood out in the crowd. Brock's.

Renee's stomach muscles seized. Brock, like his mother and father, had never been crazy about Renee, which made Brock's holding on to the divorce papers a bit unusual. He should have been eager to get rid of her. She wasn't sure she believed the tale he'd told Flynn about feeling guilty about breaking up the marriage. Brock rose from his seat at the head of the table and approached her.

"Renee. Welcome back." His eyes and voice were as cool as his handshake. Had Flynn told Brock the truth? Had he told anyone?

"Thank you. It's…good to be back," she added, since it was probably expected of her.

Flynn's arms encircled her waist, and he spooned her back from shoulders to knees with the muscled planes of his body. A wave of awareness and warmth washed over her as he leaned forward until his slightly bristly cheek pressed hers. "Everybody, this is Renee. My wife."

A chorus of hellos rained on her, then Flynn added, "You remember Celia and Lauren."

"Yes. Hello again." Both women's welcoming smiles seemed genuine.

"To Brock's right is Elle, his executive assistant. To Lauren's left is Jason, one of Madd Comm's ad execs and Lauren's husband." Renee nodded at each new person, since Flynn didn't release her to shake hands. "Next is Ash, another ad exec, and you've already met Gavin."

The names came so fast she hoped she could remember them. "Hi, everyone. Thanks for including me to-night."

She slid into the empty chair Flynn pulled out for her. Flynn shifted his chair close enough for his leg to press hers beneath the table. He offered her a menu with one hand and stretched his other arm along the back of her chair, then he twined a lock of her hair around his finger and gave a gentle tug.

She shivered. Renee's nape had always been ultra-sensitive—a fact Flynn knew all too well. She glanced up to see Celia, Elle and Lauren watching. Lauren winked and snuggled closer to Jason. Elle's gaze flicked to Brock and lingered before turning back to her menu. Was she reading Brock's expression to see how the boss felt about Renee's return?

The waitress arrived. "What can I get you?"

"A Diet Coke, please," Renee said.

"Bushmills," Flynn replied, naming the Irish whiskey he'd preferred for as long as she'd known him.

Celia leaned forward. "No martini? The Rosa Lounge is known for them."

"You're not pregnant, too, are you?" Elle asked.

Alarm trickled through Renee as all eyes focused on her. "Not that I know of."

She added a smile and hoped everyone would let the topic pass.

"Renee and I always wanted a large family. Maybe this time around we'll make it happen."

Flynn's words sent her heart crashing against her rib cage and brought her shocked gaze to his. A tender smile eased over his lips as he stroked her cheek with his knuckle. If she didn't know this was an act, she'd swear the love softening his eyes was real.

He'd wanted to make the reconciliation look believable, and he'd taken a giant step in that direction by laying their plan on the table for everyone to witness their success or failure.

And they would fail, she reminded herself. She would walk away—no matter how convincing Flynn might be in the role of the doting lover. Her sanity depended on escaping as soon as she'd fulfilled her end of their bargain.

Escaping before she broke.

A steady drumming beneath Renee's ear nagged her awake. She fought her way out of the sleepy fog and grappled for her bearings.

Friday. Tile grout.

But she didn't want to move from her snug spot. Warmth anchored her to the mattress. She opened her heavy eyelids and a male chest filled her vision. Her pulse jumped on a rush of adrenaline as she identified Flynn's bed, Flynn's arms around her and Flynn's erection pressing the thigh she'd hooked over his hips.

She shouldn't be here, but she must have fallen asleep after sex last night. Great sex. Exhausting I-can't-come-anymore sex. The kind they used to share back in the days when they couldn't get enough of each other.

Last night at the Rosa Lounge Flynn had used the ruse of their reignited love to touch her at every opportunity. He'd played with her hair, stroked her arm or shoulders and sneaked caresses on her thighs beneath the table, knowing that as per their agreement, she couldn't object. Even though she'd been aware he was shamelessly taking advantage of her predicament, he'd still had her so turned on by the time they reached the house last night that they'd barely made it inside the front door before ripping off each other's clothing.

She'd promised herself she'd leave his bed as soon as her legs regained the strength to carry her down the hall to her room, her shower and her bed. And yet here she was, with her limbs entangled in her husband's and his scent clinging to her skin.

And she didn't want to leave. That was exactly why she must. But she didn't want to wake Flynn. Didn't want to face him. Not after the way he'd played the besotted, possessive lover so convincingly in front of his brother and coworkers that she'd almost believed he still loved her.

Good thing she knew his love had died a very long time ago. He'd proved that time and time again by choosing not to come home.

Trying to slow her quick breaths, she slowly separated herself from him. She was almost free when his arms tightened, yanking her back and erasing the narrow gap she'd created between them. Her heart lurched.

"Going somewhere?" he asked in a gruff, sexy voice that rumbled through her like a passing train.

"I need to get dressed before the construction crew arrives."

He inhaled deeply and stretched, pressing his torso more firmly against hers. His hand swept down her back and curved over her bottom, stirring up a hunger that should have been more than satiated.

"Flynn, let me up."

He lifted slightly to look at the alarm clock, then sank back onto one elbow. "We have thirty minutes."

The husky intent in his voice made desire coalesce in her midsection. "I'm probably not…fertile anymore."

His palm skimmed upward over her hip, her waist, to cup her breast and thumb the nipple. A skewer of need pierced deeply and her flesh puckered. He nuzzled her temple. "You don't need to be fertile for me to make you feel good."

A pulse pounded deep inside her, and a craving for the satisfaction he could deliver swelled in her tummy. She fought it and shoved against his chest. She couldn't allow herself to become desperate for his attention ever again.

"Flynn, we're not supposed to be doing this unless the timing to conceive is right."

"There are no written rules for our agreement."

"Maybe there should be."

He held her captive with his passionate gaze and powerful arms for several more seconds as if debating changing her mind. Part of her wanted him to. And that part was the very one she had to ignore.

He relaxed his hold. "Run if you must."

She stiffened. "I'm not running. The builders will be here soon."

She scrambled from the bed and searched the floor, the bed, the room for something to cover her nakedness, but he'd removed her clothing downstairs. Short of dragging the sheet off his long, lean body or raiding his closet, she was out of luck.

She crossed her arms over her breasts and backed toward the hall. "I'm going to take a shower."

He sat up in bed. The sheets bunched around his naked hips, leaving his muscular chest and washboard abs on display—a mesmerizing view. "Tonight we'll move your stuff in here."

Panic knocked her breath from her lungs. "Flynn, I'm not sharing this room with you."

"When is the nursery furniture going to be delivered?"

She dampened her suddenly dry lips. In the excitement over her new workspace, she'd forgotten her purchase. "M-Monday."

"We'll paint the guest room this weekend before tackling your kitchen and have it ready by the time the furniture arrives." He tossed back the covers and rose in a rippling exhibition of firm, fit and aroused male.

Her fingers curled against the need to test his length and thickness. She blinked, tore her gaze from his morning erection, but she couldn't as easily banish the memory of how he'd felt in her hand, her mouth and her body mere hours ago. "What part of 'I am not sharing with you' did you not understand?"

"I heard you, but moving you in here is our only option."

"The third floor—"

"Isn't ready. The floors still need to be sanded and refinished." His gaze prowled from her head to her breasts, hips, toes and then returned at an even more leisurely pace.

Her skin prickled in response. She wanted to cover up. She wanted *him* to cover up. Concentrating when they were both naked was beyond her capabilities. "The builder—"

"Won't have time. I asked. He has to finish your kitchen by next Friday and return to his previously scheduled jobs."

She cradled her lower belly. "There's no rush. We don't know if there *is* a baby yet."

"There's no need to drag our feet. If we convert the front room into the nursery, we can work on the third floor together and get it right—the way we did with the rest of the house."

His words called to the primitive, nest-building part of her. "I'll have time to work upstairs until the bookings start coming in."

"You'll have bookings beginning next weekend."

Once more his words sent her reeling. "I won't have the permits."

"The first job is a small one. No permit required. You can work from my kitchen or the client's. Call Gretchen today and find out what she needs."

"Who's Gretchen?"

He strode into the bathroom, calling over his shoulder, "A friend."

Something in his tone made the hairs on her nape rise. She followed him and caught his gaze in the mirror. "A *girl*friend?"

His expression blanked and his hands flexed around his toothbrush. "She's a woman with connections who can give you the exposure you need to get your name out there."

His avoidance of an answer told her what she needed to know. A swarm of something ugly and uncomfortable buzzed inside her. She wasn't jealous. She was just... unsettled at the realization that once she left, there would be other women in Flynn's life. In her baby's life. Somehow that just hadn't been considered when she'd agreed to this deal.

The mirror reflected their nude bodies back at her, making her feel even more exposed. "Does she know we're still married?"

"That's irrelevant."

"Is it?" Was this Gretchen person his lover?

"Renee, don't make a big deal out of nothing."

She had no right to protest. And why was she standing here arguing when she needed to get ready? "I'm going to shower."

He captured her hand, his palm warm against hers. "You can shower here. With me."

Her breath hitched. If she stayed, any showering would be done *after* they made love again. His erection made that clear. Shared showers—with her arms braced against the tile, her legs splayed and Flynn taking her from behind, with his wet, soapy hands caressing her breasts—used to be one of her favorite ways to start the day. But not today.

She yanked free. "Flynn, don't make this into something it's not."

"And that is?"

"A real reconciliation. I am not sharing your bedroom or your bathroom."

"That's what you say, but this—" he flicked a fingertip over an erect nipple "—this says you want to."

An arrow of desire hit the bull's-eye. Turning on her heel, she retreated to the only sanctuary she had in this house—the guest room—and closed the door behind her. She sagged against the panel.

She'd been jealous twice now.

Being possessive was not the way to keep her distance. For all intents and purposes Flynn was merely her sperm donor by orthodox means. Nothing more.

And she wanted it that way.

The other woman could have him.

"But not until after I'm finished with him," she groused as she marched toward her bathroom.

The idea of him climbing from another woman's bed and into hers repulsed her. But that had absolutely nothing to do with her heart. Her only concern was her health, she assured herself. She didn't want Flynn giving her or her baby something contagious.

Renee couldn't sleep. She stared at the shadows dancing on her bedroom ceiling Friday night and willed the tension to ease from her overwrought body, but her mind kept racing with thoughts of the baby, her business, Flynn.

Especially Flynn. And the way he made her feel. How could he still get to her after all this time and all the heartache she'd endured at his hands?

She rolled over and fluffed her pillow. The clock inched toward midnight, then past it. This was how the trouble had started last time. Her drinking had begun with a simple nighttime glass of wine to help her unwind while waiting for Flynn to come home. Then it had progressed to a second glass to help her get to sleep.

She wasn't going to fall into the same trap this time. If she couldn't sleep she would find something constructive to do. But what? Play with recipes? No. Banging around the kitchen might wake Flynn. Exercise? No. That would work her up, rather than wind her down. She could paint the basement. She'd bought everything she needed this afternoon.

Decision made, she rolled out of bed, pulled on a pair of old jeans shorts and a T-shirt. She didn't bother with a bra. No one would see. Then she pulled her hair into a scrunchie and eased open her door. Only the sounds of the old house settling broke the silence. Good. Keeping an eye on the open door to Flynn's darkened bedroom, she crept down the stairs without turning on any lights, avoiding the third tread that squeaked. Being familiar with the house had its advantages.

When she reached the basement she sighed in relief at arriving undetected, then hustled to the supplies in the corner. She opened and stirred the paint while debating her options.

Tonight she needed monotonous, easy work. She'd save cutting in along the wood trim for tomorrow when her mind and her hands were steadier. After pouring the thick liquid into the tray, she coated the roller and then reached for the nearest wall. The sticky smacking sound of the paint rolling over drywall filled her with satisfaction, and the repetitive motion soothed her and allowed her mind to wander.

Marking her territory had always been important to her. Throughout her childhood and her early teens she and her mother had moved often, as her mom followed the jobs and earned her reputation as a temperamental but gifted chef. When Renee had turned thirteen, Lorraine had decided having a teenage daughter around made her look old and sent Renee to live with Emma. Renee had been thrilled at the prospect of putting down roots, but at the same time apprehensive about changing schools again.

Granny had made a party of it by inviting over the neighbors' teenagers to help paint Renee's bedroom, providing Renee with instant friends and a place to call home. That's why painting Flynn's Victorian had been so significant. Painting her space made her feel like she belonged and might not leave.

Wrong.

Bad memory. Tension returned to her muscles. She stepped back to study the ten-foot square she'd covered with French Vanilla paint.

"Good color," Flynn said behind her.

She jumped, almost dropping the roller, and turned. Flynn wore his boxer shorts and nothing else. "What are you doing up?"

He strolled closer, stepping from the shadowy area at the base of the stairs and into the brightly lit room that would become Renee's kitchen. The basement was cool, and his nipples tightened into tiny points. "I could ask you the same."

She shrugged. "I couldn't sleep. I decided to put my surplus energy to work."

"Good idea." He crossed to the pile of supplies.

"What are you doing?"

"Getting a brush."

No, no, no. "Flynn, it's one o'clock in the morning. Go back to bed."

"I will if you will."

If she quit now and retreated to her room, she'd only go back to tossing and turning and worrying.

"Could you at least put on some clothes?" How would she concentrate with all that taut golden skin, those washboard abs and ropy muscles on display?

"Not tonight. I'll have to search for clothing I don't mind getting paint on."

"But—"

"I've painted in less, Renee. So have you."

Memories hit her like a runaway trolley car. More than once she and Flynn had draped a sheet over the windows and painted in the nude. They'd had some of their happiest and most passionate moments speckled with paint.

"I'll cut in," he said as he filled a small bucket with the creamy hue.

She couldn't stop him from helping, but she didn't

have to watch him. She turned her back on him, refilled her roller and resumed her task. Struggling to maintain her focus, she covered another square yard, and then Flynn parked the stepladder beside her and climbed, putting his bare, hair-dusted muscular thighs and firm derriere directly in her line of vision.

She closed her eyes and took a fortifying breath. It was going to be a long night, and sleep…well, it wasn't going to make an appearance anytime soon.

Flynn flexed and stretched in her peripheral vision as he painted along the ceiling. She angled her body away from him, but the smooth ripple of his muscled shoulders and arms pulled her gaze back again and again. Arousal smoldered in her middle. How had they ever managed to get any work done before?

For almost an hour they painted side by side with only the hiss of the brush and the roller breaking the silence. It felt good, like the old days, when simply being in the same room had been enough to keep a smile on her face.

"What made you decide to have a baby now?" Flynn asked after they'd relocated the drop cloth and other paraphernalia to the second wall.

She stalled by refilling the paint tray and then her roller. "CGC is successful. I have time to focus on other things."

"But the real reason is…?"

She should have known she couldn't fool him. "What makes you think there's more to my decision than that?"

"Is something wrong physically to make your clock start ticking with such urgency that you were willing to pick a stranger out of a catalog to father your baby? We both know how unsettled you were not knowing anything about your father."

The concern in his voice touched her. "I'm in perfect health. I wouldn't have a child if I didn't plan to be around to care for it. But I'm tired of coming home to an empty house. With Granny gone…" Loss squeezed her throat, choking off her words. She waited until she had control of her emotions before continuing. "I always wanted a family. Waiting for Mr. Right isn't working, and I refuse to settle for Mr. Right Now."

Wasn't that exactly what she'd agreed to with Flynn? The only difference was she knew he'd be a good father. "And my assistant's daughter started school. Tamara used to bring Angel to work every day. I loved playing with her, and I miss her."

"I missed you after you left."

Surprise snatched her breath. She lowered the roller. "I'm surprised you even noticed I was gone."

His blue eyes locked on hers. "I noticed."

"You didn't come after me. You didn't even call." She winced. She hadn't meant to let that slip.

"Your note said, and I quote, 'Please don't contact me.' I had my pride. And frankly, I was angry."

"Why?"

"Because I expected you to stick it out, 'for better or for worse,' and help me through the rough patch."

Guilt burned in her belly. She wanted to take him in her arms and assure him he hadn't been the problem. But she couldn't. "You left me first, Flynn. Even though we still shared the same address, you abandoned the job you adored and me."

"I didn't have a choice. You did."

Yes, she'd had options. She could have stayed and lost herself. And then she'd have lost him, too. She'd decided it would be better to make a swift, clean break and quit him and the liquor cold turkey. "I had to go."

"Why?"

She shoved her roller across the wall, keeping her gaze fixed on the lines of paint. "Does it really matter? The past is over."

"What are you hiding, Renee?" he said an inch from her ear.

Her muscles snapped tight. If Flynn learned the truth and she wasn't already pregnant, he might refuse to give her the baby she desperately wanted. Her mother was an alcoholic. Renee could have easily become one. Their baby might carry that tendency in its genes. She was flawed and she didn't want Flynn to see her as damaged goods.

She stepped away from the heat of his bare torso under the guise of adding paint to her roller. "You're imagining things. I think I'll work another hour and finish this wall. If you're tired of painting you can head for bed."

"I'm in for the long haul. I always was."

She looked at him and held her tongue. He wouldn't have stuck around if he'd discovered the truth about her. Her mother's long line of lovers had proved time and time again that not even love could conquer the killing effects of alcoholism.

Nine

Over the next two hours Flynn focused on the cadence of Renee's roller strokes, biding his time as he plotted his next move.

As her agitation faded, the sticky sounds of paint application slowed from rapid sweeps to slow and unsteady stabs. In the past ten minutes he could tell her will to get the job done was the only thing moving her exhausted arm.

He lowered his brush and studied the droop of her shoulders. "Let's call it a night."

She startled and turned. "The room needs a second coat."

He put down his brush, crossed the room and pried the roller from her hand. "Let's have breakfast, catch a few hours of sleep and then apply the second coat."

A worry line pleated her brow. "But—"

"Renee, it's 4:00 a.m. We're both starting to lose precision." Like him, she'd always been a perfectionist. She'd understood his spending hours over the details of a blueprint because she could lose herself the same way in a recipe.

She studied the closest wall and a small dime-size spot she'd missed. "I guess so."

He brushed a lock of hair from her tired, violet eyes. "We have the entire weekend ahead of us. Your kitchen will be ready by the time the cabinets arrive on Monday. I promise."

So would the nursery, if he had his way, and Renee would be sleeping in his bed. Permanently. It might take a little finesse, but he would win this time.

"A hot shower would be nice." She rolled her shoulders as if they were stiff, and his fingers flexed in anticipation. But while he'd love to fill a hot bath for her and join her there for a slippery massage, she wasn't ready for that step.

"Go for it. I'll clean up here and get breakfast started."

She panned the painting supplies through eyes only half-open. "Are you sure?"

"I'm sure. Go."

He watched her climb the stairs, admiring her rounded bottom and smooth, pale legs. Renee didn't tan. She never had. She claimed her tone went straight from cream to lobster-red with no in-between. But he didn't care. He'd always loved her ivory skin. Tracing the lines of her breasts, inner arms and belly with his tongue had been one of his favorite pastimes. His groin pulsed at the memory.

Tamping down his unsatisfied need, he quickly put away the painting supplies, then climbed the stairs and washed up. He extracted the food he needed from the fridge and pantry and set to work on what had once been Renee's favorite breakfast. Was it still?

Fate had a twisted sense of humor. He and Renee had traded places. In the past he'd been the one who couldn't quit until a project was finished. Renee had been the one to supply him with food and urge him to rest. Giving up had never been a part of his nature. His fault-finding father had made sure Flynn always aimed for perfection. When he'd fallen short his father had relished pointing out every flaw.

Twenty minutes later the house smelled like cinnamon, melting butter and maple syrup, and Flynn had breakfast waiting on the coffee table when Renee entered the den wearing sweatpants and a T-shirt. She'd put on a bra this time, unfortunately. He'd enjoyed her beaded nipples in the cool basement almost as much as he'd enjoyed the peeks he'd caught her taking at him.

Knowing she was still attracted to him worked in his favor. He planned to agitate the chemistry between them until he achieved the desired reaction.

Her damp curly hair dragged across her shoulders, giving her a sleepy, freshly scrubbed look that called to his tired brain cells like reveille. She inhaled. "Do I smell apple-cinnamon pancakes?"

"You left your recipe card in the drawer."

"I haven't had them in years. Not since—" She bit her lip.

"We made them together?"

"Yes." Their gazes met and the shared memory stretched between them. His "help" in the kitchen had usually been more of a distraction and a hindrance. He'd pass her the ingredients she requested until his hands wandered into more intimate territory and the meals were temporarily put on hold for hot sex.

Her cheeks flushed, and she abruptly averted her face. "And is that coffee?"

"Decaf. We need sleep. You can have the real stuff after our nap."

She lifted a mug from the table and sipped, her eyes closing. "I almost fell asleep in the shower."

"It wouldn't be the first time." A smile tugged his lips. Until Renee he'd never met a woman who could work so hard she'd fall asleep as soon as she stopped moving. He'd caught her dozing in the shower numerous times.

He handed her a plate. "Eat."

"Thanks." She took a bite of pancake. "Mmm. Exactly the right amount of cinnamon."

When they'd cooked the recipe together in the past, the brown sugar and maple syrup had often ended up being licked off bare skin. Their kitchen had seen almost as much action as their bedroom.

Her lids grew heavier as her plate emptied. By the time she finished she was almost asleep sitting up. He took her dish from her and set it back on the coffee table beside his. She started to rise. He caught her hand. "Sit tight while I clear this away."

"Flynn, you don't have to wait on me."

"Consider it my turn."

Her lips parted as if she wanted to argue, but then she nodded and sank deeper into the cushions, almost limp with fatigue. He rose, gathered the breakfast dishes and carried them to the kitchen. He took his time loading them in the dishwasher and then returned to the den. As he'd expected she'd fallen asleep sitting up. He smiled at the success of his strategy, then debated his next move. As soundly as Renee slept, he could carry her upstairs and tuck her in without waking her. But waking in his bed would put her on the defensive.

He sat beside her and eased her over. She sighed, tucked her hands beneath her cheek and settled her head in his lap. Just like the good ol' days. Now all he had to do was convince her to move down the hall to his room and the battle would be all but won.

Someone had put hot rocks on her eyelids, Renee decided as she struggled to cut her way through the fog clouding her brain. And she needed a new pillow. This one was hard. And hot. And the down tickled her nose.

Down? You're allergic to down. Move before your face swells like a red balloon.

She forced her lids open and blinked against the bright sunlight streaming through the windows, trying to clear her vision. Her "pillow" resembled a man's thigh. Flynn's thigh.

Like rocks gaining momentum in an avalanche, her heart bounded into a faster rhythm as the chain of events leading up to her ending up with her face in Flynn's lap replayed on her mental movie screen.

The hands on the antique clock across the room pointed to noon. She must have fallen asleep after eating. This wasn't the first time she and Flynn had napped together on this sofa. But that was then. Now she had to be more careful. She knew how disastrous falling into a false sense of security with him could be, which was why she hadn't wanted to completely relax her guard and sleep in his bed.

Holding her breath and trying not to wake him, she

eased upright and stood. His bare chest continued rising and falling evenly. Flynn looked peaceful and relaxed tipped into the corner of the sofa with his dark lashes fanning his cheeks and the lines of stress smoothed away. A lock of hair fell across his forehead. The urge to comb her fingers through the lush strands and brush them back almost overcame her caution.

She turned away from the temptation. A piece of paper on the end table beside his lamp had caught her eye. Her slowly waking brain identified a drawing on the back of an envelope. She lifted it and her breath caught.

Flynn had sketched out a baby's nursery complete with a crib and mobile dangling above it, the dresser and even the toy box. She'd shown him the photo she'd taken of the furniture with her cell phone, and he'd accurately depicted the details in excruciating detail.

There was no mistaking which room of the house he'd placed the furniture in. Her room. The French doors leading to the balcony gave it away.

Flynn had always been a talented artist, but he'd usually limited his drawings to architectural designs. Though most of his work had been done on a computer, he'd liked to pick up a pencil when working out the rough idea.

She stroked a finger over the curving runner of a rocking horse, and emotion clogged her throat. Looking at this, she could almost believe he wanted a baby as much as she did. A baby who might have his ink-dark hair and bright blue eyes. A precious little boy or girl that would give her the family they'd once planned to share.

A hollow ache swelled in her chest. She wanted Flynn's baby probably more now than she had the first time around. And then, anger had filled the emptiness. Flynn loved to draw, to envision, to create. His misplaced loyalty to his family had robbed him of that joy. Why did he insist on denying his gift? It wasn't as if his selfish mother appreciated his sacrifice, and his father—

"What do you think?" he asked in a rough, groggy, sexier-than-sin voice.

Her pulse sprinted. She studied his beard-stubbled, sleepy-eyed face. It would be so easy to love him again. But she couldn't.

"It's beautiful."

"We can do it, Renee—have our home and family the way we once planned."

The strength of yearning for what he offered scared her so badly she grasped for mental and physical distance. "Why did you do it, Flynn?"

He eased upright in a slow flexing of muscles. "Do what?"

"Give up your dream."

He rose and towered over her, scowling. "We've been over this before."

"It pains me to see you deny your talent with a number-crunching job. I understood when you stepped in during the crisis. Your family needed you. But what about now? The crisis is over. Why can't Brock hire another VP and let you return to your dream job?"

His frown deepened. "It's not as simple as that."

"It could be."

"I never finished my internship."

"It would take less than a year to get all of your certifications."

"I'm not a college kid anymore." Shoulders tight, he headed toward the stairs.

"Denying your passion for architecture won't bring your father back, Flynn," she called after him.

He flinched as if she'd hit him, then pivoted abruptly and charged back toward her, stopping only inches away. He glared down at her. "Why do you care?"

Good question. Why did his happiness matter when she planned to get as far away from him as possible as soon as she had what she wanted from him?

The wall blocking what she'd been trying to deny shattered like glass. She realized it mattered because she was still in love with her husband.

Mentally reeling, she tried to find a safe response. "I don't want my child raised by a bitter, unhappy parent."

"I'm not your mother."

She winced at the accuracy of his barb. "No. You're not."

I won't let myself be, either.

But like Flynn had said, it wasn't as simple as wishing and making it so. Avoiding her mother's mistakes would take constant vigilance.

"I'm going to finish painting." She left him because she was very afraid he'd guess her secrets.

Renee stared up at Gretchen Mahoney's Knob Hill home late Sunday morning. While she admired the ornate architecture and beauty of the exquisitely maintained house, she had no desire to live in such formal surroundings.

This was the type of house Carol Maddox wanted her son to occupy. Instead, Flynn had chosen a diamond-in-the-rough residence and an even less polished wife. Two strikes against Renee in Carol's book.

Renee rang the bell and braced herself to face Flynn's

"friend" who had insisted on a Sunday-morning interview. Despite Renee's questions, Flynn had refused to share any more details about his relationship with the woman. Perhaps she was an acquaintance of his mother who lived in the same posh neighborhood, or a client he knew through work. Maybe she was the wife of an old friend.

The front door opened, revealing a gorgeous, willowy thirty-something brunette in four-inch heels and the kind of designer-chic suit that graced *Vogue* magazine covers. She looked Renee up and down with curiosity-filled olive-green eyes framed by sleek curtains of hair. "You must be Flynn's wife. I'm Gretchen. Come in."

Renee's fingers tightened on her leather portfolio as uneasiness swarmed down her spine and buzzed in the pit of her stomach like a hive of angry bees. "Yes, I'm Renee Maddox."

"According to Flynn, you are exactly what I need for my little soiree." Gretchen led Renee through an immense black-and-white, marble-tiled foyer with a massive staircase and an equally sizable floral arrangement to a formal living room filled with antique furniture and more expensive bouquets.

"Please have a seat." Her hostess flicked a hand toward a white French provincial chair—a ringless left hand. Not the wife of an acquaintance, then.

Was this woman Flynn's lover? Renee sat and tried to focus on the job ahead, but not knowing exactly who Gretchen was or what she was to Flynn made concentrating difficult.

She opened her notebook. "Flynn didn't tell me what kind of event you needed catered. What did you have in mind?"

"Getting right to business, are we? No chitchat?"

Renee blinked. Usually clients with this kind of wealth didn't want to mingle with the lowly help. "I'm sorry. I understood this was a rush job and that you were eager to nail down the details."

"It is and I am. My usual caterer had a heart attack last week and is unable to work."

"I'm sorry. That leaves you in a tight spot. Let's begin with the type of event, the mood you'd like to set and then work our way toward budgets."

Perfectly arched black eyebrows hiked. "Aren't you even a little curious about me? I confess I've been quite curious about you."

Renee didn't know whether to admire the woman for her candor or hate her for being beautiful, rich and poised—all the things Renee was not.

"As a prospective client, you have a right to your questions."

"I only have one question. Do you realize how badly you hurt Flynn when you left?"

Renee stiffened at the personal attack. "Perhaps I should qualify that by saying questions pertaining to my résumé."

Radiating protectiveness rather than malice, Gretchen leaned back in her chair and crossed her endlessly long legs. "Did you ever consider the gossip he'd face after you disappeared? The explanations he'd have to make?"

The woman's audacity amazed Renee. But Gretchen did have a point. After Renee had fled to L.A., she'd tried not to think about Flynn or the mess she'd left behind. She'd thrown herself into a new job and into caring for her grandmother, trying to exhaust herself each day so she could sleep at night—without the booze to help her relax. She'd firmly believed Flynn would be better off without her than with a wife who would become a liability, and she still adhered to that opinion.

"Flynn isn't the make-excuses type." Determined to get this meeting back on a business footing, she clicked her pen. "Do you have a preferred theme for your event?"

"Reputation is everything in advertising. You damaged Flynn's," Gretchen insisted, ignoring Renee's question.

"Ms. Mahoney, could we please stick with business? Unless your party was only a ruse to get me here and harass me, my personal life is really not relative to the service I offer."

"If you believe that, then you're sadly mistaken. In this competitive market, it's not just what you do, but who you know and who you've pleased or crossed in the past. But we'll play this your way. For now."

She slid an embossed invitation across the table. "As you can see I'm hosting a silent auction in my home to raise money for the local women's shelter. The shelter is a place near and dear to my heart."

"It's a worthy cause."

"My second husband rescued me from there."

Surprised, Renee didn't know what to say. Gretchen didn't look like the typical victim of abuse Renee had in her head.

"Once I found the courage to quit hiding my bruises and admit I had a problem, I escaped from my first husband with the help of friends I could count on. Flynn was one of those friends. He's a wonderful man. Supportive. Understanding. I would have married him in an instant—after my second husband died, that is. But a part of Flynn would never have been mine. That part still belongs to you."

Renee's heart stalled and her hand froze, pen clutched above paper. "You're mistaken."

"There are few things in life that I won't share, but my man tops that list."

Alarm skittered down Renee's spine. "Are you warning me off?"

"No. I'm advising you not to hurt Flynn again. He deserves better."

"Better meaning you?"

"Better meaning a woman who is strong enough to honor her commitment to him and not run when the going gets tough."

Anger and shame blended inside Renee. By running away without giving an explanation, she'd left the door open for everyone to think badly of her. She'd thought it better to let people assume the worst, rather than stay, become a drunk and confirm it. She hadn't considered her departure might cast Flynn in a negative light.

With hindsight she realized what she considered an act of self*less*ness could be construed as one of self*ish*ness by others. But admitting that to her hostess would be like handing a possible rival ammunition.

"You're judging me based on something of which you have no knowledge."

"I'm not judging you at all, Renee. I'm merely letting you know I'll be watching. All of Flynn's friends will be. And if you hurt him again, you'll find it very difficult to make a success of your catering business in San Francisco."

After delivering her threat, Gretchen uncrossed her legs and sat forward, the enmity in her eyes changing to excitement. "Now, about my little get-together, I have sixty of San Francisco's wealthiest citizens confirmed

for this Friday night. I want them feeling happy and generous. What do you suggest?"

Head reeling at the about-face, Renee mentally adjusted from defense to offense. She wanted to tell Ms.
Mahoney to stuff her party right up her designer-clad
behind. But she couldn't. She had a business to market,
and she couldn't afford to let a verbal skirmish throw
her off her game.

But her confrontation with Gretchen made one thing
very clear. She had two choices. One: give up on the
baby and expansion ideas and retreat before loving
Flynn destroyed her. Two: she could fight her demons,
charge ahead and try to win back her husband and the
life they'd once dreamed of sharing.

From her perspective either choice could be poten-
tially disastrous, but only one offered a reward.

She studied the beautiful, poised woman in front of
her. If Gretchen had taken back her life and refused to
be a victim, could Renee be any less courageous?

No. She'd kept her drinking issue under control since
that turning-point night, and she would continue to do
so. Flynn would never have to know.

Ten

Juggling three bags of groceries containing the ingredients for a special dinner consisting of Flynn's favorites, Renee climbed the front steps to the Victorian with a signed contract and a sizable deposit for her first San Francisco event in the leather portfolio swinging from her shoulder.

Deciding to try to rebuild the relationship she'd once shared with Flynn had filled her with energy that not even two stressful hours of planning a short-notice event could take away. During her time with her client, Renee had been forced to admit she wouldn't blame Flynn if he'd had an intimate relationship with the woman after his wife had left him.

Gretchen was smart, creative and, apparently, wielded a lot of clout in the wealthy social circles. She was the type of woman Carol Maddox had wanted her son to marry, and not just because of Gretchen's deceased husband's extreme wealth, but because Gretchen had been born into the same social stratum. With women like that waiting in the wings, Renee knew she had to act now.

Despite the competition, she was looking forward to Friday, to working Gretchen's party and proving to San Francisco's snobs that California Girl's Catering had the right stuff.

Renee let herself in the front door and pocketed her keys. Splatters of red on the floor stopped her. A trail of rose petals led up the staircase.

Her heart pumped harder, making her almost lightheaded with excitement. The Flynn she'd fallen in love with had made another appearance. God, she'd missed him and missed having someone to play with, to talk to and plan with. With sudden clarity she realized that's why her attempts to find Mr. Right had failed. None of her dates had understood her the way Flynn had. He got her need to create with food because he shared the same need, only his method of expression was blueprints. Each of them relished seeing something go from an abstract idea to concrete reality.

Despite everything, could the rose petals mean he still cared? Flynn had claimed he wanted her to stay, but he hadn't said he loved her.

Impatient to discover the answer, she dumped the groceries and her briefcase on the credenza and then followed the petal-strewn path. Her body hummed with anticipation. What would she find at the top of those stairs?

Similar incidents from the past rushed forward, crowding her brain with a smorgasbord of happy, sexy, tender and delicious memories of the claw-foot tub with bubbles and petals floating on the surface and Flynn waiting to be her personal bath attendant, a sexy new black cocktail dress with sinful matching lingerie and dancing shoes and Flynn struggling with the bow tie of his tux as he exited the bathroom. Or maybe she'd find Flynn, naked and hungry for her in their bed.

Scratch that thought. The roses turned away from the master suite and led to the closed door of the guest room—her room. Was he waiting in her bed?

"Flynn?"

"In here."

She pushed open her door. The ruby-speckled path led to Flynn, seated by the French doors on the only piece of furniture remaining in the room. Even the rugs had been stripped from the polished hardwood floors. He rose and stepped aside, revealing a wooden rocking chair.

"You'll need this when the baby arrives." He curved his fingers over the high back and stroked the smooth wood. "The man who made the baby furniture made this."

"Where is everything else?" She waved a hand to indicate the empty room.

"I moved your clothes to our room and the bedroom suite upstairs."

A big step, but she was okay with that. "By yourself?"

"Brock helped."

When she'd discovered the roses, she'd expected seduction and sex. Hot, steamy sex. Instead, Flynn had given her something better—a concrete visual of the future within their grasp.

He thumped a knuckle on the hand-carved back of the rocker. "Try it out."

She crossed the room and sank into the chair. The wood, retaining the warmth of Flynn's body, embraced her. Her fingers stroked the glossy armrests. This was where she'd sit and nurse their baby, where she'd rock her son or daughter to sleep. A rush of emotion squeezed her chest.

"It's beautiful, Flynn. I love it. Thank you."

His lips brushed the top of her head, then he circled and knelt in front of her. "Happy Valentine's Day."

Her breath caught. "I forgot all about the holiday. I'm sorry, I didn't get you anything."

"You're here where you belong. That's all I need." He pulled her from the chair and into his arms. His mouth teased hers tenderly at first and then with intensifying passion that made her blood race.

Yes, she was where she belonged. And she would make their marriage work this time. A bond was only as strong as its weakest link, and she would not be that weak link. She would be strong for Flynn and for their baby.

Flynn felt Renee's capitulation clear down to his bones. Her lips moved with his, her supple body melted against him, and her nails dug into his waist, pulling him closer.

Adrenaline shot through him. He'd won.

He wanted to celebrate his success in an act of making love that had nothing to do with making a baby. He swept her into his arms and carried her down the hall. Without breaking the kiss, he laid her in the center of the bed and followed her down.

Her arms slid from his neck to his chest. She tugged at his shirt as if eager to be skin to skin with him—the way she used to. But something was different. There was an urgency to her frantic movements that went beyond hunger.

She hiked his shirttail, slid her hands beneath the fabric and went straight for his erogenous zones, tracing the underside of his arms, along his rib cage, the small of his back, his hipbones. He sucked in a sharp breath when her fingertips dipped into his waistband and hunger overrode his curiosity.

He shrugged off his shirt and then swept her sweater over her head. Her nipples showed clearly through the lace of her white bra. Propping himself on an elbow, he bent and captured one peachy tip. Her scent filled his lungs and the lace abraded his tongue. He raked her puckered flesh with his teeth, tugging gently then sucking. She rewarded him with a soft "Mmm."

She cradled his head with one hand. The other worked the button and zipper of his khaki pants, and then she slid her hand inside his open fly, cupping, then stroking his erection. Desire pulsed through him, making him harder, hotter and impatient to sink into her wetness.

He rolled away from her talented hands, knelt and quickly stripped her skirt down her legs. He paused long enough to admire her white bikini panties and then those and her bra had to go, leaving her in nothing but glistening golden curls and her black heels.

Like a cat, she rolled into a kneeling position and reached for him. He evaded her grasp long enough to stand by the side of the bed and shuck the remainder of his clothing under her hungry gaze. Her palms splayed on her thighs and her full breasts called for attention. Blue-violet eyes scrolled over him and she licked her lips. His pulse rate doubled.

Why had no other woman ever affected him as strongly as Renee did? And how the hell could Renee have walked away from this as if it didn't matter? As if *he* didn't matter.

"Make love with me, Flynn. I need you. Here." Her

husky whisper followed by her fingers gliding down her torso, combing through her curls and covering what he yearned for demolished his anger and any chance he had of taking it slow.

He craved the taste of her. Lunging forward, he feasted on her mouth, her neck, her breasts, belly and navel, then finally reached her nectar. No one tasted like Renee, and no one other than her had been able to satisfy his need.

He licked, sucked and nibbled her until her cries filled his ears and her spasming body arched off the bed. He wanted to be unselfish, to bring her to orgasm multiple times, but he had to be inside her. *Now.* Palming her bottom, he lifted her. Her fingers curled around his erection, stroking him, then guiding him. He slid into her wet, welcoming warmth, and his muscles locked as he fought for control and savored the feel of her.

Her internal muscles gripped him and her fingers, digging into his butt, urged him to move. He couldn't resist. He pumped harder and faster, her slickness easing his way.

Her hands rushed over his body, as if urgently mapping his muscles, then her nails skimmed his nipples. Jaw-clenching bolts of pleasure shot through him. He tried to focus on her, on her soft gasps, on the jiggle of her full breasts with each hard thrust, on finding and caressing her center.

He lost it. His climax exploded, sending shards of ecstasy through his body.

One corner of his mind registered Renee's cries as she joined him, and along with repletion, the sense of coming home, of finally being where he belonged, overwhelmed him.

Lungs bellowing, he eased down beside her. Not knowing the reason she'd left the first time meant he couldn't prevent her leaving again. The lack of control unsettled him.

Then he rolled onto his back and stared at the ceiling. Renee shifted, hooking her thigh over his and her arm over his torso. She'd always been a snuggler. He held her close, savoring the melding of their damp bodies. He should have gotten over her. Any self-respecting man would have. And he had tried. But Renee was the only person he'd ever known who'd understood his need to create and encouraged him to follow his dream of becoming an architect when even his family cursed his choice.

Her fingers walked a path up his abdomen to his chest. She drew a shape over his left pectoral. A heart. Another blast from the past. They used to write messages on each other's skin.

"I love you, Flynn. I always have."

Her breathless declaration sent his heart slamming into his ribs beneath her hand. He turned his head, met her gaze and saw her words reflected in her gaze. He wanted to believe her, but doubts nagged at him. "Then why did you leave?"

Tension invaded her muscles and her fist clenched on his chest. Her eyes turned evasive, long lashes descending to shield her thoughts. "I didn't want to. But I had to. Please, *please* believe I thought my getting out of your life was the best thing for everyone concerned."

He couldn't blindly believe without facts. Not this time. "What happened, Renee?"

She pulled away, tugging the edge of the comforter with her as she climbed from the bed. "I—I had to go, okay? That's all I can say."

"Was there someone else?" He voiced the words that had been lurking in his subconscious—words he'd been trying to ignore.

Her shock appeared genuine. "No. Oh, no. Never. I loved you. Only you, Flynn."

He rose and faced her across the mattress. "I need more of an explanation than that."

She bit her lip. "You'll have to take my word for it. I love you, and I'll love our baby…if there is one."

"And if there isn't?"

"You said yourself we'd keep trying. I want to be with you, Flynn. I want everything we once planned. The family, the house, the fenced yard, the dog. All of it. And I want it with you. But you have to trust me."

Trust her. She had no idea how much she was asking. He'd counted on her before and she'd let him down. Did he dare risk making the same mistake twice?

High on satisfaction, Renee hummed a tune as she packed up her cooking utensils in Gretchen's kitchen Friday night.

The week with Flynn had been just short of heavenly. The nursery was perfect with its new furniture and pale mint paint. CGC's new quarters were finished and beautiful. And life with Flynn…

Renee wanted to do a happy dance. Their relationship was almost back to where it had been before his father died. He hadn't said he loved her yet, but there had been tenderness in his eyes and in every gesture. That had to mean something.

She lifted the box of utensils, noting as the edge pressed against her that her breasts were tender. Her pulse quickened. Was she pregnant? Or was the soreness a symptom of her monthly visitor, which was due any day now? Was it too soon to do a pregnancy test?

Eager to get home to Flynn and tell him how well CGC's entry into the San Francisco market had gone, she set the box of her belongings down near the servants' entrance and glanced at her watch. The event should be over in a matter of minutes. Tack on cleanup time and she should be home around one. She hoped Flynn would be up.

The kitchen door swung open. Mindy, one of Renee's three temporary workers, rushed in. Her tuxedo-skirt ensemble still looked as fresh as it had when she'd started her shift three hours ago, but the woman looked frazzled.

Mindy set the serving tray on the counter. "Red wine spill on the living room rug."

"I'll get it." Renee jumped into action, grabbing a bottle of club soda and a rag. She'd spent the entire evening in the kitchen preparing food and refilling trays. She seized the opportunity to do a walk-through and made her way toward the designated area.

Only a dozen or so of the expensively dressed and perfumed guests lingered, most of whom had spilled out the open doors on the far side of the room and into the conservatory. A massive flower arrangement on the top of the closed grand piano partially obscured Renee's view.

She spotted the stain and knelt. The club soda fizzled as she poured, diluting the red wine and bringing it to the surface of the expensive Aubusson carpet. She blotted and repeated the procedure.

"You simply must tell me how you managed to find a caterer of this caliber at the last minute," a familiar voice said, stopping Renee mid-blot.

Flynn's mother was here. Renee grimaced. Dislike

curdled in her stomach, overshadowing the compliment. Facing the witch would kill the buzz of a successful night.

"Carol, you know I never divulge my secrets," Gretchen replied.

The women paused on the opposite side of the piano just inside the open doors. The only parts of them Renee could see from her position were their thousand-dollar shoes and legs below the hems of their cocktail dresses. That meant they couldn't see her, either.

"I must hire him for my next event. The food and presentation were absolutely superb," Carol continued.

Pride filled Renee's chest. The menu she and Gretchen had chosen had turned out exquisitely, if she did say so herself.

"I'll pass on your compliments," Gretchen replied.

"You might as well stop playing games. You know I'll find out who you used. I have my ways." Carol's tone sounded more threatening than teasing.

"You are extremely well-connected, and if my caterer wishes to make your acquaintance, I'll give her your contact information and let her get in touch."

Renee debated staying hidden while she blotted up the last of the spill, but skulking behind furniture to avoid unpleasant people wasn't her way. Not anymore. Seven years ago it would have been—a fact Carol Maddox had used to her advantage.

On the other hand, Renee owed Gretchen her loyalty for taking a chance on her, but building her business would be impossible if she didn't get her name out.

The expensive heels moved in her direction, taking the decision out of her hands. She would not be on her knees in front of her mother-in-law. She rose. "Good evening, Carol."

Her mother-in-law's shocked eyes fixed on Renee like laser beams. Despite Carol's chemically paralyzed face, her distaste couldn't be clearer. She took in Renee's crisp white chef's uniform and her lip actually twitched in a sneer. "Hired help now, are you?"

Renee bit the inside of her lip on the waspish comment that came to mind. She wouldn't stoop to Carol's level. "Yes. I'm the help you're so desperate to identify. I catered the party tonight. Thank you for your compliments."

She reached into her pocket and withdrew a newly printed business card and offered it to her mother-in-law.

Carol lifted her chin, turned on her heel and stalked away—without the card.

"Why does her rudeness not surprise me?" Renee asked rhetorically.

"She is a witch," Gretchen confirmed. "But she's an influential one. Getting on her bad side isn't a good idea."

"I've been on Carol's hate list since the day Flynn brought me home to meet the family eight and a half years ago."

Gretchen made a sympathetic moue. "The only reason I'm not on the same list is because my family could buy and sell her ten times over, and since I now control all that lovely money…" She shrugged and glanced over her shoulder. "Let me share a little something I learned from being an abused wife. People can only make you feel inferior if you let them."

Renee identified the paraphrased quote. "Eleanor Roosevelt."

"Yes. I've learned to hold my head high—especially when the sharks are circling in the water. And make no mistake about it, Carol Maddox is a shark. If she smells blood in the water, she will attack from your weakest side, and she won't be particularly concerned about collateral damage."

A frisson raced over Renee, but Gretchen wasn't telling her anything she didn't already know. "I'll keep that in mind."

But she wasn't going to let Carol's snobbery dampen her good mood. Instead, Renee planned to focus on her successes and her future with Flynn.

"You exceeded my expectations for tonight, Renee. I enjoyed working with you, and you literally saved my event, and because of that I raised a lot of cash for the shelter. Leave as many business cards as you brought with you. I'll see that they end up in the right hands." With a nod, Gretchen returned to her guests.

Renee smiled. Apart from her mother-in-law, life was just about perfect right now, and Renee wasn't going to let anything or anyone ruin it for her this time, not even Carol Maddox.

Renee stuffed the party leftovers in the refrigerator and closed the door.

Bedtime.

It was just after one in the morning and she should be exhausted, but she was still too keyed up to sleep.

She couldn't help feeling a teensy bit deflated. She wanted to share her excitement with Flynn, but the lights had been off upstairs when she'd pulled into the driveway fifteen minutes ago, which meant Flynn was probably asleep. But mostly, she'd wanted to thank him for making tonight happen with his calls to Gretchen and the employment agency.

She crossed to the laundry room, stripped off her uniform and dropped it into the washer. Rolling her tense shoulders, she returned to the kitchen and jerked to a stop. Flynn waited with one hip parked against the counter. He wore nothing but his boxers.

She took in his gorgeous physique and her mouth watered. "Did I wake you?"

His eyes raked her nakedness. "Trust me, even if you had, the view is well worth the trip downstairs. I was waiting for you. I wanted to hear about your night."

She grinned. "The event went well. I have leftovers in the fridge if you're hungry."

"Maybe later. I have other plans for you."

The glint in his eyes made her heart trip. "Care to elaborate?"

"Come upstairs and find out." He extended his hand.

Desire coiled inside her belly as she laid her palm across his. Flynn jerked her close. Their bodies slapped together. He pressed a quick hard kiss on her lips and then drew back. Looking her up and down, hunger evident in his eyes and in the bulge rising in his briefs, he shook his head as if denying himself and then led her upstairs.

"Flynn, thank you for tonight," she said as she climbed. "None of this would have happened if you hadn't called Gretchen."

"You're welcome."

When she reached the landing she heard water running. In the bedroom she smelled her favorite bath salts. And then in the bathroom, she spotted the steaming claw-foot tub.

Flynn's hands landed on her shoulders. He pulled her back flush against his front. "Just as I expected. Your muscles are knotted. Nights on the town always jazzed you up before. I thought you might need to unwind. Remember how we used to end most party nights in here?"

The memories of sexy shared baths combined with his teeth grazing the curve of her shoulder made her shiver. "Yes. Does that mean you're going to join me?"

She felt his smile against her neck. "Not this time. You soak and give me a replay of the night. I'll play masseur and enjoy the view."

She tested the water and then climbed into the tub. Flynn lathered his hands and then sat on a vanity stool he'd placed behind her head. He gently dug his thumbs into her tense neck muscles, rubbing out the kinks until she sighed.

"That feels wonderful."

"Relax." He pressed a kiss on her ear and kneaded her shoulders. "I hope tonight is just the beginning of a new successful venture, but if it takes a while to get CGC off the ground, that's okay. There's nothing we can't handle if you level with me."

She knew he still wondered why she'd run seven years ago. She'd caught him watching her with a question in his eyes several times. She yearned to confess. But she said nothing. Flynn hated weakness as much as she did. He'd once claimed he'd stand by her, and he would because he was an honorable guy. But he'd lose respect for her if he learned the truth. She couldn't bear watching his love die again. The first time had nearly destroyed her.

Eleven

Flynn caught himself sketching on his blotter again Monday afternoon—this time a miniature version of the Victorian complete with a lookout tower turret—a fort/playhouse for his and Renee's children.

Children. He didn't even know if she was pregnant yet and he was already thinking in multiples. He found her confident, ambitious persona far sexier than her younger, eager-to-please version had been.

He raked a hand over his jaw and tried to refocus on the columns of numbers in front of him, but Madd Comm's rivalry with Golden Gate Promotions couldn't hold his attention.

Since Renee's return he'd had a hard time maintaining his interest in the Maddox bottom line. His mind flicked back to Friday night. When he'd heard Renee's van enter the driveway after Gretchen's party, he hadn't been able to wait for her to come upstairs. He'd wanted to share her enthusiasm—or her disappointment. The bath he'd run for her had ended with a hot make-out session followed by leftover hors d'oeuvres eaten in bed while she told him about the event.

The fire of excitement in her eyes while she'd talked had reminded him of the woman he'd fallen in love with so long ago and of what he'd stripped from her the first time around. Asking her to live without a creative outlet was the same as asking her to live without air. He knew that now. No wonder she'd left him.

Like him, Renee needed to feel pride in her accomplishments. By making her a homebody, he'd limited her outlets.

His door burst open and his brother stormed in. "Have you seen this?"

Brock held a newspaper opened to the society, aka gossip, page.

"I don't read that crap. I'm surprised you do."

"Shelby brought it to my attention. You might reconsider reading it since you, your wife and Maddox Communications are mentioned."

Flynn's senses went on red alert. "Judging by your tone, I take it the article isn't a positive recap of Renee's Friday-night catering job."

"Far from it."

Flynn took the paper and skimmed the page looking for what had sent Brock into orbit.

Ad Agency's Top Gun Shoots Blanks?

The headline hit him like a sucker punch. He gritted his teeth and read on.

What's a thirty-something woman to do when her biological clock starts ticking and she can't find suitable daddy material? Renee Landers Maddox, wife of Flynn Maddox, VP of Maddox Communications, reportedly took matters into her own hands recently and visited a local sperm bank. Rumor has it she petitioned for a deposit made by her estranged husband, but that deposit was destroyed. Now she and hubby claim to be reconciling. Meanwhile she has launched a branch of her catering business in L.A. out of his Pacific Heights basement.

Is this a case of home-is-where-the-heart-is or just a form of direct deposit? If Maddox's VP is faking his marriage, what else is he faking? Stay tuned. But I wouldn't suggest hiring California Girl's Catering with a party date of nine months from now, since Mr. and Mrs. Maddox have already purchased nursery furniture.

Flynn wanted to rip the gossip rag to shreds. But that wouldn't solve the problem. "Renee doesn't need this when she's trying to get CGC off the ground."

"Is it true? She tried to get your sperm bank deposit?"

"That is nobody's business but ours, Brock."

"It's my business if it affects Maddox Communications. And that column slanders Maddox Communications, too."

"Who in the hell would make a personal attack like this?"

"I only know one person who stands to gain if Maddox looks shady, and he happens to fight dirty."

Flynn didn't need a genius IQ to follow Brock's line of thought. "Athos Koteas? But why target Renee?"

"Because she's your weak spot. You didn't answer my question. Is your reconciliation a sham? Is she back just for a kid?"

He owed his brother the truth. "Our reunion started out that way when the clinic contacted me about Renee requesting my sample. That's why I asked about the divorce papers, and then I subsequently found out we were still married. Renee agreed to move back in if I'd father her child. But our marriage isn't a pretense anymore."

Brock cursed and strode to the window. "How many people knew about that stupid college prank?"

"Only family and the other fraternity guys involved, but they made deposits, too. Outing me would also bring their parts in the stupid bet to light." Flynn tapped his pen on his blotter. "If we have a leak in the office, the perpetrator could have gotten the info from my office. The sperm bank faxed forms to me here. I kept copies just in case something went wrong."

Brock cursed. "There is no 'if' we have a spy. Someone at Maddox is feeding proprietary information to Koteas."

"If it is Koteas." Flynn didn't know why Renee had left him the first time. Would this embarrassment be enough to send her running again? He had to fix this before that happened. But how? "I don't want Renee to find out about this."

Brock pivoted, his mouth agape. "It's a paper with a circulation of tens of thousands. You can't buy and burn every copy or keep people who've already read the column from talking."

"I need to get Renee out of town until the scandal blows over. No. Scratch that. She'll want to be here to take calls and make appointments for CGC."

"You could try to get the rag to print a retraction."

Flynn scanned the damning words again. They didn't sound any better the second time. "Technically, nothing they've printed is untrue."

The intercom on his desk buzzed. "A reporter from the *San Francisco Journal* is on line one," Cammie said. "He wants to ask you about a sperm bank?"

Reporters. Damn. "Hold all my calls. And, Cammie, don't talk to any reporters. I'm going out."

"Now?" Brock asked.

Flynn scrubbed his knotting neck muscles and rose. "I'm going to talk to Koteas. If I leave now he may still be in his office."

"What good will talking to that bastard do?"

"I don't know, but I have to do something. Or I might lose Renee again."

"Lay off my wife," Flynn growled at Athos Koteas across the man's wide desk.

The seventy-year-old founder of Golden Gate Promotions laid down the paper Flynn had thrust at him, leaned back in his massive leather chair and cracked an amused smile.

"Aah. Children. They are both a blessing and a curse. We have such high hopes for them when they are born. But my three sons—" he shook his head "—they are useless. You, on the other hand, have no interest in advertising, but like a good son, you joined your father's firm when duty called."

That duty had cost him his marriage, and then Flynn

realized Koteas knew too much about him. But that wasn't why Flynn was here. He was here because the damned reporter had refused to divulge her source when Flynn had called on his way to Golden Gate's offices. He'd had to go with his original suspect.

"Why target my wife?"

"As much as I would like to take credit for that interesting tale, I cannot. I do not waste my time on tabloids."

Flynn studied the man's heavily lined face and steady dark eyes and found no evidence that Koteas lied. "No one else stands to gain from this story."

"Are you sure? Think harder, Mr. Maddox. Everyone has enemies, including your lovely wife."

Who could dislike Renee?

"Good luck finding the viper in your nest," Koteas added.

In your nest.

Flynn clenched his teeth as his thoughts raced ahead. He had a suspicion who that poisonous snake might be. Someone who had made Renee's life difficult since the day Flynn had first brought her home.

His mother.

She wasn't pregnant.

Renee's knees buckled under the weight of disappointment. She sank into the new rocking chair and pushed off with her toe. But the repetitive back-and-forth motion didn't soothe her. She'd come so close to having everything she'd once dreamed of with Flynn.

She wanted him here, wanted his arms around her and his assurances that they could try again. Her need for him was stupid really. She was used to standing on her own feet. But she needed a sympathetic shoulder, and he was the only one who would understand and be as disappointed as she was over the negative pregnancy test.

She pulled her cell phone from her pocket and dialed his private work number. Voice mail picked up. She hung up and tried his assistant's number. "Flynn Maddox's office, Cammie speaking. How may I help you?"

"Cammie, it's Renee. I need to talk to Flynn."

"Hello, Renee. Flynn's out. I'm not sure if he'll be back today. May I take a message?"

This wasn't news he needed to hear secondhand. "No. I'll call his cell phone."

She disconnected and dialed his cell. No answer. She tried again and still received no response. She checked the new teddy-bear clock on the nursery wall. Almost five. He should be home soon.

Until then, she would hang tight and wait. The flashback to the past and waiting for Flynn to come home kinked her muscles. But this time was different. She wouldn't turn to the bottle.

She was stronger now. She had too much to lose. And she'd learned her lesson.

Hadn't she?

"What in the hell were you thinking?" Flynn asked his mother Monday evening in the living room of her lavish Knob Hill house.

She broke eye contact and fussed with her diamond earring. "You have no proof I spoke to that reporter."

"You knew about my college prank. You dislike Renee, and your driver took you to meet the reporter at Chez Mari Saturday afternoon. How much more proof do I need?"

His mother's taxidermy-tight face blanched. "Renee Landers is not good enough for you."

Anger roared through him like a canyon fire. "Maddox, mother. Renee Maddox." He enjoyed her flinch. "She's the woman I married and the one who will be having your grandchildren. That's all that matters."

"What matters is that you end this marriage before she gets her hooks into you by tying you down with her low-class, white-trash brats. I only spoke to the columnist because I wanted Renee to leave. I had hoped she'd realize she's an embarrassment and a liability to you and Madd—"

His teeth slammed together. How had he missed this vicious enmity before? "Renee is not an embarrassment or a liability. She is the only person who puts my happiness above her own."

And that had always been the case, which made her leaving seven years ago all that much more intriguing. Had she left out of some misguided belief he'd be better off without her?

"You're wrong, Flynn. I want you to be happy, and finding a suitable wife will make you happy."

"As happy as your marriage made you?"

His mother's chin jerked up. "I don't know what you mean."

"Did you ever love my father? If you did I never saw signs of it. You tolerated him because he bankrolled your spending habits. You gave him children not because of any maternal urge, but only because it was expected of you, and children guaranteed Dad would continue supporting you financially."

"That's not true."

He didn't bother to argue. He knew the facts. The

memories of growing up in a cold, unloving household were too vivid to forget. No wonder his father had spent all his time at the office.

Flynn hadn't known love until Renee had chiseled down his walls and forced her way into his heart with her humor, intelligence and generosity.

"Think very carefully before you make your choice, Mother."

"What are you saying?"

"Either you apologize to Renee, or you say good-bye to me. I'll walk out that door and we're through."

"Don't be ridiculous, Flynn. I'm your mother."

"A fact that brings me nothing but shame at the moment. I knew you were unhappy, but I didn't realize you'd become a bitter, vindictive old woman."

Ignoring her gasp, he turned on his heel and stormed out of the house. He needed his wife. Only Renee's kisses could heal the wound of dealing with a parent who would stab him in the back.

Eight o'clock. Flynn was late.

Renee stared at the kitchen counters laden with cookies, a pie and quiche. She'd needed a way to deal with her agitation—an outlet other than drinking.

Flynn hadn't called and his cell phone dumped straight to voice mail. The hospitals had no reports of anyone matching his description being brought in. She knew. She'd called all the local emergency rooms. Twice. Her stomach burned from nerves.

She had to admit Flynn's well-stocked liquor cabinet was tempting. Drinking herself into oblivion and not having to worry would certainly be easier than concocting new recipes and walking the floor. But she resisted.

She wasn't her mother. She'd developed better coping skills for dealing with her problems than numbing them out. She cooked. She cleaned. If all else failed she read cooking magazines online.

She heard a key turn in the front door and her pulse jumped like a runner hearing the starter's pistol. Wiping her hands on a towel, she raced down the hall and reached the foyer as Flynn entered. Anger combined with worry and grief tangled inside her. She wanted to scream at him for scaring her and throw herself into his arms and cry in relief because he was okay.

"Where have you been?"

He frowned at her frantic tone. "Has anyone called?"

She stared at him in disbelief. "No. Not even you. You're hours late. Answer my question, Flynn."

Silently he withdrew a folded newspaper from his briefcase. Confused, she took it from him. He pointed at a headline halfway down the page.

Ad Agency's Top Gun Shoots Blanks?

Uneasiness swirled through her like a cold, damp fog. Her heart inched up her throat as she read the rest of the article. Someone had used her to attack Flynn and Maddox Communications. Flynn had said reputation was everything, and this article wasn't helping his.

"Who would do this?"

He wiped a hand over his face. Only then did she notice his tightly clenched jaw and the lines of stress bracketing his mouth. "I spent the afternoon trying to find out. Brock and I suspected Athos Koteas, Maddox's rival. But it wasn't him."

"Then who?"

"My mother."

Reeling, Renee staggered into the den and collapsed on the sofa. "Does she hate me so badly that to get to me she'd hurt you and malign the company that pays her bills?"

"I'm sorry, Renee. My mother has always been difficult, but I had no idea she'd stoop so low."

Feeling sick to her stomach, Renee gulped. She'd never had anyone treat her so viciously and had no idea how to react. Maybe she should call her mother. Lorraine had never been one for giving advice, but most of her mother's relationships ended with the same kind of brutal emotional battles. Lorraine would know how to deal with this situation.

Never mind. Lorraine's way of coping would be to ingest large quantities of booze until she forgot. Renee wasn't interested in that kind of medicine.

But if her mother-in-law would rather humiliate her than admit she was a success, then Renee had to wonder what her child's life would be like with a witch like Carol for a grandmother. No child deserved that.

Renee rose and paced to the window.

She loved Flynn, but the sperm bank wasn't the most appalling part of her past. She couldn't risk someone digging up the sordid details and hurting him even more. She had no choice. To take the heat off him and Maddox Communications, she was going to have to leave.

"I can't live in a glass house, Flynn."

"My mother isn't going to cause us any more trouble."

"You can't know that." Her heart ached. She blinked and swallowed the tears burning her eyes and throat. "I'm going back to L.A."

"Good idea. Take a week. By the time you return this will have blown over."

She closed her eyes, took a deep breath and gathered her courage. "I'm not coming back."

He flinched. "What about the baby? What about us?"

She'd been devastated just hours ago, but maybe it was a blessing that she wasn't pregnant. "I did a pregnancy test today. It was negative. I've been trying to call you all afternoon to tell you."

The pain and disappointment on his face wrenched her. "We'll try again."

"I won't raise a family in a verbal war zone. I've been there, Flynn, and I always swore I'd never do that to any child of mine. We need to end this—end *us*."

She couldn't risk repeating her mother's mistakes. This time she'd been strong enough to resist the lure of the alcohol cabinet. Next time she might not have the strength. And what would having a drunk for a wife do for Flynn's reputation? "I'll have my attorney contact yours."

Flynn caught her upper arms. The warmth of his hands penetrated her clothing, but did nothing to warm the cold knot forming inside her. She wanted him to hug her and tell her it would be all right. But she knew it wouldn't. "That's it? You're just going to quit?"

"It's better this way. Trust me." A sob welled up inside her. She mashed her lips together to hold it in. It was because she loved him that she had to let him go.

"Trust you? Apparently, that's the last thing I should do. At the first sign of trouble you run."

Renee flinched, but she didn't explain. Flynn might not enjoy working for Maddox Communications as much as he had the architectural firm, but the VP position was the one he'd chosen, and she had to support him in any way she could. And the best way to help him was to get far away and completely disassociate from him. With her history, having her around would always be a time bomb waiting to explode and damage Maddox's credibility and reputation.

"I'm sorry, Flynn." She brushed past him and raced up the stairs, hoping to reach their room—*his* room—before her tears started falling. She closed and locked the door, then frantically threw the necessities into her suitcases.

When she couldn't stall any longer, she lugged her bags downstairs. Flynn stood stiffly in the den, hands in his pockets, staring out the window into the darkness.

Emotion choked her. She couldn't have spoken even if she'd known what to say, and she didn't.

How did you tell a man you loved him too much to stay?

You didn't.

"I'll send someone for the rest of my stuff."

And then, for the second time, she walked away from the only man she'd ever love.

"Aren't you joining us for Happy Hour at the Rosa?" Brock asked from Flynn's doorway Friday evening.

Flynn looked up from the numbers on his screen—numbers he hadn't really been seeing. His mind had been elsewhere. "No."

Brock entered and closed the door. "It's been four days since Renee left, Flynn. You have to pull yourself out of this funk."

"You're a fine one to talk. You look like hell."

Brock held up his hands. "Hey, don't shoot the messenger. And forget about me. I'll be fine as soon as we catch the Maddox snitch. The team's leaving in five minutes if you change your mind and want to walk down to the bar with us."

Flynn's head wasn't into celebrating the end of another week tonight. "I won't."

"Your loss." Brock reached for the doorknob.

"Brock, I can't do this anymore."

Frowning, Brock paused. "Do what?"

"Crunch numbers."

"You need a vacation? Fine. Take one."

"It's more than that. I'm thinking long-term."

"Flynn, you're not thinking straight. You'll get over Renee and—"

"That's just it. I am thinking straight for the first time in a long time. And if I didn't get over Renee in seven years, then I never will. She said something before she left about living in glass houses. She's right. Madd Comm requires us to live our lives open to others' inspection, commentary and judgment—even if it doesn't make us happy."

"That's because our clients stand to lose a lot of money if we do something that violates their moral code or that of the people who buy their products."

"I'm violating a moral code. Mine. I'm living a lie."

"What are you talking about?"

"I hate this job. I hate crunching numbers and pushing paper. I like designing, building, watching a plan go from a one-dimensional rough sketch on paper to a six-dimensional structure I can walk through, smell and touch. I'm happier slinging paint with Renee than I am inking multimillion-dollar deals for Madd Comm. I still love her."

The realization had hit him like a runaway trolley car when he'd awoken alone in bed this morning. He missed Renee. Her smile, her energy. The way she encouraged him to follow his dreams and loved him even when he didn't. Together they made amazing things happen. Without her he just went through the motions—living without living at all.

"You'll get over this. Trust me. I've been there."

Flynn shook his head. "Renee is right. Working here won't make Dad proud of me or bring him back. I don't want to pretend to enjoy this anymore. It's time to live for me."

"Flynn, don't do anything rash."

"This isn't a rash decision. It's all I've thought about since she left." Flynn turned off his computer and rose with a sense of satisfaction swelling his chest, as if he'd finally gotten something right after he'd been working on it for a very long time. And he had. He'd finally gotten his priorities straight.

"I refuse to give strangers the right to decide how I live my life. I'll have my resignation on your desk Monday morning."

"Take the weekend to think it over."

"There's nothing to think over. I know what I want."

"And what is that exactly?"

"I'm going to finish my architectural internship. I only had six months left when I quit. There will be some remediation, but frankly, even if I have to start over on day one and work through the whole five-year internship again, I'm willing. At least then, if I have to live alone, I'll at least like the company I keep."

"You're out of your mind."

"No, Brock, I'm finally in my right mind. And I have Renee to thank for that." He brushed by his brother on the way out the door.

"Where are you going?" Brock called after him.

"I'm going after my wife."

Twelve

Tamara lingered by the door of Renee's cottage. "Are you sure you don't want to go camping with us this weekend? The girls would love to have you."

Renee shuddered. "Your girls would love to laugh at me. I don't camp. Bugs, snakes and I are not on friendly terms. I'd squeal and scream and, suffice to say, not be a happy camper." Even though she was mentally and physically exhausted and heartbroken, she forced a light tone for her assistant's sake. She'd been faking "fine" all week.

Tamara frowned and bit her lip. "Maybe we could go another weekend."

"Don't you dare cancel on them. Besides, we have events booked for the next four Saturdays."

"But—"

"But nothing. Scram or you're fired."

Tamara stuck out her tongue. "You can't fire me. You don't know the secret ingredient in my salsa recipe."

Renee laughed at their old joke. "No. And I would go out of business without that recipe. Go and have a great time. I'll be fine. I'm going to tweak that carrot cake recipe."

Tamara sighed. "Promise me you won't work all night again."

Renee grimaced. She'd been up late cooking every night this week. The local soup kitchen appreciated her efforts even if her assistant did not. "I promise I'll be in bed before I turn into a pumpkin at midnight."

Her reluctance obvious, Tamara finally left.

Renee scanned her kitchen and her gaze landed on her granny's ladder-back chair. She found comfort in the familiar piece of furniture. It was as if her granny were here to guide her through this rough patch.

Monday, when she had her head together, she'd contact the appliance people about selling the equipment she'd installed in Flynn's basement and try to recoup some of her financial losses. But this week…she just hadn't been able to handle the idea of tearing down what she and Flynn had built together. Not yet.

With that decided, she turned back to her mixer and the notes she'd been making on the cake recipe. When the doorbell rang in what seemed like only a few minutes later, Renee glanced at her watch. *Eight?*

Three hours had passed since Tamara had left. Shouldn't she and the girls be zipped into their sleeping bags or roasting marshmallows by now? But who else would drop by unannounced at this time of night?

Renee wouldn't put it past her assistant to bring the girls and their camping gear here and insist on putting up the tent in the cottage's back garden. Tamara had been hovering ever since she'd shown up for work Tuesday morning and found Renee already busy in the kitchen surrounded by mounds of food.

Renee headed for the front door and caught a glimpse of a taxi driving away through the window. Who would take a taxi to her house? She flicked on the porch light and glanced through the peephole. Flynn stood on her welcome mat.

Heart pounding, she staggered back a step. Why was he here?

She didn't want to see him. She wasn't ready. Panic set in.

A fist pounded on the door. "Renee, I know you're in there. Open up."

Loving him and knowing she couldn't have him hurt more than she could have imagined. But leaving had been for his own good. She had to remember that.

Wiping her damp palms on her jeans, she took a deep breath and opened the door. She drank in the sight of him with his dark hair tousled and five-o'clock shadow darkening his jaw. He looked tired. His tie hung askew and the top button of his white shirt gaped open, as did the coat of his black designer suit.

She looked past him, but his BMW wasn't in the driveway. "Why did you take a taxi?"

"I chartered a plane to get me here faster. Besides, you can't throw me out if I have no way to leave."

His logic startled a laugh from her. "I could just call another cab."

"It would take at least an hour for it to get here. That's an hour I could use to talk some sense into you."

"Sense? Into me?"

"You can't leave me, Renee. I love you."

She gasped. Those were the words she'd longed to hear. But it was too late.

"We're good together, Renee. No one understands me the way you do. No one loves me the way you do." He moved forward and she automatically stepped back and let him in. Dumb move. She should have shut the door in his face.

"Flynn—"

He brushed her cheek with his fingertips and erased whatever protest she'd meant to make. "You love me. Admit it."

She couldn't deny it. "It's not that simple."

How could she make him understand? She turned and led him into the living room.

With a sinking feeling of doom, she realized she'd have to tell him the truth—all of it—and watch his love die. "It was never you, Flynn. It was about me."

He took her hands and pulled her down on the sofa beside him. "Explain."

The love and patience in his eyes tore her apart, but that love wouldn't last long when he learned the truth.

Just do it. Spit it out like ripping off a bandage. Fast.

"After your father died I...I started turning into my mother."

"How?"

She gulped down her fear. "My drinking started innocently enough. I'd open a bottle of wine to share a glass with you when you got home. Then you'd be late. I'd start thinking about what your mother said. How I didn't fit into your crowd. How I was an embarrassment to you when you had to meet with clients, and that I'd never be smart enough to carry my end of a conversation, since I didn't have a college degree. And I'd have a second glass of wine and wonder if Carol was right. Maybe you did regret marrying me. Maybe that was why you didn't want to tie yourself to me with a baby. Maybe there was someone else."

Fury filled his eyes. "My mother said all that?"

Renee nodded.

"Renee, from the day I met you in that paint store there was never another woman. I was working."

"But you weren't coming home."

He wiped his face. Regret filled his eyes. "The adjustment to the VP job wasn't going well. I felt as if I was failing and letting the team down. I was exhausted from trying to clean up the mess my father left behind, and when I came home and you wanted to make love… sometimes I was so exhausted I couldn't. I knew the rejections hurt you, and I hated the idea of failing at home, too, so I slept at the office."

With hindsight, what he said made perfect sense. "I wish you'd told me."

"I didn't want to burden you. Besides my mother's viciousness, what made you leave?"

A fresh wave of shame washed over her. "One day I woke up and there were two empty wine bottles on the floor. I didn't even remember opening the second one. I realized I was becoming my mother. So I ran. I came home to L.A., and Granny helped me find a therapist."

"You should have come to me."

"Why? So I could see you lose respect for me because I was weak? So I could watch your love die? I saw that happen over and over again with my 'uncles' when they discovered my mother was an alcoholic."

"You're saying you're an alcoholic?"

She searched his face, looking for condemnation, and found none. "I don't know, Flynn. I've talked to several counselors. They seem to think that because my drinking only lasted a couple of months and I stopped voluntarily that maybe I'm not. I've worked very hard to develop healthy coping skills for my stress. But I have my mother's genes. I can't take the chance on *maybe,* so I err on the side of caution."

"That's why you don't drink."

She nodded. "I don't want to trigger whatever it is that makes people fall into that downward spiral."

"I think you're too strong to fall."

"Even strong people falter."

He brushed his fingertips over her cheek. "What does that have to do with us not being together for the next fifty years?"

Her love for him swelled inside her. "Flynn, I would never want to force someone I love to become an enabler like my grandmother and I had to be. We had to cover for my mother, make excuses for her. You're better off without me. Not only am I a risk, but my DNA is also contaminated. Our children could carry the tendency to be alcoholics."

"Renee, if only perfect people had children, the population would cease to exist. We'll teach our children those healthy coping skills you mentioned. I love you, and I want you in my life."

Hope fizzed inside her, but she burst the bubble. "I can't live with the idea of others always watching and waiting to pounce on my weakness and use it against you or Maddox Communications."

"You won't have to. I'm leaving Madd Comm."

Surprise stole her breath. "Why?"

"You told me seven and a half years ago that if I couldn't be happy with myself, then I could never be happy with anyone else. And you were right. I finally understand what that means. I was trying to live the life my father had mapped out for me, instead of the one I wanted for myself—the one we had planned with each other.

"I'm going back to architecture. It will allow me the chance to do something that invigorates me, instead of drains me."

"I'm glad. You deserve to be happy."

"There's only one thing that would make me happier."

"What?"

"Come home with me. We're a good team. And I will be there for you this time if you'll give me that chance. I love you, Renee. Let me spend the rest of my life proving that."

"I love you, too. And there's nothing I'd like more than to spend the rest of our lives together."

* * * * *

2 in 1
GREAT
VALUE

THE DESERT PRINCE by Jennifer Lewis

Yes, Salim had once rejected Celia Davidson as a suitable bride, but now it's proving difficult to keep their relationship strictly business…

THE PLAYBOY'S PROPOSITION by Leanne Banks

When Michael Medici spotted the beautiful cocktail waitress, he made his move. One extraordinary night later, he knew he wanted more from Bella St Clair…

BILLIONAIRE'S CONTRACT ENGAGEMENT by Maya Banks

Evan is falling for stunning career woman Celia and he can tell the stunning ad exec desires him too. But will she play the role of his fake fiancée…?

MONEY MAN'S FIANCÉE NEGOTIATION by Michelle Celmer

Ash is devastated when his girlfriend leaves him but when he hears she has been in an accident he rushes to her. Why did she leave?

AFFAIR WITH THE REBEL HEIRESS by Emily McKay

CEO Ford Langley is known for his boardroom—and bedroom— conquests, but Kitty Biedermann isn't about to let Ford get his own way, in the boardroom *or* bedroom!

THE MAGNATE'S PREGNANCY PROPOSAL by Sandra Hyatt

She came to tell him the IVF has worked, Chastity is carrying Gabe's late brother's baby. Then Gabe drops the bombshell—the baby is actually his!

On sale from 21st January 2011
Don't miss out!

*Available at WHSmith, Tesco, ASDA, Eason
and all good bookshops*

www.millsandboon.co.uk

0111/51

MILLS & BOON®

are proud to present our...

Book of the Month

Prince Voronov's Virgin
by Lynn Raye Harris

from Mills & Boon® Modern™

Paige Barnes is rescued from the dark streets of
Moscow by Prince Alexei Voronov—her boss's
deadliest rival. Now he has Paige unexpectedly in
his sights, Alexei will play emotional Russian
roulette to keep her close...

Available 17th December

Something to say about our Book of the Month?
Tell us what you think!

millsandboon.co.uk/community
facebook.com/romancehq
twitter.com/millsandboonuk

2 FREE BOOKS
AND A SURPRISE GIFT

We would like to take this opportunity to thank you for reading this Mills & Boon® book by offering you the chance to take TWO more specially selected books from the Desire™ 2-in-1 series absolutely FREE! We're also making this offer to introduce you to the benefits of the Mills & Boon® Book Club™—

- **FREE home delivery**
- **FREE gifts and competitions**
- **FREE monthly Newsletter**
- **Exclusive Mills & Boon Book Club offers**
- **Books available before they're in the shops**

Accepting these FREE books and gift places you under no obligation to buy, you may cancel at any time, even after receiving your free books. Simply complete your details below and return the entire page to the address below. You don't even need a stamp!

YES Please send me 2 free Desire stories in a 2-in-1 volume and a surprise gift. I understand that unless you hear from me, I will receive 2 superb new 2-in-1 books every month for just £5.30 each, postage and packing free. I am under no obligation to purchase any books and may cancel my subscription at any time. The free books and gift will be mine to keep in any case.

Ms/Mrs/Miss/Mr _____ Initials _____

Surname _____

Address _____

_____

_____ Postcode _____

E-mail _____

Send this whole page to: Mills & Boon Book Club, Free Book Offer, FREEPOST NAT 10298, Richmond, TW9 1BR